Order the full range of Horus Heresy novels from
www.blacklibrary.com

Download the full range of Horus Heresy audiobooks and dramas from www.blacklibrary.com

THE HORUS HERESY

Dan Abnett

KNOW NO FEAR

The Battle of Calth

BLACK LIBRARY

For Remus McNeill and Argel Dembski-Bowden.

A BLACK LIBRARY PUBLICATION

First published in Great Britain in 2012 by
The Black Library,
Games Workshop Ltd.,
Willow Road, Nottingham,
NG7 2WS, UK.

10 9 8 7

Cover and page 1 illustration by Neil Roberts.

A CIP record for this book is available from the British Library.

UK ISBN13: 978 1 84970 134 1
US ISBN13: 978 1 84970 135 8

Distributed in the US by Simon & Schuster
1230 Avenue of the Americas, New York, NY 10020, US.

See the Black Library on the internet at

www.blacklibrary.com

Find out more about Games Workshop
and the world of Warhammer 40,000 at

www.games-workshop.com

Printed and bound by CPI Group (UK) Ltd, Croydon, CR0 4YY

THE HORUS HERESY

It is a time of legend.

THE GALAXY IS in flames. The Emperor's glorious vision for humanity is in ruins. His favoured son, Horus, has turned from his father's light and embraced Chaos.

His armies, the mighty and redoubtable Space Marines, are locked in a brutal civil war. Once, these ultimate warriors fought side by side as brothers, protecting the galaxy and bringing mankind back into the Emperor's light.
Now they are divided.

Some remain loyal to the Emperor, whilst others have sided with the Warmaster. Pre-eminent amongst them, the leaders of their thousands-strong Legions, are the primarchs. Magnificent, superhuman beings, they are the crowning achievement of the Emperor's genetic science. Thrust into battle against one another, victory is uncertain for either side.

Worlds are burning. At Isstvan V, Horus dealt a vicious blow and three loyal Legions were all but destroyed. War was begun, a conflict that will engulf all mankind in fire. Treachery and betrayal have usurped honour and nobility. Assassins lurk in every shadow. Armies are gathering.
All must choose a side or die.

Horus musters his armada, Terra itself the object of his wrath. Seated upon the Golden Throne, the Emperor waits for his wayward son to return. But his true enemy is Chaos, a primordial force that seeks to enslave mankind to its capricious whims.

The screams of the innocent, the pleas of the righteous resound to the cruel laughter of Dark Gods. Suffering and damnation await all should the Emperor fail and the war be lost.

The age of knowledge and enlightenment has ended.
The Age of Darkness has begun.

~ DRAMATIS PERSONAE ~

The XIII Legion 'Ultramarines'

ROBOUTE GUILLIMAN	Primarch of the XIII Legion
TAURO NICODEMUS	Tetrarch of Ultramar (Saramanth), Primarch's Champion
EIKOS LAMIAD	Tetrarch of Ultramar (Konor), Primarch's Champion
JUSTARIUS	Venerable Dreadnought
TELEMECHRUS	Contemptor Dreadnought
MARIUS GAGE	Chapter Master, 1st Chapter
REMUS VENTANUS	Captain, 4th Company
KIUZ SELATON	Sergeant, 4th Company
LYROS SYDANCE	Captain, 4th Company
ARCHO	Sergeant, 4th Company
ANKRION	Sergeant, 4th Company
BARKHA	Sergeant, 4th Company
NARON VATTIAN	Scout, 4th Company
SAUR DAMOCLES	Captain, 6th Company
DOMITIAN	Sergeant, 6th Company
BRAELLEN	6th Company
ANDROM	6th Company
EVEXIAN	Captain, 7th Company
AMANT	7th Company
LORCHAS	Captain, 9th Company

AETHON	Captain, 19th Company
ERIKON GAIUS	Captain, 21st Company
TYLOS RUBIO	21st Company
HONORIA	Captain, 23rd Company
TEUS SULLUS	Captain, 39th Company
GREAVUS	Sergeant, 39th Company
KAEN ATREUS	Chapter Master, 6th Chapter
KLORD EMPION	Chapter Master, 9th Chapter
VARED	Chapter Master, 11th Chapter
EKRITUS	Captain, 111th Company
PHRASTOREX	Captain, 112th Company
ANCHISE	Sergeant, 112th Company
SHARAD ANTOLI	Chapter Master, 13th Chapter
TAERONE	Captain, 135th Company
AEONID THIEL	Sergeant, 135th Company [marked]
EVIDO BANZOR	Chapter Master, 16th Chapter
HEUTONICUS	Captain, 161st Company
JAER	Apothecary, 161st Company
KERSO	161st Company
BORMARUS	161st Company
ZABO	161st Company

| ANTEROS | 161st Company |
| HONORIUS LUCIEL | Captain, 209th Company |

The XVII Legion 'Word Bearers'

LORGAR AURELIAN	Primarch of the XVII Legion
KOR PHAERON	The Black Cardinal
EREBUS	Dark Apostle

ARGEL TAL	Gal Vorbak
ESSEMBER ZOTE	Gal Vorbak
FOEDRAL FELL	Commander
MORPAL CXIR	Commander
HOL BELOTH	Commander
MALOQ KARTHO	Apostle to Hol Beloth
SOROT TCHURE	
ULMOR NUL	

Cults

THE USHMETAR KAUL	'The Brotherhood of the Knife'
CRIOL FOWST	Confided Lieutenant
THE TZENVAR KAUL	'The Recursive Family'
THE JEHARWANATE	'The Ring'
THE KAUL MANDARI	'The Gene-kin'
VIL TETH	Gene-named

Imperial Personae

UHL KEHAL HESST	Server of Instrumentation, Mechanicum
MEER EDV TAWREN	Magos of Analyticae
MAGOS ULDORT	
AROOK SEROTID	Master of Skitarii
CYRAMICA	Skitarii
SHIPMASTER SAZAR	*Macragge's Honour*
BOHAN ZEDOFF	
REPRESENTATIVE	*Macragge's Honour*
MAGOS PELOT	
SHIPMASTER OUON	*Sanctity of Saramanth*
HOMMED	

Imperial Army

COLONEL SPARZI	Neride 10th
BOWE HELLOCK	Sergeant, Numinus 61st
DOGENT KRANK	Numinus 61st
BALE RANE	Numinus 61st

Citizens of Calth

SENESCHAL ARBUTE	
OLL PERSSON	
GRAFT	Servitor Menial
HEBET ZYBES	
KATT	
NEVE RANE	

'When we are tired, we are attacked by ideas
we conquered long ago.'
                    – the philosopharch Nietzsche,
                                        circa M2

'They are dead, they will not live;
they are shades, they will not arise;
to that end you have visited
them with destruction and
wiped out all remembrance of them.'
                    – The Apocrypha Terra,
                                date unknown

The following document is a
chronological account extracted and
compiled from Ultima (XIII) Operational
Record 1136.271.v and the writings of
Primarch Roboute Guilliman.

TARGET//ACQUISITION

'The Phase of Acquisition, or preparatory condition, is a vital segment of any successful prosecution. Though a warrior must be prepared to battle reactively without notice or forewarning, it is when he prepares and plans for war, and accommodates the specifics of his adversary into those plans, that he is most successful... This is war as craft or science, as I have remarked before. Often the fight is won before the first shot has been fired, or even before notice of the first shot has been given.'

– Guilliman, *Notes Towards Martial Codification*, 7.3.ii

1

WHO ARE THE first to die?

Most commentaries will cite Honorius Luciel (*captain, 209th*) and seventeen others by the hand of Sorot Tchure on the company deck of the cruiser *Samothrace* at *mark: -00.19.45*, but these are not in fact the first combat fatalities.

The fleet tender *Campanile* is mob-boarded and taken off the Tarmus Apogee approximately one hundred and thirty-six hours [sidereal] before count start as a preliminary to the Calth assault.

Three thousand seven hundred and nine crew members are executed, including the ship master, the Navigator, the echelon port master, two fabricators from the yards, and a detail from the Neride Regulators 10th serving as deck protection.

Proof of the loss of the *Campanile*, delivered to Primarch Guilliman around *mark: 01:30:00* demonstrates calculation and planning on behalf of the adversary, and establishes what Primarch Guilliman refers to as a 'preparatory phase of acquisition', which refutes any claims that the conflict was born out of mistake or misadventure.

This represents a 'precondition of malice' on the part of the adversary, and strengthens Primarch Guilliman's hand in that it removes any compunction to resist or fight back with full military force.

There is no longer any point trying to reason with his brother, because his brother is not, in fact, *mistakenly* trying to kill him at all.

Lorgar has been planning it all along.

Precise details of the circumstances surrounding the loss of the *Campanile* are lost / *and alone in such darkness, on a deceleration arc past the outer moons, one small ship, overweight and wheezing, over three and a half thousand souls* / because no log record or data canister is recovered from the wreck / *which had been penetrated by something in the night, made in the night, made out of the night, a void-hard darkness with teeth and eyes, squirting through every airgate and hatch seal and vent tube like pressurised oil* / though it is assumed that the vessel was overhauled by a fighting ship from the XVII Legion's fleet and taken with all hands / *all of them screaming as they were blinded and suffocated, nowhere to flee to, no escape, no door that would open except to bare and airless space, and still the thing made of night filling the* Campanile *up, every compartment and deckway, every chamber and access, like black storm water flash-flooding an underground habitat, blinding and choking and drowning everything, filling rooms, filling mouths, filling lungs, filling ears, filling stomachs, stewing brains, smothering gunfire, blunting blades, swallowing the screams of the dying and the overcome, stealing the screams away and laughing them back in mocking voices that promised that screams were nothing more than the chamber music of dark monarchs mankind had only just begun to dream of* / so that its anchorage codes could be used to penetrate the platform yards.

Course irregularities are noticed of the *Campanile* by Calth System Control at *mark: -136.14.12* and again at *mark: -135.01.20* and *mark: -122.11.35.*

Vox contact is recorded as lost at *mark: -99.21.59.*

Two hours later, Calth System Control marks the *Campanile* 'cause for concern', and the Master of the Port determines that a support intercept should be sent out if nothing further is received by the end of shift. There are one hundred and ninety-two thousand items of shipping traffic in the Veridian System that day because of the fleet conjunction.

The support intercept is not sent out because the *Campanile* resumes code transmission at *mark: -88.10.21.*

The crew of the *Campanile* is listed on the roll of the fallen in the aftermath of the battle, though none are ever seen again / *except they were, but not in any form that they could be recognised, apart from their screams.*

[*mark: -124.24.03*]

THE FIRST OF the fleet advances have hauled their scarred hulls into the arrestor slips and come to full stop in the high anchor station above Numinus City. They are warships that have gone a long way, and killed a great many things, and they wear the insignia and colours of the XVII proudly.

Luciel opens the airgate hatch. His company has been assigned close protection of Numinus High Anchor. He has requested the duty personally.

Tall as one big man on another big man's shoulders, broad as any three muscle-heavy athletes, his bulk augmented by the massive ceramite plate of gleaming Praetor-pattern armour, Luciel opens the airgate hatch.

The light inside finds him blue and gold. His skull-close helm is in place. Behind the visor slits, Luciel's eyes react as fast as the optic augmetics in the slit rims. Involuntary combat instincts take over: a new space is revealed, so he must consider it and assess any threats.

An airgate compartment, sixty cubic metres, grav supporting decking, self-seal armoured skinning, neutral normalised atmospherics (though Luciel can feel the pressure decay of the air pumps' end-cycle). There's a reciprocal airgate hatch at the other end of the gate compartment.

There is a figure in front of the door. It is another Space Marine in full wargear.

Luciel is XIII Legion, an Ultramarine. Blue and gold, clean and sharp. Armour burnished to a silk gleam. The Praetor-pattern is a new variant, locally fabricated at Veridia Forge, not yet a formally accepted mark within the Legiones Astartes.

The other is XVII Legion, a Word Bearer. His pattern is the current Mark IV, the Maximus, built for Imperial supremacy. Its fixed frontal armour and angular helm are familiar.

Its colours are not. Dark crimson, with gunmetal edging. Company symbols and squad brands lacquered in dark shapes, almost undecipherable, as if they have been erased or are yet to be painted. Where is the plasmaetched grey of the old scheme?

The Word Bearer is almost unrecognisable. For a nanosecond, the figure registers to Luciel as an unknown, a threat.

Transhuman responses are already there, unbidden. Adrenaline spikes to heighten an already formidable reaction time. Muscle remembers. Luciel wears his boltgun, an oiled black pit bull of a weapon, in his thigh holster. He can draw, aim and fire in less than a second. The range is six metres, the target unobstructed. There is no chance of missing. Maximus plate, frontally augmented, might stop a mass-reactive shell, so Luciel will fire two and aim for the visor slits. The airgate skin-sleeve is self-repairing, and will survive las-fire damage, but a bolter shot will shred it open, so Luciel also braces for the explosive decompression of a ricochet or a miss-hit.

At a simple, subconscious neural urge, boot-sole electro-magnets charge to clamp onto the deck plates.

Luciel thinks *theoretical*, but of course there is no theoretical. There is no tactical precedent for a Space Marine to fight a Space Marine. The idea is nonsense. He thinks *practical*, and that directs him to the visor slits. He can make a clean kill headshot in less than a second and a half, two rounds for kill insurance, and probably protect the atmospheric integrity of the airgate.

All this, all this decided, unbidden, instinctive, in less than a nanosecond.

The Word Bearer raises his right hand. Moving it where? Moving it towards his primary weapon, a plasma cannon in a pull-to-unlock sheath?

The hand spreads, opens like a flower, palm forward, the light glinting off the tiny mail links.

'Luciel,' says the Word Bearer. 'Brother.'

'Tchure,' Luciel replies, his voice a growl over the helmet speaker. 'Brother,' he adds.

'Well met,' says the warrior of the XVII, stepping forward.

'A long time,' says Luciel, coming to meet him. They embrace, forearm guards clattering off backplate panels.

'Tell me, brother,' says Luciel. 'What new things have you learned to kill since last we met?'

2

AEONID THIEL, ULTRAMARINE, marked for discipline and censure, boards the blue and gold Stormbird on a landing strip two thousand kilometres south of Numinus City. The sun, which is a star named Veridia, is a dot of pearl in the pale sky. A beautiful star, Thiel has heard it said. A beautiful star and a fine world.

Before him, the Dera Caren Lowlands, the district of manufactories and assembly halls, matt metal in the sunlight. The buildings, clean, simple and utilitarian, wisp white vapours into the clear sky through rotating roof vents and cycle chimneys. Areas of forest have been preserved between the finishing concourses where the labour force can rest and mingle between shifts.

In the west, just a cloudy ghost low in the sky, one of the orbital shipyards has just risen like a moon. Thiel knows of eight others. Soon, Calth will rival Macragge's manufacturing output, perhaps in two or three decades. There is already talk of a projected superorbital plate. Like Terra. Terra has superorbital plates. The master worlds of the Imperium have plates. Calth will join Macragge, Saramanth, Konor, Occluda and Iax as one of

23

the master worlds of the Ultramar sector, and between them, they will govern a vast swathe of the Ultima Segmentum. Calth will be one of the anchor points of the coming civilisation.

Calth is an embodiment of the reward that centuries of warfare have been leading to.

For this reason, Calth must not fall. For its status as part of the dominion of Ultramar, it must not fall. For its shipbuilding capacity and its forge world, it must not fall.

Intelligence has been received from Horus. A *theoretical* has been identified. It must be a great deal more than a *theoretical*, Thiel believes, for mustering and conjunction to have been taken this far, unless the new Warmaster is anxious to prove his authority. To mobilise the XIII, the largest of all the Legions, in an essentially singular war effort, that takes balls. To tell Roboute Guilliman, the primarch with the least to prove, how to do his duty, that takes balls of adamantium. To suggest that Guilliman might need *help*...

Horus is a great man. Thiel is not ashamed to admit that. Thiel has seen him, served with him, admired him. His selection as Warmaster makes reasonable sense. It was only going to be one of three or perhaps four, no matter how other primarchs might deceive themselves. To be the Emperor's avatar, his proxy? Only Horus, Guilliman, Sanguinius, perhaps Dorn. Any other claims for viability were delusional. Even narrowed down to four, Dorn was too draconian and Sanguinius too ethereal. It was only ever going to be Horus or Guilliman. Horus always had the passion and the charisma. Guilliman was more clinical, considered. Perhaps that tipped it. So did, perhaps, the fact that Guilliman already had responsibilities. An empire, half-built. Ultramar. Administration. Populations. A culture. Guilliman had already evolved beyond the status of warlord, where Horus was still a killer of worlds and a subjugator of adversaries.

Maybe Warmaster Horus is aware of this disparity, that even in his triumphant election, he has been outstripped by a brother who does not even want for the honour of Warmaster any more. Perhaps that is why Horus needs to exercise his authority and give orders to the XIII. Perhaps that is why he is conjoining them with the XVII, a Legion they have never been comfortable with.

Or perhaps the new Warmaster is rather more creative than that, and sees this as a chance for Lorgar's rabble to borrow a little gloss from Guilliman's glory by association and example.

Aeonid Thiel, Ultramarine, has said these thoughts out loud.

They are not the reason he is marked for discipline and censure.

[mark: -111.02.36]

THEY ARE LOADING munitions crates at the docks on the south shore of the Boros River. Numinus City faces them across the wide grey water.

The work is hard, but the men, Imperial Army, every one, are laughing. After the loading, a meal break, a last drink, then lifters to orbit.

The crates are scuffed metal, like small coffins, full of local-pattern lasrifles, the *Illuminator VI*, a refined variant pressed out at Veridia Forge. The men hope to be using them within a fortnight.

The wind blows in along the estuary, bringing scents of the sea and the coastal dredgers. The men are all from the Numinus 61st, regular infantry. Some are veterans of the Great Crusade, others are new recruits inducted for the emergency.

Sergeant Hellock keeps the spirits up.

'Will it be greenskins? Will it be the greenskins?' the

rookies keep asking. They have heard about greenskins.
He assures them it will not.

'It's an exercise in cooperation,' Hellock says. 'It's an
operational show of force. This is Ultramar flexing its
muscles. This is the Warmaster flexing his muscles.'

Hellock is lying to them. He lights a lho-stick, and
smokes it under the shade of a tail boom, the collar of
his dark blue field tunic pulled open to let the sweat
on his collarbones dry. Hellock is on good terms with
his captain, and Hellock's captain confides in him.
Hellock's captain has a friend in the Ultramarines 9th
Company, part of the encouraged fraternisation. His
captain's transhuman friend says that the threat is not
theoretical. He calls it a 'likely excursion of the Ghaslakh
xenohold', which is a shit-stupid way of describing it.
Bastard greens. Bastard orks. Bastard bastards, gathering
at the sector edge, working up the courage to come and
ransack Calth. Not frigging theoretical at all.

That's why you take the whole bastard XIII *and* the
whole bastard XVII *and* all the Army units you can
scare up, and you throw them at the *Ghaslakh* bastard
xeno-bastard-*hold*, thank you so very much. You drive a
bastard system-killing compliance force through their
precious xenohold, and put them down dead before
they put you down, and you kill their barbarian empire
at the same time. Just kill it. Dead, gone, bye-bye, clap
the dust off your hands, no more threat, theoretical or
bastard otherwise.

You take a compliance force the scale of which hasn't
been seen since Ullanor or the early days of the Great
Crusade, two full Legions of the Emperor's finest, and
you pile-drive it through the septic green heart and rancid green brain and green frigging spinal cord of the
Ghaslakh xenohold, and you end them.

This is how Sergeant Hellock sees it.

Sergeant Hellock's forename is Bowe. None of the
men in his command know this, and only one or two

who survive will learn it later when they read his name on the casualty lists.

Bowe Hellock will be dead in two days' time.

It will not be an ork that kills him.

[mark: -111.05.12]

SERGEANT HELLOCK HAS gone for a smoke. The men slow the pace. Their arms are aching.

Bale Rane is the youngest of them. He is absolutely raw, a week out of accelerated muster. There's been a vague promise he'll get an hour to say goodbye to his bride of six weeks before he lifts that evening. He cannot bear the idea of not seeing her. He is beginning to suspect it was an empty promise.

Neve's on the other side of the river, waiting for him on a public wharf; waiting for him to wave from the ferry rail. He can barely stand the idea that she will be disappointed. She will wait there all night, in the hope that he's only late. It will get dark. The refinery burn-pipes will glitter yellow reflections off the black river. She will be cold.

The thought of this hurts his heart.

'Pull your collar up,' Krank tells him, clipping his ear. Krank is an older man, a veteran.

'Work in the sun,' he scolds, 'it'll burn you, boy. Cap on, collar up, even if you sweat. You don't want skin-burn. Trust me. Worse than a broken heart.'

[mark: unspecified]

THE 'MARK' OF Calth means two things. First, it refers, as per XIII Legion combat record protocol, to the elapsed time count (in Terran hours [sidereal]) of the combat. All Ultramarines operations and actions of this period may be archivally accessed for study, and their elapsed time count mark used as a navigation guide. An instructor might refer a novitiate to 'Orax mark: 12.16.10', meaning the tenth second of the sixteenth minute of the twelfth hour of the Orax Compliance record. Usually, this count begins at either the issuing of the operation order, or the actual operational start, but at Calth it is timed from the moment Guilliman ordered return of fire. Everything before that, he says, wasn't a battle: it was merely treachery.

Secondly, the 'mark' of Calth refers to the solar radiation burns suffered by many of the combatants, principally the human (specifically non-transhuman) troops.

The last of these veterans to die, many years later, still refuse graft repair and wear the mark proudly.

3

REMUS VENTANUS, CAPTAIN of the 4th, has command of the Erud Province muster. It's supposed to be an honour, but it doesn't feel like it.

It feels like a desk job. It feels like labour for a bureaucrat or an administrator. It feels as if the primarch is teaching him another valuable lesson about the responsibilities of transhumanity. Learn to take pride in the work of governance as well as war. To be a ruler as well as a leader.

Remus Ventanus understands this. When the war is done, as it must eventually be done, when there are no more enemies to end and no more worlds to conquer, what will the transhumans who have built the Imperium do then?

Retire?

Pine away and die?

Become an embarrassment? A gore-headed reminder of older, more visceral days when humans needed superhumans to forge an empire for them? War is acceptable when it is a necessary instrument of survival. When it is no longer needed, the very fact that it was ever a necessary instrument at all becomes unpalatable.

'It is the great irony of the Legiones Astartes,' Guilliman had told his captains and masters, just a week ago. 'Engineered to kill to achieve a victory of peace that they can then be no part of.'

'A conceptual failure?' Gage had asked.

'A necessary burden,' Sydance suggested. 'I build your temple, knowing that I will not worship in it.'

Guilliman had shaken his head to both. 'My father does not make mistakes of that magnitude,' he had said. 'Space Marines excel at warfare because they were designed to excel at everything. Each of you will become a leader, a ruler, the master of your world and, because there is no more fighting to be done, you will bend your transhuman talents to governance and culture.'

Remus Ventanus knows that his primarch believes in this sincerely. He doubts the likes of Primarch Angron or Primarch Russ regard the prospect of a peaceful future with such optimism.

'Why are you smiling?' asks Selaton, at his side.

Remus glances at his sergeant.

'Was I smiling?'

'You were looking at the data-slate and smiling, sir. I was wondering what was so amusing about a manifest list of eighty super-heavy armour pieces.'

'Very little,' Remus agrees.

Beyond the observation port, mass-loader engines carry four-hundred-tonne tanks into the bellies of bulk liftships.

[mark: -108.56.13]

BROTHER BRAELLEN IS young, and has not yet fought the greens. His captain has. In the sunlight of the ground camp in the Ourosene Hills, some impromptu training takes place while they wait for the signal to stow and board.

'Ork, *theoretical*,' says Captain Damocles.

'Head or spine, mass-reactive,' replies Braellen. 'Or heart.'

'Idiot,' grumbles Sergeant Domitian. 'Heart shot won't stop one. Not guaranteed. Filthy things soak up damage, even boltguns.'

'So, skull or spine,' says Braellen, corrected.

Damocles nods.

'Ork, *practical*?' he asks.

'What do I have?' asks Braellen.

'Your bolter. A combat sword.'

'Skull or spine,' says Braellen, 'or both or whatever works. Maximum trauma. If it comes to close combat, decapitation.'

Damocles nods.

'The wrinkle is, don't let it ever *get* that close,' says Domitian. 'They've got strength in them. Shred your limbs off. Sometimes, the damned things keep going when their skulls are off or open. Nerve roots, or something. Keep them at bay, if you can – ranged weapons, bolter fire. Maximum trauma.'

'Good advice,' says Captain Damocles to his grizzled sergeant. He looks at the brothers in the circle. 'And from a man who has fought greenskins six times more than I have. It is six, isn't it, Dom?'

'I think it's seven, thanking you, sir,' replies Domitian, 'but I won't grieve if you won't.'

Damocles smiles.

'You have left out one caveat on the *practical* assessment, though,' he says.

'Have I, sir?' asks Domitian, honestly surprised.

'Anyone?' asks the captain.

Braellen raises his hand.

'Round count,' he says.

Domitian laughs and tuts to himself. How could he have forgotten to cover that base?

'For the benefit of the others, Brother Braellen?' prompts Captain Damocles.

'Round count,' says Braellen. 'Maximum trauma, maximum damage, but watch your load counter and try to balance damage delivery against munitions rationing.'

'Because?' asks Damocles.

'Because, with orks,' says Domitian, 'there's always a shit load of them.'

BROTHER ANDROM HAS also not fought greenskins before. When the captain breaks the circle and sends them to duties, he speaks to Braellen.

They have both recently rotated up from the reserve companies, ready to complete their novitiate period through service in the active line. Both are grateful and proud to have been given places in the 6th Company, to serve under Saur Damocles, and to etch – if only temporarily – the company's white figure-of-eight serpent emblem onto the blue fields of their shoulder guards.

[mark: -99.12.02]

OLL HAS LAND on the estuary at Neride.

The land is about twenty hectares of good black alluvial soil. The hectares are service-shares. Oll has service, and a yellowing record book at the bottom of a storeroom drawer to prove it. Good years of service, marching behind the Emperor's standard.

Oll is Army.

His service ended on Chrysophar, eighteen standard years past. Then, he was known as 'Trooper Persson'. He got his papers, and his service ribbon, and a stamp on his record book, and service-shares, proportionate to years served. The Army always rounds down.

Oll spent two years on a cattle-boat coming to Calth from Chrysophar. The posters and the handbills all called Ultramar 'the New Empire'. The slogan seemed a little disloyal, but the point was made. The rich new

cluster of worlds that great Guilliman had made compliant, and wrangled into a brawny frontier republic,
had the look of a new empire about it. The posters were
trying to appeal to the settlers and colonists streaming
out towards the Rim on the coattails of the expedition-
ary fleets. *Come to Ultramar and share our future. Build
your new life on Calth. Settle on Octavia. New worlds, New
destinies!*

If you claimed your service-shares on a rising world
like Calth, the administration paid your passage. Oll
came with the thousand people who would be his
neighbours. By the time he reached Calth, he was known
as 'Oll', and only those who saw the fading ink on his
left forearm knew about his past in professional killing.

The fusion plants of Neride generate the power that
lights the lamps of Numinus City and Kalkas Fortalice.
The plants pump river water to wash the smudge-carbon
off their clean-stroke turbines, and thus warm the estuary with a rich black swill that makes the river valley one
of the most fertile places on the planet. It's good land.
There's always a stink of beets and cabbage in the humid
air.

Oll has no wife, and knows only toil. He grows
swathes of bright flowers to decorate the tables and vases
and buttonholes of the Numinus City gentry, and then,
on the season turn, he cycles a second crop of swartgrass
for the sacking industry. Both crops require seasonal
labour forces. Oll employs the young men and women
of neighbouring families: the women to cut and pack the
flowers, the men to harvest and roll the swartgrass. He
keeps them all in line with an ex-Army loader servitor
called Graft. Graft cannot be conditioned not to call him
'Trooper Persson'.

Oll wears a Catheric symbol around his neck on a thin
chain, the gift of a wife he had barely got to know before
she died and was replaced by Army life. The symbol, and
his faith, are two of the reasons he came to Ultramar.

It is, he feels, easier to believe out here in the Ultima Segmentum.

It's supposed to be, anyway.

Some of his neighbours, who have been his neighbours these eighteen years and whose children he employs, laugh at his faith. They call him 'pious'.

Others attend the little chapel on the edge of the fields with him.

It's swartgrass season, and the men and boys are in the fields. Two weeks of hard work to go.

There are a lot of ships in the top of the sky today. Troop ships. Munitions ferries. Oll squints into the sun as they pass over. He recognises them. Farmer, colonist, believer, whatever he is, he's still Army underneath it all.

He recognises them.

He feels an old feeling, and it reminds him of the lasrifle hanging over his fireplace.

[mark: -68.56.14]

AT BARRTOR, EAST of the Boros River, 111th and 112th Companies of the Ultramarines are stationed in pre-fab cities in the forest hem. At the word from Vared, Master of the 11th Chapter, they will mount their Land Raiders, Rhinos and long-body Rhino Advancers, and advance to Numinus Port for embarkation.

Ekritus has just taken the captaincy of the 111th from Briende, who fell on Emex. It was a hard loss for the company. Ekritus is a fine commander in the making. He wants a good fight, a fight that will hammer the 111th back into shape and show them he's a worthy replacement for the beloved Briende.

'I've never seen a man so eager to make shift,' says Phrastorex, Captain of the 112th. 'Have you, Sergeant Anchise?'

'No, sir,' says Anchise.

They've come to join Ekritus on the embankment below the trees. It forms a natural viewing platform. They can see the floodplain, the encampments of Word Bearers companies who made planetfall the night before, the tent cities of the Army, and the fields of Titans. The war-engines are powered-down, dormant, standing in groves like giant metal trees. A column of armour and towed artillery pieces is grumbling down the highway below. Interceptors flash by on a low pass. There is a blue haze.

Ekritus grins at them. Phrastorex is a veteran, an old soul. Ekritus understands that Vared has pushed Phrastorex into a mentoring role during the transition. A company is a considerable entity: you do not take on its command lightly.

'I know one should not be in haste to greet war,' Ekritus says. 'I know, I know. I have read my Machulius and my Antaxus, my Von Klowswitts–'

'And your Guilliman, I hope,' says Phrastorex.

'I've heard of him, certainly,' says Ekritus. They laugh. Even Anchise, at attention, has to cover a grin.

'I need to close the men on a target. A practical threat, not a theoretical one. There's only so many rousing speeches I can give before they need me to simply lead by example.'

Phrastorex sighs.

'I commiserate. I remember when I accepted the commander's stave after Nectus passed. I just needed that first match to blood the men. Hell, I needed it. I needed them to bond with me against an enemy, not bond against me as an outsider.'

Ekritus nods.

'Is that right, sergeant?'

Anchise hesitates.

'Perfectly correct, sir. The theory is sound. The focus of battle makes men forget other issues. It is an excellent way to bind them to a new commander. Gives them an experience they have shared. Of course, in the specific

case of Captain Phrastorex, he's never been able to bond
with us or prove his worth.'

All three of them laugh out loud.

'I might have wished for something more streamlined,'
says Ekritus. 'The scale of this mobilisation is ridiculous.
The logistics alone are slowing everything down.'

'They say we'll be away by tonight,' says Phrastorex.
'Tomorrow at the latest. Then what? Two weeks' ship
time, and you'll be up to your eyes in ork blood.'

'It can't happen soon enough,' says Ekritus, 'because
no damn thing is ever going to happen here.'

[mark: -61.20.31]

*If you start with many and end with a single victory, then the
cost in between is acceptable.*

Guilliman reads back what he has written. The tactical
sentiment is not original to him: it was told to him by a
T'Vanti war-triber. He has... polished it.

He's not even sure if he believes it, but all military
concepts and aphorisms are worth recording, if only to
understand how an enemy's mind works.

The war-tribes believed it. They were honourable
allies, able fighters. Low tech, of course, nothing compared to his Legion. The T'Vanti had agreed to serve
as auxiliaries. It had been a diplomatic move on Guilliman's part. If he allowed the locals to share in the
victory, then they might also take responsibility for
maintaining the compliance of their world. But the orks
moved mercurially that day; some unpredicted pulse of
contrariness fluttered through their mass. They turned
west, against all sense. Guilliman's force was delayed
by a day. The wartribes went ahead without them, and
took the hill at Kunduki, decapitating – literally – the
greenskin command.

The T'Vanti seemed delighted by their achievement,

and utterly oblivious to the eighty-nine thousand men it had cost them.

Guilliman turns the stylus in his hand, thoughtful. It takes discipline to die in such numbers. It is one of the reasons that a bladed T'Vanti cordulus hangs on his compartment wall. He believes he has the most disciplined military force in the Imperium, and given the quality of the other Legions, that is quite a claim. Still, he is not sure even his Ultramarines would display such a deep degree of discipline, such a *T'Vanti* degree.

'They will never have to,' he reflects, out loud.

Guilliman sits back. The seat flexes to support his armoured bulk. He is shaped like a man, but he is far more than that, far more than even the transhuman giants of his Legion. He is a primarch. There are only seventeen other beings like him left in the universe.

He is the thirteenth son of mankind's Emperor. He is the Master of the Ultramarines, the XIII Legion. He is one of the more human of his kind. Some are more like angels. Others are... *otherwise*.

From a distance, one might mistake him for a man. Only when the distance closed would you realise he is more like a god.

He is handsome, in a plain way. He is handsome the way a regent on an old coin is handsome, like a good sword is handsome. He is not handsome like a ritual weapon, the way Fulgrim is. He is not angelic, like Sanguinius. Not heartbreakingly angelic. None of them are *that* beautiful.

There is a dutiful line to his jaw, like his good brother Dorn. They share a nobility. There is the great strength of Ferrus and the vitality of Mortarion. There is, sometimes, the rogue glint of the Khan in his eyes, or the solemnity of the Lion. In the architecture of his nose and brow there is, many claim, the energy and triumph of Horus Lupercal.

There is none of the bitterness that shadows Corax, or

the persecuted despair that haunts poor Konrad. There is never any of the deliberate mystery that obscures Alpharius or Magnus, and he is more open than that buried soul Vulkan. He is accomplished, very accomplished, even by the standards of the primarchs. He knows that the breadth of his accomplishments troubles his more single-minded brothers like Lorgar and Perturabo. He never displays the pitch of fury found in Angron, nor do his eyes ever ignite with the psychotic gleam of Russ.

He is a high achiever. He knows this about himself. Sometimes it feels like a fault that he has to excuse to his brothers, but then he feels guilty for making excuses. Few of them really trust him, because, he feels, they always wonder what he's going to get from any compact or cooperation. Fewer still like him: as friends, he counts only Dorn, Ferrus, Sanguinius and Horus.

Some of his brothers are content to be the instruments of crusade they have become. Some of them don't even pause to consider that is what they are. Angron, Russ, Ferrus, Perturabo… They are just weapons, and have no ambition beyond being weapons. They know their place, like Russ, and are content to keep to it, or they have no idea that any other role might be possible or desirable, like Angron.

Guilliman believes that none of them were made to be *just* weapons. No war is meant to last forever. The Emperor, his father, has not raised disposable sons. Why would he have gifted them with such talents if they were destined to become redundant when the war is done?

He turns the stylus in his hand and reads back what he has written. He writes a great deal. He codifies everything. Information is power. Technical theory is victory. He intends to compile and systemise it all. When the war is done, perhaps, he will have time to properly compose his archives of data into some formal codification.

He uses a stylus by choice, recording in his own handwriting. The stylus marks directly onto the lumoplastek

surface of his data-slate, but even so it is considered anti-
quated. Key plates seem impersonal, and vox-recorders
or secretarial rubricators have never suited his process.
He tried a thought-tap for a time, and one of the newer
mnemo-quills, but they were both unsatisfactory. The
stylus will stay.

He turns it in his hand.

His compartment is quiet. Through the vast, tinted
armourglas doors behind him, he can see his Chapter
Masters gathering for audience. They are waiting for his
summons. There is a great deal to do. They think he's
idling, recording notes and not keeping his eye on the
dataflow.

It amuses him that they still underestimate him.

He has been writing notes on T'Vanti war practices for
seventeen minutes, but he has still noted and marked
fifteen hundred data bulletins and updates that have
tracked across the secondary screens to his left.

He sees and reconciles everything.

Information is victory.

[mark: -61.25.22]

THE CHAPTER MASTERS await their primarch. From the
antechamber, they can see him through the tinted
armourglas of the doors. He sits like a commemorative
statute in an otherwise empty chapel. Every now and
then, his hand moves as he makes a notation on the
hovering slate with his antique pen. The compartment,
Guilliman's compartment, is stark and bare. Steel-fold
floors and adamantium-ribbed walls. The far end is a
crystalflex wall through which orbital space is visible.
Stars glitter. A glare comes up through the blackness
from the radiant world below.

Marius Gage is First Master. They're not all here yet.
Twelve have arrived so far, and that is, in itself, quite an

assembly. By the day's end, there will be twenty.

The XIII Legion, largest of all the Legiones Astartes, is divided into Chapters, a throwback to the old regimental structures of the thunder warriors. Each Chapter is formed of ten companies. The basic unit currency is the company, a thousand legionaries, plus their support retinue, led by a senior captain. A company, Gage has often heard his primarch comment, is more than sufficient for most purposes. There is an old aphorism, popular in the XIII. It is, perhaps, boastful and arrogant, and there are certain opponents such as the greenskins and the eldar to which it does not apply, but it contains a basic estimation of truth:

To take a town, send a legionary; to take a city, send a squad; to take a world, send a company; to take a culture, send a Chapter.

Today, at Calth, twenty of the XIII's twenty-five Chapters will conjunct for deployment. Two hundred companies. Two hundred thousand legionaries. The remainder will maintain garrison positions throughout the Five Hundred Worlds of Ultramar.

Such a gathering is not unprecedented, but it is rare. The XIII hasn't been oathed out in such numbers since the early days of the Great Crusade.

And you can add to their mass the equivalent of five Chapters of the XVII, the Word Bearers.

The level of overkill is almost comical. What exactly does the new Warmaster think the Ghaslakh xenohold has in its magazine?

'I hope,' says Kaen Atreus, Master of the 6th Chapter, 'I hope,' he says out loud, 'we open up the heart of the biggest greenskin nest in known space.'

'You hope for trouble?' asks Gage, amused.

'Remark 56.xxi,' says Vared of the 11th. '*Never wish for danger. Danger needs no help. There is no such thing as fate that can be tempted, but morale is never improved by an active lust for war.*'

Atreus scowls.

'I would rather tempt a little fate,' he says, 'than waste my time for the glory of others.'

'Which others have you in mind?' Gage wonders.

Atreus looks at him. A scar bisects his left eye and turns the corner of his mouth down. When he smiles, it is an act of stealth.

'This compliance is designed to achieve two objectives, and neither of them is military,' he says. 'We're to lend a little gloss to the clumsy reputation of the Word Bearers by operating in concert. And we're to demonstrate the authority of Horus by jumping twenty full Chapters to his whim.'

'Is this a theoretical or a practical assessment, Atreus?' Banzor asks, and all the masters laugh.

'You've seen the tactical audits. The Ghaslakh green-skins are a joke. There is some doubt they've even advanced to Golsoria. Their threat has been over-sold. I could take a company from the reserve and crush them in a week. This is about glorification and the demon-stration of authority. This is about Horus throwing his weight around.'

Some murmurs, many of agreement.

'Horus *Lupercal*,' says Marius Gage.

'What?' says Atreus.

'Horus *Lupercal*,' says Gage. 'Or *Primarch* Horus, or *Warmaster*. You may not consider him a worthier being than our primarch, but the Emperor does, and has bestowed the rank. Even informally, among ourselves, like this, you will refer to him with respect. He's War-master, Atreus, he's our Warmaster, and if he says we go to war, we go to war.'

Atreus stiffens, and then nods.

'My apologies.'

Gage nods back. He glances around. Fourteen Chapter Masters have gathered now. He turns to the doors.

They open. Sub-deck hydraulic pistons pull them apart.

'Enter,' Guilliman calls. 'I can see you fretting out there.'

They enter, Gage leading. Their retinues and veterans remain outside.

Guilliman does not look up. He makes another mark with his stylus. Data scrolls across hololithic plates, unobserved, to his left.

Now they are in the compartment, the view through the crystalflex wall has become more spectacular. Below them, the vast hull of the flagship gleams in the sunlight as it extends away. *Macragge's Honour*. Twenty-six kilometres of polished ceramite and steel armour. Flanking it, at lateral anchor marks, eighteen fleet barges, each one the size of a city, gleam like silver-blue blades. In tiers above, grav-anchored like moons, are shining troop ships, carriers, Mechanicum bulkers, cruisers and grand cruisers and battleships. The space between is thick with small ships and cargo traffic, zipping between holds and berths.

Below, cargo-luggers raise hauls of materiel from the orbital platforms. They look like leafcutter ants, or scorpions bearing oversized prey in their claws.

Below that, a frigate test cycles its engines in the nearest orbital slip.

Below that, Calth, blue-white with reflected sunlight. Pinpricks mirror-flash in the glare: liftships coming up from the surface, catching the sun.

Gage clears his throat.

'We had no wish to disturb you, primarch, but–'

'–there is much to do,' Guilliman finishes. He glances at his First Master. 'I have been watching the datastream, Marius. Did you think I hadn't?'

Gage smiles.

'Never for a moment, sir.'

A hundred labours, simultaneously. The primarch's ability to multitask is almost frightening.

'We wanted to make sure you'd caught every detail,'

says Empion of the 9th. Youngest of them. Newest of them. Gage covers a smile. The poor fool still hasn't learned not to underestimate.

'I believe I have, Empion,' says Guilliman.

'The *Samothrace*–'

'Requires further engine certification,' says Guilliman. 'I have told Shipmaster Kulak to divert servitors from orbital slip 1123. Yes, Empion, I *had* seen that. I had seen that the *Mlatus* is eighty-two hundred tonnes overladen, and suggest the yard chiefs reassign the 41st Espandor to the *High Ascent*. The Erud Province muster is running six minutes behind schedule, so Ventanus needs to get Seneschal Arbute to increase handling rates at Numinus Port. Six minutes will expand over the next two days. Kolophraxis needs to get his ship in line. Caren Province is actually timing ahead of schedule, so compliments to Captain Taerone of the 135th, *however* I doubt he has accommodated the rainstorm predicted for later this afternoon, so he needs to be aware that surface conditions will deteriorate. Speaking of the 135th, there is a sergeant inbound. Thiel. He is marked for censure. Send him to me when he arrives.'

'That's a discipline matter that can be dealt with at master level, sir,' says Antoli. The 13th is his, and the role falls to him.

'Send him to me when he arrives,' Guilliman repeats.

Antoli glances at Gage.

'Of course, my primarch.'

Guilliman rises to his feet and looks at Antoli.

'I just want to talk to him, Antoli. And, yes, Marius, I am micromanaging again. Indulge me. Loading an army is a precise but tedious occupation, and I would like a little diversion.'

The masters smile.

'Any show of our principal guests?' Guilliman asks.

'Primarch Lorgar's fleet has been translating into the system since midnight, Calth standard,' says Gage. 'The first retinues are assembling. We understand the primarch is crossing the system terminator, inbound at high realspace velocity.'

'So... sixteen hours out?'

'Sixteen and a half,' says Gage.

'I was rounding down, like the Army does,' says Guilliman. The men laugh. The primarch looks through the crystalflex wall. Amongst the rows of starships that glint like polished sword blades there is already a scattering of darker vessels, like bloodied weapons that await cleaning.

The first of Lorgar's warships, docking and manoeuvring, taking up their places in the line.

'Hails have been received from the arriving captains and commanders,' says Gage. 'Erebus requests an audience at your convenience.'

'He can wait a while,' says Guilliman. 'The man is quite deplorable. I'd rather we tolerated them all in one go.'

His masters laugh again.

'Such indiscretions are for our circle only,' Guilliman reminds them. 'This operation is designed to demonstrate the efficiency of the new era. It is entirely designed to glorify my brother Horus and reinforce his authority.'

Guilliman looks at Atreus, who smiles, and Gage, who glances away.

'Yes, I was listening, Marius. And here's the thing. Atreus was right. This is show, and this is pomp, and this is, essentially, a waste of time. But – and here's the thing – Horus *is* Warmaster. He *deserves* glorification, and his authority *needs* to be reinforced. Marius, meanwhile, was quite correct too, Atreus. You will refer to the Warmaster at all times with full respect.'

'Yes, my primarch.'

'One last matter,' says Guilliman. 'There was a vox signal interrupt six and half minutes ago. I have the details recorded. Probably solar flare distortion, but someone check, please. It sounded for all the world like singing.'

* * *

[mark: -61.39.12]

THE INTERRUPT IS checked, and attributed to solar distortion. A vox artefact. The void forever creaks and whispers around the audible and electromagnetic ranges.

Half an hour later, a rating aboard the *Castorex* reports hearing voices singing on a vox-link. Twenty minutes later, chanting blocks out the main orbital datafeed for eleven seconds. Its source is unidentified.

An hour later, there are two more bursts, unsourced.

An hour after that, Communication Control reports 'a series of malfunction events' and warns that 'further communication disruption may be expected during the day until the problem is identified'.

An hour after that, on the night side of Calth, the first of the bad dreams begins.

[mark: -50.11.11]

THERE ARE MANY clues. There are many portents. Given the extraordinary thoroughness with which the XIII Legion maintains its readiness, it might be considered tragic, or incompetent, that so few are heeded.

The simple truth is that, in this instance, the Ultramarines do not know what to look for.

Down on the surface of Calth, in the morning light, Tylos Rubio waits with his squad to board transports. They are all of the 21st Company, under Captain Gaius.

Rubio's head aches. There is a pain behind his eyes. He ignores it. He considers, briefly, mentioning it to an Apothecary, but he does not. They have gone without rest periods for several days during the preparation phase. It has not been possible to shut down higher mental functions and sleep, or at least remedially meditate.

He puts the ache down to this, to background fatigue. It is just another frailty of human flesh that his transhuman biology will target and neutralise within an hour.

It isn't fatigue. Later, Rubio will regret not mentioning his ailment. He will regret it more bitterly than anything else that happens on Calth. The remorse will hound him to his grave, many years later.

After the death and the slaughter, after the firing and the killing, when fate has taken an extraordinary step and removed him from the field of war, when there is finally a moment to think, Tylos Rubio will realise that in his determination to follow the edicts of the Emperor, he ignored a vital warning sign.

He is not alone. Amongst the two hundred thousand or so Ultramarines on or around Calth that day, there are hundreds of gifted individuals like him, all self-lessly and obediently reduced to ordinary ranks. They all ignore the headaches.

Unlike Rubio, few survive the event long enough to regret it.

4

'I ASKED TO join the advance,' says Sorot Tchure. For the first time since their reunion, Luciel notes a discomfort in his friend's disposition.

And for the first time, he also reflects that they are not friends at all. What would be a better word? Comrades, perhaps?

They have met once before, eight years previously. Happenstance drew their companies together in the defence of Hantovania Sebros, the last of the tower cities of Caskian. Side-by-side, for four Terran months, they fought off an insect species whose name or language they never learned. Comrades of circumstance.

Circumstance makes decisions for us all.

The simple truth, unglossed, is that the Legion Astartes XIII Ultramarines and the Legion Astartes XVII Word Bearers are not close. Despite their superficial similarities, they are worlds apart in terms of their organisation and combat ideology. They are as unlike each other as the primarchs who lead them.

Any fool can see that the Emperor's original purpose, in creating his Legions and his sons, was to generate a variety of fighting forces that would embellish and complement one another. Their various strengths and characters were supposed to shine in contrast. There is, in uniformity, weakness.

And as brothers are different, so they clash. There are rivalries and arguments, fallings-out and bickering, envy and competition. This, too, is supposed to be part of the healthy organic processes of the Legiones Astartes. This is the Emperor's vision. Let his sons compete. Let his Legions challenge one another. That way, they will spur one another on. That way they will do better. The Emperor, and his oldest, wisest sons, are always there to stop things going too far.

Honorius Luciel and Sorot Tchure stand on the observation deck above the principal hold of the cruiser *Samothrace*. They have greeted each other with respect and affection, and spent the day supervising the transfer distribution of Army personnel and munitions from Tchure's warcarrier to the troop ships in Luciel's oversight. They are alike – alike in stature, alike in rank; one red, one blue, as though stamped from identical fabricatory presses and then finished in different paints.

'We have a bond, I believe,' says Tchure. 'I hope I am not wrong.'

'We do,' Luciel agrees. 'It was an honour to serve with you on Caskian.'

'We are, therefore… unusual,' Tchure ventures.

Luciel laughs.

'You asked to join the advance,' says Luciel. 'I imagine your primarch was supportive?'

'He was.'

'Just as mine was,' Luciel replies, 'when I requested the duty of close protection of Numinus High Anchor. We are cast in the roles of ambassadors, brother.'

'This is my feeling,' Tchure nods, greatly relieved that it is now, after hours in each other's company, at last being spoken of.

'We are, I believe, the only genuine point of friendship between our Legions,' says Luciel. 'No wonder we find ourselves paving the way for the conjunction.'

They walk along the deck, under the immense arches of the hold rib-vaults.

'My Legion's pride is bruised,' says Tchure.

'Of course it is,' Luciel replies. 'Wounded, I would say. And this is the remedy. Our Legions will serve alongside each other in collaborative effort, and thus bond. Our experience serves as an example in miniature.'

'There has been talk of this as an exercise,' replies Tchure. 'That the Warmaster is flexing his authority by commanding two of his brothers, especially one who is so mighty in his own right. But that is smoke. I think Warmaster Horus is displaying remarkable insight. He knows that, as things stand, the unity of any line formed by the Word Bearers and the Ultramarines will be flawed.'

'Warmaster Horus, in his infinite wisdom, has clearly studied the report on the Caskian Campaign.'

'He has, I think.'

Bad blood can take a long time to dilute. Sometimes it must be let out. The point of contention, the bruised pride, is simple. Dissatisfied with the progress and performance of the XVII during the Great Crusade, the Emperor sent the Ultramarines to chastise them. It was an absolute and humiliating rebuke, and stemmed from the Emperor's distaste for the Word Bearers' zealotry, especially when it came to the veneration of his own person as divine. The Emperor's truth was the secular Imperial truth. He tolerated more pious attitudes amongst his sons, but only so far.

It was, perhaps, the Ultramarines' misfortune to be used in such a way. Not just any Legion, but the largest, the most secular, the most efficient, the most disciplined. The most, it could be argued, successful.

Luciel is sympathetic. He has spoken, privately,

with his primarch on the subject on several occasions, because Guilliman is evidently bothered by it too. To be used as an instrument of humiliation, and as an example of perfection, does not sit comfortably. Guilliman is concerned that things will never be right in his relations with the Word Bearers. It is clear from the way he has repeatedly quizzed Luciel, the only officer of the XIII to have ever engineered a reasonable confidence with an officer of the XVII.

For the Word Bearers have only ever been loyal and devoted. Luciel knows this. He has no doubt about the level of Tchure's absolute loyalty. They had their devotion questioned and vilified by the very *object* of that devotion.

Horus Lupercal, Warmaster, is demonstrating his wisdom and perception right at the start of his command. He is healing wounds. He is actively working to set two of his largest Legions at ease with each other, and close the bitter rift.

'On Caskian,' says Luciel, 'I learned a lot from you, Sorot. I learned to wonder at the stars, and to appreciate the humbling scale of our galaxy.'

'And I learned from you,' Tchure replies. 'I learned the close analysis and appraisal of my enemies, and thus re-measured my own capacity as a warrior.'

The exchange is candid. On Caskian, Tchure reminded Luciel of his place in a greater universe. Though he did not try to convert the Ultramarines captain to any form of spiritual belief, he was able to help him glimpse the ineffable, the cosmic mystery that reminds a man, even a powerful transhuman, of his tiny part in the great design, which forms the beating, vital heart of any faith. In effect, Tchure gave Luciel perspective that beneficially diminished Luciel's sense of self in the face of the universe. It showed Luciel his place, and reminded him of his purpose.

In return, Luciel demonstrated to Tchure the rigors of

practice and theory, a robust schooling that pierced the veil of spirituality with a welcome pragmatism. Luciel reminded Tchure he was superhuman. Tchure reminded Luciel he was *only* superhuman. Both benefitted immeasurably from the exchange of perspectives.

'I would know great joy,' says Luciel, 'if our brothers on both sides could come to celebrate their common differences the way we have.'

'I have no doubt,' replies Tchure, 'that this conjunction will bring an end to the hostility between our Legions.'

[mark: -26.43.57]

AEONID THIEL, MARKED for censure, awaits his interview. He has been aboard the *Macragge's Honour* for some hours.

He was told to wait. He is expecting to be called into the presence of Sharad Antoli, Master of the 13th Chapter. He is braced for this. The rebuke will be unstinting, and discipline duties will follow.

He has already been through it once from Taerone, his company captain. During this interview, Thiel made the mistake of attempting to justify his actions. He will not repeat the error when he is called before Chapter Master Antoli.

Thiel has been obliged to wait in a huge anteroom on the fortieth deck. It is a display arsenal, lined with weapons. There are burnished practice cages on raised platforms down the centre of the chamber.

After three hours of standing perfectly still, he relents, removes his helm, and begins to wander the empty chamber, admiring the weapons on display. Most are blade weapons, many master-crafted. They represent the peak weaponcraft of a thousand cultures. This is an exemplar collection, where the highest ranking officers of the XIII come to study weapon types, rehearse and practise with them, and thus improve their theoretical and practical differentials.

Thiel knows he is unlikely to ever come so close to such perfect specimens again. He fights the temptation to take some of the weapons down and examine them. He wants to feel the comparative weights, the individual balances.

When no one has come for a great stretch of time, Thiel reaches a hand out towards a longsword suspended against the wall on a gravity hook.

'Sergeant Thiel?'

Thiel stops and quickly withdraws his hand. A deck officer in ceremonial dress has entered the chamber.

'Yes?'

'I have been asked to inform you that you will not have to wait much longer.'

'I will wait as long as I am required to,' replies Thiel.

'Well,' the officer shrugs, 'it will not be much longer. Logistical issues have taken priority. The primarch will call you shortly.'

He turns to leave.

'Wait, the primarch?'

'Yes, sergeant.'

'I was waiting to be called by Chapter Master Antoli,' says Thiel.

'No, the primarch.'

'Ah,' says Thiel.

The deck officer waits a moment longer, concludes that their conversation is done, and walks out.

The primarch.

Thiel breathes out slowly. It is safe to estimate that he is in about as much trouble as it's possible to be in.

In which case…

He takes down the longsword. It has extraordinary balance. He sweeps it twice, then turns towards the nearest practice cage.

He halts. He turns back.

Might as well be damned for the whole as a part.

He takes down a Rathian sabre, half the length of the longsword, almost the same weight. A blade in each hand, he walks to the cage.

'Rehearsal, single sparring mode. Dual wielding, extremity level eight. Commit.'

The cage hums into life, the armature system rises around him, clattering as it begins to turn.

Thiel hunkers down. He raises the two, priceless blades…

[mark: -25.15.19]

THEIR LIFT IS delayed. Something about a storm out over Caren Province. The sky in the east goes mauve, like a blood bruise.

Sergeant Hellock tells them to bed down and wait for the call. Their lift is delayed, but not in any way that will allow Trooper Bale Rane to leave the site and go see his girl.

'Standing orders apply, no exceptions,' says the sergeant. Then he softens slightly. 'Sorry, Rane. I know what you were hoping.'

Bale Rane sits down and leans his back against a loader pallet. He's beginning to think that he will spend the rest of his life looking at Sergeant Hellock's face and never see Neve's again.

The truth could hardly be more contrary.

'Is that singing?' asks Krank. He gets up.

'That's singing,' he says.

Rane can hear it. Two hundred metres away, on the other side of some perimeter fencing, is a compound occupied by Army forces that have arrived with the XVII. A ragged mob, they look. Just the sort of fringe-world vagabonds you'd expect to come scurrying along on the heels of the zealot Word Bearers. They had received a great deal of critical commentary from Sergeant Hellock as they disembarked, criticism that included uniform code, formation, equipment maintenance and parade discipline.

'Oh, that's just embarrassing,' Hellock says, lighting a lho-stick as he watches them dismount from the troop landers. 'They look like bastard vagrants. Like shit-stupid hunters from some arse-end world.'

The soldiers from off-world indeed do not look promising. They are ragged. There is a wildness to them, as though they have been deprived of something vital for too long. Their skin is pale and their frames are thin. They look like plants that have been starved of light in a cave. They look like heathens.

'That's just what we need,' says Hellock. 'Heathen auxiliary units.'

They are singing, chanting. It is not a comfortable or attractive sound. It's atonal. It's actually quite unpleasant to listen to.

'That's going to have to stop,' the sergeant says. He grinds the butt of a lho-stick under his heel.

He crosses the yard to have a word with the commander of the other unit. The chanting bothers him.

5

RAINDROPS COME OUT of the dry air like bolter rounds. They explode like black glass against the hood of the speeder that Selaton is gunning down Erud Highway.

Everything's dust: dust-dry land, dusty-caked metal, a fog raised by lifters and engines and traffic. The flat landscape is pale, harshly lit. The sky has gone oddly dark, opaque. From the passenger seat of the armoured speeder, Ventanus can see the distant line of the hills, swathed in green.

There's a rainstorm swimming up from the south. Vox says it's already a mire down in Caren.

It'll be a mire here too, before very long, Ventanus thinks. The light is so weird. The sky so black, the ground so light. The raindrops look like glass beads, like tears. They explode all over him, all over his armour, all over the speeder, wet black streaking the film of white dust all surfaces have acquired during the day.

The raindrops hit the dusty ground, the highway, the scabby verge, making millions of little black entry wounds, little black craters, little puffs of white. Far away, little silver threads of lightning glitter in the low cloud, like seams of bright ore exposed in coal.

Selaton drives like an idiot. The speeder is a hefty two-man machine with forward gunmounts, its cobalt-blue armour flaked with dust and bruised with the dents and scrapes of use. The cockpit is open. Grav plates keep the ground at bay, and the drive-plant is over-powered to help it slide all that armour around.

It's a light recon vehicle that's mean enough to fight its way out of bother. Ventanus requisitioned it for the day as staff transport.

Now Selaton's driving it like an idiot.

He's affecting just about maximum horizontal velocity, pluming a white tail of dust out behind them along the flat, straight roadway. The rain is trying to wet the dust back down, but it's too thick. A nav-track display to the left of the driver blinks a route overlay. The display is armoured and grilled against wear and tear. The speeder is a working machine with bare metal along most seams.

The twitching cursor on the illuminated display is supposed to be them. The etched line is the highway. At the foot of the screen is a blob, that's Erud station. At the top, a triangular icon.

Red hazard hatching appears on the etched line ahead of the cursor.

'Slower,' says Ventanus over the helmet link.

'Too fast?' Selaton replies, eager glee in his voice.

Ventanus doesn't even look down. He taps the screen of the nav-track.

Selaton glances, sees it, eases off the throttle immediately. They're coming up on the tail of a muster convoy. Even as they bleed off speed, they hit the dust wake of the moving column.

Selaton steers out, crosses the centre of the highway, starts to overtake. Trundling troop transports, cargo-20s, towed artillery, tank transporters, laden. Each hulking vehicle zips by and falls behind, each one glimpsed for a second as they pass it in the odd light, in the air that is both dry with dust and wet with rain. Troop truck, gone. Troop truck, gone. Troop truck, gone. Troop truck, gone. A garland of cheers and hoots from a transport load of Army troopers, waving them past.

Self-propelled guns now, zipping past, barrels up to sniff the sky. Ten, twenty, thirty units. The damn column is forty kilometres long. Shadowswords. Minotaurs. New Infernus-pattern armour and regimental troop carriers.

Ventanus watches beads of rain, black with soot, crawling and quivering over the hood of the speeder.

He's had to leave Sydance in charge at Erud, with reliable sergeants like Archo, Ankrion and Barkha to back him up. There's something to sort out with the Numinus seneschals. Local politics. Ventanus hates local politics, but this has come from the primarch's staff directly. Port affairs. Handling rates. Diplomacy.

Ventanus knows what to do with a boltgun.

This is another unnuanced exercise in teaching them the other crafts their lives will one day require. Courtesy. Effective management. Authority. Basically, anything that *doesn't* involve a boltgun. It has Guilliman's hand-prints all over it.

It's the sort of issue that Ventanus would prefer to resolve with a quick vox order, but he's been told to handle it in person. So, a forty-minute wasted trip to the port where the seneschals he needs to see *aren't*, now an hour up the Erud Highway instead to… where was it?

The Holophusikon. *Holophusikon.*

Ventanus isn't stupid. He knows what the word means. He just doesn't know what it is.

A triangular icon on the navigation display.

Selaton makes a sound. It's a murmur of something. Surprise. He's impressed by something.

He drops more speed.

They're coming up on Titans. Titans marching down the highway towards the port, single file.

They trudge. They are immense. Outrider gun-carts and skitarii speeders with flashing lights surrounding their feet, waving Ventanus wide.

They pass through their trooping shadows. Shadow, sunlight, shadow, sunlight. Each shadow is a darkness like the underworld. The Titans are caked in dust. They look weary, like ramshackle metal prisoners, giant convicts shuffling towards the stockade.

Or a gibbet.

The odd, hard sunlight catches their upper surfaces and cockpit ports. A gleam in the eye. A killer gaze. Ancient giants that have endured all wars, obediently marching towards the next one.

Ventanus finds himself looking up, looking back, gazing at them as they pass. Even he is impressed. Forty-seven Titans. He can hear the tectonic boom of their footsteps over the howl of the speeder's engines.

The biggest are filling the highway. A supply convoy moving in the opposite direction has been forced to pull onto the shoulder and wait to let them pass. Marshals wave batons and lamps.

Selaton, urgent, has pulled wide. Now the shoulder is filled with stationary transports, so he pulls wider still, crossing the highway marker, the shoulder, the culvert and ditch, riding off the transit way onto the scrub beyond, building speed again, raising a foxtail of grey dust. He uprates the grav elements, lifts another fifty centimetres for terrain clearance, and opens the throttle again. They bank, accelerating. The speeder's drive wails. They're moving parallel to the highway.

Ventanus looks back.

He fancies one or two of the Titans turn their massive heads to watch; disdainful, grumpy. Who is that in the tiny speeder, racing past? Why are they so impatient? Where are they going in such a damned hurry?

* * *

[mark: -19.12.36]

THE HOLOPHUSIKON. IT turns out it *is* a triangle, like the icon.

A pyramid. Actually, a pyramid raised on three smaller pyramids, each one supporting a base corner of the largest. It is made of faced ashlar and cream stone. Ventanus notes that it is an impressive building, in terms of both scale and design.

It might even be beautiful. He's not sure. He has no expertise in such determinations.

They can see it from ten kilometres away. The Erud Highway passes it, linking to the Holophusikon's own feeder roadways, and the township of service buildings and garrisons. Numinus City resolves as a gleaming skyline on the horizon.

The Holophusikon is stately, immense, planted in the open space of the plains. Though there is an ample town of buildings around it, it still looks new, as though it has just been built and is waiting for a city to sprout around it.

Or it looks as if it has been sent into wilderness exile for punishment.

The rain has stopped, briefly. The wind is up. The light catches the monolith's sunward faces, bright. The other aspects are deep brown shadows. Its perfect geometry is emphasised.

Approach roads are avenues hung with banners that jump and flap in the wind. Golden masts, gilt canopy poles, lamp stands. The banners bear the heraldry of the Five Hundred Worlds of Ultramar, of Terra, of the Imperium, of the XIII. Ventanus hasn't seen so many banners in one place since he last looked at picts of the Triumph at Ullanor.

There are gardens in the ground too. They are very green. Irrigation has dragged water from the Boros River out into the arid plains to create an oasis. Pools shimmer. Hydration systems fill the air with spray. Miniature rainbows form. Palms nod.

'Slow down,' says Ventanus.

They ride up under the flapping banners, and through the cool darkness under a grand arch, and coast into an inner courtyard. There is a great flight of steps like the processional advance to a temple. More banners drape from the walls of the inner precinct. There are other vehicles in sight, and dots that are people dwarfed by the immensity of the enclosure. Motorised staircases with ceramite treads flow silently on either side of the main flight.

They dismount. The speeder wobbles like a small boat as their weight leaves it. Liveried footmen approach to take care of the vehicle.

Ventanus starts up the steps, his sergeant behind him. He unclasps and removes his helm, breathes unfiltered air, feels heat and light on his face.

'The Holophusikon,' says Selaton.

'A universal museum,' says Ventanus.

'I understood that.'

Ventanus has little patience for, or interest in, such places. He is prepared to admit that this is a flaw in his character.

They arrive at the top of the towering flight. A standard human being, even an exceptionally fit one, would be slightly short of breath at the end of such a climb in the sunlight. If anything, their pace is faster by the time they reach the top.

A marble platform, a broad entrance. Beyond, a huge and airy stone space, lit by natural light through slots in the roof. Cool. The spacious echo of murmured voices.

Ventanus approaches through the broad entrance. It is rectangular, landscape in form. A vast slot. The lip of the doorway overhead is thirty metres wide.

There are a few other visitors, tiny clumps of figures in the vast interior space. Ventanus is struck by the scale of the space, by its hollow, empty sound. Around the edges of the great chamber there are alcoves, podiums, plinths, displays. The exhibits, he supposes. That's where the visitors are. Why build such a vast space and then dot the few exhibits around the edges?

'What is this supposed to be?' asks Selaton.

'I don't pretend to understand curation,' replies Ventanus.

More liveried footmen approach them.

'How may we serve, sir?' asks one.

'Ventanus, Captain, 4th Company, First Chapter, XIII,' Ventanus replies. 'I am looking for–'

He has memorised the names.

'–Seneschals Arbute, Darial and Eterwin. Or, in fact, any senior municipal servant whose portfolio encompasses the starport.'

'They are all in the building,' the footman replies. He is clearly being fed behind the eyes by some direct-to-retina datasystem. Ventanus can tell from the slightly glassy way his eyes de-focus to verify the names.

'Could you fetch them?' asks Ventanus.

'They are in session all afternoon,' replies the footman. 'Is it urgent?'

Ventanus chooses his next word carefully. It's not so much the word as the hesitation he places in front of it, the hesitation that says *I am wearing battle plate, I am armed, and I am doing my very best to be polite*.

'Yes,' he says.

The footmen hurry away.

The Ultramarines wait.

'Sir, is that–?' Selaton starts.

'It is,' Ventanus replies.

Ventanus walks towards the distant figure that they have recognised. The figure is kneeling in front of one of the exhibit plinths. Attendants wait for him at a respectful distance.

The kneeling figure sees Ventanus and gets up. The

gears and motors of his armour hum. He is taller than Ventanus, broader, the bulk of his plate master-crafted and finished with expansive golden wings, lions, eagles. He is leaning on a broadsword that is fully the height of a standard human.

'Lord champion,' Ventanus says, saluting.

'Captain Ventanus,' the giant replies. He eschews a salute, hands off the mighty sword to a bearer, and clasps Ventanus's steel-cased hand between his own.

Ventanus is flattered to be recognised by such an august person.

'What are you here for?' the giant asks. 'I thought you were running the Erud muster.'

'You are well-informed, tetrarch,' says Ventanus.

'Information is victory, my brother,' the tetrarch says, and laughs.

Ventanus explains his errand, the diplomatic function.

The tetrach listens. His name is Eikos Lamiad. His rank is tetrarch and also Primarch's Champion. The four tetrarchs represent the four master worlds that command the fiefdoms of Ultramar under the authority of Macragge: Saramanth, Konor, Occluda and Iax. Lamiad's fiefdom is Konor, the forge world. The tetrarchs are the four princes of Ultramar, and they rule the Five Hundred Worlds, standing in the hierarchy of power below Guilliman and above the Chapter Masters and the planetary lords.

'I know the seneschals,' says Lamiad. 'I can introduce you.'

'I would appreciate that, my lord.' Ventanus replies. 'It is a matter of expediency.'

Half of Eikos Lamiad's face, the right half, is heroically handsome. The other half is a pale porcelain blank seamlessly embedded into the flesh, an elegant estimation of the missing face. The left eye is a gold-pupilled mechanism that winds and counter-circles like an antique optical instrument.

Lamiad was grievously wounded during the defence of Bathor. Shuriken shrieker rounds blew his skull apart and dismembered his body, but the worshipful Mechanicum elders of Konor Forge rebuilt him, respectful of his service and his good governance of their world holding.

It is said he would inhabit a Dreadnought chassis now, but for their ministrations.

'Do you like the Holophusikon, Ventanus?' the mighty champion enquires. His entourage of servitors, bearers, aides and battle-brothers is silent and stoic. All of them are in rich, ceremonial dress.

'"Like", lord?'

'Appreciate, then?'

'I have not given it much thought, lord.'

Lamiad smiles, the half of his face that can.

'I sense a reservation, Remus,' he says.

'If I may speak candidly?' Ventanus says.

'Do.'

'I have been to many worlds, lord, Imperial and not Imperial. I have, I think, lost count of the number of repositories of all wisdom I have been shown. Every world, every culture has its great library, its archive of wonders, its data store, its trove of lore, its casket of all secrets. How many ultimate archives of all universal knowledge can there be?'

'You sound jaded, Remus.'

'I apologise.'

'Cultural archiving is important, Remus.'

'Information is victory, lord.'

'Indeed,' says Lamiad. 'We need to store our learning. We have also, during the Great Crusade, learned vast amounts by acquiring the archives of compliant cultures.'

'I understand the–'

Lamiad raises his hand, a soft gesture.

'I wasn't reprimanding you, Remus. While I acknowledge the import of careful data gathering, I am also tired of the overly reverential way in which places like this are regarded. Oh, *another* holy repository of the most secret secrets of all, you say? Pray tell me what secrets you might keep that I have not learned from a thousand crypts just like this?'

They laugh.

'You know what I like about this one, Remus?'

'No, lord. What?'

'It's empty,' says Lamiad.

The Holophusikon was commissioned thirty years before, during the development of Numinus City. It is younger than both of them, younger than their careers. Construction work has only recently been finished. Curators have just begun to import objects and data for display and storage.

'They are usually so old, aren't they?' Lamiad remarks. 'Dusty tombs of information, closed and guarded for unnumbered centuries, with special keys, and special rituals to get in, and all that tedious mystery. What I like about this place is its emptiness. Its intent. It is a proposition, Remus. It's a great undertaking that looks forward, not back. It is open, and ready to be filled with mankind's future. One day it will be a universal museum, and perhaps it will stand, alongside the libraries of Terra, as one of the greatest data repositories in the Imperium. For now, it is an ambition, built of stone. A deliberate statement of our intention to establish a robust and sophisticated culture, and to maintain it, and to record and measure it.'

'It's a museum of the future,' says Ventanus.

'Well said. It is. A museum of the future. For now, that is exactly what it is.'

'And that's why you've come here?' asks Ventanus.

Lamiad shows him the exhibit he was inspecting when Ventanus arrived. In a sterile suspension field is the stabilised corner of a fire-damaged banner. Body heat triggers the hololithic placard, revealing origin details.

It is part of the banner that Lamiad carried on Bathor. This exhibit, one of the first few hundred chosen, honours him and his achievement, and commemorates that great battle.

'I have tours of service planned that will take me from Ultramar for at least ten years,' Lamiad says. 'I felt I should come and see this before I embarked. See it with my own eyes.'

He looks at Ventanus.

'Well, with my flesh eye and the one the Mechanicum made for me.'

They talk of the muster for a while, and of the coming campaign. Neither of them mentions the XVII.

Then Lamiad says, 'They say Calth will be named a major world soon. It is developing fast, and its strengths are evident. The shipyards. The fabrication. Its status will be upgraded, and it will control a fief of its own.'

'I will not be surprised,' replies Ventanus.

'It will have its own tetrarch too,' says Lamiad. 'It will have to. As a major world, it will be obliged to appoint a military governor, and produce a champion and a champion's honour guard for the primarch.'

'Indeed.'

'There is talk of Aethon. Aethon of the 19th. As a potential candidate for the post.'

'Aethon is a fine candidate,' Ventanus agrees.

'There are others in consideration. There is, I am told by our beloved primarch, some art to the choosing of a tetrarch.'

'And it can't be a tetrarch, can it?' says Ventanus. 'Perhaps you will all become *quintarchs* once there are five of you?'

Lamiad laughs again.

'Perhaps they will coin another title, Remus,' he says. 'One that is not numerically specific. Calth won't be the last, merely the next. Ultramar grows. As we meet the future and fill this Holophusikon, we will have more than Five Hundred Worlds, and more than five fiefdoms. Like the emptiness of these halls, we must be ready to accommodate the changes and the expansions to come.'

He turns. Figures in long, pale green robes are approaching them, followed by attendants.

'Here come the seneschals,' says the Primarch's Champion. 'Let me introduce you so you can get your business done.'

6

[mark: -16.44.12]

AT THE ORBITAL Watchtower, Server of Instrumentation Uhl Kehal Hesst communes with the noosphere.

The code is speaking. It is *gabbling*.

The pleats of his floor-length Mechanicum robes are so crisp, he looks as if he has been carved by stonemasons. He stands at the summit of a Watchtower that is similarly straight and slender. The tower casts its shadow across Kalkas Fortalice, the armoured citadel that faces Numinus City across the glittering width of the Boros. It is a cauldron of walls and castellated towers, a city in its own right, but a place of defence, a lifeguard set to stand at the shoulder of Numinus and protect it from harm.

Ten thousand people work in the Watchtower, and another fifty thousand function in the gun towers and administration buildings around it. It is alert, a sentient place, its noospheric architecture designed on Hesst's forge world, Konor, and supported by technologies supplied directly from the fabricatories of Mars.

The Watchtower's command deck is vast, and bustling with staff. Windows, their blast shutters raised, gaze out across the river and the city to one side, and out towards the lowlands on the other. Hesst can image the traffic at the starport, the dust raised by marshalling on the plains, the bright land and the storm-tinted sky, but he is not interested in the view.

The tower supports its own manifold field, and is inloading data to him and the other seniors at a rate equivalent to the noospheric broadcast of eight hundred Battle Titans. Sixty moderati of the highest quality, working in amniotic armourglas caskets set into the deck, help to cushion that flow and parse it for comprehension.

From this deck, from this summit, Hesst can issue – by means of a simple code command across his permanent MIU link – the order to commit the planet's weapon grid. Two hundred and fifty thousand surface-based weapons stations, including silo launchers and automated plasma ordnance, plus tower and turret guns, field stations, polar weapon pits. He can activate the immense void shield systems that umbrella Calth's principal habitation centres. He can bring on-line the nine hundred and sixty-two orbital platforms, which include outward-facing protection systems and surface-aiming interdiction networks. Furthermore, he can harness and coordinate any and all available forces on the ground, and any fleet composition assembling at high anchor or in the shipyards.

Which means that, today, because of the conjunction, Server Hesst has immediate personal control over more firepower than Warmaster Horus. Or, it's conceivable, the Emperor himself.

This consideration does not impress Server Hesst, or fill him with anxiety. Hesst is aware, however, that Magos Meer Edv Tawren is reading his elevated adrenal levels.

Tawren is young and efficient, tall, fully modified. She has excelled in her advancement through the developmental levels of the Mechanicum, and is profoundly good at her work. She supervises the Analyticae. Hesst is fond of her. He seldom accesses his emotions, but on the rare occasions that he decides to use them, he always notices the warmth with which he perceives her. Her modifications are technically pleasing, and her base organics possess a certain aesthetic.

<You are running hot,> she blurts to him in binaric code, a microsecond transmission on the intimate direct mode. It is non-verbal, but the blurt contains code signifiers for Hesst, and for a Titan battle unit straining its drives.

<Not at all. Rumination: Today is simply demanding.>

Tawren nods. She is ghosting his overwatch. He is aware of her presence in the manifold at his shoulder, just as she is standing next to him on the deck in the fleshsphere. Her fingers are trembling, touching invisible keys, coordinating data via the subtle haptics. Today's difficulty is *not* shooting at things.

With two fleets in conjunction, traffic density above Calth is singularly high. Virtually all of it is moving according to non-standard or adjusted traffic patterns, extraordinary situational shifts of movement, course and proximity that are not coded into the regular watch registers. This is a one-time thing, for one day only: their responsibility is the safe and assured orchestration of a vast armada.

Calth's weapons grid has multiple redundancies and stratified forms of cross-check and authorisation. It cannot be abused or used in error by any single individual: not Hesst, not the forty other servers in the Watchtower, not the six thousand two hundred and seventy-eight magi and adepts stationed planet-wide, or the garrison commanders of the Army or the local divisions. Nothing can happen without his personal consent.

Every time a ship arrives, or moves, or passes another, or joins formation, or enters a yard, or docks, or begins to refuel, or begins a sunward circuit to certify its drives, an alarm sounds. Every non-standard motion or manoeuvre system-activates the grid, and Hesst has to reject a firing query.

It's actually the most superb test and demonstration of Calth's grid, but it is becoming tiresome. From the summit of the Watchtower, Server Hesst controls the effective firepower of a major fleet, that firepower distributed across the surface and orbit. The system is hyper-sensitive, so that nothing can take it by surprise and secure an advantage. Every non-standard movement triggers an automatic firing solution from the grid, which Hesst has to personally reject in discretionary mode. He's currently getting between eighteen and twenty-five a second.

Tawren knows that standard Mechanicum operating practice under such conditions, as advised by both the forgemasters of Konor and the exalted elders of Mars, is to temporarily bypass the multi-nodal automatics of the grid's alert processors and, for the duration of the fleet manoeuvres, transfer approval control to the automatic stations. Let the sentient machines of the platforms shoulder the burden. Let them cross-check the constant inload of data. Let them verify the anchorage codes and the traffic registration marks.

She also knows that Hesst is a determined individual who takes great pride in his work, and in his duties as a server. Calth's planetary grid is optimised to run on multi-nodal automatics with a server or servers supplying final approval of all operations. To switch out to auto- matics alone is to admit the weakness of the fleshbrain. It is to resort to machine alone rather than bioengine synthesis. It is to acknowledge the limits of man, and to submit to the clinical efficiency of cold code.

They have discussed this. They have even discussed it using flesh-voices and vocal chords, unplugged. Hesst has the purest vision of the Mechanicum's dream, and she adores him for it. It is not, as so many of the unmodi- fied in society believe, the adoration of the machine. It is the use of the machine to extend humanity. It is apotheosis through synthesis. To stand back and allow the machines to do the work is disgusting to Hesst. He probably finds the concept more abhorrent than an unmodified human would.

<It's not an admission of failure, you know?> she blurts. She is resuming a conversation they were having two days before, as if no intervening time had elapsed.

He acknowledges the fact, recognising the conversational marker appended to her code that reopens his saved file of that exchange.

<It is, in fact, a practice recommended by Mars.>

Hesst nods.

<If we build systems we cannot run, what is the point of building them? Tell me where that leads, Magos Tawren?>

<The annihilation of self. The abnegation of sentience.>

'Exactly,' says Hesst. His use of flesh-voice surprises her, but she instantly realises that he has switched from binaric in order to make a symbolic point. This amuses her, and she shows him that she is amused by using a facial expression.

'You think this is about my pride, don't you, Meer?' he asks.

She shrugs. Like him, she is still, simultaneously, making subtle haptic gestures and scouring the noosphere's dataflow. 'I think that no one, not even an adept of the rank server or above, has ever run an operation like this on discretionary mode alone. I think you're attempting some kind of record. Or trying to win a medal. Or trying to rupture a major organ.'

Her voice is clean, as pure as code. He sometimes wishes she would use it more.

'It is simply a question of security and efficiency,' he says. 'The grid is designed to be multi-nodal. That is its strength. It has no single heart, no single brain. It is global. Take out any point, even this Watchtower, even me, and any other ranking server or magos can take over.

The grid will adjust and recognise the discretion of the next in line. This tower could topple, and a server on the far side of the planet would instantly take over. Multi-nodal redundancy is a perfect system. You cannot kill anything that has no centre. So I'd prefer not to weaken the integrity of this planet's defence system even slightly by opting out of discretion and transferring approval oversight to the orbital engines.'

'This conjunction is expected to continue for another day or two,' she remarks. 'When would you like me to take over from you? Before or after you stroke out and tumble to the floor?'

Tawren realises he isn't listening. He has become pre-occupied with the inload.

'What is it?' she asks.

'Scrapcode.'

Any complex information system will produce scrap-code as a result of internal degradation. She knows that. She wonders what he means, and peers into the manifold.

She sees the scrapcode, dull amber threads of diseased information buried in the mass of healthy data. There is two per cent more of it than any Analyticae projection has calculated for the Calth noosphere, even under the irregular circumstances of the day. That is an unacceptable margin.

<Filtration isn't clearing it. I don't know where it's coming from.>

He has reverted to binaric blurt. There is no time for words.

[mark: -15.02.48]

CRIOL FOWST HAS been given a blade, but it proves impractical to use it. He uses his sidearm instead. The oblators need to be killed cleanly and quickly. There isn't time to fool about with a knife.

Outside the shelter, his appointed officers are rousing the men in song. Chanting fills the air. They have been encouraged to bring viols and qatars, tambours, pipes, horns and bells. It is supposed to sound like a celebration. The eve of battle, honoured allies, the anticipation of glory, all of that nonsense. It is supposed to sound joyous.

And it does, but Fowst can hear the ritual theme inside the noisy singing. He can hear it because he knows it's buried there. Old words. Words that were old before humans learned to speak. Potent words. You can set them to any tune, to the verse-and-chorus of an Army battle reel. They work just the same.

The singing is loud. It's quite a commotion, six thousand men in this corner of the muster fields alone. Loud enough to drown out his shots.

He pulls the trigger.

The matt-grey autopistol barks, bucks in his hand, and slams a single round through the temple it's pressed against. Blood and tissue spray, splashing his jacket. The kneeling man flops sideways, as if the weight of his punctured head is pulling him down. There's a whiff of fycelene in the air, a smell of powdered blood, burned flesh and blood vapour.

Fowst looks down at the man he has just shot and murmurs a blessing, the sort one might offer to a traveller embarking on a long and difficult voyage. His mercy almost came too late that time. The man's eyes had begun to melt.

Fowst nods, and two of his appointed officers step forward to drag the body aside. Now the corpses of seven oblators lie on the groundsheet spread out to one side.

The next man steps up, stone-faced, unfazed at the prospect of imminent death. Fowst embraces him and kisses his cheeks and lips.

Then he steps back.

The man, like the seven who have come before him,

knows what to do. He has prepared. He has stripped down to his undershirt and breeches. He's given everything else away, even his boots. The Brotherhood of the Knife uses whatever equipment it can gather or forage: hauberks, body armour, ballistic cloth, sometimes a little chainmesh. There's usually a coat or cloak or robe over the top to keep out the weather, always dark grey or black. With no more need for any field gear, the man has given away his good coat, his gloves and his armour to those who can use them later. His weapons too.

He's holding his bottle.

In his case, it's a blue glass drinking bottle with a stoppered cap. His oblation floats inside it. The man before him used a canteen. The man before that, a hydration pack from a medicae's kit.

He opens it and pours the water out through his fingers so the slip of paper inside is carried out into his palm. The moment it's out of suspension in the hydrolytic fluid, the moment it comes into contact with the air, it starts to warm up. The edges begin to smoulder.

The man drops the bottle, steps forward and kneels in front of the vox-caster. The key pad is ready.

He looks at the slip of paper, shivering as he reads the characters inscribed upon it. A thin wisp of white smoke is beginning to curl off the edge of the slip.

His hand trembling, the man begins to enter the word into the caster's pad, one letter at a time. It is a name. Like the seven that have been typed in before, it can be written in human letters. It can be written in any language system, just as it can be sung to any tune.

Criol Fowst is a very intelligent man. He is one of a very few members of the Brotherhood who have actively come looking for this moment. He was born and raised on Terra to an affluent family of merchants, and pursued their interests into the stars. He'd always been hungry for something: he thought it was wealth and success. Then he thought it was learning. Then he realised that learning was just another mechanism for the acquisition of power.

He'd been living on Mars when he was approached and recruited by the Cognitae. At least, that's what they thought they'd done.

Fowst knew about the Cognitae. He'd made a particular study of occult orders, secret societies, hermetic cabals of mysteries and guarded thought. Most of them were old, Strife-age or earlier. Most were myths, and most of the remainder charlatans. He'd come to Mars looking for the Illuminated, but they turned out to be a complete fabrication. The Cognitae, however, actually existed. He asked too many questions and toured datavendors looking for too many restricted works. He made them notice him.

If the Cognitae had ever been a real order, these men were not it. At best, they were some distant bastard cousin of the true bloodline. But they knew things he did not, and he was content to learn from them and tolerate their theatrical rituals and pompous rites of secrecy.

Ten months later, in possession of several priceless volumes of transgressive thought that had previously been the property of the Cognitae, Fowst took passage rimwards. The Cognitae did not pursue him to recover their property, because he had made sure that they would not be capable of doing so. The bodies, dumped into the heat vent of the hive reactor at Korata Mons, were never recovered.

Fowst went out into the interdicted sectors where the 'Great Crusade' was still being waged, away from the safety of compliant systems. He headed for the Holy Worlds where the majestic XVII Legion, the Word Bearers, were actively recruiting volunteer armies from the conquered systems.

Fowst was especially intrigued by the Word Bearers. He was intrigued by their singular vision. Though they were one of the eighteen, one of the Legiones Astartes, and thus a core part of the Imperium's infrastructure, they alone seemed to exhibit a spiritual zeal.

The Imperial truth was, in Fowst's opinion, a lie. The Palace of Terra doggedly enforced a vision of the galaxy that was rational and pragmatic, yet any fool could see that the Emperor relied upon aspects of reality that were decidedly un-rational. The mind-gifted, for example. The empyrean. Only the Word Bearers seemed to acknowledge that these things were more than just useful anomalies. They were proof of a greater and denied mystery. They were evidence of some transcendent reality beyond reality, of some divinity, perhaps. All of the Legiones Astartes were founded on unshakeable faith, but only the Word Bearers placed their belief in the divine. They worshipped the Emperor as an aspect of some greater power.

Fowst agreed with them in every detail except one. The universe contained beings worthy of adoration and worship. The Emperor, for all his ability, simply wasn't one of them.

On Zwanan, in the Veil of Aquare, a Holy World still dark with the smoke of Word Bearers compliance, Criol Fowst joined the Brotherhood of the Knife, and began his service to the XVII primarch.

He was able. He had been educated on Terra. He was no heathen backworlder energised by crude fanaticism. He rose quickly, from rank and file to appointed officer, from that to overseer, from that to his current position as a *confided lieutenant*. The name for this is *majir*. His sponsor and superior is a Word Bearers legionary called Arune Xen and, through him, Fowst has been honoured with several private audiences with Argel Tal of the Gal Vorbak. He has attended ministries, and listened to Argel Tal speak.

Xen has given Fowst his ritual blade. It is an athame blessed by the Dark Apostles. It is the most beautiful thing he has ever owned. When he holds it in his hand, byblow gods hiss at him from the shadows.

The Brotherhood of the Knife is not so-called because it favours bladework in combat. The name is not literal.

In the dialect of the Holy Worlds, the Brotherhood is the *Ushmetar Kaul*, the 'sharp edge by which false reality might be slit and pulled away to reveal god'.

Fowst's attention has wavered. The oblator has finished keying in the eighth name. The slip of paper is burning in his hand. Smoking scads are falling from his fingers. He is shaking, trying not to scream. His eyes have cooked in their sockets.

Fowst remembers himself. He raises the sidearm to deliver mercy, but its clip is empty. He tosses it away, and uses the athame that Battle-brother Xen gifted him.

It is a messier mercy.

Eight names are now in the system. Eight names broadcast into the dataflow of the Imperial communications network. No filter or noospheric barrier will block them or erase them, because they are only composed of regular characters. They are not toxic code. They are not viral data. But once they are inside the system, and especially once they have been read and absorbed by the Mechanicum's noosphere, they will grow. They will become what they are. They will stop being combinations of letters, and they will become meanings.

Caustic. Infectious. Indelible.

There are eight of them. The sacred number. The Octed.

And there can be more. Eight times eight times eight-fold eight...

Majir Fowst steps back, wipes blood from his face, and welcomes the next man up to the vox-caster with a kiss.

[mark: -14.22.39]

STILL OVER TWELVE hours out of Calth orbitspace, the fleet tender *Campanile* performs a series of course corrections, and begins the final phase of its planetary approach.

7

'I CAN ASSURE you, sir,' says Seneschal Arbute, 'the labour guilds are fully aware of the importance of this undertaking.'

She's a surprisingly young woman, plain and businesslike. Her robes are grey.

Sergeant Selaton revises his estimate. What would he know? She's not so much plain, just unadorned. No cosmetics, no jewellery. Hair cropped short. In his experience, high status females tended to be rather more decorative.

They have accompanied her from the Holophusikon to the port, following her official carrier in their speeder. She is a member of the Legislature's trade committee. Darial and Eterwin have more power, but both insist that Arbute has a much more effective relationship with the guild rank and file. Her father was a cargo porter.

The port district is loud and busy. Huge semi-auto hoists and cranes, some of them looking like quadruped Titans, are transferring cargo stacks to the giant bulk lifters on the field.

Captain Ventanus seems to have wearied of the effort.

79

He stands to one side, watching the small fliers and mes-
senger craft zip across the port like dragonflies over a
pond. He leaves Selaton to do the talking.

'With respect,' says Selaton, 'the guildsmen and porters
are falling behind the agreed schedule. We're beginning
to get back-up in the mustering areas.'

'Is this an official complaint?' she asks.

'No,' he replies. 'But it has been handed down from
the primarch. If you can put in any kind of word, my
captain would appreciate it. He's under pressure.'

She smiles quickly.

'We're all under pressure, sergeant. The guilds have
never undertaken a materiel load on this scale. The estimated schedule was as accurate as they could make it,
but it is still an estimation. The porting crew and loaders
are bound to hit unexpected delays.'

'Still,' says Selaton. 'A word to their foremen. From a
member of the city legislature. A little encouragement,
and an acknowledgement of their effort.'

'Just so I know, what is the shortfall?' asks Arbute.

'When we came looking for you, six minutes,' he says.

'Is that a joke?'

'No.'

'Six minutes is... Forgive me, sergeant. Six minutes is
nothing. It's not even a margin of error. You came to
find me, and dragged me here from the Holophusikon
ceremonies because of a *six-minute* lag?'

'It's twenty-nine minutes now,' replies Selaton. 'I do
not wish to sound rude, seneschal, but this is a Legion-led
operation. The tolerances are tighter than in commercial
or regular military circumstances. Twenty-nine minutes
is bordering on the *abominable*.'

'I'll talk to the foremen,' she says. 'I'll see if there's any
reserve they can draw on. There has been bad weather.'

'I know.'

'And some incidence of system failure. Junk information. Corrupt data.'

'That happens too. I'm sure you will do what you can.'
She looks at him, and nods.
'Wait here,' she says.

[mark: -11.16.21]

'IN YOUR CONSIDERED opinion?' Guilliman asks.

Magos Pelot is the senior serving Mechanicum representative aboard the flagship *Macragge's Honour*, and he's just been required to present the primarch with awkward news. He thinks for a moment before replying. He does not want to tar his institution with verdicts of incompetence, but he has also served the primarch long enough to know that little good ever comes of sugaring the pill.

'The scrapcode problem we have identified is a hindrance, sir,' he says. 'It is regrettable. Especially on a day like today. These things do happen. I won't pretend they don't. Natural degradation. Code errors. They can occur without warning for any number of reasons. The Mechanicum dearly wishes we weren't being plagued by them during this event.'

'Cause?'

'Perhaps the sheer scale of the conjunction itself? Precisely because today is important. The simple mass of data–'

'Is it proportional?' asks Guilliman. 'Is it the proportional increment you would naturally expect to find?'

Magos Pelot hesitates. His mechadendrite implants ripple.

'It is slightly higher. Very slightly.'

'So it's an abnormal level, in the experience of the Mechanicum? It's not natural degradation?'

'Technically,' Pelot agrees. 'But not in any way that should be deemed alarming.'

Guilliman smiles to himself.

'So this is just… for my information?'

'It would have been inappropriate not to inform you, lord.'

'What are the implications, magos?'

'The Server of Instrumentation insists he can continue to oversee the operation, but the Mechanicum believes his attention would be better spent identifying and eradicating this scrapcode problem before it develops any further. For the duration of that activity, the server would suspend discretion, and oversight would be managed automatically by the data-engines in the orbital yard hub.'

Guilliman considers this. He looks out through the crystalflex at the stars.

'A group of seniors from the Mechanicum, your esteemed colleagues, Pelot, dined with me on Macragge just a month ago. They were extolling the virtues of the newest generation cogitators that had been installed to run the Calth yards and grid. They were immensely proud of their machines.'

'So they should be, lord.'

'They spoke about them as if they were... as if they had personalities, as individuals. I took that as an indication of their near-perfection in the development of the machine-spirit.'

'Indeed, my lord.'

'We can build a world of greater perfection and higher performance than the human form, magos. We can exceed the natural limits of humanity.'

'Sir.'

'I'm saying, perhaps we should trust your wonderful machines to do the job for a time while the server removes the problem.'

Pelot nods.

'That is our feeling, lord.'

'Good. I will make our visitors aware that there is a scrapcode issue, and gently investigate if it's something they have brought with them by mistake. They have been on the fringes of late. And your server will need their cooperation in his investigation.'

'Very good, lord.'

'Pelot?'

'My lord?'

'With regard to the natural limits of humanity, it's worth noting that during our dinner, your colleagues did not really ingest any actual food.'

'Yes, my lord. In fairness, I doubt you needed to either.'

Guilliman smiles.

'Very good, magos.'

He turns to his deck officers.

'Arrange and establish a live link, please. As quickly as possible,' he instructs. 'I want to talk to my brother.'

[mark: -9.32.40]

TELEMECHRUS WAKES, BUT it is not time for war.

He has been taught things, and one of them is to control his anger until it is needed. It is not needed now, so he controls it.

He analyses. He scans. He determines.

His determination is this: he is in his casket, and his casket is being moved for transit. Something, perhaps some clumsy or inexpert handling of his casket, has woken him.

It is not time for war. This disappoints him.

He controls his disappointment, just as he has been taught. He controls his anger. He realises he needs, additionally, to control his anxiety. Anxiety is akin to fear, and fear is an abomination previously unknown to him, and he has resolved absolutely not to let it in. Thus, his anxiety increases.

Telemechrus lived his life as a legionary of the XIII. Ten years' service, from his genetic construction to his death in combat, and all that time he knew no fear.

None whatsoever. Despite everything he faced, even death when it finally came, he was never afraid.

During the first conversation he had with them, after his death, the techpriests told him that things would be different from now on. His mortal remains, the remains of Brother Gabril Telemach, 92nd Company Ultramarines, were no longer viable. Too much of his organics had been vaporised for there to be any continuation of life as he could understand it. But he was, in respect of his courage and service, and because of his compatibility, going to be honoured. His mortal remains were going to form the organic core of a cyberorganic being.

He was to be made a Dreadnought.

As a man, as flesh and blood, Gabril had thought of the Dreadnoughts as ancient things. They were veterans, brothers taken at the brink of death and installed inside indomitable war machines. They were old. Some were a century old. Some had been alive in those machine-boxes for a hundred years!

Gabril Telemach was not old. Just a decade of service.

Now he was trapped in a box forever.

There were adjustments to be made, the techpriests said. Mental adjustments. He accepted, first of all, that every Dreadnought, even the most venerable, had to be new at some point. Dreadnoughts were a vital part of the Legion's fighting power, and they were lost from time to time. So new ones needed to be constructed at intervals, when the combat chassis were available, and when war-loss produced suitable and compatible organic donors.

The techpriests told him that he would lack many things his flesh body had taken for granted. Sleep, to begin with. He would only sleep when they placed him into stasis hibernation. He would experience – or rather *not* experience – long periods of this, because they would ensure he slept most of the time. They would wake him if it was time for war and his participation was required.

The techpriests said that this was because of the pain.

There would be pain, and it would be constant. His pitiful mortal residue was sheathed in a cyberorganic web,
laced into electro-fibre systems, and shut in an armoured
sarcophagus. There would be no opportunity to manage
pain the way he had done as a man, no mechanism for
pain control.

For the same reason, he would find himself prone
to emotional variations he had not known as a man.
He would probably be prone to rage, to anger. Despite
the devastating power bequeathed to him as a Dreadnought, he would miss his mortal state. He would
resent his death, regret the circumstances of it, fixate
upon it, come to hate the cold-shell life he had been
given in exchange.

To spare him this bitterness, and the pain, and the
anger, he would be encouraged to sleep for great periods
of time.

He would also, they told him, probably be prone
to bouts of fear, especially early on. This was, they
explained, because of his profound change of state.
His consciousness had been shorn away from a linear,
mortal scale, from any timeframe he could recognise
or understand, from time itself, in fact, because of the
prolonged hibernations. Fear, anathema to the Space
Marine, was merely part of the mind's adjustment to this
extreme fate. It was natural. He would learn to control it,
and to use it, just like his anger. Eventually, fear would
evaporate, and be no more. He would be as fearless as he
had been as a legionary.

It would take time. There would be gradual and careful adjustments of his hormones and biochemical mix.
He would receive hypnotherapies and acclimation pat-
tering. He would be mentored by others of his kind, the
venerables, who had grown used to their strange fates.

He had said to the techpriests, 'I was fearless as a
battle-brother, even though I might fall. Now you have
rendered me invincible, you say I am prey to fear? Why

then call me a Dreadnought? I was a *dread nought* before. I dreaded *nothing* as a man!'

'This is the anger we spoke of,' they had replied. 'You will adjust. Sleep will help. Begin hibernation protocols.'

'Wait!' he had called out. 'Wait!'

Justarius is his mentor. Justarius is venerable. Justarius is also sullen and, despite his greater lifespan as a Dreadnought, seems not to have shed the bitterness or the anger. Justarius prefers to sleep. He is curmudgeonly when woken. He seems, at best, ambivalent to Telemechrus's concerns.

'It's Telemach,' says Telemechrus.

'My name was Justinus Phaedro,' grumbles Justarius in reply. 'They rename us like machines. Or they forget. I forget which.'

Telemechrus is the newest Dreadnought in the ranks of the XIII. He is Contemptor-pattern. He has yet to see combat.

They wake him once, during routine resuscitation in the vaults at Macragge. His implant clock tells him that he has been dormant for two years. The techpriests inform him that an operation has been announced. He will be installed in his chassis and shipped to Calth for deployment, and then woken when it is time for war. The war will be with orks. Telemechrus has questions, but they return him to his hypnotherapeutic dreams.

'Wait!' he says.

Telemechrus wakes, but it is not time for war.

He has been taught things, and one is to control his anger until it is needed. It is not needed now, so he controls it.

He analyses. He scans. He determines.

His determination is this: he is in his casket, and his casket is being moved for transit. Something, perhaps some clumsy or inexpert handling of his casket, has woken him.

His implant clock tells him it is eighteen weeks since

that routine wake-up on Macragge. Locator systems, reading noospheric tags, tell him that his casket is under transfer in the orbital yards at Calth. The staging post. The place of conjunction. He has roused too early. They're not at the war front yet.

He wonders why he has woken. Was it clumsy handling? A loader jarring his casket? Justarius and Kloton and Photornis are nearby, in their own caskets, and they are still in hiber-stasis.

Was he physically disturbed? Or was it some scrapcode abnormality causing his cogitation systems to fibrillate?

Telemechrus doesn't know. He is new to this. There are no techpriests nearby. He wants Justarius to wake so he can ask him.

Is this normal? What do these traces of scrapcode mean? He feels trapped. He feels anxiety. Fear will follow.

He is aware of the hibersystems trying to pull him back into unconsciousness where he belongs. They are trying to spare him the pain and the anger. *There is no need to wake. You woke too early. You don't need to be awake.*

The techpriests are wrong.

It's not the pain a Dreadnought is afraid of.

It's the silence. It's the oblivion. It's the sleep.

It's the inability to escape from yourself.

[mark: -8.11.47]

GUILLIMAN LOOKS AT Gage and nods.

Gage speaks to the lithocast operators and they activate the system.

Guilliman steps onto the hololithic plate as it starts to come to life. The tiered stations of the flagship's bridge rise up around the vast plate like the stalls of an amphitheatre.

Light blooms around him.

Figures resolve, there but not there at all. Light has

been captured, folded and twisted to give the illusion
of reality. Guilliman knows that, somewhere, millions
of kilometres away, other deck systems are fabricating
images of him out of light. He is appearing as a hololithic presence on the lithocast decks of other stages, for
the benefit of the august commanders whose ghosts are
manifesting to him here.

One in particular.

'My worthy brother!' Lorgar exclaims. He steps forward to greet Guilliman.

The simulation is remarkable. Though luminous,
there is true density and solidity to his flesh and his
armour. There is no lag to his audio, no desynchronisa-
tion between mouth and voice. *Remarkable.*

'I did not expect to meet you like this,' Lorgar says. His
grey eyes are bright. 'In person, so I could embrace you.
This seems premature. I was informed of your request. I
have had no time to dress in ceremonial attire–'

'Brother,' says Guilliman. 'You see that I greet you in
regular battle plate too. There will be time for personal
greeting and full dress ceremony when you arrive. You
are just a few hours out now?'

'Decelerating fast,' Lorgar replies. He looks at someone
not caught inside the hololithic field of his bridge. 'The
shipmaster says five hours.'

'We will meet together then, you and your commanders. Me and mine.' Guilliman looks at the warlords whose
images have appeared around Lorgar's. They all appear
to be connecting from different ships. He'd forgotten the
imposing bulk of Argel Tal. The lipless sneer of Foedral
Fell. The predatory curiosity of Hol Beloth. The hunched
gloom of Kor Phaeron. The lightless smile of Erebus.

'Some of you are already here,' Guilliman notes.

'I am, sir,' says Erebus.

'We will meet shortly, then,' says Guilliman.

Erebus inclines his head, more an accepting bow of
the head than a nod.

'My vessel is entering orbit,' says Kor Phaeron.

'Welcome to Calth,' says Guilliman.

The light phantoms salute him.

'I've asked for this brief communication,' Guilliman says, 'to discuss a small technical matter. I do not wish it to mar our formal conjunction, nor do I wish it to create problems for your fleet during approach and dispersal.'

'A problem?' asks Kor Phaeron.

There's a stiffness to them suddenly. Guilliman feels it, even though they are only present as handfuls of light. When they first appeared, he realises, they seemed like a pack of dogs, padding into the firelight, teeth bared in smiles that were also snarls, gleefully inquisitive. Now they seem like wild animals that he should never have brought so close to the hearth.

The Word Bearers have been fighting brutal, heathen wars of compliance in the ragged skirts of the Imperium. They've been fighting them dutifully and ferociously for decades, since that fateful day on Monarchia that changed the relationship between XIII and XVII forever. There is something coarsely barbaric about them. They have none of the praetorian nobility of Guilliman's men. They don't even evince the passionate devotion of their misguided days. They look sullen, world-weary, as though they have seen everything it is possible to see and are tired of it. They look hardened. They look as though all compassion and compunction have been drained out of them. They look like they would kill without provocation.

'A problem, lord?' Argel Tal repeats.

'A machine code problem,' Guilliman replies. 'The Mechanicum has advised me. There is a malicious scrap-code problem in the Calth datasphere. We're working to eradicate it. I wanted you to be aware of it, and to take steps accordingly.'

'That could have been summarised in a databurst, sir,' remarks Foedral Fell.

'A connected matter,' Guilliman says carefully, 'is that

the source of the scrapcode remains unidentified. There is a strong possibility that it is a data artefact that has been inadvertently brought in from outside the Calth system.'

'From outside?' asks Lorgar.

'From elsewhere,' Guilliman states.

There's a look in Lorgar's eyes that Guilliman hopes never to see again. It's hurt and it's anger, but it's also injured pride.

Lorgar raises his hand and draws it across his neck in a cut-throat gesture. It takes Guilliman a moment to realise that it's not a provocation, a curt insult.

The hololithic images of his officers and commanders freeze. Only Lorgar's remains live. He takes a step towards Guilliman.

'I have suspended their transmissions so we may speak plainly,' he says. 'Plainly and clearly. After all that has passed between us and our Legions, after all that has been toxic these last years, after all the effort to engineer this campaign as a reconciliation... Your first act is to accuse us of tainting you with scrapcode? Of... *what*? Of being so careless in our data hygiene we have infected your precious datasystem with some outworld codepox?'

'Brother–' Guilliman begins.

Lorgar gestures to the frozen light ghosts around them.

'How much humiliation do you intend to heap upon these men? They want only to please you. To earn the respect of the great Roboute Guilliman, a respect they have been lacking these last decades. It matters what you think of them.'

'Lorgar–'

'They've come to prove themselves! To show they are worthy to fight alongside the majestic Ultramarines! The warrior-kings of Ultramar! This conjunction, this campaign, it's a point of the highest honour! It matters to them. It matters very much! They have waited years for this honour to be restored!'

'I meant no insult.'

'Really not?' Lorgar laughs.

'None at all. Brother Lorgar Aurelian, why else would I have communicated informally? If I'd saved this matter to sully our ceremonial greeting, then you might have considered it an insult. A private word, between trusted commanders. That's all this is. You know scrapcode can develop anywhere, and adhere to the most carefully maintained systems. This could be us, this could be you, it could be an error from our datastacks, it could be some xenos code that's been stuck to your systems like a barnacle since you left the outworlds. There's no blame. We just need to acknowledge the problem and work together to cleanse it.'

Lorgar stares at him. Guilliman notes just how thoroughly his brother's flesh is covered with inked words.

'This was not meant to spoil our long-overdue reunion,' Guilliman says. 'This was my attempt to stop the reunion being spoiled.'

Lorgar nods. He purses his lips and nods. Then he flashes a smile.

'I see.'

He nods again, the smile flickering in and out. He raises a palm to his mouth, then laughs.

'I see. Then very well. I should not have spoken that way.'

'I should have been more circumspect,' replies Guilliman. 'I can see how it might have seemed.'

'We'll check our systems,' says Lorgar. His smile is back. He nods again, as if convincing himself.

'I should have been more circumspect,' Guilliman insists.

'No, you're right. There is clearly a tension here that needs to be overcome. An expectation.'

Lorgar looks at him.

'I'll get to it. We'll see if we can trace the code. And then we will meet, brother. In just a few hours now, we will meet, and everything will be put right.'

'I look forward to it,' says Guilliman. 'We will stand side-by-side, we will take down this ork threat that our brother Warmaster has identified, and then history will be rewritten between us.'

'I hope so.'

'It will be so, brother. If I had not believed that the unfortunate rift between our Legions could not be healed by good society and the companionship of shared martial effort, I would not have agreed to this. We will be the best of allies, Lorgar. You and I, our mighty Legions. Horus will be pleased and the Emperor our father will smile, and old slights will be forgotten.'

Lorgar smiles.

'They will be forgotten completely. They will be put to rest,' he says.

'Without delay,' says Guilliman.

[mark: -7.55.09]

CRIOL FOWST SACRIFICES his last oblator. In the landing camps of the XVII and its army auxiliaries, landing camps that are spread across the surface of Calth, hundreds of majir just like Fowst are concluding similar sacrificial rituals.

The Brotherhood is chanting. So are the men and women of the Tzenvar Kaul, the Jeharwanate and the Kaul Mandori, the other three principal cult echelons.

At the orbital Watchtower, Server Uhl Kehal Hesst of the Mechanicum has switched from discretionary mode in order to pursue and eradicate the scrapcode issue. He will fail to do so. He will spend the rest of his life failing to do so.

The scrapcode issue is no longer resolvable by means of the Mechanicum.

The Octed is implanted.

8

AEONID THIEL WAKES. He only slipped into rest mode briefly. He was bored. He has been waiting a long while. No one has come.

He wakes because he is no longer alone in the fortieth deck anteroom.

He bows at once.

'Are you Thiel?' asks Guilliman.

'Yes, lord,' Thiel replies.

The primarch seems distracted. He can probably tell which weapons have been used and put back, which practice cages have been operated.

'You've been waiting here for some time.'

'Yes, lord.'

'There's a lot to do today. My attention has been elsewhere.'

It's not an apology, it's just a basic explanation. Thiel wants to say that he doesn't really know why the primarch's dealing with it at all, but he knows better than that.

'Were you amusing yourself?' asks Guilliman, taking a broadsword off a wall rack and examining its edge.

93

'I… I decided to pass the time in practice,' Thiel answers. 'There are weapons here I am unfamiliar with. I thought that I might benefit from–'

Guilliman nods. The nod means *shut up*.

Thiel shuts up.

Guilliman studies the sword he is holding. He doesn't look at Thiel. Thiel has risen to attention, waiting. His helmet, with its crude, red paint-wash to indicate censure, is tucked under his arm.

'I didn't come here for you,' Guilliman says. 'I came away to think. I forgot you were here.'

Thiel makes no comment.

'That's a depressing thought,' says Guilliman, sliding the sword back onto the rack. 'I forgot something. I'd appreciate it if you didn't share that unguarded confession with anybody.'

'Of course, lord. Though I hardly blame you for forgetting me. I am a very minor detail.'

Now the primarch looks at him.

'Two things to note there, sergeant. One is that there is no such thing as a minor detail. Information is victory. One cannot and should not dismiss any data as inconsequential until one is in a position to evaluate its significance, and that only comes with hindsight. So all detail is important until circumstances render it redundant.'

'Yes, lord.'

'What's the second thing, Thiel?'

Aeonid Thiel hesitates slightly before answering.

'By any scale of decency,' he replies, 'my infraction was reprehensible. I am, therefore, not a minor detail anyway.'

'Quite,' says Guilliman.

The primarch turns and looks up at the high ceiling of the chamber. There is a slight heat-haze distortion in the air above the practice cages that Thiel has spent the last hours overworking.

'I think I may have offended him,' says Guilliman.

'Lord?'

Guilliman looks back at Thiel. He fixes him with a thoughtful gaze.

'This is a day of great sensitivity,' he says. 'We're building a part of the Imperium's future as surely as if we were making a star system compliant. We're cementing a relationship. Repairing a weakness. It's political. The rift between XIII and XVII is a rift in the Imperial line. Horus knows that. That's why he's sewing it up, and we can all swallow our distaste over it.'

Guilliman rubs his cheekbone with his fingertips. He is pensive.

'The future depends on the solidarity of the Legions,' he says. 'Where solidarity is weak, where it is lacking, it must be repaired or enforced. And this is forced. This is us getting along with each other for the greater good.'

Thiel chooses to remain silent.

'He is so... changeable,' Guilliman says. 'He is so prone to extremes. Eager to please, quick to take offence. There is no middle to him. He's so keen to be your best friend, and then, at the slightest perception of an insult, he's angry with you. Furious. Offended. Like a child. If he wasn't my brother, he'd be a political embarrassment and an impediment to the effective rule of the Imperium. I know what I'd do with him.'

'I'm sure I could demonstrate how, lord,' says Thiel, and then winces.

'Was that a joke, sergeant?'

'I may have just made a very unfortunate attempt at humour, lord,' Thiel admits.

'It was actually quite funny,' says Guilliman.

He turns to leave.

'Remain here. I'll get to you in due course.'

'Yes, my lord.'

* * *

[mark: -3.01.10]

'TROOPER PERSSON,' GRAFT calls as he whirrs up the track. The estuary wind is rising, swishing the swartgrass. There's an empty, metal smell of cold water and mud. It will be night soon. The lights are coming on in and around the fortalice, and their reflections are bobbing on the black river.

'Trooper Persson,' the servitor calls.

It's time to stop. The end of the day's toil. Wash up, grace and supper. Oll is weary, but he's about eight rows back from where he thought he'd be. Too much of the day spent looking up at the sky, at the running lights of ships. Too much of the day wasted watching the heavy landers glinting as they pass overhead.

Graft trundles up to him. The servitor's huge bulk-extension upper limbs, built for ammo loading, have been replaced by basic cargo shifting arms.

'Time to stop, Trooper Persson,' Graft says.

Oll nods. They've done what they can with the light.

But he doesn't feel like it's time to stop. It feels like something's about to start.

[mark: -1.43.32]

VENTANUS AND SELATON watch Arbute talking to another gang of labour guild officials. Behind them, a bulk-lander as huge and drab as a cliff face is slowly backing into a cargo silo. Oil stains shine on the rock-crete ground.

'I don't know why it's so difficult,' says Selaton. 'She tells them to work harder, they work harder. She's got the authority.'

'It's more complex than that.'

'Is it, captain? They've been doing it all day. As far as

I can tell, the main quibble seems to be the length and regularity of rest breaks.'

'Fatigue is an issue,' Ventanus reminds his sergeant. 'A human issue. We need cooperation. We have to acknowledge their qualities.'

'Weaknesses you mean.'

'Qualities.'

'It makes me profoundly glad I'm not an elective human,' says Selaton.

Ventanus laughs.

'Still, it's us who'll get strung up by the primarch if the muster falls behind.'

'No, it's me who'll get it,' said Ventanus. 'And we won't fall behind. The seneschal is pretty persuasive.'

'Really, sir?'

'I think the guild was dragging its heels because it thought bonus payments should be on offer.'

'*Deliberately* going slow?' asks Selaton, the notion alien to him.

'Yes, sergeant. They make a fuss about over-work, negotiate themselves some hefty bonus fees, and then have a little slack they can take up so they look like they're working hard. I think our new friend Seneschal Arbute has made them buck their ideas up by introducing new concepts such as patriotism, and the favourable disposition of the primarch.'

Selaton nods.

The sky over the starport is fulminous grey, with rack rides of cloud chased by the wind and backlit by the setting sun. The lights of incoming transports shine especially bright.

'We're losing the light,' says Selaton. 'Earlier than estimated.'

'A result of the storm,' says Ventanus.

'Probably,' agrees Selaton.

* * *

[mark: -1.01.20]

THE FLEET TENDER *Campanile* passes the inner Mandeville Point of the Veridian System, outer marker ring 16, and the local picket. It broadcasts full and correct anchorage codes to the watch ships at ring 14, and to the Veridius Maxim Star Fort. The Star Fort retracts its target acquisition lock and signals the tender to pass.

The ship appears to be decelerating.

[mark: -0.55.37]

TELEPORT FLARE. THE crackle of the energy burst shivers across the open hillside, and ozone taints the cold northern air.

Erebus, Dark Apostle, becomes flesh, and emerges from the scratch of light. He is not clad in ceremonial armour, he is wearing wargear that has been stripped down to fighting weight, darkened with ashes and inscribed over its entire surface with tiny, spidery script.

A strike team is waiting for him. Its leader is Essember Zote of the Gal Vorbak, a warrior of the most incendiary fury. His sword is already drawn. His armour is the colour of blood.

This is how their enemies will know them. Blood red, the colour of fire, the colour of hell, the colour of gore, the colour of the Octed.

Zote has a work party of the Tzenvar Kaul with him, seventy men, all childless. They have been working since they arrived at dawn on one of the first ships.

The Satric Plateau, two thousand kilometres north of Numinus City, is a lonely place. The hard winter has already arrived. Because of its size and terrain, the Satric region was chosen as one of the sixty-eight staging fields for the operation. Landers are parked all along the line of the slope, cargo hatches open to the grey sky.

Erebus inspects the work.

This particular area of the Satric Plateau, sheened
with frost, is especially perfect. It took several days of
comparative study with the orbital scans to determine
its perfection compared to other potential sites. It is
consistently flat in relation to sea level. It is aligned
according to magnetic north and the tidal process, and
has favourable moonrise on the day of the conjunction.
It possesses other qualities too, other qualities that could
not be disclosed by standard Imperial physics. Immaterium vectors are in alignment. The skin of the empyrean
is thin here tonight.

This is the true conjunction. Erebus reflects upon how
remarkably perfect it is. Not just workable or suitable or
acceptable. Perfect. From today, for the next sixty days. It
is as though some power somewhere manufactured the
perfection at exactly the right time.

The men of the Kaul have laid the circle. Polished black
rocks, each taken from the volcanic slopes of Isstvan V
and marked with a sigil, are arranged in a perfect circle a
kilometre in diameter.

Erebus takes the last rock from Zote. They are summoning stones. The latent power in them makes him
feel sick, just taking one in his hand.

He places it in the gap in the circle. It clacks against the
stones on either side as he sets it.

'Begin,' he tells Zote.

The men of the Tzenvar Kaul approach, carrying
other offerings from the Isstvan system. In procession,
they bear along portable stasis flasks like censers in
some Catheric worship. The fluid in the stasis flasks is
murky with blood. Harvested progenitor glands. Harvested gene-seed. The lost life of betrayed souls now
offered for the final blasphemy. There is Salamanders
gene-seed here, Iron Hands, Raven Guard. Erebus
knows that the Ruinous Powers make no distinctions,
so there is other gene-seed here besides: Emperor's

Children, Death Guard, Night Lords, Iron Warriors, Word Bearers, Alpha Legion, even Luna Wolf. Any that fell during the secret abominations of Isstvan III or V are suitable.

Erebus stops the first man in the procession, and strokes the glass of the stasis flask. He knows what's in it, the mangled tissue in the cloudy suspension.

'Tarik…' he whispers.

He nods. The Kaul start to carry the flasks into the circle. The moment they cross the stones, the bearers start to whimper and retch. Several pass out, or suffer strokes, and fall, smashing the flasks.

It doesn't matter.

The moon is rising, a pale curl in a mauve sky already busy with lights.

Zote hands Erebus a data-slate, and the Apostle checks the approach timings. He is data tracking using anchorage codes.

He hands the slate back and takes the vox-link in exchange.

'Now,' he says.

[mark: -0.40.20]

'ACKNOWLEDGED,' REPLIES SOROT Tchure.

He walks back to join the others. His men are mingling with the men of Luciel's company on the company decks of the *Samothrace*. They have finished the formal dinner that Luciel had arranged. None need to eat, certainly not the fine foodstuffs that Luciel provided, but it is a symbolic gesture. To dine as allies, as warrior-kings. To bond ahead of the coming war.

'Problem?' asks Luciel.

Tchure shakes his head.

'Some question about loading platforms.'

Tchure looks at Luciel.

'Why have you changed your markings and armour field?' asks Luciel.

'We are remaking ourselves,' Tchure replies. 'A new scheme to celebrate our new beginning. Perhaps it is down to the character of our beloved primarch, may the cosmos bless him. We have never quite found ourselves, Honorius. Not like you. We have struggled to realise a proper role for ourselves. I do not believe you appreciate how fortunate you are. The clarity of your purpose and position as Ultramarines. From the start you had a reputation that never needed to be questioned, and a function that never needed to be clarified.'

He pauses.

'For years, I have despised Lorgar,' he says quietly.

'What?'

'You heard me.'

'Sorot, you mustn't–'

'Look at your primarch, Honorius. So singular in aspect. So noble. I have envied you, envied the Imperial Fists, the Luna Wolves, the Iron Hands. And I am not alone. We struggle with a mercurial mind, Honorius. We labour under the burden of a brilliant but fallible commander. We no longer bear the word, my friend. We bear *Lorgar*.'

'Some fall into their roles quickly,' says Luciel firmly. 'I have thought about this. Some fall into their roles quickly. Others take time to evolve, to discover what their purpose is to be. Your primarch, great Lorgar, is a son of the Emperor. There will be a role for him. It may turn out to be far greater than any that falls to Guilliman or Dorn. Yes, we're lucky to have clarity. I know that. So are the Fists, the Hands, the Angels. Terra above, so are the Wolves of Fenris and the World Eaters, Sorot. Perhaps the lack of clarity you have laboured under thus far is because Lorgar's role is yet unimaginable.'

Tchure smiles.

'I can't believe you're defending him.'

'Why can't you?'

Tchure shrugs.

'I think we may be finding our purpose at last, Honorius,' he says. 'Hence our new resolve. Our change in scheme and armour colour. I… I was asked to join the advance.'

Luciel frowns, quizzical.

'You told me that.'

'I have things to prove.'

'Why?' asks Luciel.

'I have to prove my commitment to the new purpose.'

'And how do you do that?' asks Luciel.

Tchure doesn't answer. Luciel notices how the Word Bearer's fingers stir, tapping the tabletop. What agitation is that? Nerves?

'I learned something,' Tchure says suddenly, changing the subject. 'A little piece of warcraft that I thought you would appreciate.'

Luciel lifts his cup, sips wine.

'Go on,' he smiles.

Tchure toys with his own cup, a straight-sided golden beaker.

'It was on Isstvan, during the fight there.'

'Isstvan? There's been fighting in the Isstvan system?'

Tchure nods.

'It hasn't been reported. Was it a compliance?'

'It's recent,' says Tchure. 'The full reports of the campaign are still being ratified by the Warmaster. Then they will be shared.'

Luciel raises his eyebrows.

'Guilliman won't appreciate being left out of the loop for any length of time. Is this how the Warmaster intends to conduct the Great Crusade from now on? Guilliman insists on sharing all military data. And Isstvan was *compliant*–'

Tchure holds up his hand.

'It's recent. It's fresh. It's done now. Your primarch will

hear all about it in due course. The point is, the fight was bitter. The Imperium faced a foe that had discovered the mortal power of treachery.'

'Treachery?' asks Luciel.

'Not as a strategy, you understand. Not as a tactic to surprise and undermine. I mean as a property. A power.'

'I'm not sure I know what you mean,' smiles Luciel. slightly disarmed. 'It's as though you're talking about... *magic*.'

'I almost am. The enemy believed that there was power in treachery. To win the confidence of your opponent, to mask your animus, and then to turn... Well, they believed that this actually invested them with power.'

'I don't see how.'

'Don't you?' asks Tchure. 'The potency, they believed, depends on the level of betrayal. If an ally suddenly turns on an ally, that's one level. But if a trusted friend turns on a friend. That was the purest kind of power, because the treachery ran so deep. Because it required that so many moral codes be broken. Trust. Friendship. Loyalty. Reliance. Honesty. Such an act was powerful because it was beyond belief. It achieved a potency that was akin to the most powerful blood sacrifice.'

Luciel sits back.

'Interesting, certainly,' he says. 'For them to believe that. Culturally, it speaks a great deal to the strength of their honour codes. If they believed this invested them with power, then it seems like an act of superstition. It has little strategic merit in terms of warcraft or technique, of course. Except, I suppose, psychologically.'

'It certainly worked for them.'

'Until you crushed them, of course.'

Sorot Tchure does not reply.

'What's the matter?' asks Luciel.

'It's like a sacrifice,' says Tchure. 'You identify and commit the greatest betrayal possible, and it is like a sacrifice to anoint and begin a vast ceremony of victory and destruction.'

'I still don't understand. It has no tactical methodology.'

'Really? Really, Honorius? What if it does? What if there is an entirely *other* kind of warfare, one that extends beyond all practical techniques, one that defies and eclipses all the martial law codified by the Ultramarines and recognised by the Imperium? A ritual warfare? A kind of *daemonic* warfare?'

'You say that as if you believe it,' Luciel laughs.

'Think about what I'm saying,' says Tchure quietly. He looks around the chamber, at his men talking and drinking with Luciel's. 'Think of this... If the Word Bearers turned against the Ultramarines, wouldn't that be the greatest betrayal of all? Not Lorgar turning on Guilliman, for they dislike each other anyway. Here, in this chamber, between two men who have actually managed to become friends?'

'That would be the most atrocious deceit,' Luciel agrees. 'I concede it would have some power. As shock value in the Legion. We are immune to fear, but horror and surprise might unman us briefly at the unimaginable nature of the act.'

Tchure nods.

'And it would be the centrepiece,' he says. 'The sacrificial spark to ignite the ritual war.'

Luciel nods gravely.

'I suppose you're right. It would be well to understand, and allow for, an enemy who carried such conviction in the power of infamy.'

Tchure smiles.

'I wish you understood,' he says.

[mark: -0.20.20]

THE CAMPANILE CROSSES the inner ring, its codes accepted by the defence grid. The mass of the fleet disposition lies ahead of it, the yards. The bright glory of Calth.

As it passes within the orbit of Calth's moon, it begins an abrupt acceleration.

[mark: -0.19.45]

'UNDERSTAND WHAT?' ASKS Luciel.

'I was asked to join the advance,' says Tchure.

'And?'

'I have to prove my commitment to the new purpose.'

Luciel stares at him.

For just a second. A second. And in that second, he finally realises what Sorot Tchure has been trying to tell him.

That in order not to betray one impossible bond, Sorot Tchure is required to betray another.

The goblet falls from Luciel's grip. His hand is already moving, through instinct alone, for his sidearm. Only sheer, disfunctioning shock is slowing him down.

Tchure's plasma pistol is already in his hand.

The goblet hasn't even hit the tabletop yet.

Tchure fires. Point blank, the plasma bolt strikes Honorius Luciel's torso. The bolt is as hot as a main sequence star. It vaporises armour plate, carapace, reinforced bone, spinal cord. It annihilates meat, both hearts, and secondary organs. It turns blood into dust. The shot's hammer blow impact knocks Luciel down, through the table, smashing the tabletop up to meet the falling goblet, spinning it into the air in a semi-circle of wine.

Luciel's men are turning, caught by surprise, not understanding the noise and motion, not understanding the weapon discharge or the violent collapse of their captain. Tchure's men simply draw their guns. They are not distracted by the gunfire. Their eyes never leave the men they are talking to, men who are turning away in confusion.

Luciel rolls on the deck, limbs thrashing, as the

smashed table falls around him. The goblet bounces off
the deck plate beside his head. His eyes are wide, straining, staring. The plasma shot has burned a massive hole
clean through him. His body is cored. The deck plating is
visible through his twitching torso. The edges of the gap-
ing damage are scorched and cooked by superheating.
His armour is likewise punctured, the cut edges glowing.
Larraman cells cannot hope to clog or close a wound
quite so catastrophic. Tchure is on his feet, his chair tipping backwards behind him, toppling. He swings the
plasma weapon down, aims it at Luciel's face, and fires
again.

Around him, the chamber shakes with a sudden storm
of gunfire. Twenty or thirty boltguns discharge almost
simultaneously. Armoured bodies, blown backwards,
fall. Blood mist fills the air.

The goblet lands on the third bounce, rolls in a circle,
and comes to rest on its side next to Honorius Luciel's
seared and shattered skull.

ABSOLUTE//OVERWHELM

'Battle is not a state to be entered into lightly. Battle is always painful and always comes at a price, so the astute commander never commits to battle unless no other options remain. Once that commitment is made, once the Phase of Execution, or primary condition, *has begun, it must be done with the utmost efficacy: a rapid application of overwhelming force to obliterate your enemy as quickly and completely as possible. Do not give him the time or space to react. Do not leave him with any materiel or opportunity that he can use in a rallying phase. Eliminate him physically and psychologically so that his threat is entirely removed. Kill him with your first shot. Utterly annihilate him with your first strike. This may be considered the application of* attack in its purest form.*'*

– Guilliman, *Notes Towards Martial Codification*, 4.1.ix

1

AN ALARM SOUNDS. A red hazard light starts to blink on a burnished copper console.

The officer of the watch, at his station on the bridge of the *Samothrace*, reacts swiftly but with some confusion. Are the ship's systems notifying him of a malfunction? It is a high-scale alert.

He presses an ivory-cushioned key to access clarification. On the small glass screen, a phrase appears in luminous green characters.

[Weapons discharge, company deck]

That can't be correct. Even if it somehow is, a weapons discharge must be accidental. The officer of the watch is, however, highly trained and well disciplined. He knows that answers, clarifications, corrections and explanations are secondary issues. They can wait. Even informing the captain can wait. He understands protocol. He reacts as he has been trained to react.

He activates the vox systems and rouses deck protection. His hands move with rehearsed agility over the keys. He sounds general quarters. He starts to systematically close the bulkheads fore and aft of the company deck space, and to lock out the through-deck access points and elevators.

Within four seconds of the alarm sounding, the officer of the watch has begun the procedure to cordon and secure the entire company deck, and to place deck troops at all access points. His response is exemplary. Within thirty-five seconds of the alarm sounding, a full, regulation lock-down would have been enforced.

But thirty-five seconds are not available.

The captain has heard general quarters sound, and has started out of his seat to join the officer of the watch and examine the issue. There is a frown on his face.

'What's going on, Watch?' he asks.

His words are drowned out by another alarm. Then another alarm. Then another. Klaxons, bells and hooters overlap, screeching and booming.

The proximity alarm.

The collision warning alert.

The course defect advisor.

The detector array.

The passive auspex.

The primary orbital traffic alert from Calth System Control.

Something is coming at them. Something is moving into the dense and rigorously controlled shipping formations spread across the close orbit band. Something is sweeping through the orbital high anchorage without approval or authorisation.

The officer of the watch forgets, for a second, what he was in the middle of doing.

He looks at the main screen. So does the captain. So do the bridge crewmen.

What happens next, though they are looking straight at it, happens too fast for them to see.

* * *

[mark: -0.18.34]

THE CAMPANILE ACCELERATES. It lights its main realspace drives, delivering main extending thrust in a position where it should be almost coasting at correction burst only. It raises its void shielding to make itself as unstoppable as possible. It fires itself like a bullet at the planet Calth.

The screams of its crew can still be heard, but no one is listening.

Main extending thrust is a drive condition used for principal acceleration, the maximum output that takes a starship to the brink of realspace velocity as it makes the translation to the empyrean. It is a condition that is used as a starship moves away from a planet towards the nearest viable Mandeville Point, a distance that is roughly half the radius of an average star system.

There is no such long run-up here. The *Campanile* is already inside the orbit of Calth's satellite. There is not enough range for it to reach anything like maximum output or velocity. Even so, it is travelling at something close to the order of forty per cent of the realspace limit as it reaches the edge of the atmosphere. It is travelling too fast for anything physical, such as an eye or a pict-corder or a visual monitor, to see it. It is only visible to scanning systems and sensors, to detectors and auspex. They shriek at its sudden, savage, shockwave approach.

Their shrieks are as futile as the unheard screams of its lost crew.

It does not hit Calth.

There is something in the way.

[mark: -0.18.32]

THE CAMPANILE STREAKS like a missile into Calth's orbital shipping belt. It punches through the formations of ships in parking orbit, the rows of freighters, barges and troop vessels at high anchor, the precisely spaced lines of vast cruisers and frigates, the glittering clouds of small craft, loaders, lifters and boats attending the parent ships.

It is like a bolter round fired into a crowd.

It misses the *Mlatus*, the *Cavascor*, the *Lutine* and the *Samothrace* by less than a ship's length. It passes under the beam of the battleship *Ultimus Mundi* and skims the back of the gargantuan carrier ship *Testament of Andromeda*. Its shields graze the hull of the strike craft *Mlekrus*, vaporising the masts and arrays of its starboard detectors. It slices between the battle-barges *Gauntlet of Victory* and *Gauntlet of Glory*. By the time it crosses the bow of the grand cruiser *Suspiria Majestrix*, shredding the mooring and fuelling lines that secure the famous vessel to its bulk tenders, the *Campanile* has begun to swat aside small craft, annihilating them against the front of its shields. The small ships disintegrate, fierce blue sparks fizzle against the shield shimmer: cargo boats, lighters, ferries, maintenance riggers. The *Campanile's* shield displacement hurls others out of the way like a tidal bore, swirling into each other, compressing them with gravimetric thrust, crashing them against the hulls of larger ships or the support cradles of the outer orbital yards.

Then the *Campanile* reaches the main shipyard.

The Calth Yards are orbiting islands, the fledgling beginnings of the planet's first proper superorbital plate. There are a dozen of them orbiting Calth. This is Calth Veridian Anchor, the largest and oldest of them. It is a massive edifice of jetties and slips, ship cradles and docks, suspension manufactories, habitats, depots and docking platforms. It is a little over three hundred kilometres across, a raft of metal and activity and life.

The *Campanile* hits it, creating light. Void shields moving at high sub-light velocities strike physical matter, and mutually annihilate. The tender simply vaporises the Ultramar Azimuth Graving Dock, shredding the superstructure of the giant berth cradle, and the cruiser *Antipathy* docked inside it. Cut in half, the nine kilometre-long *Antipathy* vanishes in a ripple of rapidly expanding heat and light as its drives detonate, and six thousand lives disappear with it. The blast incinerates the two manufactory modules adjoining the graving dock, instantly killing another thirty thousand artificers and engineers, and shears the superstructure away from arrestor silos A112 and A114, both of which collapse sideways, spilling the escort *Burnabus* into the fast escort *Jeriko Rex*. Both vessels suffer catastrophic hull damage. The *Burnabus* crushes and deforms like a spent shell case.

The *Campanile* is still moving. As the Ultramar Azimuth Graving Dock disintegrates behind it, it punches on through Assembly 919, a hollow spheroid currently housing the *Menace of Fortis*, the *Deliverance of Terra* and the Mechanicum fabrication ship *Phobos Encoder*. All three ships are obliterated. The assembly spheroid ruptures like a glass ball. Propelled debris rips into attached habitat modules, voiding them to space. Part of the *Phobos Encoder* is flung out of the explosion and spins into the yard's principal cargo facility, which buckles laterally. This secondary impact destroys forty-nine lift ships and one hundred and sixty-eight small lighters and ferries. Cargo pods and transportation containers spew out like beads from a snapped necklace, like grains of rice from a ripped sack. They spill, tumbling. Some start to glow blowtorch blue as they plunge into the high atmosphere.

Calth Veridian Anchor shudders. Internal explosions propagate through it, driven along by the devastating trajectory of the *Campanile*. Habitats and depots blow out. Jetties collapse. Manipulator cranes buckle and fold like wading birds struck by a hunter's buckshot. The *Aegis of Occluda* catches fire, all seven kilometres of it, in its ship cradle. The *Triumph of Iax*, secured in an arrestor slip, is crippled as a storm of debris penetrates it. Its secondary drives implode, ripping the massive ship through ninety degrees like a man being swung by his ankles. The bow, still encased in its slip housing framework, encounters the *Tarmus Usurper*, which is being fitted out in the adjacent slip. The collision mangles them, tears them, lacerates their hulls. Atmospherics void explosively from rent hull plates, aerosol jets filled with particles that are tiny, tumbling bodies.

Light blossoms. The annihilation of matter is vast, and light is the only form in which it can escape. The battleship *Spirit of Konor*, seventeen kilometres long and one of the most powerful warships in the fleet of the Five Hundred Worlds, ignites, and then vanishes as critical damage compromises its power plants and vast munitions stockpiles. Huge, burning sections of the yard structure are ejected upwards, whirling, into space, or are spat down at the world beneath. The Ultramar Zenith Graving Dock suffers integral gravimetric failure and drops out, breaking and twisting towards the planet below. The grand cruiser *Antrodamicus*, supported by that dock, rips free of its moorings and begins to slide backwards out of the collapsing cradle, in some ghastly parody of a ship launch. Its drives are off-line. It has no power to prevent its slide or stabilise its position, at least nothing that can be lit or brought to bear fast enough. It is a huge ship, twelve kilometres long. It simply slips away backwards, like a vast promontory of ice calving from a glacier into the sea.

The *Campanile* is still moving. Its shields finally fail and it is just a solid projectile, a mass of metal. It annihilates two more slipways, and the ships within them, cripples the anchored carrier *Johanipus Artemisia*, and then rams through the data-engine hub in the centre of the yard structure. All the data-engines are destroyed instantly. The automatics fail. The noosphere experiences a critical and fatal interrupt. Another thirty-five thousand individuals perish as the yard's core is obliterated.

Impact has virtually erased the unshielded mass of the *Campanile*. Its structure is atomised, except for the largest chunks of it, which punch onwards as the ship breaks up, still travelling at immensely high realspace velocities, communicating billions of tonnes of force. The largest surviving piece, a part of the *Campanile's* solid-core drive section, spins out like a ricochet and kills the battleship *Remonstrance of Narthan Dume* like a slingshot pellet to the brainpan.

The final pieces of the *Campanile* clear the far side of Calth Veridian Anchor and spray on out across the planet, scattering, dipping and burning like meteorites.

This entire catastrophe has taken less than a second to occur. It has been entirely silent, a light-blink in the soundless void.

All that any observers – either on nearby vessels or the surface of the planet – would have seen was a blinding flash, like a star going nova, that was instantly replaced by a propagating series of overlapping, expanding fireballs that consume the entire sky.

[mark: -0.18.30]

THE LIGHTSHOCK OVERLOADS the resolution of the bridge screens aboard the *Macragge's Honour*. They brown out, fizzling. Plugged servitors squeal and chatter. Automatic systems slam the blast shutters on every bridge window port, shutting them in a ruddy, armoured gloom.

Marius Gage rises from his seat.

'What the hell was that?' he demands.

No one answers.

'Find out!' he roars.

The shockwave hits.

* * *

[mark: -0.18.30]

THERE IS A blink. Ventanus knows what it is. Instinct identifies it in a fraction of the time it would take his conscious mind to explain it. It's the electromagnetic pulse that precedes a major explosion.

He has time to see that Selaton has sensed it. The seneschal has not. Her human senses are too modest to register the blink. She's saying something.

Ventanus grabs her and pulls her down. Arbute cries out, not understanding at all. He knows his armoured fingers are breaking some of her ribs. There is still a chance he can shield her with his body.

A brand-new sun fills the heavens above Numinus starport.

[mark: -0.18.30]

LIGHT SEARS, THEN fire fills the sky over the fields and the estuary at Neride like a roasting surge from god's own flamer.

Oll Persson flinches, though the heat and wind are still half a minute away. He's seen ships explode in orbit. He's never seen anything this big.

The twilight flushes orange. Evening shadows stretch behind them. The crop workers look up, baffled, horrified.

'Trooper Persson?' Graft asks, unable to frame a more complex question.

'God save us all,' Oll says.

The swartgrass stirs, swishes.

The wind hits, hot, as though a furnace door has opened nearby.

* * *

[mark: -0.18.30]

A THUNDERCLAP. THAT'S what it sounds like to Hellock.

'What the bastard shitfire is–' he starts to say to anyone near enough to hear him, plucking his latest smoke out from between his lips. Trooper Rane is right in front of him. Rane is suddenly a silhouette, so are the stacks and spires of the city over the river: black shapes against a sky that's turned white, like some excess of dawn, like sheet bastard lightning, but as bright as the forked stuff.

Hellock doesn't know what's just happened, but he already senses it's the worst thing he's ever going to experience.

He's wrong.

[mark: -0.18.30]

THE SKY EXPLODES over Numinus City. Braellen and Androm stand up, snapping out of rest mode. They don't speak because there's nothing factual to state yet, but they draw their weapons without waiting for an instruction from Captain Damocles.

It's a high altitude detonation, high altitude or low orbit. Multiple detonations, overlapping, that's clear a second later as the flashes chop and flicker like a strobe, blooming fire inside fire inside fire.

'We just lost a ship,' says Androm.

'That wasn't just one ship,' Captain Damocles corrects.

[mark: -0.18.30]

'DID YOU SEE that?' Captain Phrastorex cries. 'Did you see that?'

'I saw it, captain,' replies Sergeant Anchise.

The sky to the west of their camp is rippling with light,

as if someone's moving a glow-globe behind a veil of silk. There's a growl, a long rumble that seems to be coming from space and shows no sign of ending.

'Get the men up,' Phrastorex yells.

The vox is screwed up. Weird sounds spit and cough through his helmet every time Phrastorex tries to open a link. Is that screaming?

Is that... *chanting*?

'Get the men up and ready!' he repeats, and then starts to pound across the clearing to the areas marked out for the 111th. Ekritus needs to get his men moving too. Something's going on. Phrastorex hasn't felt an intuitive wince this bad since the firefight on Cavolotus V. Ekritus needs to get ready for whatever this turns out to be.

A strange wind is stirring the trees, making them swish. The wind's warm, dry. It feels like something bad has exhaled.

'Ekritus!' Phrastorex yells.

Down on the plains below the woods, even the Word Bearers are rousing. Phrastorex can see them forming up. He can see their Army units assembling. That's good. *Damn* good. Far better drill than he expected of the XVII, given their reputation as heathen berserkers. *Far* faster response.

Good. *Good*, then. They're all standing ready, ready to face this. United as one. It gladdens his heart.

They can face this together, whatever *this* is.

[mark: -0.18.30]

THE DATASHOCK KILLS Server Uhl Kehal Hesst.

It doesn't kill him instantly the way it kills forty-six of the data moderati in the cogitation wells around him, but it bursts and fries key sections of his cerebral architecture. This is brain damage that cannot be repaired, and from which he will never recover. Synaptic junctions are burned out like faulty wiring. A brain-bleed begins in his frontal lobe.

He remains standing.

Light hits the orbital Watchtower at Kalkas Fortalice a nanosecond after the shockwave of data. The noosphere collapses like an ice sculpture in an oven. The tower's manifold field stutters out. Hesst feels and absorbs the shared agony of several thousand deaths: his modified brethren aboard the primary shipyard, aboard docked vessels, in the tower around him. Some deaths are quick: flashes of annihilation. Others, still fast, are physically traumatic: the liquid spatter of compression, the explosive misery of decompression, the blunt fury of impact, the screaming hell of immolation.

Some deaths are slower. They take whole parts of seconds to end. The plugged men and women in the amniotic armourglas caskets around him reel as hammer blows of data assault their brains. Information overload. Sensory overload. Hypertraumatic inload syndrome.

He is almost relieved when the noosphere fails.

He sways. The windows of the tower have automatically tinted to reduce the flare of the orbital explosions. Hesst's permanent MIU link burns like a white-hot wire through his soul. His entire bioengineered self is fatally compromised.

Only one thought, captured in simple binaric form, remains within his grasp.

Hesst surrendered discretionary mode four hundred and sixty-two minutes ago. He surrendered it to the orbital bioengines.

The bioengines, *all* the orbital automatics, have died.

Calth's planetary weapons grid has just ceased to function.

* * *

[mark: -0.18.30]

TELEMECHRUS WAKES AGAIN. He wakes bolt upright awake, screaming awake, howling awake, as if from a nightmare. There's cold sweat on his back, but he doesn't have a back. There's blood in his mouth, but he doesn't have a mouth. His eyes are open, but he doesn't have eyes.

A flash-flood of data has shocked him into ignition, shocked him so hard that for a moment he is given a physical memory of his life before transformation. Not his recent transformation. From before that, from before his formative transformation by biogenetic engineering to Space Marine. For a second he was granted a memory of waking from a nightmare as an unmodified human being.

As a child.

He realises it wasn't just a data shock. There was a significant physical shock too. His casket has been violently disturbed, thrown, dropped.

His implant clock tells him that he has been dormant for a little over nine hours and ten minutes. External sensors are down. He can't see. He can't open the casket. There is no noosphere. There is no data inload.

His own sensors, the cyberorganic sensors of his combat chassis mount, tell him the external temperature of the casket is over five thousand degrees Celsius. His inertial locators tell him that he is upside down and falling.

At terminal velocity.

[mark: -0.18.30]

THE SKY ERUPTS. Criol Fowst clutches his athame so tightly against his breast that the blade draws blood from his fingers.

Staring up at the firestorm that is devouring the sky, the Brotherhood of the Knife starts to chant the litany of the Octed.

Ushkul Thu! Ushkul Thu!

Fowst wants to join in, but he is too busy laughing, laughing uncontrollably, like a maniac.

[mark: -0.18.30]

EREBUS LOOKS UP from the circle of black stones. The centre of the ritual circle, where the bodies of many of the Tzenvar Kaul processionals lie smouldering or twitching, has not been a focused reality for almost ten minutes. Matter squirms there. The membrane of the universe has turned liquid. There's a smell like the smell of weird dreams, strong but not in any way identifiable.

Essember Zote of the Gal Vorbak mutters something as the first flash hits the southern skies. Erebus is already watching. Fire, light, *first light*, a dawn of sorts. Erebus understands that several clear strategic benefits will be achieved by their plan, but they are all military objectives and they count little to him. To the first of the Dark Apostles, it is the meaning that matters: the significance, the art, the context.

The light in the sky, that huge bright flare they have wrought upon this day, that is the *Ushkul Thu*. In the archaic language of the Holy Worlds, the words mean 'Offering Sun' or 'Tribute Star'. It is hard to translate it precisely. There is a sense of sacrifice, a sense of the promise represented by dawn, and the sense of something greater to follow.

There is a greater sunrise to come.

2

[mark: -0.18.20]

CALTH VERIDIAN ANCHOR, the vast shipyard, is ablaze and dying. Damaged beyond the possibility of salvation or stabilisation, its giant platform structure is tipping, shredding, pulsing like a white dwarf star that has suddenly been placed in Calth's orbit.

It is an energy fire, a nuclear fire, spherical and incandescent, throbbing. The nearby orbital platforms shiver at the series of shockwaves thumping out of the stricken orbital. Some have taken collateral damage from outflung superstructure debris or parts of exploding ships, and are now burning or holed. Along the anchorage line, ships of the fleet are combusting or crippled. Debris and ejecta continue to tumble from the underside of the foundering orbital, caught by Calth's gravity.

It is chaos. Electromagnetic slams have crippled communication networks, and what little vox and pict remains is choked with frantic intership traffic: questions, demands, entreaties, insistences. *What has happened? What is happening? You will tell me immediately what is happening!*

There is no information, no data. The Mechanicum's

throat is cut, its voice-box torn out, its brain mush. The only facts are those available to anyone with eyes, or a window port, or a functioning picter. An act of unimaginable violence has been perpetrated. Calth high anchor is a firestorm. The death toll is huge. The injury to the fleet and the yard infrastructure is unthinkable.

It is an attack. It can only be an attack. An act of war. No accident could have been so far-reaching in its effect. The Veridian system and its approaches are protected by scrupulous systems of check and countercheck, by peerless levels of redundant security. This magnitude of catastrophic damage would have required malice in order to achieve it: a deliberate and inimical intent to circumvent the secure cordon.

This is no accident. This is an attack.

Someone, somewhere, gabbling in the flash flood of unfiltered vox traffic, uses the word 'ork' or 'greenskin'. The enemy has got wind of the Veridian mobilisation. It has received warning of the force poised to launch at it, and it has struck first.

Within ten or twenty seconds of the first impact, ships across the high anchorage have desperately begun to power drives and weapon systems. Some are generating power in the hope of raising shields, or even preparing to slip authorised moorings so that they can reposition.

Then a battle-barge opens fire. The massive barge is known to the Ultramarines as the *Raptorus Rex*, but it has been renamed, with as little notice as the Word Bearers gave when they changed their battledress colours, the *Infidus Imperator*.

The *Infidus Imperator* is the barge of Kor Phaeron.

It discharges all of its primary lance weapons at the battle-barge *Sons of Ultramar* and reduces it to a whizzing cloud of metal chaff carried outwards in all directions by an expanding ball of fire.

The *Infidus Imperator* chooses its next target. In formation behind the mighty craft, the *Crown of Colchis* starts to fire too. So does the battleship *Kamiel*. So do the *Flame of Purity* and the *Spear of Sedros*.

And so does the flagship of Dark Apostle Erebus, the battle-barge *Destiny's Hand*.

[mark: -0.17.32]

SHIPMASTER OUON HOMMED, captain of the heavy destroyer *Sanctity of Saramanth*, sees the *Infidus* begin its merciless prowl along the anchorage line. He understands precisely what the vast Word Bearers barge is doing. It's executing the ships in the line beside it the way a man might execute a row of helpless prisoners.

He's done it before himself. At Farnol High Harbour, after the Ephigenia Compliance, he crawled the *Sanctity* along the slipways, scuttling the captured enemy ships so they could not be reactivated and re-used. It was a graceless, unrewarding task, utterly pragmatic. The ships were too dangerous to leave intact.

As a shipman, as a person whose life has been dedicated to the service of the great starships, he's never taken pleasure in scuttling duties.

Why does it seem like the *Infidus* is relishing it?

Hommed is screaming at his command staff, demanding yield of power, weapons, shields, data... anything they can give him. The *Sanctity* was sitting at slip cold, drives tamped down. With the best will in all the worlds, it will take fifty minutes to rouse the ship to operational readiness.

This is true of the entire fleet. The starships of Ultramar were sitting cold at high anchor for the conjunction. All of their power plants were at lowest yield for the purposes of maintenance, loading and embarkation checks. None of them needed ready drives or weapons or shields. They were all under the protective aegis of the planet's weapon grid.

'Power!' he yells. 'I want power!'

'Yield is rising, sir,' his first officer replies.

'Nothing like fast enough. I need active condition!'

'The Drive Room says we can't hope to raise the yield any faster than–'

'Tell the bastards in the Drive Room I want power, not excuses!'

There's no time. The *Infidus* is coming. Whatever has happened, whatever outrage has occurred, the ships of the XVII clearly believe it to be an attack, and clearly regard the ships of Ultramar as a threat. They're killing everything they can pre-emptively, killing everything before…

Hommed stops. He forces his mind to clear for a second. He realises how stricken he is with panic and extreme stress. Everyone is. The bridge around him is pandemonium. A clear head is the only hope he has to salvage anything, anything at *all*, from the situation.

The *Infidus* is coming. That's the point. *That's* the point. The thrice-damned *Infidus* is coming. Every ship was powered down at the time of the attack, which is why they're all helpless and shield-less now.

Except the *Infidus* is coming. It's moving. So are other ships from the Word Bearers fleet. It's not that they're responding hastily. It's not that they're taking wild shots at imagined targets before finding out what's really going on.

It's the fact that they're moving at all.

They weren't powered down. They were sitting at anchor hot.

They knew what was coming.

They were ready.

'Those *bastards*,' he breathes.

The *Infidus* closes. It's firing callous broadsides; the whole length of it lighting up with multicoloured fury. Each salvo causes the counter-active gravimetrics to tense and brace the ship against the monumental discharge.

Each salvo murders another helpless vessel.

The *Constellation of Tarmus* disappears in a clap of heat and metal.

The *Infidus* closes.

'Power?' Hommed asks.

His first officer shakes his head.

The *Infidus* shivers and looses another broadside. Enough firepower to scorch and split a moon.

The *Sanctity of Saramanth*, struck amidships, bursts asunder.

[mark: -0.17.01]

MAGOS MEER EDV Tawren registers her own hyper-elevated adrenal levels. She has survived the great data-death that has ripped through the orbital Watchtower. Hesst saved her. Basic operational procedure saved her.

She does not want to think about that irony. That happenstance. That kindness.

There's too much to do. They are in the middle of an unthinkable crisis. A disaster. She has to rescue the situation.

She has to save Hesst.

The tower's elevators and lifting platforms are out. She hauls up the skirts of her long robe and rushes up the main spiral staircase. Smoke hangs in the air. The buzz of alarms. Voices echo from above and below. Outside, the sky is unnaturally luminous.

She passes servitors that are stumbling and mindless, trailing torn plugs, drooling. Some have slumped. Some are whining or replaying bursts of their favourite data like nursery rhymes. Some are smacking their heads against the staircase wall.

Toxic-data. Data-death. Overload.

Let Hesst be alive.

He was plugged in. He would have taken the brunt of the shock–

Don't think about it. Just get upstairs.

She trips over the sprawled body of a high-grade servitor. A hand steadies her arm.

'Do not fall, magos,' a meatvoice requests.

Tawren looks up into the menacing face of Arook Serotid, the master of the tower's skitarii brigades. Arook is a creature modified for war, not data. His ornate armour is part ceremonial, part ritual, a deliberately baroque throwback to the eras of threat-pattern and fear-posture.

'Indeed, I will not,' she agrees. He helps her up the stairs, moving blind and mindless servitors out of her way. He is a metre taller than her. His eyes are hololithic crimson slits in his copper visor. She notices that one of them is flickering.

'We took a hit,' he says.

'A major datashock,' she says. 'Hypertraumatic inload syndrome.'

'Worse than that,' he replies. 'Explosions in orbit. We've lost ships, orbitals.'

'An attack?'

'I fear so.'

They're both using fleshvoice mode. She's painfully aware of it. It's so slow, so painstaking. No canting, no data-blurts. No simultaneous and instant transmissions of ideas and data. She doesn't believe she's ever spoken to Arook in fleshvoice before, and he's clearly not used to talking at all.

But the mannered effort is necessary. They were both insulated from the data-shock. They must stay insulated.

'I need to reach the server,' she explains.

He nods. That one red eye is still blinking. A malfunction? Arook has taken some damage. Like all skitarii, he would have been linked to the noosphere, so the data-shock would have hit him like everyone else. However, the skitarii also have their own dedicated emergency manifold, a crisis back-up. Arook has been hurt by the inload shock, but he's switched to the reinforced, military code system of his brigade.

He leads the way up.

'You are undamaged, magos?' he asks over his shoulder.

'What?'

'Are you hurt, magos?'

'No. The data shock missed me. I was unplugged.'

'That was fortunate for you,' Arook says.

'It was. There was a scrapcode problem. Server Hesst switched from discretionary to deal with it.'

Arook glances at her. His visor looks like a raptor's beak. His shoulders and upper body are huge, like a bull simian. He understands. It is simple protocol. When dealing with a significant scrapcode problem, a server will have his second-in-command unplug so that there is no danger of the second-in-command being compromised by the scrapcode. It is an operational safety measure.

It has saved Tawren from far more than just a scrapcode infection.

'Might the scrapcode be an issue?' Arook asks.

Tawren has already thought of that. A serious noospheric failure brought on by a critical code corruption… that might have caused orbital collisions or accidents. It might have even caused the grid to misfire, or a ship to discharge weapons in error.

They reach the command deck. There's a pall of smoke in the air. Technicians are struggling to free injured moderati from broken amniotic pods. Servitors hang limply from their plug sheafs. The screens are fizzling with blizzard noise.

Hesst is crumpled on the platform.

'Out of my way!' Tawren cries, shoving through the hesitant servitors and sensori clustered around him.

There's a pool of dark fluid beside his head. She can smell the toxic hormones and excess chemicals that have seared through his bloodstream and ruptured his vessels.

'We must disconnect him,' she says.

Arook nods.

A technograde servitor blurts something.

'In voice, damn you!' Tawren snaps. 'The noosphere's gone.'

'Disengaging the server could result in extreme cerebral trauma,' the technograde clacks. 'We need a cybersurgical team to properly detach him from the MIU.'

'He's dying,' says Arook, looking down at the server. Arook has seen death many times, so he knows what he is looking at.

'He is severely injured,' the technograde clicks. 'Expert disengagement may save him, but–'

'We understand,' says Tawren. She looks at Arook.

'We need the specialists,' she says. 'If there's any chance of saving him, we have to take it.'

'Of course.'

She kneels beside Hesst, getting blood on her robes.

'I'm here, server,' she says, leaning in. 'I'm here. It's Meer Tawren. You must hold on. I'm ready to relieve you, but we need a surgical crew. Just hold on.'

Hesst stirs, a flicker of life.

He murmurs something.

'Just hold on. I'm here,' she says.

'Unplug me,' Hesst gurgles, flecking his chin with blood.

'We need a surgical crew first, server. There has been a major incident.'

'Never mind me. The grid is off. It's off, Tawren. Unplug me and take over. You have to see if you can get it restarted.'

'Wait,' she soothes. 'The surgeons are coming. Wait.'

'Now!'

'You'll die, server.'

His eyelids flutter.

'I don't care. It doesn't matter. *I* don't matter. The orbital bioengines have gone, Meer.'

Her eyes go wide. She glances at Arook.

'They've gone,' Hesst repeats, his voice a sigh. 'You have to plug in, Meer. You have to take my place, plug in, and see what can be salvaged. See what control can be re-established.'

'Server–'

'You have to reconstruct the noosphere. Without the grid, Calth is defenceless.'

Tawren looks at the heavy cable-trunking of Hesst's permanent MIU link, coiled on the floor under him like a dead constrictor snake. She can't detach that without killing him, surely? Especially not with him in such a fragile state–

One of the sensori cries out.

They look up.

Debris is falling from the clouds from the orbital explosions. The first scraps of metal are raining down across the river valley, trailing fire like meteorites. She sees them strike the river in columns of steam, or scratch across the rooftops of Kalkas Fortalice. Some heavier chunks strike like rockets, exploding buildings. Something smacks against the command deck's windows, crazing the armourglas.

The hail of debris is just the beginning. Larger objects are falling. Parts of ships. Parts of orbitals. Parts of docking yards.

Tawren sees it before the sensori do. The grand cruiser *Antrodamicus*, twelve kilometres from bow to stern, falling backwards into the atmosphere from its ruptured drydock in a cloud of micro-debris, falling slowly and majestically, like a mountainside collapsing.

Falling, stern first, towards them and Kalkas Fortalice.

* * *

[mark: -0.16.11]

'I DON'T CARE what there *isn't*, show me what there is!' Marius Gage roars.

Zedoff, master of the *Macragge's Honour*, starts to argue again.

'Show him,' a voice booms.

Guilliman is on the bridge.

'Better still, show me,' he growls.

'Assessments! Everything you've got!' Zedoff yells at his crew.

Impact was less than two minutes ago. The flagship's screens are blind. There's no data, no noospheric link, no contact with the grid. What comms traffic exists is a stew of screaming voices.

'We're blind,' the Master of the First Chapter tells his primarch.

'Some impact in orbit?' Guilliman says. He casts a look at Magos Pelot, who is seizing on the deck. Most of the other Mechanicum personnel are faring no better.

Crewmen start handing the primarch data-slates. He scans fragments of the record. Gage knows that Guilliman is putting them together in his mind. A line of data from here, the last snatch recorded from there, a pict, the most recent auspex scan...

'Something hit the yards, we think,' says Gage. 'Scanners are down, screens are dead.'

'Use your damned brain, Marius,' Guilliman says. He turns to the bridge crew.

'Open the shutters! All of them. All the window ports!'

Servo systems begin to raise the blast shutters that have sealed the bridge's vast crystalflex panels. Some of the wall protective shutters have to be hand-wound back to reset. Deck stewards rush to find the crank handles.

The main shutter crawls up. An alarming quality of light, unsteady and flickering, spills in through the opening gap.

'In the name of Terra,' Gage murmurs.

'Shipmaster,' Guilliman says, turning to Zedoff. 'Your priorities are as follows. Power up. Shields up. Restore our sensory ability. Restore the vox. Inform me as any of these are achieved, and if any of them are going to take more than five minutes, I want an accurate time estimate.'

'Yes, sir.'

'Once we have vox, I want links to the following: each ship of the line commander, the server at the Watchtower, the ground commanders, the orbital station masters, not to mention my dear brother. Then–'

He stops as he hears Gage curse.

The shutters are raised high enough for them to see out. The bridge is bathed in firelight. They are looking out across the planet, across the vast and explosive destruction of Calth's primary yards. Ships are on fire everywhere they look. Some are shaking and exploding, like live rounds left too close to ignition.

It's an image Roboute Guilliman will never forget. It is more terrible than anything he could have imagined when the shockwave rattled him in his compartment and sent him running for the bridge.

It's about to get worse.

'That's ship fire,' he says, pointing at a blink of light.

'That's definitely ship fire,' Zedoff agrees, a break in his voice.

'Who the hell is firing?' Guilliman asks. 'What the hell are they shooting at?'

He doesn't wait for an answer. He strides to the main detection console and pushes the bewildered staffers out of his way. They are so transfixed by the scene beyond the open shutters, they stumble aside like sleepwalkers.

'Any auspex? Any at all?' Guilliman asks.

One of the detection officers remembers where he is.

'The pulse,' he says. He coughs. 'The electromagnetic pulse, my lord. It has rendered us insensible for a moment. Automatic restoration programs will–'

'Take time,' Guilliman finishes.

'We could…' the man stammers. 'That is, I could authorise a restart of the detection array. But it might blow the links.'

'And we'd lose everything and need a month in the yards to have the array refitted?'

'Yes, my primarch,' the man says.

'Do it anyway,' says Guilliman.

The man hesitates.

'For your own good, hurry,' Gage whispers to him. The officer jumps to work.

'If this is a fight and you blow the array, we're no use for anything,' Gage says quietly.

'We're no use for anything already,' Guilliman responds. He is staring at the view, absorbing every detail he can. He's already mentally logged the names of several ships that have been crippled or destroyed.

'The ship fire,' he ponders. 'It's coming from… from the southern dayside. Close in, too. That's not coming in from interplanetary space. That's in amongst the anchorage.'

Gage says nothing. He's not quite sure how the primarch is determining this from an eyes-only view of distance, space, burning gas, energy flares and backscattered light.

'I think so,' says Zedoff, who is more used to the view from a bridge window. 'I think you're correct, sir.'

'Someone could be trigger happy,' Guilliman says. 'Firing because they think it's an attack.'

'It may *be* an attack,' Gage says.

Guilliman nods. He's still staring at the scene.

His calm is almost terrifying. Gage is transhuman: both bred and trained to know no fear. The acceleration of his own hearts and adrenal levels are simply a response to the situation, a readiness to act faster and more efficiently.

But Guilliman is at another level entirely. He is watching a critical disaster unfold on one of his most beloved planets: the miserable loss of a vital shipyard facility, the collateral damage, the destruction of ships, a portion of the fleet crippled, surface locations caught in the debris rain...

Even if it's an accident, it's a dire turn of events. And on this day of days, when so much prestige and statecraft was to be achieved.

It's not an accident. Gage knows in his gut it's not. And he knows the primarch knows it too.

But the primarch is considering things as though he's contemplating the next move in a game of regicide.

'Hurry with that auspex!' Gage yells.

'Put the vox on speaker,' Guilliman tells the shipmaster.

'It's a jumble, sir–'

'On speaker.'

A cacophony screeches across the massive bridge. Static, pulse-noise, code squeals, voices. There's overlap, interrupt, distortion, bad signal. It's as if the whole universe is screaming at them. The only voices Gage can hear with any clarity are the ones screaming for help, for answers, for permission to leave orbit or open fire.

Gage watches Guilliman listening.

'They're not speaking,' Guilliman says.

'What, sir?' asks Gage.

Guilliman is listening intently. He's teasing out every piece of detail from the uproar.

'They're not speaking,' he repeats.

'Who are not speaking?' Gage asks.

'The Word Bearers. The traffic, it's all us.'

'How do you know?'

Guilliman shrugs lightly, still listening. He's recognising ship names, voices, keel numbers, transmission codes. Would that the Mechanicum could design a bio-engine half as efficient as Guilliman's mind.

'We're the ones requesting help, requesting clarification,'

he says. 'We're the ones asking for instructions, for permission to fire back. We're the ones dying.'

He looks at Gage.

'The Word Bearers are shooting at us,' he says.

'No. No, they simply would not–'

Guilliman silences him.

'Whatever this is, whatever has happened, they think it's an attack, and they think we're part of it. Everything they believe about us has just appeared to come true, Marius, and they're shooting at us.'

He turns to Zedoff.

'Forget the auspex. Activate the lithocast and show me Lorgar. Nothing has greater priority.'

[mark: -0.16.05]

THE FIRST OBJECT hits. It's a piece of debris. Oll Persson doesn't know what it is *exactly*. He scarcely cares. A lump of ship. A piece of orbital.

It's the size of a habitat; it comes down out of the burning sky at a forty-five degree angle. It's blazing super-hot like a meteor. It punches home like a rocket strike.

It hits the scrub land on the far side of the estuary. The impact shock throws them all over onto the ground. The swartgrass in the field around them is shredded up like chaff. Heat and air smack them, tumbling Oll and the workers, and then dust, and a storm of particulate debris. Then it rains. The rain is scalding hot. It's river water from the estuary thrown up to steam and back by the hit.

A second later, another few million gallons of river hit them. The impact has thumped the river out of its bed, and driven a two-metre-high tidal bore up across Oll Persson's land.

'Get up!' Oll yells to his paid-by-the-day workers. 'Get up and run!'

The wave swallows him, sweeping him under.

He hits a fence post, grabs on, choking, dragged around by the ferocious surge, and then back as the water recedes in a sucking rush.

More objects are hitting. Two more big pieces strike on the far shore, like missiles. Vast plumes of fire spit into the sky. Smaller pieces of debris are hitting all around, like shells, like shots from light field guns. They blow holes in the ground like grenade blasts: shell bursts of mud and water and matted vegetation. Whizz and whistle, crump, ground-shake, backspatter of mud. It's as if he's back on Chrysophar, on that last tour from hell. He feels the old fear return, and prays to his god. His lungs are full of water. He's covered in mud, black mud, that good, black alluvial soil.

The thunder is like the guns of Krasentine Ridge. A boom like sheets flapping in the wind. The shudder inside your ribs as the pressure hits you, quivering your diaphragm.

Dear god, dear god, let me live, let me live, I am your servant…

Not shells. Not shells from field guns in flak-sacked redoubts. Not shells. No stink of fycelene. But just as bad.

It's raining on them now, raining burning debris. Pelting. Each hit is like a bomb.

'Find cover!' Oll yells.

Stupid. How stupid. Where is cover going to be in this? The sky is falling in.

Some of his workers are already dead. He sees a man clutching the squirting stump of an arm, writhing in the black mire, screaming. He sees parts of a woman he quite liked protruding from the steaming lip of an impact crater. He sees one boy dead, crushed, and another dragging himself along, his legs blown off.

Like Krasentine, just like Krasentine. The ridge. He came to Calth to leave that life behind, and it's found him again.

Something burning like a falling star hits one of the fusion plants at Neride, and the ground leaps.

This time the tidal wave is four metres high and feels like a rockcrete wall.

[mark: -0.16.03]

SENESCHAL ARBUTE COMES to. She looks at Ventanus as if he has attacked her. There's a graze on the side of her face and she's clutching her torso with both arms. Broken ribs.

'Wh-what did you do?' she asks.

She still has no idea.

'Listen to me,' Ventanus says. He kneels in front of her, towering over her even so. 'Seneschal, listen. We're going to find you a medicae and–'

'Why did you hurt me? You hurt me!'

'Seneschal, you must listen to me. There's been–'

What has there been, Captain Ventanus? What should he say to her?

He has carried her into the shelter of an underpass walkway. The tiles are cool, but they can feel the heat of the fires at ground level. The sidelong light falling into the underpass is twitching orange.

'What has happened?' she asks. She's starting to realise the extent of the situation.

Selaton approaches, herding some of her staff and a few dock workers. They're bloody and dazed. One of them is hurt quite badly.

'I can't reach the company or the Chapter,' Selaton tells Ventanus. 'Vox is scorched out.'

Ventanus nods. Information is what they need right now. Information is victory. To get that, they'll need a high-gain transmitter, a primary caster, something robust enough to have survived the electromagnetic shock.

He hears a noise. It vibrates the rockcrete beneath him. He strides to the mouth of the underpass.

The sky is a firestorm, ruddy and bright. Spikes and fronds of searing yellow and orange spit across it. There's lightning too, massive electrical discharge. Burning debris is hurtling down. It's as though they're caught in a meteorite shower.

The starport is in chaos. Parts of it, especially the masts and higher gantries, have been damaged by the air-blast or the rain of debris. Heat-sear and overpressure have blown down cranes, rigs, loaders and illumination towers. Thick plumes of black smoke are rising from promethium tanks and sundered refineries.

Many loading vehicles, including two heavy lifters, have been brought down by the shock, and their crash sites are ablaze. Personnel are running in every direction. Ventanus sees bewildered crash teams and fire fighters. He sees bodies on the ground.

The noise is coming from a bulk transport. Trailing smoke and flames, it is passing low overhead, so low he feels the urge to duck. Fragments of debris are tumbling off it. It's struggling to rise, but it's never going to get enough lift. Two missiles of debris streaking down from high altitude spear into its back, exploding, causing it to lurch.

It ploughs on, engines howling, ground shaking, and crawls out of sight behind the towering hive habs and the outer docks.

There's a blink of light. He feels it hit. How far away? Six kilometres? Seven? It feels like an earthquake. The air turns gritty and the vibration is so intense his vision blurs for a second.

Behind him, Arbute screams. The scream is so sudden, it makes Ventanus jump slightly. She's limped up to join him at the mouth of the underpass, and she's just seen everything else.

'What is this? What's happening?'

'Stay calm. Please,' Sclaton says, reaching them.

'Is this an attack?' she asks.

The heat is intense. The smell of burning is dry and caustic. She has to shield her eyes from the glare. They do not.

'No,' says Selaton. 'An accident. It has to be.'

Ventanus doesn't know what to say.

'Sir!'

An Ultramarine has appeared. He's spotted them. He's got a kill team with him. It's Amant, a squad leader from 7th Company.

'Do you know what this is?' Ventanus asks.

'No, captain.'

'How many are with you?'

'I've got three squads on port protection detail,' replies Amant. 'We can't find or contact our sergeant.'

'Do you have vox?'

Amant shakes his head. 'Nothing working.'

'There's a listening station on the far side of the concourse,' Arbute says. Ventanus looks at her. She's leaning on Selaton's arm to get up, wincing at the pain.

'A listening station?'

'Part of the port's original traffic control system, before the upgrade. It has old but powerful casters.'

Ventanus nods at Arbute.

'Good. Let's find out what's going on.'

'Maybe we can find out about this gunfire too,' says Amant.

'What gunfire?' Ventanus snaps.

'Reports of shooting along the western perimeter, sir,' says Amant. 'I think it's most likely a payload of munitions that's been set off by fire, but it's not confirmed yet.'

'Let's move. Quickly,' says Ventanus. 'I don't think this is an accident at all.'

The moment it's out of his mouth, he regrets saying it aloud.

'Why not?' asks Selaton.

'Because I'm a pessimist,' says Ventanus.

Selaton looks at him. They start to help the injured seneschal along.

'Look,' Ventanus tells his sergeant, 'I couldn't have caused this much disruption to Calth's transport network if I'd *tried*.'

Amant glances at them.

'Of course it's an accident,' he says. 'What else could it be?'

Ventanus isn't listening. He can feel a tremble in the air.

Everything turns black. A deep shadow has swept over them. He hears Arbute and her aides exclaim in mortal fear.

A ship is falling backwards across the sky. A grand cruiser. It's immense. To see something so big and space-borne in scale comparison with a world's surface is fundamentally shocking. It makes the ship look like the biggest object any of them has ever seen.

It is falling so slowly. It is sliding down the sky, spilling clouds of debris, trailing the disintegrating remains of its drydock. It's as though Calth's atmosphere is a deep lake and the ship is a tree trunk sinking gracefully into it. There is a primal majesty to such destruction. The descent they are witnessing feels mythical. It is like a moon that has slipped from the firmament. A god that has forgotten how to fly. It is like a fall from the old fables. Good's plunge into evil. The bright to the dark.

'The *Antrodamicus*,' Ventanus whispers, recognising the lines of the cyclopean shape.

It seems as if it's hanging, but it's only moments from impact. It's going to crush the world. The fires of its demise will scorch the continent.

'Back,' he starts to say. 'Back!'

3

BROTHER BRAELLEN ASSUMES they're going to head for the city. Captain Damocles has already ordered the transport crews to get ready. Whatever's going on, it's bad, and the people in Numinus are going to need help. Disaster control. Lock-down. From the Ourosene Hills, they can probably be there in two hours.

No one's giving any orders. No one's giving any *anything*. There's no coordination.

So the captain is the ultimate authority 6th Company has. That's fine with Braellen. They'll move in, deploy, secure. Rescue and secure, they've trained for that.

And if it's not an accident, if it's an attack... They've trained for that too.

He's thinking that when things change and their plans change with them.

It starts raining main battle tanks.

The first impact is surreal. Braellen sees it plainly. A Shadowsword super-heavy, almost perfectly intact apart from one trailing track section, drops out of the stained sky about sixteen hundred metres ahead of him. The tank's hull plating is faintly glowing pink from re-entry.

143

It hits. Hammer blow. Blinding light. Shock-wash.

The impact creates an explosion akin to a primary plasma mine. Battle-brothers are thrown through the air like toys. Some bounce off transports or stacked freight. Braellen's squad is at the edge of the blast force. They stay upright as their power armour auto-locks and braces, sensing the explosion. Inertial dampers straining. Braellen feels grit and micro-debris spattering off his armour like small-arms fire.

The shock passes, the auto-lock relaxes. Discipline wavers for a second. No fear, just bemusement. A tank doesn't just fall out of the–

A second one does. A Baneblade, this time. It's tumbling end over end. It hits the company shelters a kilometre west, and causes an impact blast that splits the ground and triggers a landslip on the facing hill. Then two more, both Fellblades, in quick succession. One crushes a pair of parked Thunderhawks. The other hits just off the trackway a split-second later and punches a crater, but doesn't explode. It actually bounces, disintegrating. It bounces and tumbles through a scattering line of battle-brothers, mowing them down, shedding torn plate and wheel assemblies.

More fall, all around. Like bombs. Like impossible hail. Like playthings tipped out of a child's toybox. Some explode. Some fracture on impact and bounce. Some bury themselves in the open ground like bullets in flesh.

Braellen looks up into the sky. It's almost blue apart from the smoke stains from the city. It's full of falling objects: tanks, armoured fighting vehicles, troop carriers, cargo pods, lumps of debris. They turn in the air, catching the sunlight, glinting, spinning, some fast, some slow. Ash and metal-fibres rain down with them. Strands of cable. Wire. Optical leads. Pieces of haptic keyboard. Pieces of data-slate. Glass and brass splinters. Flakes of ceramite.

Somewhere, far above, a low orbit depot has broken

up and the packed contents have spilled out like treasure from a sack. Enough war machines and equipment for a full division have been thrown down to be smashed by gravity. They're too low to fully burn up. Air friction is simply heating them.

To his west, amongst the impossible skyfall, Braellen spots the flashing delta-shape of a Stormbird, rotating as it falls.

Then he sees falling bodies too.

They have not endured the drop as well as the machine parts. They have scorched and cooked. They land like bundles of wet branches, and burst.

They do not gouge vast craters and explode like the falling armour, but their impacts are somehow far more devastating.

[mark: -0.15.48]

THE WATCHTOWER SENSORI start shrieking in anticipation. Even half-blind, unplugged and shock-numbed, they can feel the immensity of the material objects sweeping towards them, the radiation flood, the momentum, the displacement of atmosphere, the distortion of gravity.

The *Antrodamicus* looms through the tortured sky, electrical discharge clinging to its hull like a neon spiderweb. It comes through the vast palls of smoke spreading horizontally from the burning starport, and parts the bright plumes of volcanic flame that are suddenly emanating from a fusion plant on the estuary. Coming through the thick and wallowing smoke, it looks like a galleon from Old Terra running aground, a great barque of the sea, gilded with fretwork and figureheads, coasting through foamy breakers onto the foreshore.

It fills the windows of the Watchtower. It is as tall as them, as high as them. It is like a city swinging towards them on a slow pendulum arc. Shooting-star chunks of falling debris streak down around it, tiny bright specks, fast moving compared to the starship's slow descent. Some debris meteors strike the ship, producing flowers of flame. Others whizz past and hit the ground, the city, the river.

Tawren knows each one of those strikes would, on another day, be a civic disaster, a hab block or a street area laid waste by a massive impact blast.

Today they are minor and extraneous injuries.

'Arook!' she yells. She holds up a stretch of Hesst's permanent MIU link like a coil of mooring rope.

The skitarii looks at her. One red eyeslit fizzles.

His tulwar is drawn in a second. The blade slices clean through the plaited cables. Sparks crack and spit. Hesst goes into a grand mal seizure.

Arook sweeps the server up, flops his jerking body over one massive shoulder. He grabs Tawren's left hand in his right fist and starts to run. Around them, on the server's platform, the sensori and magi are shrieking and weeping. Some are fleeing to the stairs. A few have jumped to their deaths from the shattered tower windows.

The massive engine ducts of the *Antrodamicus*, cold and dead-black, their fires unlit, dwarf the windows, growing bigger and still bigger.

Hesst is dead. He has stopped spasming. Bloody matter is streaming from his mouth and nose and down the master of skitarii's burnished back plate. Tawren scoops up her skirts so she can run. Arook is so fast.

Where does he hope to escape to? She trusts him, but she has no idea. She has no idea what she was hoping he could do when she got him to cut the MIU. There's not enough time. Not enough time for anything. Is he trying to reach the tower-top landing pads? A shuttle? A lighter? There isn't enough time to unseal a hatch, let alone fire its engines and lift off.

No. No. He's making for the escape pods. There are concussion caskets in bays around the tower-top. They are intended to let senior magi descend to the armoured bunkers under the Watchtower's foundations. They're crude things, just counterweight mechanisms.

Would they be enough? Is there even enough time left to reach the bunkers? The bunkers might protect from an air raid, but this? A starship is falling on the city!

Arook yanks open a pod hatch. He throws Hesst in, then hurls Tawren after him.

The *Antrodamicus* hits. Its dipped tail strikes first, biting into the land just short of the north curtain wall of Kalkas Fortalice. The keel and hull are designed to withstand the stresses of the empyrean. They only slightly deform on impact.

They dig in. The starship, all twelve kilometres of it, continues to move, sliding backwards, cutting a groove in the planet's crust five hundred metres deep. The keel splits the earth like a giant ploughshare, turning it up on either side of the immense furrow. Soil and subsoil rip open. The furrow rips across arterial highways and a memorial park. It hits the curtain wall, annihilating it. Still sliding, the *Antrodamicus* demolishes a path through the teeming city of Kalkas Fortalice, a path two and half kilometres wide. Meteoric debris is still slicing down from the sky all around it, bombarding the city and the landscape. The starship's impact is lifting a wall of dust higher than the Watchtower, a smog of particulates from atomised buildings.

The planet's crust is shaking, a long, drawn-out vibration of the most apocalyptic sort. There is a tearing, screeching shriek in the air as hull and city grind each other apart.

Now stress fractures win. The *Antrodamicus* starts to crumple. Its entire mass lands, belly down, splitting its massive frame across the waist and the prow. Hull skin rips. Command towers and masts buckle and topple. The remnants of the drydock cage, wrapping it like a garland, slough off.

Internal explosions begin to riddle it. Upper plating sections blow out. Ribs are exposed, backlit by nuclear coals in the starship's stricken heart.

It is *still* moving. It is *still* grinding backwards, disintegrating, ploughing the city in half, uprooting hab towers and hive stacks, flattening steeples and palaces. The quake-shock of the impact is levelling parts of Kalkas Fortalice that the ship hasn't even touched.

The orbital Watchtower shivers as the mounting vibrations begin to overwhelm its structural integrity. Pieces of it start to splinter and fall off. It begins to sway, like a tree in a typhoon wind.

When the sliding tail-end of the starship finally reaches it and rams it down, it is starting to fall anyway.

The *Antrodamicus* ploughs it into the ground so hard that no trace of its proud structure remains whatsoever.

[mark: -0.14.20]

AT BARRTOR, THEY can feel the earth quaking under their plasteel boots. Aftershock. Calth's tectonic system shivering from the appalling blow. The forest is thrashing, shaking loose leaves.

'Theoretical?' Phrastorex asks.

Ekritus is utterly cold and focused.

'A major orbital incident. Accident or attack. Considerable fleet loss, considerable loss of support infrastructure, catastrophic collateral damage suffered on the surface due to the orbital destruction…'

He pauses and looks at Phrastorex.

'The starport's gone. All comms are out. No link to the fleet. No link to other surface units beyond anything we can establish. No data feed. No estimation of the type or extent of the situation.'

'Practical?' Phrastorex asks.

'Obvious,' replies Ekritus.

It is? thinks Phrastorex.

'We form up. Everything we have. Your company and mine, the Army, the Mechanicum, the XVII. Everything that's this side of the river and still intact. We form up, and we pull it back east into the Sharud Province. All hell's falling out of the sky and this world is turning, Phrastorex. If we sit here wide-eyed, we could end up in a debris bombardment. Or worse. Let's salvage everything we can from this muster point and pull it east, out of harm's way, so it remains intact and battle ready.'

'What if this is an attack?' asks Phrastorex.

'Then we'll be *battle ready*!' Ekritus barks.

Phrastorex nods. His instinct is to run towards the danger. To know no fear and advance into hell, but he knows the younger captain is right. They have a duty to preserve what they've got and re-form. The primarch will be expecting no less. Between them, he and Ekritus and the captains of the Word Bearers companies in the valley command an armed force that could crush a world. They have a duty to move it out of harm's way into a holding position, so that it's ready and able to do whatever Guilliman needs it to do.

'Start leading the disposition out through the forest,' Ekritus begins. 'I'll link up with the Word Bearers and the Army and–'

'No,' says Phrastorex firmly. 'You lead the march. Get the men behind you, *literally*. Show them the way. I'll order the XVII around, the Mechanicum too. Go. Go!'

Ekritus holds up an armoured fist.

'We march for Macragge,' he says.

Phrastorex punches the fist with his mailed knuckles.

'Always,' he agrees.

He starts away down the slope, through the ranks of his own men and Ekritus's cobalt-blue warriors. Behind him, he hears Ekritus, Anchise and the other officers of both companies calling the men to order, getting them mobile. The aftershocks keep coming. Light-flash and thunder rattles the sky.

He sees 23rd squad.

'With me!' he yells. They fall in with him, moving fast. Phrastorex wants an escort. If he's going to order around Word Bearers officers and Army stuffed shirts, he needs an honour company to emphasise his authority.

'What's the order, captain?' asks Battle-brother Karends.

'The job right now is to salvage and preserve as much of this fighting strength as we can,' says Phrastorex. Ultramarines units are moving past them on both flanks, heading in the opposite direction. Down on the flood-plain, tank engines have hit start-up. Lights are coming on. Phrastorex is surprised how impressed he is by the Word Bearers' response time. Maybe he needs to revise his opinion of the wretched XVII.

He sees figures in red armour. They're advancing up the hill. Word Bearers, moving already. That's good. Maybe they won't be so hard to persuade.

Phrastorex raises a hand, calling out to the nearest Word Bearers officer.

A boltgun fires.

Battle-brother Karends explodes at the waist and collapses.

The second bolt blows the fingers off Phrastorex's raised hand.

Coming uphill at the hindquarters of the Ultra-marines companies, the Word Bearers form a line. They're advancing through the dry, ferny brush, weapons raised, firing at will.

Phrastorex has fallen to one knee. His ruined hand hurts, but the wounds have already clotted. He tries to draw his weapon with his left hand. His mind is where the real pain lies. Sheer incredulity has almost crippled him for a second. There is no theoretical, there is no comprehensible *practical*. They're being fired on. They're being fired on by the Legiones Astartes XVII *Word Bearers*. They're being fired on by their *own kind*.

He's got his gun in his sound hand. He's not sure what

he's going to do with it. Even under fire, the notion of firing back at Space Marines is abhorrent.

Phrastorex looks up. Bolter rounds are exploding in the ranks of the Ultramarines, blowing blue armour plate apart, throwing men into the air. Plasma beams, searing like blatant lies, rip through his company. Ultramarines fall, shot in the back, in the legs, split open, sliced in half. Men topple face down, the backs of their Praetor helms caved in and smoking.

It's a massacre. It's a slaughter. In seconds, before the main strength of the men can even turn in surprise, the ferny slope is littered with dead and dying. The leaves of the nodding fern brush are jewelled with blood. The trees shiver and hiss in disgust. The ground heaves as though it cannot bear to touch the proof of such infamy, as though it wants to shake the Ultramarines dead off itself so it is not implicated.

Heavier guns open fire. Lascannons. Graviton guns. Meltas. Storm bolters.

Rotary autocannons wither the rows of men in the forest space, shredding the brush cover into a green haze, spattering tree trunks with blood and chips of blue metal. Splintered trees collapse alongside splintered men.

The brothers in the squad accompanying the captain are mown down around him. A broken fragment of armour, outflung from a toppling Ultramarine, gashes Phrastorex's right eye socket, damaging the optics. The impact snaps his head sideways.

It snaps him awake, out of his stupor, out of his shocked daze.

He rises, aiming his weapon.

The crimson Space Marines are advancing towards him, up the blood-soaked slope. He can hear them chanting. Their weapons are blazing.

'You bastards!' he yells as a headshot slays him.

* * *

AT THE TOP of the slope, in the deeper forest, Ekritus turns as he hears the gunfire.

He doesn't understand what he's seeing.

Around him, other men turn and stand, dumbfounded. They watch the slaughter unfolding as though it is some trick or illusion that will be explained later.

Men in the stunned formation around Ekritus start getting hit. Heads snap back. Carapaces explode. Brothers are flung backwards. Others sag, life leaking out of them.

Ekritus shakes, too stunned to make a decision. What he's seeing is impossible. *Impossible*.

He sees Phrastorex, far below.

He sees him rise, gun in hand. In the wrong hand.

Then he sees him smashed backwards, headshot. Dead.

Ekritus roars in fury. He starts down the slope, into the hail of gunfire. Anchise grabs him and stops him.

'No,' the sergeant shouts. 'No!'

He shakes Ekritus and turns him.

Titans advance through the forest to their right. Trees crash down, uprooted or snapped by the massive fighting engines. War horns boom. Ekritus smells the stink of void shields.

The Titans begin to shoot.

[mark: -0.11.21]

SERGEANT HELLOCK SHOUTS orders. No one is listening.

Bale Rane stands, open-mouthed, dazed by the overload of shock. Men run in all directions. Fireballs scream down out of the blood-clotted sky and explode all around them. Rane tenses and ducks as the pieces of orbital debris swoop over and hit. A kitchen tent explodes on the far side of the parade ground. The medicae section is thrown into the air as though mines have been triggered beneath it.

Each blast makes Rane flinch, but his eyes never leave the main wonder. A ship just crashed about thirty kilometres west of them. A whole ship. It's sitting there now like a newly raised mountain range, broken, smoking. Ripples of explosions fire-cracker across its fractured hull.

It's beyond anything he can imagine. It's too big to be real.

All he can think of is Neve on the far side of the river. She'll be scared. She should be alive; he reassures himself of that, at least. The starship fell on the Kalkas side of the river. Numinus was spared, though debris is fire-balling the whole region. Whoever knew there was so much stuff up there in space that could fall out of it? She'll have gone to her aunt's, most likely. She's a smart girl. She'll have gone to her aunt's and got in the cellar. Safe as houses.

Rane swallows hard.

He realises he doesn't love her. He probably never did. He sees that with clarity, suddenly. It was all so easy, so romantic. He was going to be a soldier, and go off with the Army muster, so their time was precious. They'd probably never see each other again. So it was easy. It was easy to commit. It was easy to make grand gestures when nothing had to last. Everything was romantic. Everything was poignant. Everything took on a significance because they had so little time. They got married. It was like a huge send-off. Everyone cried. So romantic. *So romantic*.

So unreal. As unreal and unlikely as a broken starship sitting where Kalkas Fortalice used to be. As unreal as this whole day.

It's as though he's gone from a daydream into a living nightmare where everything makes more sense.

Krank knocks him over.

'What the hell–?' Rane gasps.

Something that is almost definitely a wheel from a battle tank, glowing red hot, has come bouncing across the compound, flattening tents and water bowsers. It would have mowed him down, but for Krank.

'We're moving!' yells Krank.

'Where?'

'The dug-outs!' Sergeant Hellock is shouting. 'Get into the dug-outs!'

That makes no sense either. There are several thousand troopers in the immediate zone, and a few dozen dug-outs, constructed for air raids as per regulations. And if another starship falls on them, a bastard hole in the ground isn't going to save them anyway.

'Look!' Trooper Yusuf calls out. 'Look at the wire!'

They look at the fence dividing their compound from the Army auxiliaries serving the XVII. They were chanting earlier. Now they're up against the fence. They're pressing pale hands and woeful faces against the metal link. They're calling out. Rane can see flames licking on the far side of the neighbouring compound.

'They're trapped,' Hellock says. 'Bloody bastards. They're trapped in there. They can't get out.'

Some of the men run forward to see if they can open the connecting gate.

'Wait,' says Rane. 'Don't.'

They're too close. His squad mates are too close to the wire, too close to the pale, staring faces.

The fence goes down. It's been cut in places, and it simply falls flat on the ground, jingling and rattling. The foreign auxiliaries spill over into the compound of the Numinus 61st.

'What the bastard hell is this?' Hellock says.

The foreigners have guns. Rifles. Side arms. Blades. Hafted weapons. They've got bastard *spears*.

The first shots take out the nearest Numinus troops. They buckle and drop. The heathens are howling as they charge in. One rams a spear through Yusuf's gut. Yusuf screams like no one ought to ever have to scream, and the scream carries on, in broken sections, as the heathen twists and jerks the haft. Seddom, another man Rane has got to know, takes a las-round to the cheek, and his head goes a peculiar shape as he falls over. Zwaytis is shot as he turns to run. Bardra is stabbed repeatedly. Urt Vass is shot, then Keyson, then Gorben.

Rane and Krank start to run. Haspian turns to flee with them, but he trips over Seddom, and then the heathens are on him, pounding him to death with spears like washer women using beetles at the river side.

Hellock screams out a curse, draws his autopistol and fires. He makes the first active loyalist kill of the Battle of Calth, though the fact is not remembered by posterity. He shoots a heathen with a spear and puts him down dead.

Then a spear goes through his arm and another splits his thigh, and he falls. He's screaming as they pin him to the ground, screaming every insult he can dredge up.

The Ushmetar Kaul pour past, slaughtering his men. Hellock, through his rage and pain, realises they are chanting again.

One of the bastards pinning him bends down to slit his throat with a knife, but another bastard stops him.

CRIOL FOWST LOOKS down at the man his soldiers have pinned. An officer. Rank has value, ritual significance.

He can use the wounded sergeant. There are things that will have to be fed, after all.

[mark: -0.09.39]

VENTANUS CARRIES ARBUTE through the burning port complex, but she directs the way. Selaton and the seneschal's aides follow them, escorted by Amant and his squad.

'This way,' she says. 'Down that ramp. Down there.'

There are two huge listening pylons ahead of them, scaffold-frame monsters with a dish receiver set between them. It's old stuff, very basic, probably constructed by the first pioneers when they began the Calth colonies. It's military grade, though. No frills. Built to last.

'My father worked the port for thirty years. I spent time here. This was part of the original port authority traffic system, before the Mechanicum arrived and set up a proper manifold. It should have been scrapped a century ago, but they kept it serviced.'

'Why?' asked Vantanus.

'Because it's reliable. When the solar storms kick off, every fifteen years or so, they're much more resilient during the radiation flares than the manifold systems.'

'Good,' says Ventanus.

Flaming debris bombs are still slicing overhead. None of the party has quite got over the sight of the *Antrodamicus* hitting the surface. Some of the aides are tearful.

The pylons are built on a platform in the middle of a rockcrete basin beside landing platform sixty. It's a natural shelter. About two hundred port workers and cargo-men have huddled there, under the lip of the platform. It's not much of a refuge, but it's better than nothing. Hot ash is raining down, burning scraps. Every now and then something small but heavy, like a sheared mooring bolt or an airgate handle, hits the ground like a bullet.

The sheltering personnel move forward when they see the Space Marines. There are questions, a lot of questions, and pleas for help.

'We don't know anything,' Ventanus tells them, putting Arbute down and raising his hands. 'A state of emergency is now in force, obviously. I need to get that listening post operational. Maybe we'll get some answers that way. I need vox operators.'

Several men step forward as volunteers. He chooses two.

'Let's move,' Ventanus says.

He's getting edgy. It's been almost ten minutes

since the disaster struck, and he still knows absolutely
nothing.

The control rooms for the post are a trio of standard
pattern module habitats mounted thirty-five metres up
on the girder-work frame of the pylon array. An open
switchback staircase of grilled steps leads up to them.

Ventanus picks up Arbute again, and leads the way.
The vox volunteers follow, along with a couple of the
seneschal's aides, Selaton and Amant. Amant's troops
spread out to quell the agitated crowd.

They open one of the modules. There's still power.
The technicians get to work warming up the station's
main caster grid. Ventanus takes a data-slate and
records the channel frequencies he wants to raise.
Erud muster control. Fleet command. His own company command.

The vox operators sit down at the main caster desks
facing the module's windows. Whooping static and radiation distort sobs through the old, hefty speakers.

'Was that gunfire?' Selaton asks.

'Not that I heard,' Ventanus replies. 'Probably more
debris hits.'

He goes out onto the narrow gantry outside the module. The view is excellent, though what he can see is
not. Large sections of the port facility are now ablaze.
The sky over both sides of the river is blacked out with
smoke. Meteoritic streaks still stripe against the darkness, like las-bolts. It's hard to see the huge shipwreck
any more, though the pall in the direction of what used
to be Kalkas Fortalice is throbbing red like the mouth
of hell.

There's definitely a distant sound, a booming. It's
almost like a planetary bombardment. Ships firing from
orbit.

He's still clinging to the notion this is all an accident.

There's a shout from far below. Three more squads of
Space Marines have entered the basin at the foot of the

pylons. They're dressed in red. XVII. That's good. Good to get a little collaboration going in this hour of dire need. Maybe the Word Bearers' comms networks have come through the incident a little more intact.

He sees Amant's men and the crowd of port workers moving to greet them.

Ventanus steps back into the listening station module.

'I'm going back down,' he tells Selaton. 'Reinforcements just arrived and I want to find out what they know.'

He looks at the vox operators, hard at work.

'The moment they get anything, call me back up.'

Selaton nods.

Ventanus turns. Pauses.

'What?' asks Selaton. 'What's the matter, sir?'

Ventanus isn't sure. He opens his mouth to reply.

No warning. *No damned warning*. Just a nanosecond prickle, a sting of intuition, that something isn't right.

A nanosecond. Too little, and too damned late.

Mass-reactive rounds slam into the floor and front wall of the listening station module. *Mass-reactive rounds fired from below*.

The floor and front wall shred. Disintegrating metal plating becomes splinters and lethal tatters. Light and flame compress upwards into the module through its ruptured shell from the blast points, driving the splinters in with it.

The air inside the module fills with expanding flame and whizzing fragments. The forced pressure of the strike blows out the window ports and annihilates the vox-caster desks. Seneschal Arbute is knocked backwards. The head and shoulders of one of her aides become red mist as a round strikes and detonates. White-hot spalling and jagged shrapnel from the floor macerates the two vox-operator volunteers. The other staff aide, a clerk, is thrown into the module's ceiling by the upward pressure of the blasts. His broken body then falls back and drops out through a floor that is no longer intact.

Selaton sees the murdered clerk fall, cartwheeling away, dislocated and loose. His corpse disappears down through the girder work of the pylons, just one more chunk in a hailstorm of spinning debris and burning fragments.

The deck begins to break away from the front wall.

'Back! Back!' Ventanus orders. The entire module is already shrieking and tilting, as if it is about to shear clean off its mounting. Part of the metal cage supporting the entry staircase rips away and topples.

The unseen killers fire again. Another rain of explosive rounds brackets and punishes the module. Ventanus assesses frantically, his weapon drawn. The attack is coming from positions down below, on the pylon base.

Mass-reactive. Detonating on impact. *Legiones Astartes munition.* Not possible. Not possible. Unless–

'Error,' exclaims Selaton beside him. 'False fire. Error. Someone has made an–'

'I said get back!' Ventanus screams, grabbing Selaton and pulling him towards the rear of the module.

Ventanus and Selaton start to return fire, blasting down through the hole created as the floor section collapses and peels away. There is only smoke below, no clear target, no true thermal print. They fire anyway. Discouragement.

Armour inertials don't lie. The module is slumping backwards. It is going to separate from its mountings and fall.

Arbute is dead. There isn't a wound on her, but Ventanus knows that the overpressure and kinetic slam of the mass-reactive strikes will have pulped her human organs. Amant has been dropped. Two, perhaps three mass-reactive rounds have taken him from below. He is lying on his back on the rapidly perishing deck. His feet are gone, and the blasts have sliced the armour and flesh from his shins and thighs, his torso and his face. He is still alive, clotting blood filling the cavities of his wounds.

A few moments to stabilise, and they could get him clear. Get him to reconstruction. Even with the front of his body skinned and scourged away, a month or two in biotech conditioning would see him fighting again.

The module doesn't have a few moments.

They don't have a few moments.

Ventanus sees Amant's eyes, wide in a mask of blood and broken visor, staring in helpless disbelief. Ventanus understands what he sees there. Amant knows it's the end, not just of his own existence, but of the galaxy as they understand it.

Ventanus kicks out the rear hatch with one savage thump of his heel. The support staircase is gone. There is nowhere to go. The module starts to fall, like a boat rolling over in a rush as the water it is taking on suddenly hits the tipping point.

'Jump!' yells Ventanus.

An order is a damned order.

They jump.

[mark: -0.03.59]

GUILLIMAN IS ALMOST rigid with fury. He's got a stylus out, a pen, and he's at the bridge windows, recording everything he can see on his data-slate. Ship losses, dispersement. Formation.

The moment the flagship's system reboot and power comes to active yield, he wants data he can act on.

'I want that link!' he yells over his shoulder, sketching the relative placements of the *Cornucopia* and the *Vernax Absolom*.

'Do we raise shields?' asks Gage.

'The moment you have them,' Guilliman replies.

'Communicate that to the whole fleet the moment we have capability.'

Gage nods.

'Do we return fire?' he asks.

Guilliman looks at him.

'This is a tragedy. A tragedy, a *mistake*. As soon as we can protect ourselves, we do that. But do not make this worse. We do not add to the death toll.'

Gage's jaw tenses.

'I would kill them for this,' he says. 'Forgive me, but this is a crime. They must know this is wrong. They shame us–'

'They are hurt,' Guilliman says. 'They believe they are under mortal threat. All their fears are *real* to them. Marius, we do not compound their folly. We do not add our mistake to theirs, no matter what the cost.'

'We have a link!' Zedoff cries.

Guilliman turns. 'Lithocast?'

'Barely. Principally audio.'

Guilliman shoves the data-slate to Gage and moves to the hololithic platform.

Light blooms around him again. It is not as healthy as it was before, not as stable. There are figures that aren't quite there, crackling phantoms at the edge of resolution. Guilliman sees only the outline of Argel Tal, the shadow of Hol Beloth, a skeletal sketch of light that might be Foedral Fell.

Only Lorgar is visible. His resolution is black and white, jumping and interrupted. His eyes are in shadow, his head down. Wherever he is standing, there is a very local light, a glow just above him that casts his face in inky darkness.

'Stop this,' Guilliman says.

Lorgar does not answer.

'Brother. Cease fire now!' Guilliman says. 'Cease fire. This is a mistake. You have made a grave error. Stop your reprisal. We are not your enemy.'

'You are against us,' Lorgar whispers, his voice made of white noise whine.

'We have not attacked you,' Guilliman insists. 'This I swear.'

'You turned on us once. You shamed us and humiliated us. You will not do so again.'

'Lorgar! Listen to me. This is a mistake!'

'Why in all the stars would you presume this to be a mistake?' asks Lorgar. He still does not look up.

'Cease fire,' Guilliman says. 'We have not attacked you, nor allowed you to be attacked. I swear this, upon our father's life.'

Lorgar's reply is lost in a crackle of noise. Then the image of him vanishes too, and the hololithic platform dies.

'Contact lost,' Zedoff announces. 'He's refusing our attempts to restore the link.'

Guilliman looks at Gage.

'He's not going to back down,' Guilliman says. 'He's not going to stop this unless we stop him.'

Gage can see the pain in Guilliman's eyes, the enormity of what this means.

'What was that thing he said, my primarch?' Gage asks. 'That last thing?'

Guilliman hesitates.

'He said, "I am an orphan".'

Gage straightens up and glances at the senior crew.

'Your orders, sir?' he says firmly.

'Issue the instruction as best you can,' Guilliman says, stepping down from the platform. 'To all XIII Legion units and auxiliaries, upon my authority code. Priority one. Defend yourselves by all means at your disposal.'

Gage clears his throat.

'My primarch, I need your confirmation. Have you just authorised actions up to and including return of fire?'

There is a long pause.

'Return of fire is so ordered,' says Guilliman.

Zedoff and the senior gunnery officers start barking orders. Gage turns to the rubricator waiting ready at his station beside the shipmaster's throne.

'Officer of record,' he says. 'Start the mark.'

The rubricator nods and activates his cogitator.

'Initiating XIII Legion combat record, elapsed time count,' the rubricator says. 'Count begins. Calth mark: 00.00.00.'

SYSTEM//KILL

'It is necessary under some circumstances, even – in extremis – actions of compliance, to methodically destroy an opponent's infrastructure along with the opponent himself. Sometimes an emphatic military victory is not enough: sometimes the very earth must be salted, as the ancient texts put it. The principal arguments for this kind of action may be psychological (against a defiant people or species) or a matter of security (in that you are purifying a region of something too dangerous to exist). Neither of these arguments is especially comforting to a pragmatic commander. War is about accomplishment as well as victory; it should not be about supreme destruction. This kind of total war, this process of razing, is most commonly seen with shock or hyper-aggressive forces. The warriors of Angron, my brother primarch of the XII Legion, refer to it as Totality, *and even they employ it rarely to its full extent. From my brother Russ, and the Wurgen war-cant of the Vlka Fenryka we borrow the term* Skira Vordrotta, *which may most usefully be rendered as* System Kill.*'*

– Guilliman, *Notes Towards Martial Codification*, 4.1.ix

1

'MY BROTHER, HEAR me. Warriors of the XVII Legion, hear me. This violence is against the code of the Legiones Astartes and against the will of our father, the Emperor. In the name of the Five Hundred Worlds of Ultramar, I implore you to cease fire and stand down. Open communication with me. Let us speak. Let us settle this. This action is an error of the most tragic kind. Cease fire. I, Roboute Guilliman, give you my solemn pledge that we will deal with each other frankly and fairly if these hostilities can be suspended. I urge you to respond.'

Guilliman puts the speaker horn down and looks at Gage and the Master of Vox.

'As soon as we are able,' he tells them, 'transmit that message on repeat. Cycle transmissions. No interruptions.'

'Yes, sir,' says the Master of Vox.

[mark: 0.00.10]

LEVIATHANS STIR. BIGGER than the human mind can comfortably conceive, starships move through the burning

167

clouds of dust above Calth. Their dark hulks emerge from glittering banks of debris, through swirling flares of ejected energy, like marine monsters surfacing for air.

They are flying blind. They are fighting blind. They scream challenges and threats into the burning void through shorted vox systems and blown speakers. They detach themselves from the super-massive gantries, derricks and anchorages of the yards, some shearing cables, lines and airgates in their desperation to run free.

A moving target is harder to hit. That's the logic. In truth, a moving target makes itself alone and vulnerable.

The warships of the XVII Legion make the kills appear effortless. Coasting, almost stately, they run forward, shields lit, creating bright halos around their hulls as dust and particulate matter burns off the fields. Their snarling gunports are open, their primary weapons extended in their silo bays. Charge batteries and plasma capacitors seethe with power, ready for lethal discharge. They are supposed to be deaf and blind too, but they are not. Detection and target systems beyond the darkest imaginings of the Mechanicum peer out into the noisy darkness and alight upon the scattering cobalt-blue vessels of the Ultramar fleet as though they were hot coals on cold ash. They find them, and they bind them, tracking them relentlessly, scrutinising them in lascivious detail, weighing and assessing their shielding and hull strength, while weapons batteries train and align, and munitions loads are ordered up. Bulk magazines chug and clatter as projectile shells and missiles are conveyed by automatic loaders, through-deck hoists or ordnance chutes.

Munitions fill the void like seed pods, like blizzards. Columns of scorching plasma and las, hundreds of kilometres long, stripe afterimages on the retinas of those who witness them. Main lance batteries vomit bright energy and spit light in beams, in gobs, in splinters, in twitching withies of lightning.

Ships burst in the darkness. The *Gladius*, a four-kilometre-long escort from the Saramanth Wing, serially detonates as it draws clear of its slipway, its armoured hull sectioned and chewed apart by internal explosions. The barge *Hope of Narmenia* is caught by a missile spread that strikes it like a storm of needles, puncturing its upper hull and stern in a hundred places, peppering it, engulfing its interior in white-hot fire. The support carriers *Valediction* and *Vospherus* are wrecked by sustained broadside fire from a battle-barge of the XVII. The *Valediction* breaks up first, its hullplates unwrapping around a core explosion like a time-lapse feed of a flower's petals opening, blooming and dying. Hastily deployed lifeboats are swept away by the super-heat wash. The *Vospherus*, shielded by the fate of its sister ship, turns away to run, but the enemy guns reach it and pulp its drive section. Drive vents and engine bells explode, and the inward pressure forces a drive plant event, a series of star-hot overblasts in the engineering spaces that burst the stern of the carrier like a pipe bomb. The force of the blasts throws the ruined carrier forward on a pressure wave and slams the ship into the troop transport *Antropheles*, cutting it in two. Eighty thousand lives lost in five seconds.

The Infernus-class battleship *Flame of Purity*, one of the true monsters of the XVII fleet, runs into the Asertis Orbital Yard, firing cannonades to maximise collateral damage. Its prow is armoured: a vast, burnished ramming blade, a giant's chisel gilded with seraphs, narwhals and eagles. It ploughs through the smaller, berthed ships in its path, bisecting some, ripping others open, shattering hulls. Its main spinal lance mount, a primary magnitude exo-las weapon, wakes and screams, uttering a shaft of matter-annihilating light that sends the picket cruiser *Stations of Ultramar* reeling from a hammering concussion as it attempts to defend the yard space. The cruiser tries to rally, trailing debris from a blackened and molten port side. It turns about, dazed, clumsily glancing against support stations and yard gantries. Clouds of pink flame belch from its stricken engines. It raises its shields. The *Flame of Purity* fires its recharged exo-laser again. The shields surrounding the *Stations of Ultramar* do not even retard the beam. They pop like soap bubbles. The beam vaporises the cruiser's central mass, until it's merely a toroid of hull metal around a glowing white-hot hole. The *Flame of Purity* powers on, bumping the drifting ruin of the *Stations of Ultramar* aside on its magnetic bow-wave.

In the dark pits of drive rooms and engineering chambers, hosts of stokers and allworks slave away with furious effort. The chambers are infernal, soot-caked and lit by the ruddy glare of the vast engines and reactor furnaces. Armies of stokers, sweat-sheened and roaring, eyes like white stones in blackened faces, shovel fuel ores and promethium pellets into the iron chutes. Servitor crews, their metal skins colour-bruised like old kettles by the constant heat, lever and haul on the throbbing activator rods that quicken the drive plants. Coal-black chains swing. Bellows wheeze and flush dragon-breath balls of roiling fire up flues and vent pipes. Abhuman labourers, troll-like and grunting, swelter as they drag in monolithic payload carts of raw fuel from the silo decks.

There is frenzy here, panic that is barely kept at bay by the lashes and orders of the engine room masters. There are no windows, no way of appreciating the outer universe or the threats it may contain.

In truth, the envied bridge crews in their glass and gilt towers far above have no better understanding of the calamity than the blind stokers down in the dark below. Knowledge of this irony may not have enhanced the stokers' confidence.

Many will never know the light again. Some of the ships slain during the Calth Atrocity will continue to circle the tortured star for a hundred thousand years as frozen wrecks, as tomb ships for the silent dead, mummified and preserved in the act of screaming their final screams.

[mark: 0.00.20]

VENTANUS AND SELATON hit the ground. The drop is severe. Their strength and their armour absorb the impact, and they come up, bolters ready. Dust and ash films their armour plate.

They move.

The module reaches the ground behind them, shredding open as it lands. The noise is huge, a splintering of metal. Behind the module comes the best part of one of the pylons. They can hear steel hawsers parting like bolter shots. Broken fastener pins, released by the extreme tension, whistle through the air like micro-missiles.

Selaton and his captain outrun the falling pylon. It collapses like a tranquillised animal, buckling at the knees, and then falling from loose hips, then from a slack neck that turns back against the direction of the fall. Dust erupts in a rolling wall, as if driven by the sound of tearing steel. Ventanus and Selaton bound out of the dust wall.

The landing platforms ahead of them are covered with debris and corpses. Ventanus blanches as he sees fallen Ultramarines. Bolter fire has reamed and split their beautiful cobalt-and-gold armour. He sees one man who died carrying a regimental standard. It is a golden symbol of the Legion surmounting a double eagle. The banner pole is clenched so tightly in his armoured fists that his grip has marked the haft.

This was an honour guard. A ceremonial squad cut down as it prepared to board. Nearby, the bodies of city dignitaries, of trade officials, of seneschals, of aides and cargo foremen. They are bloody ruins: split sacks of meat and torn clothing. They were cut down by weapons designed for post-human war, weapons that could slay and have now slain the Legiones Astartes.

Weapons whose effects on unmodified, un-enhanced, unarmoured humans amount to overkill.

Selaton slows to a halt. He regards the litter of dead.

'Move!' Ventanus orders.

'They were waiting to board,' says Selaton, as if this matters.

Ventanus stops and looks at his sergeant.

It is so obvious, and yet, he missed it. It has taken Selaton's less experienced mind to see the simple truth.

They were waiting to board. They died waiting to board, banners and standards raised. But it is, perhaps, fifteen or twenty minutes since the disaster struck, fifteen or twenty minutes since the orbital detonation that began the deluge of fire.

Did they stand there all that time, still waiting to board as the world caught light around them?

'They were already dead,' says Ventanus. 'Dead, or dying.'

This murder pre-dated the disaster. At best, it was simultaneous. The disaster was no accident.

Gunfire shrieks across the platforms. Las-fire spanks off the blast walls behind them. Bolter shells corkscrew the smoke they cut through. Impacts occur all around.

Ventanus sees Word Bearers advancing out of the filthy air. Troops move up with them, Army cohorts with lasrifles and halberds.

They're shooting at any target they can see.

Selaton, still confined by the ethical parameters of the universe he used to understand, asks the obvious question.

'What do we do?' he says. 'What do we do?'

2

[mark: 0.01.00]

ABOARD THE SAMOTHRACE, Sorot Tchure performs his second ministry.

His men are already killing most of the ship's primary crew. Advancing to the main bridge, burning through blast hatches that had been closed in desperation, Tchure comes face-to-face with the ship's captain, who solemnly announces his disinclination to assist Tchure, no matter what threat is made.

Tchure ignores the officer. He is a yapping gatehouse dog that is too ignorant to know better. He is barking futile defiance at the carnodon that has just entered through the gates.

Tchure grasps the captain's head in his right hand and squashes it like an uncooked egg. He lets the body drop. The bridge crew gawps at him, realising that their predicament is far worse than they ever imagined. When a ship is seized, bridge crew can ordinarily safeguard their lives in exchange for their vital technical services.

The bridge officers of the *Samothrace* see their captain murdered, and realise their services are not required.

Several pull sidearms, despite the fact that they are

unmodified humans dressed in cloth and braid, despite the fact that they are outnumbered by martial transhumans who have just cut their way into the main bridge space, despite the fact that their laspistols will not even dent the armour of the invaders.

Tchure is in the newer Maximus plate, as befits his command status. Crimson is the first colour his suit has ever been painted.

'Death,' he instructs as a las-round *tangs* off his shoulder plate.

The Word Bearers use their fists, guns slung. Tchure doesn't want mass-reactive shells destroying the vital control stations of the bridge. They break men. They grab them and snap spines and necks, or mash skulls, or tear out soft throats. The officers have nowhere to run, but they run anyway, screaming in terror. They are grabbed and picked up by the hair, by the coat-tails, by the ankles and wrists, grabbed and picked up and killed. The bodies are slung in a pile in the centre of the deck in front of the late captain's throne.

Tchure observes the work. He raises his left wrist, and speaks into the glass-and-wire mechanism welded there. It is inscribed with the mark of the sacred Octed. The dark, glistening thing living inside the wire-wrapped bottle does not send his words like a vox. It simply repeats them through other mouths in other places.

Hearing the signal through their own warp-flasks, the Mechanicum magi advance onto the bridge. They are all of the cadre that has sided with the Warmaster. They have turned their backs on Mars and Terra. Subtle variations in their robes and insignia already show this change of alignment, but most of all there is a darkness to them. They wear the mystery of their technological craft around them like a shadow.

'The ship is seized,' Tchure tells their leader. The magos nods, and instructs his men to bridge positions.

'Ten minutes, and we will be mobile,' the magos tells

Tchure. 'Motivation is coming to yield.'

'Zetsun Verid Yard,' says Tchure, naming his destination. The yard is a smaller, specialist facility that forms part of the orbital archipelago where the *Samothrace* has docked.

The magos nods again. Under the deck, systems are humming up to active power.

Tchure turns to his second, Heral.

'Locator,' he says.

Heral's squad brings forward the locator unit, a warp-flask the size of an urn, and places it in the middle of the deck. They wedge it into the pile of corpses to hold it upright. Blood is sliming the floor under their feet.

They stand back. Something in the flask pulses and ripples, gleaming slug-black. Something whispers in the darkness. Something withdraws into its shell like a glistening mollusc, except the shell is not there, in the flask, on the bridge of the *Samothrace*, it is *else*where, in another universe, recessed through the coils and loops and whorls of an interstitial architecture.

Frost forms on the corpse pile. Some of the dead muscles stiffen into rictus, and cause the corpses to jerk and lurch as though they are trying to wriggle out from under the tangle of limbs.

Corposant ignites around the flask, lights up the bodies, twitches and crackles along the ceiling beams like neon ivy. It grows impossibly bright. Tchure looks away.

When he looks back, the glow is fading, the piled corpses have been burned black, and a new figure has joined them, still smoking with teleportation energy.

'Welcome to the *Samothrace*,' says Tchure, bowing his head. The air smells of cooked fat from the incinerated bodies.

'Sorot. Let us begin,' says Kor Phaeron.

* * *

[mark: 0.20.34]

AT BARRTOR, THE forests east of the Boros are on fire. Traitor Titans lumber through the sparks and smoke billowing up from the canopy. They look like woodsmen tending a brushfire. Their weapon mounts pour destruction into the glades and cavities of the forest.

Air support howls past. Down in the woods, the shattered remnants of the 111th and 112th Companies, Ultramarines, retreat before the reaping assault of the betrayers. Achilles- and Proteus-pattern Land Raiders, dressed in crimson and badged with abominable designs, demolish the tree cover and men alike. Mega bolters, grinding like unoiled fabrication plants, lacerate the world, reducing trees to fibres, rocks to dust, and bodies to paste.

Ekritus moves backwards, firing as he goes. Anchise is nearby, doing the same. Beyond him, a few other trusted men. Ekritus isn't even thinking about what's happening any more. To do so would be to confront the unthinkable, and to leave his mind and wits with as much protection as the flimsy trees are currently affording his body.

He is simply surviving. He is firing at anything he can cleanly target, and falling back. They are buying time for the squads he has sent off at an expedited rate of retreat. Throne alone knows if they will draw clear, or find any shelter from the aircover that is sweeping across them.

What's left of his companies are cut off from their heavy support. They haven't got anything in their arsenal that will stop the Land Raiders. Each of those beasts is felling a swathe of the forest ahead of it. Nothing at all will stop the Titans. Every time one of the marching giants speaks, booming its speaker horn in a howl of scorn and triumph, Ekritus feels his bones shake.

He scrambles through brush, reloading his weapon on clips taken from the dead. The blood of others paints his armour, turning him crimson, a colour he has an unexpectedly painful need to wash off. Bolt-rounds snap and whine through the trees. One pulps leaves in a mist of sap. One hits a tree trunk, explodes, and collapses the ancient tree wholesale. One destroys Brother Caladin's head, and flips his corpse into a ditch.

Ekritus finds a mossy slope, ducks under a root mass, and clambers up. Old stonework, the retaining wall of some earthwork built in the early years, when this was estate land. Smoke bores through the woodland space as if driven by an ocean current. Animals and avians are mobbing out of the devastated environment in teeming plague-year swarms.

Nature in rout. A world turned upside down.

He clambers higher still. He is above the tree line. He can see for many kilometres. He can see the world burning. On the plains beyond the forest expanse, he can see vast hosts assaulting the towns along the river and the port. Waves of men, tens of thousands strong, Army or what until an hour ago passed for Army. Waves of men, of armour, formations of Titan engines, phalanxes of Space Marines, all of them hazed in the dust and smoke of their advance.

The blot of their insult.

The stain of their crime.

Here alone, east of the river, he can see a mobilised force large enough to take a continent. A world, probably. And this, just one muster of the Calth conjunction. He watches as it surges, a fluid mass, sweeping aside everything in its path.

There are so many burning ships and orbitals in the sky, it looks like a hundred sunsets all happening at once. The actual sun, the Veridian system's pure, blue-white star, is lost behind circumfulgent smoke.

Ekritus wants to kill them all. He wants to face them and kill them, one by one, until there are none left, and the heat of his outrage is finally quelled.

He senses movement. The first of the Word Bearers appears. Behind him, two more, toiling up the earth-work slope. More come behind them. Ekritus stands to meet them.

They do not shoot him.

He hesitates, boltgun in one hand, power sword in the other.

He is red, like them. Except not by choice.

They see his true markings under the sticky sheen of blood only as they draw close. By this time, as they react, he is already killing them.

He shoots the first in the face. There is no time to appreciate the satisfaction of seeing the grilled helm explode, the pieces of bone and hair and brain-matter eject in all directions. The second he hits in the gut. The third in the left shoulder, tipping him backwards down the hill into the men behind him.

The fourth is another headshot.

There is no fifth. No rounds left.

Ekritus goes into them with his sword. He severs a wrist, a thigh, a neck. He impales a body and lifts it, hurling it like a sack down the earthwork rise. It crashes into its kin below. Two-handed, he buries the edge of the blade in the cranium of another helm, splitting it in half.

One has dropped a bolt pistol. He snatches it up out of the bloody moss and fires twice into the chest of the next traitor on him, killing him cold. He kills the next two, then side slashes a man off the bulwark ridge to his left.

But they're on him. There are too many. Enough to take a world. Enough to bring a Legion to its knees. They hit him. They beat him with gun-butts and sword hilts. They pin him and club him down to his knees, chipping and denting his armour until some of the blue shows through again.

One of them tears off his helm.

'Bastards! Bastards!' he yells at them. A fist pulps his
face, repeated blows to mash flesh and crush bone. He
drools blood and teeth through swollen lips. One eye
has gone.

They drag him up. He's a captain. He's a trophy.

A figure towers over him. Ekritus, half-blind, realises
it's one of the Titans, advanced to face the earthwork. Its
speaker horns boom. The Word Bearers roar an answer
and punch the air.

When the Titan resumes its advance, knocking down
the old earthwork and trampling the trees, Ekritus is cru-
cified on its torso plates.

[mark: 0.32.31]

HOL BELOTH, RECENTLY teleported to the surface, commands the advance on the port at Lanshear. Hosts of the
Kaul Mandori, the Jeharwanate, and the Ushmetar Kaul
sweep before his engine formations. A brigade of the
Tzenvar Kaul is encircling the port to the north.

The brotherhoods fight with supreme devotion. Beloth
or his immediate officers have selected and anointed
many of the zealots personally. They are conduits for the
warp-magicks used by the highest ordinals of the XVII to
enrapture their warhosts.

Hol Beloth is ambitious. He wishes to be more than
a commander and more than a conduit. Such status has
been promised to him by Erebus and Maloq Kartho and
other, unnamed shadows that stand beside them sometimes and mutter in the twilight. He will be invested. He
will be greater than even the Gal Vorbak. But he must
prove himself, though he has proved himself in war a
thousand times before.

This is a new form of war. This is a warfare that has
never been unleashed openly before. Beloth must
achieve his objectives, and perform his duties well. He

must prove that he can command and control men and *un*-men alike.

He is hungry for power. Erebus and Kor Phaeron were always the greatest adepts, since the earliest days, but now the primarch seems to have exceeded them. His essence is frightening. Lorgar is transcendent. It is not simply the power, it is the fluid subtlety with which he employs it. Just being near Lorgar is a privilege. Being apart from, like here on Calth... it feels like the sun has gone out.

Hol Beloth believes that Erebus and Kor Phaeron are painfully aware of the way they have fallen behind. He believes they watch the primarch and crib from him, borrowing tricks and talents they have learned by observation, and then deploying them with stiff, crude proficiency. They are not *adept* any more. They are struggling to keep up with Lorgar's mastery.

It is as though they are borrowing from another place, while Lorgar has become one with that place.

Hol Beloth intends to ascend to a place beside his primarch. He will burn Lanshear for the right to do so.

[mark: 0.45.17]

NUMINUS CITY IS mortally wounded. Actinic light shivers along the skyline. Criol Fowst knows that the blessed dark masters of the XVII are already loosening the interstices of Calth. They are displacing it; they are rocking it in its clasp like a thief twisting a jewel out of its setting. Hoar frosts keep forming then thawing on the walls and roofs of the city. Fires gutter and die for no reason, and then reignite spontaneously. Twice, Fowst has looked up and seen, through the smoke cover, patterns of stars that do not belong to Calth or the Veridian System; patterns of stars, indeed, that he has never seen before, but which seem so familiar they make him weep for joy.

He rallies his men. The Ushmetar Kaul are dedicated. They have already gutted the Army encampments along the south bend of the river and left them in flames. They have killed thousands. Fowst has inspected the heaped dead. Almost a division of men went into the river in a thrashing attempt to escape, and were cut down by cannon and rifle. Their bodies, those which have not washed away downstream, have formed several new jetties at the water's edge; slipway ramps of corpses jutting out into the stained current.

Where there is resistance, the Brotherhood does not flinch. They walk into return fire, soaking up the hits. It is a process of gleeful sacrifice that leads to overwhelm. Some of his men are strapped up with explosives, and walk in amongst the masses of the fleeing enemy to find their ascension.

In the ransacked encampments of the Numinus 61st, the Brotherhood has found crates of rifles, las-weapons, new issue Illuminators ready for distribution. The Ushmetar Kaul took them, ditching their old pieces in favour of the powerful new firearms. Fowst has one. It is tough and lightweight, with virtually no kick. It has a folding wire stock that he can clip back out of the way. He has killed six men with it already.

He is an educated man. The irony is not lost on him.

Orders are coming from the Legion. The spaceport must be secured, and then the outlying palaces on the plains.

Fowst wonders about the planet's southern hemisphere, primarily ocean and more sparsely inhabited. He believes it is about to have more comprehensive fury meted out upon it. Great power, both ritual and actual, has been unsheathed today. But the task at hand will take much more than that.

* * *

[mark: 0.58.08]

THE SAMOTHRACE STEERS in through the slip gates of the Zetsun Verid Yard. Behind it, Calth's main shipyard is burning. No one challenges the *Samothrace*. It's a vessel of the XIII fleet, running for cover, and besides, the vox is choked and the noosphere is dead.

No one aboard the Zetsun Verid Yard questions the fact that the yard structure has remained untouched either. Too small? Overlooked? Yet it is a vital specialist facility, and yards around it have been targeted and obliterated.

The ship docks between the two fast escorts sheltering in the yard space.

'How long?' Kor Phaeron asks the senior magos of his shadow techpriests.

'Three hours, provided we are not interrupted, majir,' the priest replies.

'They will not be interrupted,' says Sorot Tchure.

Kor Phaeron is breathing hard. He seems desiccated and frail inside his armour, as though he is drawing off great quantities of his own vitality. Space has worn thin around him.

Calth is his operation, far more than it is Lorgar's. Kor Phaeron has planned this for his primarch meticulously, and executed it with the aid of Erebus. The punishment and annihilation of the XIII is its principal aim; the humiliation and execution of the wretched Roboute Guilliman. But it is also an advancement, another step on the spiral path of the Great Ritual. It will allow their beloved primarch to progress.

Sorot Tchure is aware of his commander's burden. There is no room for failure. There is a priceless and vital military objective to be won, but even that pales into nothing beside the greater intent.

He will support his commander every step of the way. It has been Sorot Tchure's privilege to be one of Kor

Phaeron's senior assault leaders for several years. The novelty of their Legion's transmutation has simply deepened his commitment to their cause. They were always driven by faith in a higher power. Now they are inspired by proof of that power. It has invested them all. It has answered them. It has blessed them. It has revealed to them the truths that underpin all mysteries of creation.

And the greatest truths are these: the Emperor of Terra is no god, as they once believed. He is a small and pitiful spark in the blackness of the cosmos, and in no way deserving of their devotion. He rebuked the Word Bearers for their faith, and he was right to do so: he was probably afraid of what the real gods would do when they saw him being worshipped.

The faith of the Word Bearers was misplaced. It was mis-assigned. They were looking for a god, and they found merely a false idol, hungry for adoration.

Now they have found a power in the heavens worthy of their faith.

The docking clamps seal the airgate hatches open. As he did during the first act of the ritual, Sorot Tchure leads the way through.

3

IN A STAR formation, led by the barge *Destiny's Hand*, seventeen ships of the XVII fleet enter low orbit and prosecute the southern hemisphere.

As they descend, the ships snipe and barrage at the local orbitals, destroying two yards outright and crippling a third. Attempts to block their advance are met with dogged fury. The frigate *Janiverse* is killed by multiple main lance blasts as it attempts to disrupt the planetary assault formation. The carriers *Steinhart* and *Courage of Konor* are driven back, and then crippled in a direct confrontation. The *Steinhart* suffers a critical power failure, loses all vital support mechanisms, and slides into a ragged, thousand-year death orbit of the sun with its crew ice-locked at their posts. The *Courage of Konor*, void-holed twice by broadsides and struggling to pull clear of the advancing formation, is caught a third time by cannonfire. Hull plates fail. The keel fractures. A meson beam ruptures the carrier's exposed reactor core, and it immolates, dropping away into the atmosphere.

It becomes, therefore, the second capital-class ship to hit Calth.

Its plunge is not stately and slow like the dying fall of
the grand cruiser *Antrodamicus*. The *Courage of Konor* is
a plenilunar ball of white fire, consumed by fluorescent
radiation from bow to stern. It falls like a meteor, turning and spinning. It strikes the cold, open ocean near the
planet's southern pole.

The impact is akin to an extinction event meteor strike.
The atmosphere buckles for five hundred kilometres in
all directions as the released heat and light squirt outwards in a distorted, epipolic flash. Trillions of tonnes
of ocean water are vaporised instantly, and trillions
more are upflung in an ejection cone. Tectonic damage
occurs. The consequential tidal wave, a rolling wall of
black water, hits the continental coast six minutes later
and wipes out the littoral to a distance of four kilometres
inland.

It is merely a prelude, collateral damage that forms a
savage precursor to the assault proper.

The assault formation descends to the lowest possible
operational altitude, their sizzling void shields squeak-
ing and howling against the thin upper atmosphere.
Ventral lance batteries and bombardment cannon begin
to fire.

The systematic destruction begins.

There is no finesse involved. The northern hemisphere
is dense with strategic targets and population centres
that need to be targeted and secured. The northern
hemisphere is also where most of the XVII ground forces
could be landed prior to the hostilities without raising
questions.

The southern hemisphere can, largely, be decimated.

The *Hand's* formation does just that. Magma bombs
blitz the bleak antipodean continents, scouring them
with hellish firestorms. Lance fire turns seawater into
steam, and rips oceans from their beds. Meson con-
vertors and ion beamers dislocate the ancient tectonic
patterns, buckle the crust, and send seismic spasms

through the mantle. Smoke, ash and ejected matter stain the atmosphere. Steam clouds the polar latitudes.

Forests burn. Jungles scorch. Rivers vanish. Glaciers melt. Mountains collapse. Marshlands desiccate. Deserts fuse into glass.

Millions die in the scattered southern cities.

[mark: 01.37.26]

GUILLIMAN WATCHES.

His stylus has snapped in his hand. He calls for another. The console in front of him is piled with notes and sketched plans.

The magi of the Mechanicum, those who were not crippled or killed or driven insane by the first outrage, have begun to reboot the flagship's crippled systems. Limited vox has been restored. Guilliman has motive power, shields and weapons.

But even the mighty *Macragge's Honour* cannot take on the XVII fleet alone. The Ultramar fleet elements are scattered. There is no way to coordinate them.

There is no way to coordinate them fast enough to counter and check the planetary assault.

Calth is burning. Calth, jewel of Veridia, one of the great worlds of the Five Hundred, is violated, perhaps beyond any hope of recovery.

Guilliman turns his back. He cannot watch.

'Is it still on repeat?' he asks.

'My lord?' Gage responds.

'My declaration? My message to my brother?'

'Yes, my lord,' says Marius Gage. 'It is on constant repeat via what little comms capability we have.'

The primarch nods.

'Should I… cancel it?' the First Master asks.

Guilliman doesn't reply. Aides have delivered more data to his bridge position. Lacking cogitator function and active grids, he has had scribes and rubricators stationed on all observation decks, recording data by hand on slate and paper. Runners bring all documents to him every four minutes. The heap of information is growing.

The primarch has noticed something. He has noticed some detail amongst all the others. He scoops it up. Other papers and info-tiles slither to the deck, disturbed.

'What is it?' asks Gage.

[mark: 01.40.41]

THE WORLD IS trembling. On the far side of the globe, the planetary bombardment is under way, scourging the other hemisphere. The trauma, transmitted as a subterranean micro-shock and an atmospheric flicker of overpressure, can be felt even here.

Here. Numinus starport. Enormous sections of its sprawl are still on fire. The drumming of heavy artillery is coming from the city. Formations of attack craft rush overhead every few minutes, roaring bright coals of afterburner heat. Smoke has blackened the sky, apart from the bright pinpricks of debris burning up, of ship-fire up in space, of dying orbital yards combusting.

There's dust everywhere. It's fine, yellowish, a by-product of ash and the up-cast of surface impacts. It films the air and coats upper surfaces. The micro-shocks are making it trickle and sift in places. It seeps through vents. It dribbles down gutters. It wafts like smoke where the breeze stirs it.

It sticks to blood.

It has adhered to the blood-soaked skin and armour of the fallen. It has clotted the pools of blood like sawdust. It covers dead faces like powder, so the corpses look painted and preserved, formally prepared by mortuary assistants.

Vil Teth, gene-named leader of a Kaul Mandori strike

team, advances along one of the transit causeways, las-rifle trained. His brown leather boots scuff up the yellow dust. Eight men of his immediate brotherhood squad follow him, with another twelve holding back with the heavy support, an armoured speeder with an auto-cannon mount. Zorator, their watcher, is somewhere nearby.

The zone has to be cleared. The commanders have ordered this. By midnight, the entire port must be sectioned and secure. There are survivors hiding every-where. Teth is cautious because he knows that some of these so called 'survivors' are XIII Legion warriors, gone to ground. His men are not equipped for that kind of opposition, no matter how broken or cornered it might be.

That's why they have the heavy support and the watcher.

It's not death that Teth fears. They're Kaul Mandori. They are immortal. This is the promise that has been made to them, the vow they have accepted. This is the promise that lured him from his life in the Army and made him join the brotherhood. Immortality for service: it seemed, to Vil Teth, a fair exchange.

It's not the death he fears. But he's seen enough action in his career to know that he'd prefer to avoid the pain.

Zorator's presence in the area is spooking the enemy from cover. Teth rises sharply as three men break into the open ahead, and begin to flee across the field of smouldering rubble. They are non-heterosic humans, which relieves him. They are wearing the livery uniforms of the cargo handling guild. They are unarmed.

Teth raises his rifle, takes aim, and shoots the first of them. A seventy-five metre shot at a moving target. Back of the legs, as he intended. Not bad. The man falls, wail-ing in pain. Alive. Alive is good. As well as clearing the zone, his strike team has been told to forage for food.

Around him, the Kaul Mandori raise their weapons

and take aim. Two make shots that miss the fleeing
pair, and skim the dusty rubble. Garel, Teth's second,
squeezes a las-bolt off and clips one of the targets. The
man topples, headshot. Dead is good too.

Teth laughs. Garel laughs back, white teeth in a dust-
caked face.

There's another shot. It's not a las. It's a gut-deep *boom*.
Bolter. Garel explodes. There's meat and black blood
everywhere in a splatter pattern, covering them all, dark
gore and liquidised tissue coating the dust that's coating
them. Teth flinches as he is hit by a whizzing chunk of
Garel's spine. He blinks blood out of his eyes. He sees
teeth on the ground, teeth embedded in a chunk of jaw,
teeth that just that second were grinning at him.

Teth's men are scattering. He yells an order.

'Support! Support!'

There's a fugging Ultramarine coming at them. Coming out of cover. Coming like a blue blur. The bastard's
huge.

They open fire. Five lasrifles find the giant, clip him
with zagging neon las-bolts. The impacts chip his dusty
blue armour. They check him, but they don't stop him.
He's got a fugging sword in one hand, and a battered
golden standard in the other.

He puts the sword through Forb, clean fugging
through, and then carves Grocus. Grocus rotates as the
sword catches him. He spins like a dancer pirouetting,
twirling blood like an out-flung cape, then falls.

The Ultramarine kills Sorc, then Teth's world turns
upside down as he gets knocked flat. The Ultramarine
isn't stopping. He's going for the heavy support. He
knows that's the real threat.

Teth rolls over, spitting out blood, dust and the part
of his tongue he bit off when the Ultramarine smashed
into him.

'Kill him! Kill him!'

The support unit's coming up. The men are firing,

some kneeling to steady their shots. The Ultramarine's running right at them. He's brandishing the fugging standard pole. Idiot. Autocannon's going to fug him up.

The speeder spurs forward. Why the fug isn't it firing?

Teth realises how clever the Ultramarine has been. That's why he came through them, head on. He wants to take the speeder. If the speeder opens up at him, Teth and the others are in its field of fire.

You idiots, Teth thinks. You *idiots*. What the fug's the universe going to look like with you ruling it? I don't matter? I'm fugging immortal! Gene-named! Remember? We're gene-kin! They've taken our blood. They'll bring us back. That's what the Word Bearers promised us if we served them. If we die for them, they bring us back. they can do that. They have gene-tech.

Forget me! Fugging shoot the bastard!

The speeder kicks forward to meet the bounding Ultramarine. The fugger's so fast. Something that big and heavy ought not to be able to move that f–

Teth realises something.

Garel got ruined by a bolter, but the Ultramarine hasn't got a bolter. He hasn't got a bolter, so–

The second giant in cobalt blue shows himself. He *has* got a bolter.

He comes off the roof of a fab-shop twenty metres back. A running jump off a six-metre drop. Transhuman muscle puts some real distance on that. His feet stride out as he sails down. He was waiting until the speeder passed under him. He was waiting for it to come to meet his partner.

The newcomer bangs down on the lid of the speeder, both feet planted, denting the roof panel. The landing is as loud as a bolter round hitting. The speeder bounces on its grav-field, soaking the impact.

The newcomer, feet braced, bends over and fires his boltgun through the roof. *Thud. Thud.* Two shots. Two kills.

The first Ultramarine reaches him, running head-on into the support squad's frantic small-arms fire. Teth sees point-blank las shot flecking clean off his armour. More sword work. Arterial blood hoses the side of the speeder. The Ultramarine swings the standard like a club, spading one of the Kaul clean out of his boots.

The second Ultramarine jumps off the speeder's roof and joins the melee. He's put the bolter up. Saving ammo. He's laying in with his combat blade. Eight of the twelve are dead in fewer seconds.

Teth shouts. He shouts so hard he feels like he's going to turn his lungs inside out.

VENTANUS HEARS THE yell. He turns. The battered golden standard in his hands is dripping blood.

'What did you bring that for?' Selaton growls, withdrawing his blade from his last kill.

Ventanus isn't listening. Some of the enemy foot troops are still alive. The leader is yelling.

'We should shut him up,' says Selaton. He's opened the side hatch of the speeder, and is dragging an exploded body out. The cabin interior is painted with blood. He needs to find the levers to adjust the seats.

The Word Bearer appears. Cataphractii. *Terminator*.

'Zorator! My watcher! Kill them!' Teth shrieks.

The Terminator is massive. The enhanced armour, cumbersome, is also as solid as a tank. The lorica segmentata of the huge shoulder plates rise up above the crested helm. The bulky gorget is part snarling mouth, part cage. Studded leather pteruges and mail skirts protect the weaker joints. He looks like a Titan engine: the vast shoulders and upper body, the stocky legs.

Lightning crackles around his left-hand claw. He starts to fire his giant combi-bolter.

Mass-reactive shells rip up the concourse. They explode and kill two of the Kaul Mandori that Ventanus had subdued but not slain. They knock Ventanus off his feet, driving armour splinters into his shin and thigh, and rip a considerable bite out of the speeder's nose plating.

Selaton throws himself down in rolling cover, using the speeder as a block. He tries to return fire. His aim is good, but the cataphractii soaks up his rounds. Flames from the mass-reactive impacts gout around the reinforced carapace.

The Word Bearer heavy fires at Selaton. The speeder takes more serious damage, including a bolt that scalps the crew bay, peeling the metal skin of the cabin roof up like the tongue of a shoe.

Ventanus is hurt. His leg is punctured. The bleeding's already stopped. He churns to his feet. He's got the speed the hulking Terminator lacks. It's a blood-red beast, maned with crimson horsehair. He rushes it.

It swings its aim back to him. Ventanus is transhuman fast, but he can't outrun shells of a combi-bolter, and his armour won't stop them either.

There's a *ping* of tearing metal, of bolts popping. It's the sound Selaton makes as he wrenches the speeder's autocannon off its mount. He's standing on the speeder, half inside the cab, one foot on the seats, one braced on the nose plate, the cabin roof peeled back as if to reveal him like a theatrical surprise. He's got the multi-barrelled cannon wedged against his hip, the metal snake of the munition feeder coiling back, fat and heavy, into the crew bay.

He fires. The heavy weapon makes a grinding metal noise like bells being crushed through some kind of mill. A jumping lick of burning gases flickers around the rotating barrels.

The storm of shots brackets the cataphractii and rips across him. Fragments of metal flake off his armour in a puff of abraded smoke. Rubble on either side of him explodes. Pieces of the gorget and visor fly off, along with scraps of leather pteruges, shreds of horsehair, and broken mail rings. The shots penetrate in four places, allowing blood to glug out of the bare metal craters.

The Terminator stays upright for a long time, staggering backwards under the hail of fire. Finally, he goes down on his back with a crash.

Ventanus stands over him. Smoke, blue and pungent, streaks the air. The Word Bearer, gurgling the blood that is filling his helmet and throat brace, stirs. He's dying, but he's a long way from dead. He starts lifting the oil-black combi-bolter.

Ventanus brings the blade of the standard shaft down through the visor slot with both hands, driving it and turning it and screwing it, until it meets the inside back of the armoured helmet. Blood wells out over the eye slits and gorget lip, and runs down the sides of the helmet to mat the horsehair broom of the crest.

Ventanus steps back, leaving the standard planted there, crooked. Selaton approaches.

'We must move,' he says.

'Is the speeder functional?'

'Just about.'

Ventanus pulls out the standard and carries it towards the shot-up vehicle.

'That's why,' he says.

'What?' asks Selaton.

'That's why I brought this,' Ventanus replies, raising the bloody standard. 'Precisely for things like that.'

[mark: 01.57.42]

'WHAT DOES IT mean?' asks Marius Gage.

'It means…' Guilliman begins. He takes the data-slate back, ponders it. 'It means a precondition of malice.'

He looks out of the flagship's vast crystalflex ports at the bombarded planet below.

'Not that it's really in any doubt,' he adds. 'If this started as an accident or mistake, then it has truly passed beyond any limit of forgiveness. It is, however, salutary to know that my brother's crime is entirely proven.'

Guilliman summons the Master of Vox with a quick gesture.

'Rescind my previous looped broadcast,' he says, taking the speaker horn. 'Replace it with this.'

He hesitates, thinking, and then lifts his head and speaks cleanly and quickly into the device.

'Lorgar of Colchis. You may consider the following. One: I entirely withdraw my previous offer of solemn ceasefire. It is cancelled, and will not be made again, to you or to any other of your motherless bastards. Two, you are no longer any brother of mine. I will find you, I will kill you, and I will hurl your toxic corpse into hell's mouth.'

He hands the horn back to the vox-officer.

'Put that on repeat immediately,' he says.

Guilliman ushers Gage, Shipmaster Zedoff and a group of other senior executives towards the strategium.

'In the absence of vox, we will need to use direct link laser comms and sealed orders physically carried by fast lighters to coordinate the fleet,' he begins. 'I have sketched a hasty tactical plan. Specific ship orders must be communicated to each master and captain by the most expedient means available. Within the hour – the hour, you understand – I want this fleet operating to purpose. We will deny that bombardment.'

'That is our objective?' asks Zedoff.

'No,' Guilliman admits. 'I am going to put that trust in the *Mlatus* and the *Solonim Woe*. They will lead the formations against the planetary attack. Our specific objective will be the *Fidelitas Lex*.'

Zedoff raises his eyebrows.

'A personal score, then,' he says.

Guilliman doesn't try to hide it.

'I will kill him. I will literally kill him. With my bare hands.'

He looks at Gage.

'Don't say anything, Marius,' he says. 'You'll be transferring to the *Mlatus* to lead the attack. With a sober head and a proper plan. I know that going after the enemy flag has serious demerits, tactically. I don't care. This is the one battle of my career I'm going to fight with my heart rather than my head. The bastard will die. The *bastard*.'

'I was merely going to object to being absent at the moment you kill him,' says Gage.

'My primarch!'

They turn. The Master of Vox is pale.

'Lithocast, sir. Long-range signal from the *Fidelitas Lex*.'

Guilliman nods.

'So he ignores my plea for ceasefire, but I tell him to go and screw himself and he makes contact immediately. Put it on.'

'My primarch, I–' Gage begins.

Guilliman pushes past him, heading for the lithocaster plate.

'There is no way you will stop me having this conversation, Marius,' he says.

Guilliman steps onto the hololithic platform. Light bends and bubbles in front of him. Images form and fade, re-form and decay, like scratches of light on film. Then Lorgar is standing there, life-size, facing Guilliman. His face is in shadow again, but the light construction makes him look utterly real. Other shapes crowd around him, sections and fragments of shadow, no longer recognisable as his minions and lieutenants.

'Have you lost your temper, Roboute?' Lorgar asks. They can hear the smile.

'I am going to gut you,' Guilliman replies softly.

'You have lost your temper. The great and calm and level-headed Roboute Guilliman has finally succumbed to passion.'

'I will gut you. I will skin you. I will behead you.'

'Ah, Roboute,' Lorgar murmurs. 'Here, at the very end,

I finally hear you talk in a way that actually makes me like you.'

'Precondition of malice,' says Guilliman, barely a whisper. 'You took the *Campanile*. By my estimation, you took it at least a hundred and forty hours ago. You took the ship, and you staged this. You organised this atrocity, Lorgar, and you made it seem like a terrible accident so you could capitalise on our mercy. You made us stay our hand while you committed murder.'

'It's called treachery, Roboute. It works very well. How did you find out?'

'We back-plotted the *Campanile's* route once we'd worked out what had hit the yards. When you look at the plot, the notion that it was any kind of accident becomes laughable.'

'As is the notion you can hurt me.'

'We're not going to debate it, you maggot, you treacherous bastard,' says Guilliman. 'I just wanted you to know that I will rip your living heart out. And I want to know why. Why? *Why*? If this is our puerile old feud, boiled to the surface, then you are the most pathetic soul in the cosmos. Pathetic. Our father should have left you out in the snow at birth. He should have fed you to Russ. You worm. You *maggot*.'

Lorgar raises his face slightly so that Guilliman can see a hint of his smile in the shadows of his face.

'This has nothing to do with our enmity, Roboute... Except that it affords me the opportunity to avenge my honour on you and your ridiculous toy soldiers. That is just a delicious bonus. No, this is the *Ushkul Thu*. Calth is the *Ushkul Thu*. The offering. It is the sunrise of the new galaxy. A new order.'

'You're rambling, you bastard.'

'The galaxy is changing, Roboute. It is turning upside down. Up will be down, and down will be up. Our father will be tossed out of his throne. He will fall down, and no one will put him back together again.'

'Lorgar, you–'

'Listen to me, Roboute. You think you're so clever. So wise. So informed. But this has started *already*. It's *already* under way. The galaxy is turning on its head. You will die, and our father will die, and so will all the others, because you are all too stupid to see the truth.'

Guilliman steps towards the lithocast phantom, as though he might strike it down or snap its neck.

'Listen to me, Roboute,' the light ghost hisses. 'Listen to me. The Imperium is finished. It is falling. It is going to burn. Our father is done. His malicious dreams are over. Horus is rising.'

'Horus?'

'Horus Lupercal is rising, Roboute. You have no idea of his ability. He is above us all. We stand with him, or we perish entirely.'

'You *shit*, Lorgar. Are you drugged? Are you mad? What kind of insanity is–'

'Horus!'

'Horus *what*?'

'He's rising! He's *coming*! He will kill anyone who stands in his way! He will rule! He will be what the Emperor could *never* be!'

'Horus would–' Guilliman clears his throat. He swallows. He is dazed by the sheer extent of Lorgar's dementia. 'Horus would never turn. If any of us turned, the others would–'

'Horus has risen against our cruel and abusive parent, Roboute,' says Lorgar. 'Accept that, and you will die with greater peace in your heart. Horus Lupercal has come to overthrow the Imperial corruption and punish the abuser. It is already happening. And Horus is not alone. I am with him, sworn and true. So is Fulgrim. Angron. Perturabo. Magnus. Mortarion. Curze. Alpharius. Your loyalty is *air* and *paper*, Roboute. Our loyalty is *blood*.'

'You're lying!'

'You're *dying*. Isstvan V burns. Brothers are dead already.'

'Dead? Who are–'

'Ferrus Manus. Corax. Vulkan. All dead and gone. Slaughtered like pigs.'

'*These are all lies!*'

'Look at me, Roboute. You know they are not. You know it. You have studied every one of us. You know our strengths and our failings. Theoretical, Roboute! *Theoretical*! You *know* this is possible. You know *from the very facts* that this is a possible outcome.'

Guilliman steps back. He opens his mouth, but he is too stunned to reply.

'Whatever you think of me, Roboute,' says Lorgar, 'whatever your opinion, and I know it is about as low as it can be, you know I'm not a stupid man. I would betray my brother and attack the assembled might of the XIII Legion... for a *grudge*? Really? *Really*? Practical, Roboute! I am here to exterminate you and the Ultramarines because you are the *only* force left in the Emperor's camp that can possibly stop Horus. You are too dangerous to *live*, and I am here to make sure you do *not*.'

Lorgar leans forward. The light catches his teeth.

'I'm here to remove you from the game, Roboute.'

Guilliman steps back.

'Either you're insane, or the galaxy has gone mad,' he says with remarkable steadiness. 'Whichever, I am coming for you, and I will put you and your heathen killers down. Excommunicate Traitoris. You will not have any opportunity to reflect upon the *monstrosity* of this crime.'

'Oh, Roboute, I can always rely on you to sound like a giant pompous arsehole. Come and get me. We'll see who burns first.'

Lorgar turns to step out of the light, and then hesitates.

'One last thing you need to know, Roboute. You really don't appreciate what you're up against.'

'A madman,' snaps Guilliman, turning his back.

Lorgar alters.

His holocast form shifts, like fat melting, like bones deforming, like wax dripping. His smile tears in half and something rises up out of his human shape. It is not human.

Guilliman senses it. He turns back. He sees it.

His eyes widen.

He can smell it. He can smell the pitch-black nightmare, the cosmic stench of the warp. The thing is growing, still growing. Lorgar's empty skin sloughs off like a snake's.

It is a horror from the most lightless voids. It is glistening black flesh and tangled veins, it is frogspawn mucus and beads of blinking eyes, it is teeth and bat-wings. It is an anatomical atrocity. It is teratology, the shaping of monsters.

Filthy light veils it and invests it like velvet robes. It is a shadow and it is smoke. Its crest is the horns of an aurochs, four metres high, ribbed and brown. It snorts. There is a rumble of intestines and gas, of a predator's growl. A smell of blood. A whiff of acid. A tang of venom.

The things that hovered behind Lorgar are transforming too. They turn beetle-black, gleaming, iridescent blue. Their boneless limbs and pseudopods writhe. They stir vibrissae and clack like insects. Multiple faces fold and ooze into one another, mutating into ghastly diprosopia. Overlapping mouths pucker and lisp Guilliman's name.

Guilliman steadies himself. He will know no fear.

'I've seen enough of his charlatan tricks,' he says. 'Break the lithocast link.'

'The... link...' begins the Master of Vox. 'Sir, the link is already broken.'

Guilliman sweeps back to face the nightmare, the thing-that-is-no-longer-Lorgar. His hand reaches for the hilt of his sword.

The thing speaks. Its voice is madness.

'Roboute,' it says. 'Let the galaxy burn.'

It lunges, jaws wide, spittle flying.

Blood, many hundreds of litres of human blood, suddenly sprays the walls of the flagship's bridge under pressure. The crystalflex window ports blow out in blizzards of shards, voiding into space.

The bridge tower of the immense battleship *Macragge's Honour* explodes.

TARGET//ENGAGEMENT

'In the Phase of Open Warfare, especially when one is placed in a position of defending or countering, one must be proactive. Determine what commodities or resources you will need to gain the advantage and place your opponent on the defensive. Establish which of these commodities or resources your opponent possesses. Take them from him. Do not chase glory. Do not force unwinnable confrontations. Do not try to match his strength if you know his strength over-matches yours. Do not waste time. Decide what will make you strong enough, and then acquire those things. Your most desired commodity is always your continued ability to prosecute the war.'

– Guilliman, *Notes Towards Martial Codification*, 14.2.xi

1

[mark: 4.12.45]

IT GETS LIGHT early. Another beautiful day on the estuary. The light's so good, Oll reckons they can get an extra hour or so's work done. An hour is an additional two loads of swartgrass. A day of hard labour for good returns.

His hands are sore from the harvest work, but he has slept well and his spirits are good. Strong sunlight always lifts him.

He rises, says a prayer. In the whitewashed lean-to at the back of the hab, there's a gravity shower. He pulls the cord and stands under its downpour. As he washes, he can hear her singing in the kitchen.

When he goes into the kitchen, dried and dressed, she's not there. He can smell warm bread. The kitchen door is open, and sunlight streams in across the flagstones. She must have just stepped out for a moment. Stepped out to get eggs. He can smell the swartgrass straw on the warm air.

He sits down at the worn kitchen table.

'It's time to get to work, Oll.'

He looks up. There's a man standing in the doorway,

backlit by the sun so that Oll can't see his face for shadow.

But Oll Persson knows him anyway. Oll touches the little symbol around his neck, an instinctive gesture of protection.

'I said–'

'I heard you. I'll get there when I'm good and ready. My wife's making breakfast.'

'You'll lose the light, Oll.'

'My wife's making breakfast.'

'She isn't, Oll.'

The man comes into the kitchen. He hasn't changed. He wouldn't though, would he? He never will. That confidence. That good-looking… *charm*.

'I don't recall inviting you in,' says Oll.

'No one ever does,' replies the man. He helps himself to a cup of milk.

'I'm not interested in this,' Oll says firmly. 'Whatever you've come to say, I'm not interested. You've wasted a trip. This is my life now.'

The man sits down facing him.

'It isn't, Oll.'

Oll sighs.

'It's great to see you again, John. Now get out of my hab.'

'Don't be like that, Oll. How've you been? Still pious and devoted?'

'This is my life now, John.'

'It isn't,' the man says.

'Get out. I don't want anything to do with anything.'

'You don't have a choice, I'm afraid. Sorry. Things have escalated a little.'

'John–' Oll almost growls the warning.

'I'm serious. There aren't many of us, Oll. You know that. You and me, we could set our hands on the table here, and count them off, and we'd still have fingers spare. There never were many of us. Now there are even fewer.'

Oll gets up.

'John, listen. Let me be as plain as I can. I never had time for this. I never wanted to be part of anything. I don't want to know what trouble you've brought to my door. I like you, John. Honestly, I do. But I hoped never to see you again. I just want to live my life.'

'Don't be greedy. You've lived several.'

'John–'

'Come on, Oll! You and me? Anatol Hive? Come on. The Panpacific? Tell me that doesn't count for anything.'

'It was a lifetime ago.'

'Several. Several lifetimes.'

'This is my life now.'

'No, it isn't.'

Oll glares at him.

'I'd like you to go, John. Go. Now. Before my wife gets back from the coops.'

'She's not coming back from the coops, Oll. She never went out to the coops.'

'Get out, John.'

'This is your life, is it? This? An ex-soldier turned farmer? Retired to a life of bucolic harmony? Good honest toil in exchange for plain food and a good night's rest? Really, Oll? This is your life?'

'This is my life now.'

The man shakes his head.

'And what will you do when you've had enough of that? Will you quit it and move on to something else? When you're tired of farming, what next? Teaching? Button-making? Will you join the Navy? You might as well, you've been Army already. What will you do? An ex-soldier-farmer-widower?'

'Widower?' Oll snaps, flinching from the word as though it was buzzing in his face to sting him. 'What are you talking about, widower?'

'Oh, come on, Oll. Don't make me do all the hard work. You know this. She's not out at the coop. She's not making you breakfast. She wasn't in here just now singing. She never came to settle on Calth. She was gone, the poor love, before you ever joined the Army. *Last* time you joined the Army. Come on, Oll, your mind's a bit mixed up. It's the shock.'

'Leave me alone, John.'

'You know I'm right. You know it. I can see it in your face.'

'Leave me alone.'

'Come on. Think.'

Oll stares at him.

'Are you in my head, John Grammaticus? Are you in my bloody head?'

'I swear I'm not, Oll. I wouldn't do that uninvited. This is all you. Trauma. It'll pass.'

Oll sits down again.

'What's happening?' he whispers.

'I haven't got much time. I'm not here long. Just talking to you is taking a huge effort. We need you, Oll.'

'They sent you? I bet they did.'

'Yes, they did. They did. But I didn't mean them. I meant humans. The human race needs you, Oll. Everything's gone to shit. So, *so* badly. You wouldn't believe it. He's going to lose, and if he loses, we all lose.'

'Who's going to lose?' asks Oll.

'Who do you think?'

'What's he going to lose?'

'The war,' says John. 'This is it, Oll. This is the big one, the one we always talked about. The one that we always saw coming. It's happening already. Bloody primarchs killing each other. And the latest round of executions happens here, today. Right here on Calth.'

'I don't want any part of it. I never did.'

'Tough shit, Oll. You're one of the Perpetuals, whether you like it or not.'

'I'm not like you, John.'

John Grammaticus sits back and smiles, pointing a finger at Oll.

'No, you're bloody not. I'm only what I am now thanks to xenos intervention. You, you're still a true Perpetual. You're still like him.'

'I'm not. And I don't have what you have. The talents. The psyk.'

'It doesn't matter. Maybe that's why you're important. Maybe you're just important because you're here. There are only three like us in the whole Five Hundred Worlds right now, and only one of them on Calth. Ground zero. That's you. This is down to you. You don't have a choice. This is down to you.'

'Get someone else, John. Explain it to someone else.'

'You know that doesn't work. No one else is old enough. No one else understands as much. No one else has the... perspective. I tell anyone about this, they'll just dismiss me as insane. And I don't have time to spend another eighteen years in an asylum like last time I tried it. You've got to do this.'

'Do what?'

'Get out of here. They're going to slide this world. An interstitial vortex. The old Immaterium sidestep. You've got to be ready to step through that door when it opens.'

'And go where?'

It's fallen dark outside. The sun's gone in. Grammaticus looks up, and shivers.

'You've got to get something, and you've got to bring it to me. Step through the door when it opens, and bring it to me. I'll wait for you.'

He hesitates.

'I'll try my damnedest to wait for you, anyway.'

'Where am I going, John?'

It's getting dark so fast. Grammaticus shrugs.

'We're running out of time, Oll. With your permission, I'll show you.'

'Don't you bloody d–'

* * *

[mark: unspecified]

SOMEWHERE. IT STINKS of the warp, of burning void
shields. The walls are polished ebony and etched
ceramite, inlaid with crystal and ivory and rubies. Gold
leaf edges the hatch frames. The place is so big. So very
big. Vaults and chambers, dark and monumental, like
the naves of cathedrals. Of a tomb. Of a necropolis cata-
comb. The ground is black marble.

It's not the ground. It's a deck.

He can feel the throb of engines coming through it.
Drive engines. The air is dry, artificially maintained. He
can smell smoke.

'Why can I smell smoke, John?' he asks.

He can't read whatever it is that's etched into the polished walls. He realises he's glad he can't.

'John? Where did you go?'

There are starfields outside the windows. There's
blood on the floor. Bloody footprints on the marble,
bloody handprints on the walls. Tapestries have been
torn down. There are bullet holes in the bulkhead panels: craters blown by bolt-rounds, gouges cut by lasers,
by claws. There are bodies on the floor.

It's not a floor, it's a deck.

He can hear fighting. A huge battle. Millions of voices
yelling and screaming, weapons clashing, weapons firing. The din is coming up through the deck. It's echoing,
muffled, through distant archways and half-seen hatches.
It's as if monumental, cataclysmic history is happening
just around the corner.

'John?'

There's no sign of John. But he can feel the back-of-
the-neck prickle of other minds. Minds as bright as main
sequence stars.

'John, I don't want to be here. I don't want to be here
at all.'

He moves forward, through an archway twenty times

as tall as he is, into a chamber fifty times as tall. The walls and pillars are cyclopean. The air is filled with smoke and dying echoes.

There is an angel dead on the floor. On the *deck*. The angel is a giant. He was beautiful. His sword is broken. His golden plate is cracked. His wings are crushed. Blood streaks his armour and soaks the carnodon-skin mantle he wears. His hair is as golden as his armour. He has teardrops on his cheek.

His killer is waiting nearby, black as night, made of rage, masked by shadow. The edges of his wargear are chased with gold, giving his darkness a regal outline and shape. The gold encircles the eyes he wears on his chest and harness: baleful, red, staring eyes. He fumes with power. He prickles hot, like a lethal radiation leak. He's polluting the galaxy just by standing in it. There's a crackle. A fizzle. Malice so terrible a rad-counter could pick it up.

The killer is huge. His shoulder plates are draped with a cloak of furs and human pelts. A spiked framework surrounds his head: a psychic cage, an armoured box. There is a light glowing inside the box, a ruddy glow. The killer's head is shaved. He is looking down, his face in shadow. He is looking down at the angel he has just killed. Cortical plugs and bio-feeds thread his scalp like dreadlocks. He is a beast made flesh, and shod in iron. He is made of pure hatred.

Oll Persson realises he should not be here. Anywhere, anywhere in the cosmos but here. He starts to back away.

The killer hears him move or senses him. The killer slowly raises his massive head. Light seeps up from the gorget, underlighting his face. Arrogant. Proud. Evil. He opens his eyes. He stares at Oll.

'I... I renounce you, evil one,' Oll stammers. He touches the little symbol around his neck, an instinctive gesture of protection.

'You... *what*?'

'I renounce you as evil.'

'There is no evil,' says the killer, his voice a landslip rumble of mountains falling. 'There is only indifference.'

The killer takes a step towards Oll. The floor – the *deck* – trembles under the weight.

He halts. He's looking at something. He's looking at something in Oll's hand.

Oll glances down, confused. He realises he's been holding something in his other hand all along.

He sees what it is.

The killer makes a sound. A sigh. His lips part, connected by tiny strands of spittle. He looks Oll straight in the face. Straight into his soul.

Oll turns away. He cannot bear to look into those eyes any more. He turns to run.

He sees the light behind him.

He was so captivated by the killer, by the prickling, enveloping darkness, he almost didn't see the light to begin with.

Now he sees it. It's not the light it used to be. It's not the light he used to know.

The light is fading. It was once the most beautiful light, but it's dwindling. It's ebbing away and growing dim. Golden, broken, like the angel. And, like the angel, brought low by the killer made out of darkness.

Beyond the light is a vast window port.

Through it, Oll sees the hazy glory of Terra.

The human homeworld is burning.

'I've seen enough,' says Oll Persson.

[mark: 4.12.45]

It's the shock. It's just the shock. You've been hurt, and I've shown you plenty. Plenty. I'm sorry, I really am. No one should have to see that. No one should have to deal with all of that in one go. But there really isn't time to be gentle about this.

You saw what you had to see. I showed you where you have to go.

Now, this will hurt. This will be hard. You can do it. You've done hard before. Come on, Oll. Come on, my old, dear friend Ollanius.

It's time to wake up. It's time to w–

Oll wakes.

No sunlight. No bed. No singing from the kitchen.

Grey light. Fog. Cold.

Pain.

He's fallen on his back, twisted. His hands are sore, and so is his back, and one of his hips too. His head feels as though iron screws have been driven into it.

He sits up. The pain gets worse.

Oll realises the worst of the pain isn't his aches and sprains and bruises.

It's the aftershock. The aftershock of the vision. He rolls onto all fours and dry-heaves, as if he's trying to vomit out the memory and be rid of it.

It would be tempting to think it was just a nightmare. Tempting and easy. Just a bad dream that happened because he'd had a bump on the head.

But Oll knows the human mind doesn't imagine things like that. Not *like that*. Grammaticus was here. The bastard was here. Not in the flesh, but as good as. He was here, and that's what he had to show.

It says a lot that John made the superhuman effort, and took such an immense risk, to come. It says a lot, and what it says doesn't sit comfortably with Oll Persson.

He gets to his feet, unsteady. He's battered and bruised. His clothes are caked in mud that's just beginning to dry and stiffen. He tries to get his bearings.

There's not much to see. A dense grey mist is shrouding the entire world. There are rumbling sounds, and dull flashes up behind the clouds. Far away – Oll's guess would be to the north – there's a glow, as if something big on the other side of the fog is burning.

Something big like a city.

He looks around. The ground's a slick of stinking black mud and ooze, of mangled agricultural machinery and broken fence posts. This is the spew the tidal wave left in its wake. This is what's left of his land, of his fields.

He stumbles along, his boots squelching in the muck. The thick fog is part smoke, part vapour from the flood. The ground stinks of mineral cores and riverbed mire. All of his crops have gone.

He sees a line of fence posts, still standing. From the height of them above the muck, the flood wave left about a metre of silt and soil behind it. Everything's buried. Worse than damned Krasentine Ridge. He sees a hand, a man's hand, sticking up out of the black ooze, pale and wrinkled. It looks as if he's reaching up, grasping for air.

Nothing to be done about it.

Oll reaches the fence posts and leans on one of them. He realises that it's the gate at the end of the west field level. He's not where he thought he was at all. He's about half a kilometre west. The force of the flood water must have carried him, carried him like flood litter, like flotsam. Bloody wonder he didn't break his limbs or get his brains dashed out against an upright post; it was a wonder he didn't drown.

Re-aligned, he turns around and heads back the way he came. Now he's got his bearings, he knows where the farmhab is.

He passes a cultivator unit, on its side and half-sunk in black mud. Then he finds the lane, or what used to be the lane. It's a groove of ooze, a muddy furrow, knee deep in violet water along its belly. He sloshes along.

'Master Persson?'

He stops, shocked at the sound of a voice.

A man sits at the edge of the track, his back against what's left of the fence. He's plastered in mud.

'Who's that?' asks Oll.

'It's me. It's Zybes.'

Zybes. Hebet Zybes. One of the labourers. One of the
pay-by-the-days.

'Get yourself up,' Oll says.

'I can't,' says Zybes. He's sitting oddly against the
fence. Oll realises that the man's left arm and shoulder
are wrapped to the fence post with barbed wire. They've
become tangled together in the flood surge.

'Hold on,' says Oll. He reaches into his belt, but his
work tools are long since lost. He goes back to the overturned cultivator unit and digs around in the thick mud
until he finds the tool box in the cab. Then he comes
back with a pair of cutters, and sets Zybes free. The man's
flesh is pretty torn up by the wire.

'Come on,' says Oll.

'Where to?'

'We've got places to be,' says Oll.

It takes twenty minutes to trek across the mire, through
the fog, to the farmhab. What's left of it.

On the way, Zybes keeps asking questions, questions
like, 'What happened?' and 'Why did it happen to us?'

Oll doesn't have any answers. None that he has the
time or desire to explain, anyway.

Five minutes from the hab, they come across Katt,
short for Kattereena. Ekatterina. Something like that, Oll
forgets. She's a paid-by-day too, like Zybes, works in the
kiln store, drying the sheaves. She's about seventeen; his
neighbour's girl.

She's just standing there, in the fog, smirched in mud,
looking vacant, staring at something there's no possibility of seeing because there's no distance visible, thanks
to the fog. Maybe she's staring at something comforting,
like the day before, or her fifth birthday.

'You all right there, girl?' Oll asks her.

She doesn't reply. Shock. Plain shock.

'You all right? Katt, come with us.'

She doesn't make eye contact. She doesn't even nod.

But when they start walking again, she follows them at a distance.

The hab is a mess. The floodwash swept right through it, taking away the doors, the windows, and most of the furniture, leaving a half-metre carpet of silt and wreckage in exchange. Oll thinks about looking for that pict of his wife, the one that used to stand on the dresser in the kitchen, but the dresser's gone, so he doesn't see much hope of finding a picture that he last saw standing on it.

He tells Zybes and Katt to wait, and goes in. His room's upstairs, in the roof, so it's weathered the smash better than the rest. He finds his old service kitbag, made of faded green canvas, and packs it with a few useful bits and pieces. Then he strips off to his work boots, and puts on dry clothes. The best he can find are his old Army-issue breeches and jacket, also green and faded.

He picks up a last few items, choosing things to take and things to leave. There's a spare coat for Zybes, plus a medicae pack, and a blanket from the bed to keep Katt warm. He goes back down the stairs to find them.

His old lasrifle is still hanging over the fireplace. He takes it down. From the niche in the chimney breast he retrieves a small wooden box. Three magazines, fully charged. He puts two in his pocket and gets ready to slot one into the weapon.

He hears Zybes cry out, and rushes into the muddy yard, slipping and slithering. The bloody mag won't slot. It's been a long time since he drilled with a rifle, and he's forgotten the knack.

He's scared too. More scared than he's ever been in his life, and that's saying something, because his life has included Krasentine Ridge.

'What's going on?' he asks, reaching Zybes, who has ducked behind a toppled stack of grass crates.

'There's something over there,' he says, pointing at the side barn. 'Something big. Moving around.'

Oll can't see anything. He looks around to check

where Katt is. She's standing by the kitchen door, gazing at the past again, oblivious to Zybes's panic.

'Stay here,' Oll tells the injured man. He gets up and moves towards the barn, rifle trained. He hears something move. Zybes wasn't lying. It is big, whatever it is.

Oll knows he'll need a clear shot. A kill shot. If it's big, he'll need to stop it fast.

He wrenches open the barn door.

He sees Graft. The big loader servitor is rolling around in the barn, bashing into things. Mud and riverweed have totally baffled its sensors and visual systems.

'Graft?'

'Trooper Persson?' the servitor replies, recognising his voice.

'Stay still. Just stay still.'

The big cyborganism halts. Oll reaches up and yanks the ropes of weed away. He gets a cloth and cleans the optics, and gets the mud out of the fine sensor grids.

'Trooper Persson,' says Graft. 'Thank you for the assistance, Trooper Persson.'

'Follow me,' says Oll.

'Follow you where, Trooper Persson?'

'We've got work to do,' says Oll.

2

'EXPLAIN THIS,' SAYS the Word Bearer. His name is Ulmor Nul.

'There was an ambush,' says Vil Teth. 'Two of the Ultramarines.'

Nul looks down at the corpse of the cataphractii.

'They did this?'

'They did this,' agrees Teth. 'They killed my watcher, killed members of my team, and then took the speeder. One was a captain.'

'Why didn't you stop them?' asks Nul.

'The cataphractii couldn't stop them,' says Teth, in surprise. 'What makes you think I could?'

He pauses.

'Forgiveness, majir. They were legionaries. We had no *means*.'

'You have stayed in position since the attack, waiting for support?'

'Yes, majir.'

Ulmor Nul raises his warp-flask. He speaks into it, alerting the formation officers that at least two more of the enemy elite are loose in that section of the starport.

'They might have transport,' he adds.

Nul looks at his squad members.

'They need to be hunted down,' he says, simply.

One of his men, Kelter, nods and brings the tracker forward. He has to use the electric goad. The tracker is angry and uncooperative.

It's about the size of an adult mastiff, but it's bulkier and it's not canine. It growls and snuffles, drooling mucus from its flared black-flesh nostrils.

'We need something they touched,' says Nul.

'The captain touched me,' says Teth. 'He knocked me down–'

He's still saying it when he realises he's an idiot.

Nul looks at him and nods.

'Majir, no–' Teth begins to say.

The tracker surges forward. It's on him. Teth shrieks as it begins to eat him alive.

'IT'S GOT THE taste,' Kelter says. He pulls the tracker off the Kaul Mandori warrior. Teth's not dead. He should be. He ought to be. Too much of him is missing and gnawed away for him to ever mend or lead any kind of life. He can't speak. He can't even express his overwhelming agony, except to paddle his fingerless hands and churn what's left of his jaw.

The tracker starts to move, following the psyk-sense it has devoured. The Word Bearers fall in behind it.

'What about him?' one of them says to Ulmor Nul, indicating the twitching remains. 'You could end his pain.'

'Pain is something we learn from,' says Nul, 'and mercy is a waste of ammunition.'

[mark: 4.26.11]

THE ULTRAMARINES CAPTAIN puts up a decent fight. Cornered and outnumbered, he tries to do as much damage as possible before the inevitable.

Sorot Tchure makes the kill. He puts two mass-reactives into the bulkhead behind the Ultramarine, and the force of the blasts, in the enclosed space, rams the cobalt-blue figure out of cover.

He tries to get up, but it's too late. A third shell takes his head off.

Tchure walks back to the yard's master control room. He masses his squads marshalling human prisoners, or dragging out the bodies of the enemy dead. A sheen of blue smoke hangs in the air. The Zetsun Verid Yard is now secure.

It's taken longer than expected. This irks Tchure. He had hoped that sheer bewilderment would knock the fight out of the XIII, but they stuck to it.

His only solace is that the shadow magi have exceeded their estimates too. They're still at work, recalibrating the yard's main systems. Kor Phaeron's displeasure will mostly be reserved for them.

In the master control room, some magi are working with power tools, removing still more deckplates and wall panels to access sheafs of cables. Others are performing more delicate processes, probing intricate circuitry with watch-maker instruments, many of which are fused into their digits. A few have linked directly via the MIU ports, freeing their minds into an improvised noospheric environment in which they can rebuild the yard's shattered manifold architecture. They are bathing in the warm essence of the Octed code loose in the systems.

Kor Phaeron, Master of the Faith, is not exasperated. Tchure finds him in a control office overlooking the main chamber, a glazed brass box like an ecclesiastical confessional. He is reading from a roughly-bound book. The Book of Lorgar. It is not the whole book, of course, merely one volume. The Book of Lorgar fills an entire data-stack, and has been transcribed by hand into nine thousand seven hundred and fifty-two volumes. The number

increases regularly. Kor Phaeron has personally gathered
a ten-thousand-strong staff of rubricators and scribes to
copy the book, and to multiply those copies. Each senior
officer of the XVII, and each planetary overlord appointed
by the Word Bearers, is expected to own and study a set.
Tchure understands that sets are also being prepared as
gifts for each of the primarchs who have thrown their loyalty behind Horus. Copies of copies of copies. Perturabo's
edition will be bound in etched steel. Fulgrim's will be
bound in living flesh. Alpharius will be presented with
two editions, each subtly different from the other.

Horus's set will be wrapped in the tanned hide of
betrayed legionaries.

Copies of copies of copies. Lorgar reviews each edition, line by line. Transcription errors are punished by
death, or worse. Just the day before they translated into
the Veridian System, a rubricator was disembowelled for
missing a comma.

Tchure enters the control office. He can see, now he
is closer, that the book Kor Phaeron is reading is one of
the master copies, one of the original manuscripts. It is
in the primarch's own hand, directly as he composed it.
This is the latest volume, ready for dissemination. Kor
Phaeron always makes a close, personal study of the new
instalments before passing them to his staff for copying,
archiving and publication.

Kor Phaeron is reading secrets that no one else has yet
seen.

'I apologise for the delay,' says Tchure.

Kor Phaeron shakes his head, raising a claw hand, still
reading.

'The magi have explained it,' he says. 'Our devastation
of the Calth noospherics was more fundamental than we
hoped. There is a lot to rebuild. Another ten minutes, as
I understand it.'

'I will be happy when you are securely back aboard
your ship, master,' says Tchure.

Now Kor Phaeron looks up. He smiles.

'Your care is noted. But I am safe here, Sorot.'

He looks frailer than ever. A halo of filthy empyrean light flickers around him. Tchure can see flashes of his bones through his skin, like sporadic X-rays. Kor Phaeron is maintaining a vast degree of warpcraft.

'Come, Sorot,' he says. 'Read with me, for a moment.'

Sorot Tchure steps to the console and looks at the open book. He notes the intricate beauty of the handwriting. There is barely a hint of blank paper on the pages.

'He uses a stylus. And ink,' says Kor Phaeron, as if marvelling. 'In this day and age. A stylus. Of course, I have the rubricators do the same thing.'

'I understand that–'

Kor Phaeron looks at him.

'What, Sorot?'

'I was going to say, master, that I understand Guilliman also uses a stylus.'

'Indeed. Who told you that?'

'Luciel.'

'The one you killed?'

'The first sacrifice, yes.'

'He was your friend.'

'That is why the death had value,' says Tchure.

'Yes, I believe that Roboute Guilliman uses a stylus,' says Kor Phaeron. 'He writes. A lot of words, as I have been told. Not a great deal of content, however. He writes… a treatise. On warfare. On combat mechanics. On the theory of fighting. Childish concerns. The man clearly has no soul or character. And no interest in the metaphysical subjects that challenge those of more considerable intellect. Our beloved primarch already knows all there is to know about killing. He has no need or reason to write it down. The principles are simple. That is why he is able to go beyond records of gross practicality, and invest his time and energy in consideration of the great mysteries. The workings of this universe, and others. The nature of existence.'

Kor Phaeron looks at him.

'You know, Lorgar simply records what is dictated to him? What is whispered to him and him alone?'

'By the gods?' asks Tchure.

'By the powers of eight,' replies Kor Phaeron. 'By the speakers of the void and the voices of the abyss. By the Primordial Annihilator, out of the throat of the warp.'

There is a call from outside. The magi have finished their work.

Kor Phaeron closes the book and rises to his feet.

'Let us put their good work to use, shall we?' he asks.

[mark: 4.55.34]

THE ZETSUN VERID Yard systems come on-line, restarted by the shadow Mechanicum. A data-engine resumes operation. Sensing that the planetary weapons grid is inactive, and that the inactivity has been caused by the inexplicable loss of the data-engine hub located aboard Calth Veridian Anchor, the engine automatically obeys protocol and assumes control, taking up the slack reins of the grid system. Zetsun Verid contains one of the advanced engine hubs capable of substituting, in an emergency, for the primary orbital hub.

The Calth weapons grid goes back on-line. Its manifold re-ignites.

Kor Phaeron observes the work, observes how the scrapcode of the Octed is firmly established in the noospheric architecture. He determines his target, and the magi hurry to set and lock the coordinates.

All the orbiting weapons platforms, as well as several ground-based stations including the polar weapon pits, activate and begin to track as their power reservoirs come up to yield.

It takes approximately ten minutes before authority

lights flicker green along the master control room's main console.

'Target resolution achieved,' reports the senior magos, scrapcode binaric chattering behind his meatvoice.

'You may fire when ready,' says Kor Phaeron.

There is a glimmer. A flash. Beams of coherent energy, beams of staggering magnitude, rip from Calth and from its orbital stations.

Calth has a weapons grid capable of keeping at bay an entire expedition fleet or primary battlegroup. Only the most devious and ingenious treachery has circumvented it today.

The weapons grid begins to discharge. Calth begins to kill the neighbouring planets in the Veridian system.

It starts with a massive asteroid world that orbits the system beyond the circuit of Calth's moons. The asteroid, called Alamasta, is the main remnant of a planet that once occupied that orbital slot. It is now a rock the size of a major satellite.

It is no longer called Alamasta. It is known as Veridia Forge. It is the system's principal Mechanicum station, and the most significant manufacturing venue in six systems.

Veridia Forge is helpless, its systems crashed by the same scrapcode that brought the Calth grid down.

It has no shields, no responsive weaponry, and no means of evasion.

It takes four prolonged strikes from the weapons grid. The first two burn away surface rock and immolate rockcrete bastions or adamantine bulwarks. The third voids the main fabricatory to space, and combusts the forge world's reactor power systems.

The fourth causes Veridia Forge to explode like a newborn star.

For the next eighteen minutes, Calth has no nightside.

3

VENTANUS THROWS THE speeder into reverse thrust. The auspex is smashed and useless. He only saw the gun-carriage when he cleared the corner.

The speeder reverses down the slipway with a violence that lurches Ventanus and Selaton forward in their seats. Cannon-fire is already chasing them. Rapid fire from the grav-compensated carriage, a quad-weapon monster, shreds the barns and storeblocks around them. Cargo-fabs and payload warehouses explode or disintegrate. Rockcrete walls shiver and exhale dust as shots pummel through them. Window ports burst out.

'Not that way either,' says Ventanus.

'Agreed,' says Selaton. He's got the autocannon across his knees, and he's checking the munitions feed. There's not much left in the hopper.

Ventanus swings left, and they race down a dank rockcrete underpass, zip between two huge aerospace manufactories, and skirt the perimeter of a burning excise facility. There are bodies everywhere. Civilians, Army, and far too many Ultramarines for Ventanus to be even slightly sanguine about. Men are dead with their weapons still sheathed or covered. Men cut down without the opportunity to face their deaths.

Heaps of cobalt-blue armour – limp corpses inside scuffed plate – line the roadways and arterials. Some have been stacked against fences and walls like firewood. Some have been cut open and emptied. A few have been nailed to posts, or against the sheet-metal sides of buildings.

Some appear to have been butchered or… eaten.

Ventanus doesn't understand this. He presumes they are victims of some explosive weapon type new to the arsenal of the XVII. Theoretical. That's the best case theoretical. Ventanus hopes it turns out to be the practical too. The theoretical alternatives are too indecent to consider. The Word Bearers are allied with some species of carnivorous xenoform. The Word Bearers are indulging in some ritual cannibalism…

Ventanus doesn't need much more of a reason to make war to the death against the Word Bearers. The injury they have done to Calth and to the XIII, that is cause enough. Their treachery, that is cause enough. Their relentless, merciless prosecution of attack, beyond any measure of honour, that is enough.

But this desecration, this takes his *casus belli* to a whole new level. This is not a just war, this is a war crime. It defies and shames the codes and precepts of the Legiones Astartes, codes and precepts set down by the primo-genitor Emperor. The Word Bearers have perverted any semblance of the true and legal path of the Imperium, or the moral code of mankind.

Here and there, Ventanus spots signs that have been daubed on walls, presumably in blood. Eight-pointed stars and other devices he is not familiar with, and the sight of which make him uncomfortable.

Over the chug of the speeder's engine – a chug that is developing a worrying, clattering under-note – Ventanus can hear the rattle of other gun-carriages moving through the nearby streets. They are in the industrial hinterland between the starport proper and the city. Ventanus is desperate to find a route that they can use to break out and head north-west to Erud. His primary concern is re-establishing contact with his company and the other units in the Erud muster. If they've come through this intact, or approximately intact, he intends to make them the spearhead of a counter-strike.

A haze washes across the city and the port. It's smoke, in vast quantities, but it's also vapour. Steam. A fog swathes the skyline, blanketing the river basin and turning millions of individual fires into soft orange smudges. Ventanus has seen that phenomenon before, when large bodies of water have been flash-evaporated by sustained energy discharge. A dead ocean condenses over the city lowlands.

They turn another corner, and see six Word Bearers advancing down the freight lane ahead of them. The Word Bearers challenge them, and then open fire.

The speeder rocks under the hits as it starts to reverse. Its armour is pretty solid, but Ventanus knows it's taken quite enough punishment. He glides backwards, hoping to swing-turn on the hardpan in front of a fabricator shed and find another path. More Word Bearers open up on them, firing from an overwalk, and from a girder bridge between two manufactories. A mass-reactive round explodes against the side of the cab, where the roof is already peeled back and torn. The shock lurches Selaton hard.

They're running out of ways to turn.

Ventanus reverses faster. He runs down two Word Bearers who emerge behind them. Their crimson-armoured forms are slung out from the repulsors at the speeder's plated back end and fall, bouncing and clattering across the rockcrete.

But he can't simply run down the gun-carriage that's rolling out, facing their back end. It's twice their size, twice their mass, and it starts traversing its quad-guns to target them.

'Go!' Selaton shouts. 'Go! Through them!'

Ventanus kicks the speeder forward again, cranking thrust. He knocks down one of the Word Bearers they have already smashed aside once. The brute was regaining his footing. The right front wing catches him hard, folds him around the reinforced fender, and tosses him sidelong. He tumbles, and lands in a way that speaks of a severed spinal cord.

Selaton rises in his seat, bracing the autocannon against the sill of the screen. They're heading directly for the Word Bearers squad that cut them off in the freight lane. They're also running right through the hail of fire chopping down from the overwalk and girder bridge. Shells slam into the ground around them, pluming fire and grit. Others thump the bodywork like piledrivers.

Selaton kicks off with the cannon. He gets a good angle, given the improvised circumstances, and stitches a line of shots along the girder bridge, ripping handrail spars and shredding the metal balustrade. He knocks two of the enemy shooters off their feet, and then licks across a third. Ventanus sees a helmet explode like a red paint flare. The casualty rocks backwards off the bridge and hits the ground a second after they've passed underneath.

Selaton drops his angle and guns down one of the ground troops. The rotating cannon chews the figure up, shredding him like a sack of meat and metal chaff. The others stand their ground, firing straight at them. Ventanus, his grip unflinching, sees a mass-reactive round pass through the cabin between his head and Selaton's and exit through the back port-slot.

He knocks one Word Bearer down, throwing him over the racing speeder. Then he hits another and catches him on the speeder's plated fender, upper body spread across the nose, legs caught under the machine. A huge wake of sparks kicks out from the underside of the speeder as it carries the road kill along, abrading the heels and calves of the pinned Word Bearer's heavy Mark III battle plate. There is a terrible noise of squealing and scraping. Ventanus can't dislodge the man.

A wall collapses into the freight lane ahead of them, and a crimson Land Raider lumbers into the open, its hull tipping up and over the rubble of the demolished structure. It swings around, weapon mounts lining up.

Ventanus peels left. There's no other practical. He rams the sheet metal wall of a warehouse unit and blows clean through it to escape the Land Raider's hail of fire. The Word Bearer pinned to their front end takes the force of the impact. If he wasn't dead already, he is now.

But so is the speeder. The impact has killed the drive reactor. It starts coughing and rasping, leaking smoke from its vents. The speeder coasts to a halt in the darkness of the warehouse.

Ventanus and Selaton dismount. Selaton has the autocannon and the last of the ammo hoppers. Ventanus gets the standard, and then pauses and goes back to prise the boltgun out of the dead grip of the Word Bearer now all but fused into the mangled nose. There's very little of him intact from the waist down. There's a smell of superheated metal, of friction, of cooked bone marrow.

The first of the Word Bearers force their way in through the gap the speeder created. Selaton rakes them, cutting two down and sewing more holes in the wall for the light to shine in.

His hopper is spent. He ditches the cannon and pulls his boltgun.

They start retreating across the jumbled floor space of the warehouse, trading shots with the Word Bearers who are breaching their way in through the gap. Bolter shells spit to and fro. Ventanus scores a hit, but he can't be sure if it's a clean kill. Sheer weight of numbers is stacked against them.

He keeps expecting a wall to cave in and the Land Raider to storm the barn, hunting for them. He can hear it outside, rumbling and revving.

Suddenly, there's a staggering explosion outside. A brilliant light-flash pushes into the warehouse for a second, through every slit and bullet hole and window. The buildings shake, and whizzing pieces of superhot machine parts and plating debris punch through the wallskin.

Ventanus and Selaton pick themselves up. The Word Bearers who have forced entry after them are getting up too. They attempt to re-lock target finders on the fleeing Ultramarines, but they are bewildered. What was the blast? Did something just kill the Land Raider?

Searing plasma beams chop the gloom and slice them apart as they turn. The beams – scintillating green – fuse through and through blast holes in their armour and pop their helmets like balloons.

Ventanus and Selaton back into cover, weapons ready.

Lugging their powerful, close-quarter plasma blasters, skitarii of the Mechanicum flood into the building. Without compromise, they finish off any of the Word Bearers not cleanly killed.

There are dozens of the fearsome Mechanicum fighters.

'Warriors of the XIII,' one of them broadcasts in loudhailer mode. 'Make yourself known to us. Hurry, time is against us.'

Ventanus gets up, raising the battered standard.

'Remus Ventanus, 4th Company,' he announces.

The skitarii commander comes to face him. He's a big veteran, scarred and ugly, gaudy in his aposematistic wargear. One of the red eyeslits in his copper visor is flickering.

'Arook Serotid, Skitarii Kalkas Cohort,' he replies. His voice is slightly halting, as if he is not practised at talking. 'We realised from the Word Bearers activity there had to be XIII strengths in the vicinity. Just the two of you?'

'Yes. We thank you for your intervention.'

'It will count as nothing if we remain here much longer, captain,' replies Arook. 'We have the firepower to assault a small squad, a vehicle or two. But power reserves are limited, and we cannot take on the mass of the enemy forces.'

'Can you get us out of here?' asks Ventanus.

'We can get you to our senior magos,' says Arook. 'It is hoped we can begin to coordinate our resistance.'

Ventanus nods. The skitarii lead the way to the closest exit point.

Arook notes the standard that Ventanus is carrying.

'That is bulky,' he says. 'There is no need to bring it.'

'There really is,' says Selaton.

[mark: 6.12.33]

SHE USES HER fleshvoice.

'I am Meer Edv Tawren,' she says. 'I hold the rank of magos. I am the acting Server of Instrumentation for Calth/Numinus.'

'There doesn't appear to be much left to instrument,' says Ventanus.

'True enough,' replies Tawren. 'This is a hateful day. Both of our institutions have lost grievously–'

'The Imperium has lost grievously,' says Ventanus. 'Indeed, something more awful than that has occurred. For reasons I cannot even make a theoretical about, the Word Bearers have turned on us. They have unleashed open war on Calth, on the XIII, on the Five Hundred Worlds of Ultramar, and on the Imperium of Mankind.'

She nods. She is tall and solemn. Her ceremonial robes of office are dirty and torn, and they are stiff with bloodstains. In the last few hours, someone has died while being cradled in her arms.

They are standing in a sub-ground cistern several

hundred metres north of the main Numinus arterial. It is a dank cavern, a storm drain for the river system. Arook has suggested that the density of rockcrete above their heads can deter the detection systems the Word Bearers are using.

'My direct superior is dead,' says Tawren. 'We escaped from the Watchtower at the time of the ship impact, but it was too late for him. Responsibility for command and coordination falls to me.'

'What resources do you have?' asks Ventanus.

'I have a force of about three hundred skitarii, with portable weapons and some light support,' she replies, 'and that number is growing as we contact other survivor groups. We have no manifold capacity, no noosphere, and absolutely no operational control of the data-engines or the Veridian system weapons grid.'

'None at all?'

She shakes her head.

'This is due to scrapcode infection that immediately preceded the start of hostilities. We believe that the XVII Legion deliberately introduced a scrapcode plague into the Calth noospherics prior to attack in order to destabilise then cripple the Mechanicum's capability.'

'Since when does a Legion technologically outflank the Mechanicum, magos?' Ventanus asks.

'Since today, captain.'

'So... this scrapcode, it was new to you?'

'It was like nothing we had ever encountered before. Not just the coding language. The very basis of it. We are still not entirely sure what it is or how it operates.'

'Further evidence that this was planned and orchestrated well in advance,' says Selaton.

No one speaks. For a moment, the only sound is dirty water *plinking* down from the overflow chutes.

'What is your intention at this point?' Ventanus asks.

Tawren looks at him.

'I will use every means at my disposal to regain control

of the data-engines. To oust the enemy from our systems and retake the noosphere.'

'The weapons grid would certainly be a considerable asset,' says Ventanus. 'Not to say a crucial one. I fear the XIII has been worse than decimated. I fear for the fleet too.'

'We have very little in terms of accurate projections,' says Arook, 'but at least fifty per cent of the fleet assembly and the ground forces appear to be lost.'

Ventanus tries to focus. He tries to get into theoretical so that he can assist the strategy planning. He tries not to dwell on the practical that over one hundred thousand Ultramarines may already be dead. Dead in just a few hours. It is the greatest Legion loss in history, by an appreciable margin.

'How do you contact them?' Selaton asks, suddenly.

'I beg your pardon?' replies Tawren.

'You said the skitarii numbers are increasing as you contact other survivor groups. How do you contact them? There is no vox.'

'True, but the skitarii have a dedicated emergency manifold, a crisis back-up,' says Tawren. 'Arook has switched to the reinforced, military code system of his brigade. The range is limited, but secure.'

'You have limited secure comms?' asks Ventanus.

She nods.

'I need to contact Legion Command,' he says.

'Not possible,' replies Arook. 'We have no orbital links.'

'Then I need to contact my company,' Ventanus counters. 'There are skitarii units stationed with the Mechanicum support at the Erud muster. I need to contact them.'

'Erud Station?' Arook echoes. He glares his red eyes at the server. One of them flickers on and off, sporadically.

'Of course,' she says.

Ventanus slots open the cuff of his armour, and lights

up a small hololithic chart. He scans the terrain, zipping back and forth. Selaton looks over his shoulder.

'Theoretical,' says Ventanus. 'If we can get the muster moving, we could coordinate a rendezvous. Somewhere here. On the Plains of Dera. Zetaya, perhaps.'

'It's defensible, but open to the west,' Selaton points out. 'Lernaea might be a better choice.'

'They'd be too exposed crossing the valley floor,' says Ventanus. He alters the projection.

'What about Melatis? It's got a good position, and it's agricultural. With fortune on our side, it won't have been hit in the first strike. Not an important enough asset.'

'Fortune does not seem to have been on our side much so far today, captain,' says Selaton.

'What are you talking about, Kiuz?' Ventanus snaps. 'We're here, aren't we?'

He turns to Arook and Tawren.

'When you establish contact, I can give you an authority code to identify me. Try to find out who you're talking to. Ideally, Captain Sydance or Captain Yaulus. I need them to advance any units they have to Melatis on the plains. I'll meet them there.'

'You intend to go overland to Melatis?' asks Tawren.

'Yes,' says Ventanus simply.

'It is probably an over-ambitious goal,' she says gently.

'Severe bombing north of the river,' says Arook. 'They've taken out the highway. The enemy is also massing engines along the Neride Wall.'

'Titans?' asks Ventanus.

Arook hesitates.

'It shocks me too, sir,' he says stiffly. 'I have no idea how any Mechanicum engine could have been so miserably corrupted. Loyalty and devotion seem to be in short supply at this hour.'

'Leptius Numinus,' says Tawren.

They all look at her.

'The old gubernatorial palace, on the plains,' she

explains. 'It was high on my list of potential destinations. The palace has a non-active but functional data-engine, as well as a high-cast vox array. Neither are operational when the governor is not in residence, but they are maintained. I was hoping that, because both systems were off-line, they might have been spared scrapcode infection and electromagnetic damage.'

'We could contact the fleet?' asks Ventanus.

'If we could make them work,' she agrees, 'we could contact the fleet.'

'We've already identified Leptius Numinus as one of the most viable options,' says Arook. 'As an added advantage, the sub-ground network will make passage there easier than to any open target on the plains.'

'Are they part of the Calth arcology?' asks Ventanus. He recalls that significant systems of natural caverns lace the planet, and many are being developed as habitats. They are commonly used as population shelters when the local star undergoes its infrequent periods of maximum solar activity.

'Not fully, a branch,' replies Tawren. 'The early governors created a secure underground link between the city and the palace.'

'Military support from the XIII Legion at Leptius would be of great assistance while we begin our recovery program,' says Arook.

He looks at Ventanus. That defective red eye glimmers. It fades out and in again. Ventanus can hear a burble of binaric cant issuing from Arook's cybernetics.

'I have made contact,' he says. 'I have a manifold link with Skitarii Commander Gargoz. Gargoz has your Captain Sydance with him.'

'What is the situation?' asks Ventanus. 'Ask him what the situation is.'

There is a binaric crackle.

'Grim,' relays Arook. 'The muster site has been bombarded. Many are dead. Very little survives in the way of vehicles or transports. Sydance reports that strengths from the Ultramarines 4th, and eight other companies, have managed to shelter at the Braxas Wall. Approximately seven hundred men. They are ready to move at your instruction.'

Arook looks directly at Ventanus.

'Captain Sydance apparently wishes to emphasise that he is pleased to hear from you. He is pleased to know that you are alive.'

'Tell him where we need them to be. Ask him to see what other forces he can mobilise. As muster commander, I am giving authority to the movement of troops. Ask him to send an arrival estimate.'

Arook nods and relays.

'We will need a shibboleth,' says Selaton.

Ventanus hesitates.

'They have cracked everything. They've broken Mechanicum code,' says Selaton. 'Even our authority codes can't be trusted.'

Ventanus nods.

'Tell Sydance that he can only trust a message from someone who knows the number of the painted eldar. Tell him I will only trust the same.'

'It is done,' says Arook. 'What does it mean?'

Ventanus doesn't answer.

'Tell him I'll see him at Leptius Numinus in a few hours,' he says.

4

CHAPTER MASTER MARIUS Gage hits the bulkhead and slides down it with a wet squeak, leaving a smear of blood.

The wound's bad. Envenomed somehow. It's actually beating his transhuman clotting factor. He can feel his body fighting the fever.

He can feel his mind fighting the fear.

It's not fear of death or fear of pain. It's not even fear of failure.

It's the undermining disquiet of the unknown.

It's what mankind had to overcome in order to come out of his cave, in order to set forth from his birthworld. It's the thing mankind had to conquer in order to face down the xenos and the horrors that lurked in Old Night.

It's the fear his kind was bred to lack.

It amazes him.

He thought he had seen everything. His career has been a long and successful one. His status as the first Chapter Master attests to that. He has been with the Ultramarines since the very beginning.

239

They are genetically adjusted to register diminished levels of fear response. They are psychologically programmed to eschew its weakness, to resist the critical and dismaying shocks that fear can induce. Part of that programming is to study every threat and hazard, every new xenos form and mutant, that the Imperium might encounter during its outward expansion. Nothing must come as a surprise. Every possible horror must be explored. They must be exposed to every new possibility. An immunity must be built up. A disregard. Some say this makes the Ultramarines seem callous, but it is only the same kind of callous that a labourer might build up on his hands through graft work.

They must be unflinching. They must be impervious to fright.

And Gage thought he was. He really thought he was. Fear was a stranger to him.

Sweat begins to bead on his forehead. He struggles to get up, but he can't. There is a lesson here, he considers, the practical application of a theoretical paradigm. Pride is our weakness. Over-confidence. We are so sure of ourselves and our vaunted fearlessness, of such conviction that the galaxy no longer contains anything that can scare us, we make ourselves vulnerable.

Gage is sure that Guilliman has already thought of this. He is sure that Guilliman has already written the notion down somewhere in his codification notes. The sin of over-confidence. Yes, Guilliman has definitely schooled against this in his writings. He has admonished the XIII not to assume mastery of anything, including fear, because that instantly creates a vulnerability.

Now Gage thinks of it, the primarch certainly has said this several times.

Certainly. Certainly, he has.

He has said it.

He has warned. Warned of it.

In case he hasn't. In case. In case he hasn't, in that case,

Gage hopes he can get to... He can mention it to Guilliman. Mention it later.

Except. Except there may not be a later.

Guilliman.

On the bridge when... The bridge just...

That thing. That *thing*.

So much blood. Then open to the void. That *thing*. There may never be a chance now. Guilliman. Guilliman may be... He was ripped into space when the ports blew.

He may be...

Guilliman may already be dead.

That thing.

That damned *thing*.

He–

–COMES BACK OUT of the blackness. Acid bile in his throat. Tears in his eyes. Agony in his back and ribs where that thing bit him.

He blacked out there. Blacked out. Slid away into a red fog of unconsciousness as the toxins momentarily overwhelmed him.

Gage is breathing hard. Every push of his lungs is a neural fire. He looks down the hallway.

There's smoke in the air. It's moving like a river along the ceiling, gusted by the steady breeze. The flagship's air pumps are fighting to restore onboard atmospheric pressure after the bridgespace voided. Hazard lamps flash. He can see an Ultramarine dead about five metres away. The fellow's head is twisted the wrong way. Beyond him, three bridge officers sit with their backs against the bulkhead wall, resting against each other like comrades back from a drunken night's shore leave. They are entirely covered in blood, every shred of them apart from the whites of their glazed, staring eyes.

Beyond them, there's a bloody ribcage with one arm attached to it. Beyond that, a second Ultramarine has been split open like a fibrous seed.

Then he sees the thing.

Gage isn't sure if the thing on the bridge, the thing that… *killed* Guilliman… Gage isn't sure if it was *one* thing, or many in one amorphous shape. The thing picking its way towards him might be one of the many, or a piece of the whole.

It's humanoid, roughly, and about twice the size of a legionary. Its proportions are simian, though its true outline is hard to discern. Reality seems to contort around it. The air festers. It moves like a fog of the unreal, like the fluid black flow of the deepest, most subterranean nightmare.

Like a great ape, it shambles on all fours, its massive arms like tree trunks. It is bristled black, like a blowfly, but its flesh between the coarse bristles is iridescent.

It has no eyes. Its skull is all jaw and no cranium. Its face is a shrivelled grey scrap of skin drawn tight over a deformed human skull, the empty eyes like lunar craters. Its mouth is an eruption of curved tusks and huge yellow teeth like chisel blades. Venom, like sticky brown syrup, droops from its lipless gums.

It is making a snuffling sound. It smells of battery acid and spun sugar.

Is it the same thing that bit him? He doesn't want it to bite him again. He wonders if it can see him.

Of course it can see him. He's sprawled out in the open, right in its path.

But it hasn't got any eyes, so–

Gage takes a deep breath. He appreciates that the venom is making his mind swim. He knows it's making him think stupid, illogical, foolish things. He knows his transhuman metabolism is fighting it, but he's not sure if it will win the battle.

If it does win, Gage isn't sure it will win it in time.

The thing is right on him.

He reaches for his boltgun.

The weapon is long gone. He realises that several of

the fingers of his gun-hand are missing too.

His power sword is on the deck near his outstretched left leg. He leans and reaches for it. He stretches. He strains. By the old gods of Terra, he has barely the strength to move!

Gage utters an involuntary bark of frustration.

The thing hears him. It turns its tusked maw towards him. It bobs its head slightly, a feline habit, and then pounces.

Gage screams in rage and horror. He lashes out with his right hand to try to catch its throat and keep it at arm's length before it lands its full weight on him. If that happens, he's done.

His hand misses the throat. He manages to ram it up to the forearm in the thing's mouth.

The thing bites.

There is a crack of armour shattering, a crunch of forearm bones shearing. It bites his hand off beyond the wrist. There is a generous spill of blood. Pain cores up his arm like a hot wire. Gage howls. His heart rates spike.

The savage pain jacks up his metabolic reaction so hard it clears the fog of the toxin from his befuddled mind. He smashes around with his left fist, and cracks the thing in the side of the skull, knocking out two molars in a squirt of pink saliva.

The blow drives the thing back and to the side. Its mouth is still full of his hand. Gage rolls to grab his sword, but the thing is standing on his knee, and he can't twist far enough.

It opens its mouth impossibly wide and comes in for his face. He can see his severed hand flopping down its gullet.

Blue impact slams it aside. Black ichor is suddenly painted across all the nearby surfaces, including Gage's face. The thing is down, cut badly. An Ultramarine stands over Gage. He's a sergeant. His armour is battered. His helmet is painted red, indicating he has been marked for censure. He has an electromagnetic longsword in one hand and a Kehletai friction axe in the other.

'Go back to hell!' he tells the thing. It is screaming and caterwauling, its black shape swirling and re-forming, as though reality is trying to heal itself.

The sergeant puts the axe into it. The Kehletai, before they were extinguished during the bitter Kraal Compliance, made paper-thin blades that cut on a molecular level. The nanoedge blade of the axe is huge, bigger than a Fenrisian battle axe. It goes right through the thing, exploding rotten gore in all directions.

For good measure, the sergeant spears it with the longsword. Dead, it is nothing more than a stain.

The sergeant turns.

'Move up!' he yells. A fighting party appears, moving urgently down the corridor. There are several Ultramarines in it, but it is also composed of Army troopers and Navy personnel, including at least one abhuman stoker. They are armed with the most mismatched and exotic weapons Gage has ever seen outside Guilliman's private arsenal of–

They are *all* from the primarch's private arsenal.

'Move up. Secure the section!' the sergeant yells. 'Brother Kerso, scope the next corridor. Flamers to the front! Apothecary Jaer, get to the Chapter Master! Right now!'

He bends down beside Gage, setting his weapons on the deck where they will be in easy reach. Close up, Gage can see the scratch marks adorning the sergeant's armour.

'You've got an Apothecary?' Gage asks, his voice a husk of its normal baritone.

'Just coming, sir.'

'Your name?'

'Thiel, sir. Aeonid Thiel. 135th Company.'

'Marked for censure?'

'Today started in a different place, sir.'

'That it did, Thiel. Well said. Who put you in charge?'

'I put myself in charge. I was awaiting interview on deck forty when everything went to pieces. There was no chain of command. I decided I needed to build one.'

'Good work.'

'What happened, sir?' Thiel asks. He steps back slightly to allow the Apothecary to start work on Gage's wounds.

'Something attacked us. Blew the whole main bridge. Some of us got out. More than that, I can't say.'

'Who did we lose?' Thiel asks.

He's impertinent, Gage thinks. He's–

No, he's not. He's level-headed. He's practical. He's fearless. He's asking questions because he needs to know the answers.

'The shipmaster, certainly,' says Gage. 'Most of the bridge seniors. Chapter Master Vared. Chapter Master Banzor. Your Chapter Master, Antoli.'

'Terrible losses. What about the primarch?'

'I did not see him die, but I fear the worst,' replies Gage.

Thiel is silent for a moment.

'What are your orders, sir?' he asks.

'What was your operational plan, sergeant?'

'Practical: I was attempting to consolidate and coordinate a shipboard fighting force, sir, and begin to retake the ship. These daemons are everywhere.'

'Daemons, Thiel? I don't think we believe in daemons these days.'

'Then I don't know what you want to call them, sir, because they are not xenos. They are byblows. Monsters. Warp-things. It takes everything we've got to kill them.'

'Is that why you raided the primarch's collection?' asks Gage.

'No. I raided the primarch's collection because of the Word Bearers, sir.'

'Theoretical: explain that logic,' Gage asks. Then he says, 'Wait, wait. Apothecary, help me to my feet.'

'My lord, you are in no condition to–' the Apothecary begins.

'Help me to damn well stand up, Apothecary,' Gage snaps.

They help him up. He is unsteady. The Apothecary resumes dressing his wrist stump.

'Now, continue,' says Gage. 'Theoretical?'

'We are attacked by the Word Bearers,' says Thiel.

'Agreed.'

'These byblow daemons may be allied to them, some form of creature they have enslaved to their service. Or they may be controlling the XVII. It would certainly explain why our brothers have turned against us in such a fundamental fashion.'

'Agreed. Continue.'

'The daemons present a significant threat, but they appear to be… receding.'

'Receding? Explain.'

'It's like a tide going out, sir. They are fewer and weaker than they were an hour ago. As though they are draining back into hell or the warp. However, the Word Bearers have three cruisers alongside us, and they are in the process of boarding. Within the next hour they will be through the airgates and the hull, and we will be compelled to fight our own kind. This form of combat is unprecedented. Their advantage is shock and surprise. Our counter-advantage must be a lack of convention.'

'Expand.'

'They know what we are, for they are us. They know the attributes of our armour and our weapons. They also know our tactics and formulae of war, for our beloved primarch has made his codifications available to all his brothers. We never thought we would need to conceal our combat methods from our own kind. Today, we have been disabused of that notion. So we must fight them in ways that they do not expect from us. We must use the unconventional, the improvised and the makeshift.

In order to properly honour the combat teachings of Roboute Guilliman, we must cast his rules aside for the day. I have always considered his greatest wisdom to be Remark 101.x–'

Gage nods.

'I know it. *"What wins the fight is what wins the fight. Ultimately, nothing should be excluded if that exclusion leads to defeat".*'

'Precisely so, sir.'

'The "by any means" edict,' Gage says. 'The ultimate rule that no rule is unbreakable. You know, that idea always troubled him. He told me he often thought to excise the remark. He thought it too dangerous. He feared it would stand, in posterity, as a justification for any action.'

'I think the XVII have already dispensed with any such rationale, sir,' replies Thiel. 'I also would urge you not to refer to the primarch in the past tense in front of the men.'

Gage catches himself.

'Quite correct, sergeant.'

'Are my theory and my practice approved, sir?' Thiel asks.

'They are. Let us coordinate. What other officers can we contact?'

'There is a possibility that Chapter Master Empion is operational on deck thirty-five with a resistance force, and Captain Heutonicus on deck twenty.'

'A decent beginning,' says Gage. He picks up his fallen power sword and slides it into its scabbard. 'Let's move before this day goes altogether. That friction axe?'

'Sir?'

'Can it be wielded one-handed?'

Thiel hands it over.

'It's light enough, sir.'

'Lead the way. Let's cut a line towards the bridge tower.'

Thiel salutes. He turns, raising his longsword and shouting instructions to the clearance team.

Gage glances at the Apothecary.

'Are we done?' he asks.

'I'd prefer to get you to–'

'Are we done, Jaer?'

'We are, sir. For now.'

Gage hefts the axe in his good hand.

'Sergeant Thiel. Do you happen to know why he was under censure?'

'I do, sir,' says Jaer. 'His commanding officer discovered that he was running theoreticals on how to fight and defeat Space Marines, sir. Thiel claimed, in his defence, that he had run theoreticals on all other major adversaries, and it was a tactical blind spot not to know how to fight the Legions. He said, as I understand it, that the Space Marines of the Imperium were the greatest warriors in the galaxy, and thus had an obligation to understand how to fight and defeat the greatest warriors in the galaxy. Thiel declared that Space Marines were the only opponents left worth any theoretical study. His theoreticals were regarded as treasonous thought, and he was referred to the flagship for censure.'

'That was his infraction?' asks Gage.

'Looks bloody pitiful from where we're standing, doesn't it?' asks Jaer.

[mark: 7.44.02]

TROOPER BALE RANE and Trooper Dogent Krank are running for their lives through the burning streets. Trooper Maxilid was with them for a while, but some fugging thing from hell, something they didn't even see properly, swept out of the fog and bit Maxilid's bloody head off, thank you, so now they're on their own.

They're only alive because the thing was too busy chomping Maxilid down. Blood fugging everywhere.

Rane is pretty numb. He's seen it all today. All of it.

Everything it's possible to see. Every horror show. Every shock, every terror. He's seen men die. He's seen friends die. He's seen cities burn and starships fall out of the bloody sky. He's seen more dead bodies than he thought it was possible to see. He's seen men torn apart. He's seen daemons in the fog.

Worst of all, somehow, worse even than the daemons, is that he's seen men who should be friends, men who were supposed to be friends, turn towards him with unalloyed murder in their eyes. The basis of the Imperium has been up-ended. The fundamental tenets of loyalty to the fugging Throne of Terra have been torn down and pissed on.

Bale Rane knew that death would probably hurt. War would probably hurt. Breaking up with your brand-new bride and leaving her to go off to war, that would hurt too. Like a bastard.

He never, ever, in a million light years, expected treachery to hurt so much.

They've been betrayed. Calth, Primarch Guilliman, Ultramar, the Emperor, the fugging Imperium and Bale Rane of the Numinus 61st; they've all been betrayed.

Rane wants to kill someone for turning his world upside down. He wants to kill one of those bloody Word bloody Bearers, although he knows he wouldn't stand a single, solitary chance, not for a *second*.

What the fug are they thinking? What are they after? What bloody toxic poison shit is in their heads that they thought this was something they should do?

Krank is falling behind. He's getting tired. The fog's all around them, and it's getting hard to know which way to go. They've both got rifles, Illuminators, though neither of them are the weapons they were issued with at muster. They took them from corpses during their escape. When they were running from the bloody heathen Army forces that butchered their regiment.

'Come on, Krank,' Rane mutters. 'Come on now,

Kranky mate. We can keep going. We can get out of here.'

Krank nods, but he's weary. There's shock in his blood, in his spirit. Rane dare not let him stop or sleep. He might not wake up.

It ought to be the other way around. It ought to be Krank, the veteran, bucking up Rane, the rookie. That's the way it's supposed to work. That's the way it's been until today.

Rane thinks about Neve a little bit. He thinks he needs to go and find her, and take her out of the city with them. He had convinced himself she was pretty safe, tucked up in the cellar at her aunt's. But that was before the Word Bearers turned, before the Word Bearers and their heathen fugging cult troops turned and started killing everything, before it turned out not to be an accident at all.

That was before the daemons in the fog.

Bale Rane knows that it's his moral duty to go and find his young bride. He has to go and find her, and her bloody aunt too, if needs be, and get them out of the city before the city becomes an entirely dead place. That's all. That's the up and down of it.

He tells Krank that's what he's going to do.

'You can come along, if you like. Won't blame you if you don't want to.'

Krank tells him how stupid he is, but he doesn't stop walking along beside him.

The funny thing is, and Rane doesn't mention this to Krank because he knows it sounds strange, but the funny thing is, Rane doesn't believe it will take long to find Neve. He can feel her. He can feel, somehow, that she's close. She's almost calling to him. She's right there, close by, waiting for him.

They say that about people who are in love. They can find each other, find each other through thick and thin, against all the odds. He's going to find Neve, and she's going to find him.

The fog is like a silk curtain. Everywhere is grey. Fuzzy amber lights pulse where fires burn in the distance. The ruins are black and smell of smoke, of fycelene, of mud and broken drains.

Bale.

'What?' Rane asks Krank.

'What *what*?' Krank replies.

Bale. Bale. Where are you?

'You hear that?' Rane asks. 'Kranky, can you hear that?'

He can hear her. It's Neve. She's close. She's very close and she's calling to him. It's like a miracle play where the lovers are finally united at last curtain.

'Neve?'

He stops. He sees her. Just across the street, through the mist, standing in a doorway. She's pale. It looks like she's made out of mist. How the hell did she manage to track him down?

He's never been so happy to see anyone in his entire life. He feels love. He feels uplifted by love.

He takes a step forward to cross the cratered street.

Krank grabs his arm. Krank can't speak because his mouth is stoppered up with terror.

What Krank can see doesn't look like Bale Rane's young bride at all.

[mark: 8.10.32]

THE TUNNEL SYSTEM opens out on the perimeter of Leptius Numinus. For the last few kilometres, the subsurface structure is fractured, and the tunnels are flooded to knee-height. Liquid from the dislocated water table and sewage from city treatment plants has seeped up and washed out the tunnel system. They are obliged to wade.

Ventanus leads them out into the palace grounds, flanked by Arook's primary squad. They've added to their force during the journey. Several squads of skitarii have joined them, swelling the Mechanicum numbers to close to one thousand. They've also connected with about thirty Ultramarines from various decimated units, and four hundred men from the Neride Regulators 10th, nominally under a Colonel Sparzi.

The palace is elegant, a rectilinear villa complex. It reveals its stately lines slowly through the thick mist. The gardens of the estate are tumbledown. Shockwave winds and blast scorching have denuded the ploin, haps and pistachio orchards, and turned the vines into charred ropes. Ornamental walls have spilled over. Carp ponds are dry basins, the water evaporated. They find the cowering, burned skeletons of gardeners and groundsmen behind splintered trees.

The palace is closed for the winter. The city governor was in residence at Dera Tower in the city. Ventanus reflects that the governor is probably dead by now. All the casements, apart from armourglas and crystalflex reinforced sections, have been blown in by the savage transcontinental winds. The rooms, most of them filled with furniture covered by dustcloths, are littered with broken glass and snapped muntins.

Outside, the valley and the plains beyond are dark under a blanket of fog. There is no wind. Everywhere is eerily tranquil. A calm that recalls the obligatory stillness of death.

To the north-west, the Mountains of Twilight form a grey limit to the fogbound plains. To the south and south-east, the dark shape of the Shield Wall hems the city. A rugged natural formation, the back of the ridge rises above the languid, unctuous fog. Its famous forests are spines of tattered wood, stripped of limbs and leaves.

Numinus burns, a giant haze of golden light. It is not the only massive blaze they can see. Others show up in the distant fog in almost every direction, and the brutalised sky is speckled with them. Every now and then, something falls down the back of the heavens, trailing a tail of flame, and *crumps* into the hidden landscape with a distant tremor.

They move into the palace, breaking down doors where necessary. Some of the halls and chambers are littered with broken masonry where walls or ceilings have fallen. Ventanus sees fragments of moulded plasterwork, some of it painted. He sees shattered heroes from the early days of the Five Hundred Worlds. He sees the Ultima symbol, the one they all wear on their armour, broken in pieces.

Tawren assembles a working party of magi to locate and prepare the palace's data-engine and the high-cast vox array. Ventanus, in consultation with Selaton, Arook, Sparzi and Captain Sullus, a survivor from 39th Company, prepares the defences. Though its perimeter wall and ditch are quite considerable, the palace proper is not designed for military resistance of any appreciable magnitude. Sparzi's men find some tractor guns and light field pieces in a stable block to the west, and set them up facing the plains.

'If they find us here,' says Sullus, 'they will punish us.'

'If they find us here,' replies Ventanus, 'I will kill them.'

Sullus nods. A half-smile crosses his mouth. He has lost most of his company brethren since dawn. He has seen other sections of the XIII cut down by troop fire or obliterated by heavy weapons. Ventanus knows that, to keep Sullus effective, he has to spur him out of his despondency. Ventanus has already considered putting Greavus, Sullus's sergeant, in his place in the chain of command. Sullus is old, a veteran. It is as though the wind has been struck out of him.

Greavus walks over to them. He is carrying his helm under his arm. There is chalky dust on his face and in his hair. Greavus's close-cropped fair hair is red, like dirty gold. The dust makes him look as though he is prematurely aging.

'Report from the server, sir,' he says, addressing

Ventanus not Sullus. 'They've found the vox-caster system. There are some power issues, but they hope to make a test broadcast within the hour.'

'Good. The data-engine?'

'Nothing on that yet, sir,' replies Greavus.

Arook suddenly moves, raising his main weapon limb.

'Contact,' he reports. 'Two kilometres from the north gate, coming this way out of the fog.'

'Identity?' asks Ventanus.

'Concealed.'

Ventanus picks up the standard.

'Selaton, cover the south line. Colonel Sparzi, the north-east. The rest of you with me.'

They head for the gate, crossing once-ornamental lawns. Fireteams of Army troopers are setting up in hastily dug foxholes. Ventanus notes good practical distribution of the few crew-served weapons and mortars. Sparzi has read a manual or two. Probably some of Guilliman's.

They pass the field guns and reach the gate. Outside, the approach bridge spans the earthwork ditch. Beyond two obelisk mile marks, the road stretches off across scrub, the beginnings of the famous and majestic Plains of Dera. Fog and murk spoil the view.

'We've got heat-sources,' reports Arook. 'Warm bodies.'

'Confirming that,' says Greavus, using a hand-held auspex.

'They're using the fog as cover,' says Sullus dourly. 'That can't be good.'

'If I was leading reinforcements here from Erud Station,' says Ventanus, 'I'd be using the fog as cover too.'

He looks at the skitarii master.

'Vox signals?'

Arook shakes his head. The light in his damaged red eye is fading slowly in and out.

'You mentioned a code term,' says Arook.

'Yes,' says Ventanus. 'Wait.'

A slight breeze stirs. Leaf litter rattles amongst the rubble at their feet.

'A signal,' says Arook. They can all hear the muted background binarics. 'Attention palace,' he translates. 'Identify occupation.'

'Is that Mechanicum?' asks Ventanus.

'I can confirm the signal code source is Mechanicum,' says Arook. 'Not that it proves anything. If it's Gargoz, he's being circumspect.'

'Again,' says Ventanus, 'I would be if I were approaching this location hoping to find friends and fearing I was about to find enemies.'

'The signal has repeated twice,' says Arook.

'Answer it,' says Ventanus. 'Request identity.'

Arook makes a quick blurt.

'Reply reads,' he relays. 'Support elements from Erud muster, seeking shelter.'

Ventanus sticks his standard point in the earth so he can clamp on his helm.

'Too easy,' he says. 'No one from my company would expose himself that readily. Not on a day like today. No one from my company, or any other company. Ask them the question.'

'The number of the painted eldar?' asks Arook.

'That's the one.'

They wait for a second.

'No response. They repeat the claim that they are support elements from Erud muster.'

'Ask again,' says Ventanus. He glances at Sparzi. 'Get your boys up,' he says.

The colonel nods and hurries off.

'Response,' says Arook. 'A request for confirmation of xenos activity in this zone. Confirm, eldar forces?'

'They don't understand the question,' says Ventanus.

'I don't understand the question,' remarks Arook.

'The point is, Sydance would,' replies Ventanus. 'And so would any other officer of the 4th Company. Ask them to verify their response. Tell them we will stand by.'

Arook does so.

After a long pause, he says, 'They ask us to confirm xenos activity in this zone.'

Ventanus lifts the standard. 'Arook, have your skitarii paint heat-source targets in that fog bank for the benefit of the artillery crews. Tell Colonel Sparzi we will open fire in sixty seconds.'

'You're going to open fire?' Sullus barks. 'Are you mad? If it's our own kind–'

'It isn't. And I'm not going to allow it to get any closer.'

'But if they are XIII!' Sullus insists. 'If they are of Ultramar!'

'They are not, captain,' says Ventanus firmly.

Beyond the ditch, at the very edge of the miserable fog, the first figures begin to loom. The feeble sunlight catches the dull sheen of crimson armour.

'Fire!' says Ventanus.

[mark: 8.19.27]

'LET ME GO back.' cries Bale Rane. 'Let me go the fug back!'

Krank punches him in the gut and winds him badly, just to get him to stop fussing.

'Sorry,' Krank says. 'Sorry, Rane. Sorry, kid. I can't let you.'

Rane gasps out words, doubled up.

'I did not shoot at your bloody wife, Bale,' says Krank. 'I did not do that. I opened up full auto on something and it definitely weren't your wife. It most surely weren't.'

'It was Neve. She was calling to me!'

'Rane, shut up. Just shut up. Thank me, why don't you? You showed me picts of your wife. She was pretty. That thing calling to you, it wasn't pretty.'

Krank sighs. He sinks down beside Rane.

'It weren't your wife, kid. Even if you hadn't shown me picts, I'd have known. Your wife, she's got eyes, right? And she ain't got horns. I don't know what it was, Rane, but it wasn't good. It was some xenos thing. Some bloody daemon.'

The foul wind stirs the fog on the blown-out street. Out in the distance, a city hab explodes in a gout of flames, and the rumble of it falling lasts three or four minutes. Artillery thumps. Things boom above, in orbit.

Bale Rane murmurs his wife's name, tears in his eyes, snot on his lip.

Krank hears running.

'Get up, get up!' he says, pulling Rane up by the sleeves. He bundles him into cover.

Two men, Army, run past them, down the street, and then a third. They are tattered and dirty, and they're running from something. One of them is sobbing like a child.

They're fleeing. That's what they're doing.

Krank pushes Rane up against the wall as the pursuers run into view. They're Army too, but not the same Army. They're ragged, wrapped in black, brotherhood cultists like the ones who slaughtered Krank's unit. There are two of them. One laughs, raises his autorifle, and brings down the lagging trooper with a spine shot.

The other two fugitives skid up, halting. Two more cultists have appeared in their path.

The hounded men back up. The cultists stroll towards them out of the fog. The ones who were chasing drop to an amble, closing in behind.

'Please!' Krank hears one of the men beg. 'Please!'

He gets a headshot for asking nicely. He goes down like a commercia mannequin.

The other tries to run, but the cultists grab him. They pin him between the four of them, drag his head back by the hair, and cross his exposed throat with a ritual knife. His blood makes a dark red mirror in the gutter under his body.

Rane makes a noise. An involuntary sob.

The four knife brothers turn from their kill. Their eyes are sunken shadows. In the half-light, their faces look like death's-heads.

Krank fumbles with his rifle. He's not going to get it aimed in time. One of the killers sees him, and fires. The rounds whine into the brickwork beside them, and spatter them with grit and slime. Krank fires back, but Rane is tangled with him, and his aim is rubbish. His shots go wide.

The knife brothers rush them.

Krank hits one in the chest with a clean shot, point blank, and drops him on his back. Then he gets a rifle-butt in the face and collapses, his nose and mouth a bloody mash. The other two cultists grab Rane and twist his arms. One drags Rane's head back by the hair.

'This one first,' says the one who stock-smashed Krank. He stoops over his chosen victim, dagger drawn. Krank is moaning, clutching his nose. The man turns Krank's head by the chin, and aims the point of his dagger at Krank's wide left eye.

Rane goes berserk. He kicks one of his captors in the balls, then tears free and punches the other in the throat. As both of them stumble backwards, Rane hurls himself headlong at the bastard with the knife and tackles him clear of Krank.

They roll together. They writhe. Rane is nothing like strong enough. He's just a kid. The cultist is big and rangy, thin and hard. His limbs are long, and he is as tough as a wild animal.

The other two rush back in to help him, cursing. Krank reaches for his rifle, but he gets kicked down. One of them puts a pistol to his head.

The gun goes off. Krank feels surprisingly little pain considering he's been shot through the forehead. Blood runs down his face. It's hot. But there's no pain. There's not even any recoil or blowback.

The man with the pistol falls over. It's his blood decorating Krank's face. The side of the cultist's skull has been shot off. It's all matted hair and white bone shards and leaking pink.

Another man stands on the roadway. He's got a lasrifle. He fires it again, and snaps the second cultist over on his back. Headshot. A really clean headshot. Marksman standard.

Krank blinks. Where did this guy come from? He's Army. Krank can't tell which unit. The shooter clambers off the street to join them.

Rane and the other cultist have stopped fighting. Rane rolls the dead cultist off him. The big, rangy freak has got a dagger wedged in his heart. Somehow, in the frenzy, Rane managed to stick the bastard with his own knife.

'Probably an accident,' Rane says, sitting up, saying what Krank was thinking. Krank laughs, despite the fact that absolutely fugging nothing in the world is funny.

They look up at the shooter.

'Thanks,' says Krank.

'You needed help,' says the man. He's a veteran. His face is lined and his kit is faded. He's got silver in his hair.

'We all need help today, friend,' says Krank.

'True words,' says the man, offering his hand. He pulls Krank to his feet.

'I'm Krank. The kid is Rane. Bale Rane. We're Numinus 61st. Well, we were. For whatever that counts.'

'Ollanius Persson, retired,' says the man. 'I'm trying to fight my way out of this shit hole. You boys want to come along?'

Krank nods.

'Safety in numbers,' he says.

'Or company in death,' replies the old guy. 'But I'll take either. Grab your guns.'

Persson looks at Bale Rane.

'You all right, boy?' he asks.

'Yes,' replies Rane.

'He had a shake-up,' says Krank. 'He thought he saw his bride. His little wife. But it wasn't her. It wasn't human.'

'I *saw* her,' Rane insists.

'Nothing looks like what it's supposed to today,' says Persson. 'You can't trust your eyes. The warp's at work, and it's cursing us all.'

'But–' Rane begins.

'Your friend is right,' says Persson. 'It wasn't your wife.'

'How do you know so much about it?' asks Rane.

'I got old,' says Persson. 'I saw plenty.'

'You're not that old,' says Rane.

'Not compared to some, I suppose,' says Persson.

He crouches down, and plucks the ritual knife out of the cultist's blood-soaked chest. It's a black stone blade with a hand-wound wire handle, home-made. An athame. It reminds Oll Persson of something, but it's not quite right. He tosses the wretched thing away.

'Come and meet the others,' he says to the two troopers.

'Others?' asks Krank.

5

THE ENEMY COMES at Leptius Numinus. It's hard to assess numbers because of the terrible visibility, but Ventanus estimates at least six thousand. The core of the force is made up of Army units auxiliary to the XVII, the so-called brotherhoods. They look more like ritual fanatics than soldiers to Ventanus, typical of that zealot XVII mindset. Ventanus is certain that the root of many of the day's ills lies there: the fanaticism of the Word Bearers. They were always borderline and unstable, always of a religious inclination. They worshipped the Imperium as a creed and the Emperor as a god. That's why they were rebuked in the first place. That's why the Emperor used the XIII, surely his most rational warriors, to do the job.

It should have been enough. It should have ended the Word Bearers' wayward thinking, and brought them and their spurned primarch back into the common fold.

Evidently, it did not.

The Word Bearers have been fomenting dissent since that day. Reaching some crisis of faith, some epistemological crossroads, they have turned. They have turned against the Emperor they once adored.

261

But for what, Ventanus wonders? What do you replace your notion of god with?

Ventanus fears that the Calth Conjunction was an opportunity seized by the XVII to demonstrate their new alignment. The choice of Calth cannot have been chance. This was an opportunity to hurt and shame the Legion that chastised them all those years ago. By being the instrument of the savage reprimand on Monarchia forty-four years earlier, the Ultramarines made themselves a target. They made all of Ultramar's Five Hundred Worlds targets.

There are still too many questions for Ventanus's comfort. What force or concept has usurped the Emperor as the Word Bearers' all-consuming cause? What, apart from malicious vengeance, are they hoping to achieve in the Veridian system? If they crush the Ultramarines at Calth, what is their next step?

Just how many of them are there out there in the fog?

The enemy leaders press the cultists forward in serious numbers. The brotherhood warriors, swathed in black, are chanting, and Ventanus can hear drumming too. The Word Bearers are holding back, driving the cultists forward as shock troops into the earthwork ditch and against the gate.

Sparzi's gun crews have been shelling into the enemy line for about twenty minutes. They've done some serious damage considering the comparatively light nature of the field pieces. The ground beyond the earthwork is peppered with craters and littered with dead. Shot callers on the palace walls are directing the gunners in on the moving mass. Shells fall into the ranged lines, lifting tattered bodies into the air with blasts of flaming debris.

Still they come, wave after wave.

'Small-arms!' Ventanus instructs the defenders at the gate and wall. His practical is to let the Army bear the brunt of this, because the legionaries need to spare their boltguns and heavier munitions for the Word Bearers.

The Army force seems content with this. Greavus and some of the other legionaries have co-opted spare lasrifles and other weapons, and are joining the line. Others stand, blades ready, to meet any strength that reaches the gate.

Only Sullus seems distracted. His boltgun is drawn and ready. He wants to act, to fight. He's angry and frustrated, and it's fuelling his impatience.

'Steady yourself,' Ventanus warns him. 'I'll need you when the XVII come at us.'

Sullus spits out a snarl of a reply.

'Then they'd better come soon!' he snaps.

Ventanus leaves him to stew. The cultists renew their attacks. The outer walls of the palace are scarred with thousands of shot marks. Parts of some parapets have collapsed. There's an endless supply of the black-robed figures. They keep rushing the gate bridge. The bridge is littered with enemy dead, and black figures have tumbled into the ditch in significant numbers.

Rockets squeal and lash up at the walls. Sparzi's artillery tries to bracket the rocket launchers.

Ventanus has a growing concern about munitions supplies.

Ventanus locates Arook on a wall section beside the gate that is defended by the skitarii.

'Any signal from outside?' he asks.

'No,' says Arook.

'And the server? Anything from her?'

'No,' says Arook. He seems slightly embarrassed.

Mortars *tunk* and cough behind them. Ventanus hears more rockets wailing in at the wall.

'Can your men pinpoint the rocket sources? Sparzi's guns need to end that pain fast before they bring the walls down.'

Arook nods.

'I wonder how they found us so quickly?' Arook murmurs as soon as he's issued command blurts to his warriors.

'Listening in to our comms?' Ventanus suggests.

'No chance,' says Arook. 'The skitarii emergency link is secure.'

'Then just bad luck,' says Ventanus. 'There's more than enough of that to go around today.'

[mark: 9.07.32]

THE WARP OPENS broad, black wings. Kor Phaeron manifests.

'Explain your delay,' he hisses. Creatures of unlight and the outside fidget and gibber around him.

Morpal Cxir, force commander, bows his head to his manifested superior. Dirty light from the warp-flask swaddles them both.

'Resistance here, lord,' Cxir says. 'Leptius Numinus.'

'I know it,' replies Kor Phaeron. 'A summer palace. No strategic importance. No tactical viability. Burn it. Move on.'

'There is resistance, lord.'

The Black Cardinal exhales.

'Your host is expected at the Shield Wall in two hours, Cxir. Do not waste effort and lives on a non-essential target that can be razed by orbital weapons later.'

'With respect, lord,' says Cxir. 'I believe there is more to it.'

He gestures to the warriors grouped around him. One of them is Ulmor Nul, his tracker beast growling and straining at its leash.

'Nul was pursuing an Ultramarines captain who was discovered fleeing the starport. He obtained an indelible scent. The track led here, to the palace.'

'Just a survivor, running to the nearest place of shelter,' remarks Kor Phaeron.

'It is a very direct and deliberate route to take, lord,' says Nul. 'I believe the target has Mechanicum forces with him, and other survivors assembled into a reasonable fighting force.'

'The defence of the palace complex is resolute,' adds Cxir. 'It is organised and purposeful. I believe it has tactical credibility. The XIII is trying to achieve something here.'

Kor Phaeron pauses. The Primordial Truth whispers around him, a hiss like waves breaking on an endless shoreline.

'You are redirected, Cxir,' he says. 'Pursue this prosecution. Exterminate them.'

[mark: 9.20.00]

THE CHANTING AND drumming get louder. The next wave of cultists throws itself at the palace.

'They're wired,' warns Greavus sharply.

Ventanus amps up his visor view. There are brotherhood warriors in the front ranks wearing bomb vests or carrying flasks and tubs of explosives.

'Take them down before they reach the bridge!' Ventanus orders. Marksmen on the wall line, some of them skitarii using needle laser weapons, start to pick off the bombers. Some detonate as they are brought down. One is caught at the far end of the bridge, his vest exploding with a huge, sickle-shaped rip of fire. Ventanus feels the ground shake.

'They are renewing their efforts,' says Sullus.

'They are,' Ventanus agrees.

'Prelude to an attack by their Legiones Astartes, I'll wager,' says Sullus.

'They'll want to weaken the walls first,' says Ventanus.

'Let me take the fight to them!' Sullus barks. 'Practical: into the heart of them. Kill their leader. Break their focus.'

'Theoretical: you die, and so do the men I'm fool enough to let you take with you. Munitions and strength are squandered. No.'

Sullus glares at Ventanus.

'Do you doubt my courage?' he asks.

'In a way, I do,' says Ventanus. 'We know no fear, but I think, just now, you do.'

Sullus takes a furious step towards Ventanus.

'I'll break your back for that insult! I'm not afraid to die!'

'I know you're not, Sullus. But I think you're afraid that our way of life is dying. That the universe as we understand it is dying. That's what I'm afraid of.'

Sullus blinks.

'Practical: loss of faith in our philosophy will lead to over-emphatic and reckless actions. Our combat efficiency will be lost. Our performance as warriors will suffer.'

Sullus swallows.

'What if… Guilliman's dead, Remus?' he asks.

'Then we avenge him, Teus.'

Sullus looks away.

'Go find the server,' Ventanus tells him. 'Get an update on her progress. If they come at the walls, I want you to protect her.'

Sullus nods and strides away.

IN THE CAVERNOUS sub-basements of the palace, several levels underground, Tawren hears the dull *crump* of explosions from above ground. Trickles of dust skitter from the disturbed ceiling. She hears detonations, small-arms rattle, the steady tolling of artillery, the crazy ebb of chants and drums.

In chambers nearby, her magi are scrambling to re-activate the palace's old high-cast system. The vox seems to be intact, but there is a singular lack of viable power.

With a skitarii aide, a female called Cyramica, Tawren has just gained entry to the ceramite-lined well under the palace centre where the data-engine and stacks are held. The data-engine is cold, off-line. She examines it, running her agile hand along its dusty, brown plastek casing. She peers into its inspection windows, observing the etched circuitry, the brass key systems. It is old, an old pattern, probably one of the first data-engines active on Calth at the time of first settlement. It employs Konor-Gantz sub-aetheric systems, and linear binaric cogitation. Old. Quite beautiful.

But not very potent. Tawren understands that the engine was only brought on-line when the governor was in residence at the palace, and then only as a back-up for state records.

'It will have to be enough,' she declares out loud. Cyramica glances at her.

Tawren calls in some of the magi, and they begin work on ignition and data-agitation. The engine has its own power supply, a Gysson fusion module set into the floor. The chamber grows warm as the module starts working.

'If we had one of these for the vox-caster...' remarks one of the magi.

'Let us bring it to yield and then measure what it appreciates,' suggests Tawren. 'Its power output should be rated in excess of the engine's needs, to cover all circumstances. Perhaps we can divert some energy to the vox once the engine is operational.'

The magos nods. Tawren has moved laterally around a problem that was confounding him.

Tawren oversees the work. Her gaze lingers on the MIU socket. She will, of course, have to plug herself in. When the time comes. If the engine is tainted with scrapcode, all her efforts may be for nothing, and she will die in the process. Die like Hesst, die the brain-death, the data-death. She remembers Hesst passing in her arms.

A voice interrupts her thoughts. 'Will it work?'

She turns. An Ultramarines captain has entered the stack room. It is Sullus. She is not sure what to make of Sullus. From observation of micro-expressions during the journey to the palace, she believes that Ventanus does not trust his judgement or reliability.

'It will work,' she says with a conviction she does not entirely feel.

'And the vox system?' he asks, looking at the ancient engine with a dubious expression.

'That too. Another half an hour, perhaps.'

'We don't have anything like that, server,' says Sullus. 'They are at the wall. Can't you hear them? They're at the gate, and they will burn this if they get to it.'

'Then make sure, captain,' she replies, 'that they do not get to it.'

One of the magi nods to her. She clears her throat, and walks up to the MIU socket.

The plug connectors lock into place.

The data-engine purrs.

[mark: 9.33.01]

THIEL BLOWS OPEN the next hatch. The daemon-thing on the other side lunges at him, howling. It has teeth – rotten, broken pegs of teeth – all the way around its yawning mouth, which is big enough to swallow him whole. Its legs are back-jointed, with bird's feet.

Thiel rips the electromagnetic longsword through its maw, severing the upper and lower jaws. Then he puts two bolt-rounds down its sputtering gullet.

Kerso moves in to back him up, hosing the daemon-thing with fire. The thing is already shrieking and spasming, spraying the flagship hallway liberally with ichor. It starts thrashing as the fire wraps around it.

From behind them, Chapter Master Empion yells a warning. A second daemon, a thing made of hair and arachnoid limbs and antlers, has scuttled out of the shadows. It grabs Kerso before he can turn, splitting his armour down the length of his spine, peeling his carapace away like foil. Kerso is screaming. His flamer unit tumbles away, weeping fire.

Thiel hacks off two of the spider-thing's legs. They are like black willow trunks, ropey and matted with brown fuzz. More ichor spatters. Another leg lashes at Thiel. Too many limbs.

Kerso is done screaming. A lack of skull has silenced him. The thing pinning and peeling him has vomited acid juices onto his head and shoulders to render him more palatable. Kerso's head is a fused, smoking lump of tissue.

The thing has one eye, a huge white orb that throbs with a sickening, celestial light. It is crowned with a spreading tree of sixty-point antlers.

Brother Bormarus has a heavy bolter. He slugs repeated shots into the creature's wizened form. Rounds detonate under the skin, pulsing the slack flesh out or tearing it and spraying gobs of meat and pus.

Empion leaps forward alongside Thiel. He has a thunder hammer, and he breaks legs with it. He smashes at the daemon-thing's body. The energised strikes fracture chitin and pulp tissue. The daemon-thing rears back, dropping Kerso's corpse, waving its spider legs in a defensive posture. Some legs trail, broken and useless. It has hundreds of them.

Bormarus fires again, aiming at the exposed belly. Something bursts, and the hallway is filled with a noxious stench. Flies swarm everywhere. The daemon-thing flops forward. Thiel ducks a slicing limb, and stabs his longsword into the baleful eye, twists it, and keeps twisting and digging until the unholy light goes out.

Zabo recovers Kerso's flame-unit and burns the twitching hulk.

'Every door, a new horror,' says Empion to Thiel.

'And every moment a moment lost,' Thiel replies.

They're fighting their way down-ship towards the auxiliary bridge. The banging and scraping on the outside

hull is getting louder and more persistent: the Word
Bearers are on the verge of boarding from their ships
alongside. But there is no point fighting for a ship that
they can't control. The auxiliary bridge is a vital practical
asset. The *Macragge's Honour* has lost its primary bridge
tower and its shipmaster, but a replacement for Zedoff
has been located among survivors picked up from the
Sanctity of Saramanth. Master Hommed, along with a
contingent of ready and prepped command officers, is
following on behind Thiel's desperate advance.

The fight is chamber by chamber, companionway by
companionway. Daemons lurk in every shadow and
around every turn. They spilled into the flagship from
loose folds of the warp when the main bridge was compromised, and flow through the vast vessel like a flash
flood of ink, of pitch, of liquid tar.

Thiel, Empion and the rest of the ship's defenders are learning how to daemon-fight under practical
conditions. Fire and blades have greater efficacy than
projectiles or energy weapons. It seems that the primordial entities suffer greater harm from simple, basic
injuries: the primitive qualities of edge, and blunt force,
and flame.

Thiel has a theoretical developing, a proposition that
suggests a link between damage and ritual function. Fire
and cutting or stabbing tools were essential elements of
ancient magic-working. It seems more than coincidental
that their symbolic provenance should be retained. It is
as if the daemons, products of the primeval void before
man's birth, remember the sacred instruments that were
used to summon them.

He doubts he will ever have the opportunity to write
down or propose this theoretical. He believes that, if he
ever should, he would be scorned as a superstitious fool.

Urgency is renewed. Bormarus leads the way. Flies buzz
in the clefts of the hall, and gather in frenzies around the
bulkhead lights. Mould has formed on ceilings and wall

ribs, and slime is dribbling up through deck seams.

Beyond the next blast hatch, a broad prep chamber is littered with dead men. They are almost all flagship crew, most of them ratings, but Thiel spies at least four Ultramarines among the dead. All of the corpses look as though they have been crushed under the treads of a Baneblade convoy. The bodies form a broken, mangled carpet of flesh, bone and armour. The floor of the chamber is slick with blood. Flies buzz.

Thiel can hear dripping.

He looks up. The ceiling is covered, just like the deck. Bodies have been crushed into it, crushed and squashed into the ceiling like papier maché. Small pieces drop or splat down as gravity works its gradual influence.

'What did this?' Empion murmurs, marvelling at the sheer ingenuity of the horror.

There is a scraping sound. They turn, and find out the answer to his question.

6

'HERE THEY COME!' cries Arook Serotid.

The Word Bearers charge out of the fog, their huge red figures dwarfing their cultist troops. They drive the ragged brotherhood warriors ahead of them like packs of dogs into the onslaught of the palace guns. They use the cultists as shields.

'Meet them! Deny them!' Ventanus orders. At last, he fires his boltgun. Along the line of the walls and the gate, bolters open up, jagging, jumping and crackling with muzzle-flash. Heavier Legion weapons join in. Autocannons. Lascannons. The precious instruments they reserved for this moment.

The firepower slaps into the enemy charge, properly hurting it, slowing it, breaking it. Thousands of separate explosions and blasts tear men apart or throw them into the air. Tracer-bright streaks of las and plasma stitch across the enemy line. Black-robed humans are mown down. Ventanus smiles under his helm as he sees crimson-armoured figures shudder and fall amongst them.

But there is an inevitable balance. Because it is finally time to utilise the Legion-issue weapons, it is also

273

time to suffer equivalent wrath. The assaulting Word
Bearers open fire with bolters and heavy cannons, sup-
plementing the light infantry weapons of the chanting
brotherhoods. Mass-reactive shells punch into the walls,
scattering large chunks of stone, and rip into the gate.
The loyalist forces start taking much heavier casualties.

Loyalist, Ventanus thinks. How bitterly natural was it
to arrive at that name?

Crimson shapes, fast as darts, loft out of the fogbank.
Assault squads. Shock troops launching on jump packs.
They come thundering in like missiles, clearing the
broad ditch, plunging down onto the defences. Their
attack leap-frogs the main assaulting host. They arrive
killing, armed with bolters and chainblades, reaping
the Army troops like ripe crops. Angry, whining chains-
words rip screaming men apart, making red ribbons of
flesh, hurling matted body parts into the air.

'Drive them off the walls!' Ventanus yells.

Arook opens fire, spearing one Word Bearers assaulter
out of the air with a surgical intercept shot. The Word
Bearer veers away on a twisting plume of black smoke.

Four of them land on their feet at the head of the bridge,
in front of the gate. They hack and shoot their way into
the dug-in Army fireteams. The chainblades score through
sandbags, through cannon barrels, through shielding,
through flesh, through bone. The strangled, oddly mod-
ulated shrieks of the Army troopers unable to defend
themselves mark the savage progress of the Word Bearers.

Ventanus bounds forward, Greavus at his side. They
reach the defensive line under the gate, where the
ground flows with a preposterous, spreading quantity of
blood. There's a pulsing pressure to it, a flow driven by
the scampering hearts of men who bleed out through
unimaginable wounds. Streams spray and gurgle along
the gutters of the bridge, gutters designed to handle rain-
fall. The torrents void into the ditch below like rusty
water from iron pipework.

Ventanus reaches one of the Word Bearers while he is busy disarticulating an Army corporal. Ventanus catches the traitor under the chin of the helm with the thrusting wings of the standard. He drives him backwards, and then blasts him in the torso, point blank, with his boltgun. The shot augurs clean through the Word Bearer and his jump pack in a violent belch of flames and sparks.

The Assault Marine falls, but grabs the thrusting standard as he collapses, dragging it out of Ventanus's grip. Ventanus doesn't have time to recover it. Still firing with his right hand, he draws his power sword underhand with his left, and then rotates the freed blade in a semicircle, catching it full grip.

Greavus has engaged the second of the jump infantry warriors, swinging his power fist to meet the Word Bearer's moaning chainsword. The chainsword is kicking out exhaust fumes of blood and tissue fibre from its fresh kills. The augmented gauntlet, sizzling with force, shatters the grip and blade drivers of the chainsword, seizing its function.

The Traitor Marine discards his broken sword, and fires his bolt pistol. The round explodes against the side of Greavus's helm, throwing him sideways into the gateway wall. The Marine steps forward to put a second shot into him.

Ventanus's bolter roars, and the Word Bearer takes one hit in the throat and another in the chest. The twin impacts stagger him backwards, spalling slivers of armour off him in a cloud like ice chips. Blood pours through the ruptures. The Word Bearer sags against the gate wall, bubbles of blood aspirating through his mouthguard. He tries to raise his pistol again.

Ventanus's clip is spent. He clamps the bolter, bringing the power sword home with both hands. He finishes the wounded, swaying Word Bearer with a brutal scything zigzag slash. The upper part of the cut goes sideways through the faceplate, the lower return through the abdomen, clean to the backbone. Clutching his almost bisected waist, the Word Bearer buckles.

Ventanus turns in time to meet a third. The Assault Marine rushes him. Ventanus notices there are grim figures etched and marked on the Word Bearer's shoulder guards, and gibberish litanies inscribed down the length of his body plates. It is the heraldry of the insane.

Ventanus blocks the chainsword swing with his blade. More sparks dance. The chainblade, a two-handed monster, chatters as it bites against the energised edge of the power sword. They break. Ventanus parries the next stroke, blocks another, and then runs his blade, tip first, clean through his adversary's gut. The stab misses the spine, but the end of the blade merges through the plating above the Word Bearer's left hip.

Ventanus attempts to slide the blade out, but it's stuck. Nor is his opponent dead. He swings for Ventanus again, and Ventanus is forced to evade as the chainsword mutters towards his face. He has to let go of his sword, and leave it impaling the warrior's abdomen.

The Word Bearer lunges at him, set on finishing the contest. He's wielding the massive chainsword two-handed, stroking left and right in an attempt to catch the now unarmed Ultramarine. A skitarii warrior leaps to Ventanus's defence, but the Word Bearer cleaves him in half in a swirling red haze.

Open-handed, Ventanus leaps at him, tackling him bodily to the ground while his chainsword is still tearing through the Mechanicum soldier. Pinning the Word Bearer's right arm so the brute can't make a swing across his body, Ventanus punches his confined enemy in the head repeatedly. After three blows, the helmet buckles slightly. A fourth fractures part of the gorget. A fifth crazes a visor lens.

The Word Bearer roars, throwing Ventanus off him. Ventanus allows himself to be knocked clear.

He has regained his grip on the hilt of his power sword.

He wrenches it out of the Word Bearer. Sideways.

Greavus, his head streaming gore, isn't finished. He has risen again, throwing aside his ruptured, ruined helm. He has recovered a bolt pistol and is firing it past Ventanus. The fourth of the assaulters is cleaving his way through Army regulars and skitarii.

Arook and the largest of the heavyweight skitarii have retrenched. They open up with their plasma inbuilds, and slice the traitor apart. Ventanus hears Greavus yelling tactical commands to rally the head of the bridge and drive back the storm force. They're holding, but the line's going to break. Hundreds of cultists and Word Bearers are on the bridge, and some are actually swarming up the slopes of the ditch. The defenders on the walls can't get an angle of fire steep enough.

Selaton arrives with several more of the Ultramarines contingent. He moves in to support Greavus at the bridge. Ventanus reloads his boltgun, and takes a place in the line.

The force of fire now being directed at the palace gate and frontage is immense. Men are being felled by the hail. They are even being hit and killed by the stone shrapnel kicked up by shots striking the wall.

'I have a signal!' Arook yells to Ventanus over the din. 'A new signal.'

'Relay it!'

'Inbound force of XIII Legion requesting position specifics.'

'Challenge them,' Ventanus orders. 'Ask them the number of the painted eldar!'

Arook sends the message.

'Reply,' he says. 'The number is twelve. Message continues, "As anyone will tell you".'

He looks at Ventanus. Droplets of blood from dozens of bodies bead his golden armour. His defective red eye ebbs and flares.

'Captain?' he asks. 'Response?'

'The correct answer is thirteen,' says Ventanus. He takes a deep breath. 'Supply them with the coordinates and tell them that time is not on our side.'

[mark: 9.44.12]

THE DAEMON HAS a beak. It has a beak and feathers, and hundreds of vestigial limbs that end in hooves. But its body, all thirty tonnes of it, is that of a serpent, a fat, bloated constrictor. A Space Marine could stand with his arms outstretched and not match the diameter of its scaled girth.

It emerges from the vault shadows to the side of the prep chamber, spooling its vast, swaying bulk up through a massive deck hatch that leads into a magazine store. Thiel realises how the crushed carpet of victims was manufactured.

The vast beak clacks. Thiel sees that secondary snake bodies, dozens of them, form a beard, a frill under the chin of the beak. They writhe like tentacles, like pseudo-pods. The daemon is a hundred giant snakes fused into one titanic abomination, sharing one beaked head.

Bormarus rakes with his heavy bolter, and Zabo spears scalding flame. The daemon-snake rears back, and then lashes out with its frilled head. The beak catches one of the squad, a battle-brother called Domnis, and shears him in a line from the groin to the left shoulder.

Empion wades in, unflinching, circling his thunder hammer to gather momentum. The daemon-snake strikes at him, and he meets the strike, turning its beak aside with a staggering blow. The impact shakes the chamber and causes a pop of overpressure.

The beak is cracked. Ichor trickles out. Thiel strides in to support the Chapter Master, and when the daemon-snake strikes again it is greeted by the hammer and the electromagnetic longsword.

The hammer connects above the bridge of the massive beak, and deconstructs a brittle, avian eye-socket. Simultaneously, Thiel runs his longsword's razor edge up the rising belly and throat under the beard of secondary tails. The sword parts white scaled flesh, and opens bright pink meat and transparent bone. Internal pink sacs, swirled with white fat, burst and an alimentary canal ruptures.

The daemon-snake rears, its beak wide. Its secondary snake bodies and vestigial hooves thrash and spasm furiously. Partially digested, dismembered parts of human beings and Space Marines spatter out of the deep, gutting wound Thiel has delivered. The body parts spew wide in an outrush of gastric fluid.

The Ultramarines can all hear a colossal booming noise. It is the daemon's immense tail end, still coiled in the magazine below, thrashing in pained frenzy against the metal walls of the compartment.

The daemon slides back through the hatch to escape its tormentors.

'The hatch! Close the hatch!' Zabo yells. He has a locked string of ten frag grenades in his hand. As Empion punches the hatch control, Zabo arms one and lobs the whole string into the deck hatch.

The hatch is almost shut when the grenades go off. The blast jams the hatch a few centimetres from full closure, and the narrow slit focuses the contained blast pressure into a tight, extreme geyser of flame and debris that jets up and burns out across the chamber ceiling.

The booming stops.

Empion glances at Thiel.

'Every door, a new horror,' he says.

'And every moment a moment lost,' Thiel replies.

It is not the last time they will echo this call and return.

It is not the last compartment of the flagship they will have to clear a path through.

7

THE WORD BEARERS launch a third wave of Assault
Marines at the palace.

Ventanus, Selaton and Greavus have held the defence
force together, and kept the gate and the bridge, though
the bridge is chewed down to shreds of its former majesty. The second wave almost pushed them out of the
gate into the inner yard, but for serious counter-fire from
Arook's skitarii.

The third wave, Ventanus knows, will be the critical
phase. He sees it coming: one formation of jump troops
swooping for the bitterly contested gate, another veer-
ing south to hit the wall further around the perimeter.
Their intention will be to break in on Sparzi's artillery
positions.

Remus Ventanus is resolved to endure whatever he
must endure, but he knows that resistance must crumble
eventually. It is a calculable inevitability. It is a matter of
numbers. It is a solid practical.

He clings to one hope. He clings to the whispered,
relayed message from his home company. *Let it not be a
lie or a trick,* he thinks. *I've had enough of tricks this day. If*

it isn't a lie, let them be fast enough. Let them be fleet of foot
and tread. Let them get here while being here still matters.

He knows the wave is coming. There are precursor signs. The brotherhood cultists swarm yet again at
the gate and ditch. The chanting becomes so loud that
Ventanus imagines the pulse of it, the massed breath
of it, will blow away the fetid smog. The enemy strikes
at the walls with more rockets, with mortars, and with
medium artillery. Shells punch holes in the old walls, or
drop long into the gardens and compounds, scattering
gun-crews and reserve positions. Selaton reports hearing
tracks clattering in the fog, suggesting that the shelling is
coming from enemy tanks or self-propelled guns. Ventanus doesn't hear anything: his hearing is dulled by the
sheer pitch of the intense combat in which he has been
locked.

The Assault Marines shriek down. Their jump packs
generate rasping, heat-shimmered forks of blue flame.
The brotherhood charges crush the bridge barricades.
Part of the top arch of the gate explodes and collapses
in a slip of dust and loose stones. The defenders brace.

Greavus curses, blood matting his already red hair.

A Baneblade, a crimson behemoth, looms out of the
fog on the far side of the earthwork and lines up on the
gate and west wall. Brotherhood warriors swarm around
the bulk of the massive tank.

The super-heavy tank takes aim with its primary siege
weapon. The Demolisher cannon clanks into alignment.
Its skirts and side-plating are painted with eight-pointed
star designs and what appears to be considerable quantities of scrawled handwriting.

A Baneblade.

Ventanus knows the balance has finally and firmly
tipped in favour of the Word Bearers.

The close combat has already begun. There's no time
to think about the tank.

He is too busy fighting off a pair of Assault Marines.

One has wounded him in the side. The other is laying in with a power axe. The confines of the gate cramp the full measure of the axe-wielder's swing, but the Word Bearer has already killed two Army troopers and a skitarii.

Selaton covers his captain's back, turning aside the power axe with a battered combat shield whose surface decoration has been obliterated into a billion raw metals, nicks and scratches. Ventanus and Selaton fight back-to-back. Ventanus clashes his power sword with his opponent's kinetic mace. Selaton drives a chainsword across the guard of the axe-wielder.

All the while, Ventanus has half an eye on the tank.

Selaton takes a hit. The power axe gets past his combat shield and hacks into his shoulder guard. It doesn't bite through to the flesh underneath, but the damage is deep, and it jams the articulation of his arm.

Selaton tries to compensate, but his balance is twisted. He stumbles sideways, lurched by the momentum of the axe wrenching out.

His guard is therefore poor as he takes the second swing in the chest.

The wound is bloody. The force of it knocks Selaton down, and it looks as though he has the entire bite of the axe buried in his chest. In truth, his carapace has absorbed the lethal part of the hit, but the flesh is sliced and – until Selaton's transhuman biology kicks in to staunch it – bleeds copiously.

Ventanus is too committed to protect his fallen sergeant. The Assault Marine with the power axe closes down for the finishing blow.

Greavus punches him in the side of the head with his power fist, compacting his helm like a foil ration tray.

Greavus hauls Selaton back to his feet. They struggle for a second to free the axe from Selaton's armour.

Ventanus kills his opponent. Fury directs his hand. He plants his blade through the Word Bearer's helmet, slicing off the right-hand third of it. Something that for all the galaxy resembles an anatomy scholam cross-section is visible as the Assault Marine sags aside.

Ventanus can feel the heat seething inside him like a fever. Since the fighting broke out, he's taken about eighteen minor wounds, including a through and through las-hit to the meat of his right thigh, a fracture to a bone in his forearm, and a crushed fifth finger. The others are knocks, scars, and serious concussion-transmitted bruising.

His metabolism is cranking up, trying to compensate, trying to fight or delay pain, trying to maintain peak performance, trying to accelerate healing and repair. The energy debt has raised his body temperature by several degrees. He is flash-burning body fat fuel reserves. He knows he will soon need hydrolytes and additional pain-buffers if he is going to retain his battlefield edge.

He looks at the tank again. Why hasn't it fired? Why–

The Baneblade abruptly revs its powerful engine plant, throbs jets of black exhaust into the air, and starts a rapid reverse. Ventanus can hear its track sections clattering. Its massive hull rocks tail-to-nose, and its main turret begins to traverse to the left, the battle cannon elevating.

The host of brotherhood warriors mobbing around it has to break frantically to avoid being crushed by its hasty redeployment.

What's it doing? Is it turning? Is it *turning*?

There's something in the oily fog. Something to the north-west.

The Word Bearers Baneblade fires its battle cannon. The muzzle-shock is huge, and the pressure smack puffs dust up from the ground all around it. The shell spits into the fog, creating a corkscrew ripple that slowly dissolves. Ventanus does not hear it hit.

But he hears the response.

There is an oscillating scream of energy and pressure, accompanied by a micro-pulse of electromagnetics. A thick beam of blinding energy shears out of the fog and strikes the Baneblade. The impact shakes the tank, all three hundred tonnes of it. It shakes it. It rattles it like a tin toy. It rocks it off the ground for a second and skids it sideways. Dozens of brotherhood warriors perish under its violently dislodged mass.

The energy beam bangs painfully as it connects. Huge chunks of armour plating eject, some spinning high into the air. Half the turret structure is burned away. Smoke begins to plume, and then gutters and pours up and out of the damaged section. The Baneblade shudders. Ventanus can hear it attempting to restart its main drive, stalled by the body-blow. He can hear the multi-fuel plant gagging and choking.

A second energy beam, bright as the first, scores out of the fog and misses the tank by a few metres. It hits the ground, spontaneously excavating a huge trench of super-heated, fused rock, and incinerating two dozen of the brotherhood and four of the Word Bearers. Other cultists caught in the immediate target zones scream as the secondary heat-sear ignites their robes and their ammo.

The third beam, coming just a moment after the second, kills the Baneblade. It hits the hull square, under the throat of the turret, and the tank ruptures and explodes. For a millisecond, it resembles one of the wood-and-canvas vehicle dummies, little more than covered frame tents, are used in basic training exercises by the Army. It looks like a tank dummy where the wind has got up under the hem of the cover tarp and billowed it out off the underframe, lifting it, twisting the painted outline and edges.

Then the internal blast comes, sudden and bright, and hot and vast, and the twisted outline of the tank vanishes, atomised.

Two Shadowsword tanks plough out of the fog, roiling it around their cobalt-blue hulls.

Cobalt-blue. *Cobalt-blue*, wearing the white and gold heraldry of the Ultima.

Land Raiders and Rhinos churn through after them, then a trio of Whirlwinds, and a walking line of Ultramarines, forty bodies wide. They fire as they advance on the Word Bearers positions from the north, passing the smoking crater-grave of the Baneblade. Two or three bikes and speeders scoot after the massive battle tanks, romping over the churned-up ground.

The brotherhood formations at the head of the bridge baulk, under fire from a new angle. Hundreds are slaughtered where they stand. Some leap into the corpse-choked ditch to evade the hammering fire of Land Raiders. The Shadowswords are already firing into the fog, targeting high-value Word Bearers assets hidden from the palace by the haze. Their main guns screech out columns of energy that cook through the mist vapour. Objects in the blanket of fog explode. Flames gust high into the air over the mist cover. The smell in the air changes, like the turn from summer to autumn. New energies, new machines, new chemical interactions.

Full-scale battle is joined. For the first time since the attack on the palace began, the Word Bearers force is thrown into a defensive mode, prosecuted hard by an unexpected, mobile foe.

The cultist warriors break. Their chanting stops. Behind the first walking line of Ultramarines is a second, and a third. Their gold and blue armour is slightly dulled by the atmospheric conditions, but still it gleams. Salvation never looked so splendid. Death never looked so noble.

The cultists begin to flee. They run south down the earthwork, or flee into the mist. Those trying to follow the earthwork line, picking their way, scrambling, draw fire from the wall. Sparzi's troopers and Arook's skitarii lace them with opportunist weapons-fire, dropping them like sticks. Some turn back, and then turn back again, pinned and bracketed by gunfire that creeps in and slays them. Bodies slither and tumble into the death-pit of the ditch.

Ventanus sends an order to the colonel to suspend artillery. He wants to ensure the counter-strike has an unimpeded run into the enemy formation.

'Captain Sydance,' says Selaton, noting a standard and pointing.

'The 4th,' Ventanus agrees. He is surprised by the level of emotion he registers. It's not just relief from the physical hazard. It's honest pride of association. His company. *His* company.

It's a heterogeneous mix, in all truth. Sydance has composed his battlelines out of men from several XIII Legion companies. All of them were assembled at the Erud muster. He's patched holes and losses in the 4th Company structure with reinforcements from other broken units. One of the Shadowswords is an 8th Company asset, two of the Land Raiders are from 3rd. Ventanus notes the battle colours of Captain Lorchas, the second officer of the 9th.

The palace defenders watch whatever is visible. Most of the fighting boils back into the fog. Long-range armour duels rip through the cloudy murk. Nearer at hand, the Ultramarines finally dismember the last of the cult resistance, and engage in vicious close-quarter melee with the warriors of the XVII.

To their credit, the Word Bearers do not break like their chanting followers. They have significant numbers – a two- or three-company strength, by Ventanus's estimate – and even caught out of position and by surprise, they dig in. From the savagery of Sydance's assault, 4th Company and its reinforcing elements have seen too much already today to think about quarter. Ventanus wonders – dreads – what they might have witnessed and experienced out at Erud Station as the main part of the treachery broke. Did the Word Bearers encamped alongside the Ultramarines zones just turn? Did they simply rise and draw their weapons, and begin killing, without notice or warning?

He is sure they did. Ventanus is sure the Word Bearers have nothing but the absolute extermination of the XIII as an objective.

You do not just *kill* the Ultramarines Legion.

Lorgar's barbarians would not have risked a fair fight. They would have gathered every advantage that surprise, deceit and entrapment could offer. They would have wanted to blitz and kill their enemy, kill him before he even realised he *was* an enemy.

It did not work. It *did not work*. The XIII has been hurt. The last ten hours on Calth might even have mortally wounded the Legion to such an extent that it will never fully recover, and, as a consequence, will always be a weaker, smaller fighting force.

But the Word Bearers did not make the clean kill they intended. They fumbled it, or they underestimated the effort required. They made a bloody mess, and left a wounded foe that could still move and fight; a wounded, mangled foe that was fuelled by pain and hatred and vengeance, and by the bright shock of moral outrage.

Always make sure your enemy is dead.

If you must fight an Ultramarine, pray you kill him. If he is still alive, then *you* are dead.

You are dead, Lorgar. You are *dead*. *You are dead*.

'Did you say something?' Arook says to Ventanus.

Ventanus wonders if he did.

'No,' he replies. He unbuckles his helm, removes it, and wipes a smear of blood off the pitted, chipped visor. Much of the cobalt-blue paint has been scratched or spalled off. Arook Serotid, similarly, is covered in metal scrapes and dents, his ornate golden armour battered and streaked with blood and oil.

Around them, wounded, weary, filthy men gather to watch the brutal fighting on the far side of the earthwork. Army, Ultramarine and skitarii alike stand together, weapons lowered. Residue smoke coils under the chewed-up arch of the gate. Broken pieces of stone slither down from the wall, some of it jarred loose by the earth-trembling assault of the armoured vehicles. The precious few medical personnel among Ventanus's force take advantage of the suspended fire to move up and tend the injured and dying. Virtually every single one of the palace defenders has taken an injury of some kind. There are nothing like enough dressings or drugs to go around.

'Why the code?' asks Arook.

'What?'

'The number of the painted eldar?'

'The war against Jielthwa Craftworld,' Ventanus replies quietly. 'Eight years ago. Sydance had the main assault. A privilege. During the charge, he was briefly cut off and made a personal stand, taking on a dozen eldar warriors. It was an outstanding achievement. He was decorated for it. I arrived to relieve him just as the fight was ending, and he was finishing his last opponent.'

Ventanus glances at the skitarii master.

'The primarch decorated him for twelve kills in one accelerated bout of combat. Twelve of the painted eldar. But there were thirteen eldar dead on the hall floor when I reached him. I came in firing, anxious for his welfare. It is a high probability that my shots, loosed into the smoke, killed the thirteenth. So it is a standing joke between us. He famously slew twelve and was decorated for it. I slew one. But that one may have been crucial. It might have been the one who, at last, overcame him. Sydance might have died at the hands of the thirteenth, and never lived to celebrate his glory and prowess. So which was more important, his twelve or my one?'

Arook stares at him.

'This is the sort of thing you joke about?' he asks. 'This passes for humour among your kind?'

'I thought you might understand,' says Ventanus, shaking his head. 'Most humans would not.'

Arook shrugs his mighty shoulders.

'I suppose I do. We skitarii enjoy similar boasts and rivalries. We just do it in binary and keep it to ourselves.'

The force of the armour battle has become so intense the field of fog west of the palace is rippling and churning like a troubled sea. Fierce beams of light flash and burn in the murk. A troop transport, hoisted by a considerable explosion, bursts out of the mist like a breaching cetacean. Debris and fragments shower off its burning carcass as it flops back into the vapour sea.

Closer at hand, at the edges of the mist, Ultramarines are locked in hand-to-hand fighting with Word Bearers. Loyal blue against traitor red. No quarter given or taken.

Ventanus reloads his boltgun, checks his sword, and gathers up the standard. Its haft is streaked with runs of blood, and badged with bloody palm prints.

'I'm rejoining the fight,' he tells Selaton. 'Secure the palace.'

He hears a buzz from beneath his left ear, and responds instinctively before he realises what it is.

'Ventanus? This is Sullus.'

'Sullus?'

'I'm in the palace sub-basement, Remus. She did it. The server did it. Vox-link is live. Repeat, vox-link is back and live.'

Ventanus acknowledges. He turns to Selaton and the other officers.

'Change of plan,' he says. 'I'm returning to the palace building. Hold the line, and let me know the moment the nature of the fight out there changes.'

He turns and begins to walk away, through the gate, across the cratered gardens, towards the battered facade of the summer palace.

Blue smoke wreathes the air, and there's a stink of fycelene from the artillery emplacements.

He has hope. For the first time since the day began, Ventanus has decent, proper hope in his heart.

* * *

[*mark: 10.40.21*]

VENTANUS ENTERS THE sub-basement. He can feel the soft heat of the working machines. Mechanicum magi stand around, observing, monitoring. A few work at exposed circuit integrators, making final adjustments.

Tawren stands in the stack room, connected to the chattering data-engine by an MIU umbilical. She looks serene.

She glances at him as he approaches, but is too busy reconfiguring a data-transfer structure in her head to speak.

Sullus glances at Ventanus.

'4th Company just relieved us,' Ventanus tells him.

'So she said,' Sullus replies, nodding towards the server. 'She's constructing a tactical overview. I don't understand the details, but I gather she's collecting and collating strategic data from every system and information source she can link to.'

'Across the planet? Orbital?' asks Ventanus.

'Not yet, captain,' says Cyramica, the server's aide. 'For now, it is just on a local, continental level. Because it was dormant and isolated, the data-engine was not infected with pernicious scrapcode. The server is extending her reach one step at a time, maintaining code-protected cordons, so that she does not contaminate herself by infected data-transfer. There is also some doubt that this engine will be powerful enough to coordinate a full, global noosphere.'

Ventanus nods. He appreciates the way the Mechanicum have of never sugar-coating any news.

'What about taking control of the planetary weapons grid?' asks Sullus.

'No,' replies Cyramica bluntly. 'The active grid is under enemy control, and it is infected with their invasive scrapcode. All the server can do is gather data in passive mode. The engine is not powerful enough to wrest grid control from the enemy-operated data-engines, and even if it were, such a process would require active MIU function, which would allow the scrapcode a viable cross-infection route. As was demonstrated today, we do not have a code-protection cordon or "killcode" powerful enough to eliminate and cleanse the scrapcode.'

'So Tawren's forced to remain passive?' asks Ventanus.

'To protect the integrity of what we have here,' says Cyramica.

'But she can assemble and compile tactical data for us?'

'Extensively. Her magi are already assembling the first databriefs.'

Ventanus looks at Sullus. 'She can prep us with material to formulate proper theoreticals. We can then use the vox to coordinate the practicals.'

'Any coordinated reprisal is going to be bloody welcome,' says Sydance, walking into the chamber. He wrenches off his blood-stained helm and grins at Ventanus. 'Thought you were dead, Remus,' he says.

'Hoped you might be,' Ventanus replies.

'Hope all you like,' says Sydance.

They embrace with a clatter of armour.

'There's always a thirteenth eldar, Lyros,' says Ventanus.

'Twelve, only ever twelve,' Sydance replies.

He breaks the bearhug and grins at Sullus.

'Good to see you standing, Teus,' he says.

'We march for Macragge,' Sullus replies stiffly.

'You march where the hell you like,' says Sydance. 'I'm marching straight for Lorgar's throat today. I've seen...'

He hesitates, and wrinkles his mouth in distaste.

'Men are dead and gone, brothers,' he says quietly, his smile behind a cloud. 'I'll spare you the list for now, but so many. Friends, warriors, heroes. The catalogue of the fallen will make you weep. Weep. The bastards slaughtered us. Unguarded. In our sleep. Surprise attack is an honourable tradition of war, but not from a supposed friend. Ah, I'm sure you saw plenty on your way from the port, Remus.'

'I did.'

'I will make an ocean of blood,' says Sydance. 'An ocean. I will soak the soil in the blood of these bastards. I will bleed them beyond the limits of their clotting factor. I will leave their heads on spikes.'

'Vengeance, yes,' Sullus nods. 'Quite. We should however formulate a solid theoretical.'

'Screw theoreticals!' Sydance growls. 'This is one occasion when we are excused our usual approach to war as a science. This is war as art. This is war as emotion.'

'Yes,' says Sullus. 'Let us paint our faces and charge the enemy guns. They only outnumber us four-fold, after all. The few of us that remain will die, but at least we'll have died expressing our anger. So that makes it all right.'

Sydance makes a contemptuous sound.

'I'm with Sydance,' says Ventanus, but quickly raises a warning finger before Sullus can object. 'With one caveat. Given our losses, given our enemy's numerical and technical superiority, I think our spirit, our rage for vengeance, our furious need for restitution... those things may be the only qualities that give us an advantage. They have made the mistake of hurting us instead of killing us. We are more dangerous. We will use the hurt.'

He looks at Sydance.

'But there is always a thirteenth eldar.'

Sydance laughs.

Sullus is unable to cover a tiny smile.

'We must cover our backs,' Ventanus says. 'We must channel our rage, and temper it with strategy. We must use every weapon: fury, vengeance, intelligence. Fury is our practical. Intelligence is our theoretical. Neither works alone. We would disgrace Guilliman in this hour if we forgot that. Information is victory.'

He turns to Cyramica.

'Please, inform the server I wish to begin vox transmissions. I need the best signal encryption she can give me, and any source modifiers. Anything she can do to disguise our position.'

Cyramica nods.

Flanked by Sydance and Sullus, Ventanus walks into the vox-caster room. He takes up the speaker horn.

9

IT'S DARKER ABOVE ground than beneath it.

The open air is a poison fog, and the dense blackness moves hard on a wind that pushes through the Ourosene Hills.

Brother Braellen doesn't believe it's a natural wind. A natural weather pattern. During a break in the gunfire, he heard Sergeant Domitian speculate that it was atmospheric displacement: major pressure and air patterns thrown into upheaval by orbital bombardment.

There's certainly a line of firestorm glow around the lip of the southern sky.

6th Company, supported by the Army and stragglers from two other Ultramarines companies at the Ourosene muster, has pulled back from the devastated ground camp areas, and taken up position defending the surface tower of one of the northern arcologies.

Braellen hasn't seen inside the arcologies, but he knows they are huge sub-ground complexes. Some of them are habs. This one, apparently. There are hundreds of thousands of citizen workers down there, and the 6th is the only thing stopping the enemy from getting at them.

The surface tower is a small fortress, a significant fortified structure that covers and defends the mouth of the arcology system. Its sublevels contain entrances to the main underground arterial, to walkways and cargo-freight systems, and even maglev rail lines, all feeding the huge subterranean complex.

The tower is a good place to make a stand.

The enemy has been coming up the pass all day. Brotherhood cultists at the fore, then Word Bearers, then armour. The cultists seem mindless, frenzied. They are drumming and chanting nonsense. Heedless of their own lives, they rush the walls and gates, and are cut down. Some are wired to explode, and detonate themselves against the walls in the hope of bringing them over.

Braellen is intrigued by their behaviour. The cultists seem willing and eager. That is clear from their chanting and drumming and mindless sacrifice. But it is a group mentality, a hysteria. He has observed Word Bearers at the back of the vast host spurring them on, driving them forward with pain and threats. They are enslaved killers, their hysteria enforced by cruel authority.

Perhaps they have been promised some redemption, some metaphysical reward for their bloody efforts. Perhaps they hope that if they survive devoted service, they might be freed.

Perhaps they know that refusing the XVII is a more unpleasant option.

A fresh wave comes at the tower. Captain Damocles has ordered that the Army provide fusillades for the instrumentation of each repulse. The legionaries must withhold, saving their more precious munitions for Legiones Astartes targets.

The link to the arcology is vital. Significant reserves of standard Army munitions can be raised from arcology silos to supply the human defenders. But the reserves of Legion-specific munitions, including ordnance for their fighting vehicles, is limited to the supplies carried by the battle-brothers, or retrieved from the muster camp before it was abandoned.

Every bolter round must count. Las-bolts and small-arms hard-rounds can be hosed at the waves of screaming knife brothers.

Legion weapons are withheld for more significant targets.

Those targets are coming. Apart from the Word Bearers, who are yet to commit in serious numbers, there are signs of major armour massing down the throat of the pass, perhaps even war-engines.

Braellen both understands and supports his commander's practical. Tempting though it is, the legionaries must wait until their abilities are the only ones that will do.

He doesn't understand the enemy.

What has transformed them so? What has turned them? They have all heard Domitian's stories about the old rivalry and the competition.

So what? Show him two Legions that *don't* compete for glory and distinction? The rebuke was just that: a rebuke for impoverished service and performance. And it was more than four decades ago!

What is this now? Are the Word Bearers and their demented master so addled that they can brood for forty years, and finally act with such disproportionate ignominy that the galaxy draws a gasp of surprise?

Braellen can tell that Captain Damocles is wounded by it. He has never seen him so driven or grim. It is the treachery more than the loss of life. The treachery has taken his breath away, and shaken his belief in the sanctity of the Imperial truth.

That's all before you even begin to consider the transformation of the Word Bearers: their altered schemes and heraldry, their expressed choice to decorate their armour with esoteric and frankly bizarre symbols and modifications. Their willingness to consort with super-stitious, heathen zealots.

Have they been consumed by some mass delusion of sorcery?

Or has something darker and more insidious got its poison into their veins and twisted their minds against their kin?

The next wave is coming. Braellen sees them running up the slopes, a mass of swirling black robes and brandished weapons. The knife brothers, thousands of them, stampede over the dead left by the last charge and roll like a river breaking its banks towards the gate and storm walls.

The Army – 19th Numinus, 21st Numinus, 6th Neride 'Westerners' and 2nd Erud Ultima – opens fire. Lasrifles volley, light support guns and crew-serveds chatter, grenade launchers clunk and pop. Heavier autocannon emplacements crank up, chewing into the moving lines.

Another slaughter. Black figures are mown down. Some explode in shooting fireballs as they die, slaying the men round them.

Braellen clutches his bolter, fighting back the urge to shoot.

'Captain! Captain!'

Sergeant Domitian moves through the back of the line. Men turn as he passes.

Domitian reaches Captain Damocles.

'Sir,' he says. 'The damn vox just lit.'

[mark: 11.10.13]

SERGEANT ANCHISE TURNS sharply.

'What did you say?' he asks.

They're on the fringes of Sharud Province, moving at best speed ahead of the conflagration that's consuming the forests. They are the pitiful remnants of the 111th and the 112th.

Anchise has taken command now that the company captains are gone. He's trying to rally something out of the men, but there's no time to stand still. Pursuit is right there, constantly pressing them: Titans, Titans of the traitor Mechanicum, plus heavy armour columns.

The Word Bearers are in the burning woods, and every kilometre further means greater losses inflicted.

Warhorns, deep, lingering, mournful, echo through the blackness of the forest, summoning the Ultramarines to their doom.

'We're detecting a sporadic pulse code on the vox, sir,' says Cantis, who's been carrying the only caster set they dragged out of Barrtor with them.

'Is it on the helm pick-ups?' Anchise asks.

'Too weak,' says Cantis. 'I really need to set this down, erect the portable mast.'

Anchise doesn't have to tell him why he can't. Three or four mass-reactive rounds spit through the canopy above them like game birds bolting for freedom, and punch into a mature quaren. The bole splinters in a spray of fire, and the head limbs of the tree come tearing down through the canopy spread in a blizzard of sparks.

'Move! Move it!' Anchise yells. Damn they're close! He can hear whirring, the chug of treads. That's a damn Whirlwind, or maybe one of the Sabre tank hunters.

There is simply no let up. They are going to be hounded until the last of them are dead.

Two Word Bearers rush the clearing. The trees are stark black, back-lit by fierce fires that have erupted close by. Anchise can smell woodsmoke, burning brush, sparks, the burnwash of explosives.

The first of the XVII brutes fires his storm bolter, and kills Brother Ferthun with a hit to the lower back that blows out his spine and hips. The other is hefting a lascannon. He braces it and lets rip, flattening trees and retreating Space Marines with bright spears of las-energy.

Anchise decides to face his death. He goes at them,

boltgun blasting in one fist, kinetic mace in the other. The mace belonged to his captain, Phrastorex. The captain never even got the chance to unlock it from its case this morning.

Anchise's bolts blow the face off the Word Bearer with the cannon. The visor of the man's helmet explodes, and he falls back, hard. The other clips Anchise on the shoulder, and then makes a cleaner hit to his left leg. The detonation of the mass-reactive shell hurls Anchise onto the loamy ground. Rolling, he swings the mace, and breaks both of the Word Bearer's legs. The warrior goes down. Anchise finishes the job with another mace swing.

His own leg is broken. He can feel the bone trying to reknit, but the damage may be too great.

He looks around in time to see that the other Word Bearer is not dead.

He's getting up. Anchise's shots shredded his helmet, his gorget and part of his upper chest plate. The Word Bearer's head and face are exposed.

It may just be injury: burns, contusions, swelling. The warrior has, of course, just taken substantial damage from a boltgun.

But the horror doesn't look like that to Anchise. The flesh is puffed taut, like the necrotised swelling of a venom bite. The mouth is misaligned, but it looks as though it has grown that way, not been brutally configured by kinetic shockwaves. Blood streams down the side of the Word Bearer's face and neck.

There are yellow scutes on his brow that look disturbingly like budding horns.

He throws himself at Anchise, a combat blade in his right hand. The dagger looks as though it's made of obsidian or polished black rock. Its grip is wound with fine chains. Is it some kind of trophy?

Anchise lapses to automatic practical, taking his foe on in basic, close-hand measures to stop the blade. He half-rises to meet the Word Bearer, turning his left palm out to run in past the lunging knife, and turn the right wrist and forearm away. Simultaneously, he brings his right forearm up as a crossed block against the enemy's face and chest.

Transhuman versus transhuman. It's about mass and speed and power, about the application of accelerated strength and enhanced reaction time. Anchise's hard block breaks the Word Bearer's cheek, his pass turning the knife aside. But the Word Bearer is strong, and driven by a murderous fury. He circles the blade, stabbing at Anchise's side and left arm. Anchise turns his right arm block into a jabbing punch, ramming his steel fist into the enemy's throat which has been exposed thanks to the damaged gorget. The impact crushes something in the Word Bearer's throat. His eyes bulge for a second, and blood jets from his mouth and nostrils. He attempts another savage stab, and the knifeblade scores Anchise's right forearm through armour, flesh and muscle to the very bone.

Anchise is not going to lose the advantage. He places a second punch into the throat, and then a third, higher, into the misshapen jaw.

The Word Bearer's head snaps back. Anchise feels rather than hears a sharp crack. He punches again to be sure. Then, as his foe drops, he wrenches the dagger out of his hand to make certain of things.

The hand that he uses to grasp it tingles. The wound made by the knife in his forearm throbs.

He freezes.

Something opens in his mind. Despite the burning forest around him, everything is very cold. There is a sterile blue light. Something pulses. Anchise can hear a deep, cosmic heartbeat. He can smell neurotoxin and molecular acid. He cannot see it, but he has a sense of something uncoiling, something vast, something black, something scaled and greasy, something coated in a heavy caul of grey mucus. He can feel it unwrapping, expanding out of a pit that's older than all the eons, moving up through the eternal darkness of Old Night and the interstellar gulf, moving towards the light of the burning forest. Moving towards him.

It can smell him. It can taste his pain. It can hear his thoughts.

Closer. Closer. Closer.

Anchise cries out and hurls the black glass dagger away. The door in his mind slams shut.

He is breathing hard, shaking. The wound in his arm will not stop bleeding.

He knows he needs the vox. It doesn't matter if they haven't got the time or opportunity to stop and set up. He needs the vox.

If someone's out there, if anyone's listening, they need to hear him. They need to know.

They need to know what they're facing.

[mark: 11.16.39]

ON. OFF.

On. *Off.*

On.

Maintain activation. Maintain. Wake.

Trapped and blind. Helpless. Deprived of consciousness for so long, he has lost all sense of when now is or what now is.

He knows fear.

He is Telemechrus.

He has been taught things, and one of them is to control his anger until it is needed. It is probably needed now.

He lets his go. He lets it replace the abomination fear.

He analyses. He scans. He determines.

His determination is this: he is still in his casket, and

his hibersystems have shut down. No, they have been interrupted. By a comm signal. An encrypted vox signal.

He was woken by an encrypted vox transmission that triggered an auto-response in his casket support system.

His casket is damaged. Telemechrus does not believe he can get out of it. He calls out, but there are no venerables around to counsel or help him.

There is no one around.

He will know no fear. He will know *no fear*.

His implant clock tells him that he has been dormant for a little over eleven hours. External sensors are down. He can't see. He can't open the casket. There is no noosphere. There is no data inload.

There is only the vox signal that woke him. He clings to that. He tries to decrypt it.

His inertial locators tell him that he is stationary. They record, eleven hours earlier, an extreme displacement followed by a kinetic trauma spike that was too intense to fully measure. He does not remember that. Hiberstasis must have shut him down before it happened.

Motion sensors light.

There is something close by. Something approaching his casket.

Friend or foe? He has no data. No means of determination. He cannot target. The casket is trapping him. He cannot even discharge his weapons while he is locked in the box.

Friend or foe?

Something strikes the outer shell of his casket and slices through the clamps. Something pulls the hatch open.

'Are you alive in there?' a voice asks.

Telemechrus suddenly gets optic feed input. Light. He can feel air flow against his skin, even though he has no skin.

The voice comes from the figure silhouetted against the light.

'Respond,' the voice says. 'Are you capable of activity, friend?'

Telemechrus tries to reply, but his voice does not work. There is a whirr. A whine. A dry gasp of sonics. He engages his cyberorganics, drives power to his articulated limbs, shakes off the tingling numbness of stasis, and levers himself forward.

Clumsy and inelegant, he clambers out of the casket. The figure moves back to let him out.

He steps out of the casket, crushing rock fragments and glass to powder beneath his feet. He feels sunlight on his face, though he has no face. He stretches out his ghost spine, stretches his remembered arms.

His weapon pods engage. Power couplings light up. Feeds flow live. He looks down at the figure who freed him.

'Thank. You. Lord,' he manages to say.

'You know me?' the warrior asks.

'Yes. Tetrarch. I. Identified. Your voice. Pattern.'

Eikos Lamiad nods.

'That's good. My face is not as recognisable as it once was.'

Telemechrus adjusts his optic feed and zooms in on the great tetrarch. Lamiad's visual profile does not match the one stored in Telemechrus's autostack memory.

Lamiad's glorious golden armour is dented and scorched. The famous porcelain half of his face is cracked and disfigured. The intricate mechanism of the left eye is ruined.

His left arm is missing from just above the elbow, leaving nothing but a buckled stump of armour, and a cluster of torn fibernetic cables, broken ceramite boneform, and frayed artificial muscles. With his right hand, Lamiad leans on his broadsword as though it were a walking staff.

'You. Are. Hurt. Lord Champion.'

'Nothing that can't be repaired,' replies Lamiad. 'Except, perhaps, my heart.'

'You. have. Sustained. Cardiac damage? Which. Vessel?'

'No, friend. I meant it metaphorically. Do you understand what's happened today?'

'No. Where. Am I?'

Lamiad turns and gestures. Telemechrus adjusts his optic scope and pans out, wide, tracking. A desert area. The sky is dark and mottled with heat-strong blotches. A heat-blotch in the near distance represents a building structure of significant size, which is on fire. More distant but perhaps larger heat-blotch/fires can be identified and plotted. The desert is littered with debris, much of it Legion materiel, much of it apparently destroyed by impact. Telemechrus tracks around. He scans his own casket, crumpled, half-buried in an impact crater. Smashed storage pods and equipment containers are scattered all around. There are two other caskets.

Telemechrus checks for a noospheric, but there is none. He cannot patch and configure a global position with any accuracy.

'You fell from a low orbit facility,' says Lamiad. 'Two of your kind fell at the same time, but their caskets were already damaged and they did not survive.'

Telemechrus zooms in on the half-open caskets beside his own.

'Oh,' he says.

'What is your name, friend?' asks Lamiad.

'Gabril. No. It is. Not. It is. Telemechrus. Lord.'

'Telemechrus, we have been attacked in the most underhand and cowardly fashion. The XVII Legion has turned on us. They have slaughtered us, crippled the fleet and the orbital facilities, and laid waste to vast tracts of Calth. We are close to defeat. We are close to death.'

'I have seen. Death, lord. We have both. Seen it. Come close to. Us and yet in neither. Case. Did it claim. Us.'

Lamiad listens. He nods slowly.

'I had not considered it that way. You are new-forged,

Telemechrus, but you already display the wisdom of a venerable. The techpriests selected you well for this honour.'

'I was. Told. It was. Because I. Was compatible. Lord.'

'I think that is so. And not just biologically. I was almost made like you, after Bathor. The Mechanicum of Konor blessed me with a more subtle rebuild. It is not, however, as robust.'

Lamiad glances down at his shattered arm-stub.

'Today, your Dreadnought build has allowed you to endure better than me.'

'Without you. Lord. I could not. Even. Have got. Out of. My. Box.'

Lamiad laughs.

'Please. Inload me. With full. Tactical,' says Telemechrus.'

'I was over there,' Lamiad says, pointing towards the burning buildings in the middle distance. 'The Holophusikon. That was supposed to be a commemoration of our future, Telemechrus. The orbital strike rained debris across this entire area. Large pieces. They struck the whole zone like a meteor storm.'

'I was. One. Of them.'

Lamiad nods.

'A whole ship came down over there,' he says. 'And that way, a section of orbital platform that struck like a rogue atomic. The Holophusikon took direct hits. There was no protection. I was hurt. Most others present were killed by the collision trauma, the shock concussion, and the subsequent fire.'

'That's Numinus City,' he says, pointing in another direction.

Telemechrus scans another vast heat-source. He compares the stored grid positions of the city and the Holophusikon, and calculates his position relative to them, to within two hundred metres.

'There is. No. Data,' says Telemechrus. 'There is. No. Central. Command.'

'There is not.'

'Have you. Determined. A theoretical. Lord?'

'I am trying to assemble whatever strengths I can salvage,' says Lamiad. 'Then I intend to take the war back against the traitors who did this.'

'What is. The strength. of your. Force. So far. Lord?'

'It's you, and it's me, Telemechrus.'

'Why?'

'Why what?' asks Lamiad.

'Why did. Our brothers. Turn. On. Us?'

'I have no idea, friend. I am almost afraid to know the answer. In that explanation, I fear, our future will burn again. Brother against brother. Legion versus Legion. A civil war, Telemechrus. It is the one blight the Imperium never even considered.'

'We shall. Know. No fear. Lord.'

Lamiad nods again.

'I. Await. Your. Orders. Lord.'

'The city,' says Lamiad. 'Numinus. If we must make anywhere our killing ground, it's there. That's where the enemy will be.'

'Yes.'

Lamiad turns.

'What. About the. Vox-signal, lord?'

'What vox-signal?'

'The. Encrypted. Signal.'

'My vox-link is smashed, Telemechrus. Tell me what signal you mean? Is someone out there? Is someone talking?'

[mark: 11.40.02]

THE ENORMOUS SECURITY hatches, twice the height of a legionary, hiss open, retracting into the armoured frame. Internal blast shutters, like nictitating eyelids, open in sequence after them.

The auxiliary bridge of the *Macragge's Honour* is revealed. One by one, starting from just inside the hatch to the right, and moving around the room, the consoles and bridge stations begin to light up, commencing automatic activation cycles. The auxiliary command has interlaced redundancy parameters. It will be, for now, clean of scrapcode. Cryptocept keys, reserved for only the most senior personnel, empower the auxiliary command to re-integrate with the flagship's primary service and control system, to purge and rewrite the command codes, and, if necessary, to assume control of the ship.

Shipmaster Zedoff had a key, and he's dead. Guilliman had one, and he is missing.

Marius Gage has the third.

He looks at Shipmaster Hommed and the two ranking functionary magi they have rescued during the fight downhull. Hommed is bruised, and his uniform is stiff with the blood of others. He only survived the death of his ship, the *Sanctity of Saramanth*, because his first officer bundled his unconscious form into an escape pod. He would have preferred to die with his ancient and honoured vessel.

Hommed also accepts that the duty thrust upon him now is as critical as it is unexpected. A qualified and experienced shipmaster must take Zedoff's place at the helm of the *Macragge's Honour*.

'Ready?' asks Gage. There's no room for 'if' in his question. He does not even allow for a theoretical where Hommed will decline the command. The Ultramar fleet is dying. Scattered across Calth nearspace, it is being hunted, hounded and picked off by the predator warships of the XVII and the unstoppable fury of the weapons grid. Something must be done. It may already be too late, but something must at least be attempted.

'I am ready, Chapter Master,' replied Hommed.

Flanked by Hommed, the magi and a gaggle of deck officers and command servitors, Gage crosses to the master console, and inserts the last cryptocept key. His authority is requested, taken by gene-scan and retina print, then verified by voice and pheromone. Hommed then steps forward, and allows his biometrics to be recorded, verified, and imprinted.

'Command is yours, shipmaster,' says a magos.

'Command accepted, with honour,' replies Hommed. 'Begin primary service and control system purge and rewrite. On three, two, one.'

'Purge under way, shipmaster.'

'Prepare override protocols,' says Hommed. He walks towards the strategium with rapidly mounting confidence, or at least the determination not to look like a fool. As he goes, he starts pointing left and right to direct his officers to their stations. They hurry to respond, strapping in or, in the case of magi and servitors, plugging up.

'Everybody to readiness,' says Hommed. 'All stations, all stations. I will be asserting override in three minutes, and I want every station to gather and present all and any data they can the moment we are live. Priority to drive, shields, weapons and sensors.'

'Strategium tactical externals are to be built and viewable within two minutes of re-start,' Gage adds.

'Let him call it,' Empion hisses to Gage. 'Hommed knows what he's doing. He needs to know that chair is his.'

'And I need to know what the battle looks like,' says Gage. What he doesn't say is, *I need to know if, by any miraculous chance, Guilliman is still alive.*

Thiel and the strikeforce watch proceedings from the hatchway, guarding against possible attack. It's a high theoretical that the Word Bearers have already boarded the flagship. Even with Hommed installed in command, the ship may not actually belong to them at all. Thiel itches to lead squads to the main airgates and the hangar decks.

They are the sites he would use to storm-board a ship.

'Override complete,' announces a magos.

'Auxiliary command is active,' calls a deck officer.

'I have control,' agrees Hommed.

Almost immediately, the newly-assigned Master of Vox calls out.

'Signal!' he cries. 'Encrypted signal from the surface!'

'The surface?' says Empion, amazed. 'But–'

Gage steps forward. He nods at the Master of Vox to activate full encrypt, and takes the speaker horn.

'This is Marius Gage,' he says. 'Who speaks for Calth?'

10

'VENTANUS OF THE 4th,' says Ventanus. 'Please stand by as we verify your code authority and identity.'

Ventanus lowers the speaker horn and waits until Cyramica relays a confirmation from the server.

'Ventanus again,' he says. 'It is good to hear your voice, Chapter Master.'

'And yours, Ventanus,' the reply crackles back, tonally altered by the signal encrypt. 'We were blind until a few moments ago. We thought the surface was dead.'

'Not quite, sir,' Ventanus replies, 'but I can't pretend the picture is good. Our losses have been severe. We have spent the hours since the attack trying to re-establish a vox-net and regain some data capacity. In the next few minutes, I will begin passing to you details of surviving surface strengths and their positions, as they come to me. We have the Mechanicum server here, and she is processing the inload for us.'

'Ventanus, can you restore the weapons grid?' the vox crackles. 'Is the server able to do that? The enemy has control of it, and is using it to obliterate the fleet. We cannot hope to achieve anything in the face of their grid control.'

'Stand by,' replies Ventanus. 'I believe the cogitation power of this data-engine is insufficient, but the server is examining the issue. I'm going to talk with her now. Data should be inloading to you. Captain Sydance will remain on the link for further voice contact.'

'Gage, acknowledged.'

Ventanus hands the speaker horn to Sydance and walks back into the stack room with Cyramica. There is a tranquil but dead look on Tawren's face, as if her body is empty, as if her mind has fled deep into remote sub-aetheric reaches and left the physical shell behind.

'Vox contact has now been made with sixty-seven survivor groups,' Cyramica tells him, 'including two engine squadrons in North Erud, an armour company near the Bay of Lisko, and the 14th Garnide Heavy Infantry, who survived virtually intact at a bunker complex in Sylator Province.'

'Keep compiling. The primarch will coordinate the active practical.'

'The Chapter Master responded from the flagship,' observes Cyramica. 'Not your primarch. Have you discussed the orbital losses yet?'

'What do you mean?'

'Orbital losses are extreme, and they are increasing every minute as the grid hunts new targets. Is your primarch still alive? Is an active practical even possible?'

Ventanus glares at her.

'Can I speak to the server?' he asks.

'She is in deep interface.'

'And I appreciate her efforts, but I need to talk to her.'

Cyramica nods. She issues a gentle binaric signal.

Tawren opens her eyes.

'Captain,' she nods, an underlying, tremulous carrier signal clicking along behind her voice.

'Our priority is the weapons grid, server. What progress have you made?'

'I can confirm,' she says calmly, 'that this engine is

not capable of either overriding control of the grid, or of managing the grid's operation after an override. It is simply not powerful enough.'

'Is there an alternative?'

'I am attempting to decide that,' she replies. 'So far there does not appear to be a single, functioning data-engine on Calth rated sufficient for the job that is not also infected with the enemy scrapcode. For a definitive answer, however, you must wait until my final determination.'

'How long will that take?' asks Ventanus.

'I do not know, captain,' she replies.

Ventanus hears footsteps behind him, and looks around.

Selaton stands in the doorway.

'You'd better come, sir,' he says.

Ventanus nods.

'Inform me the moment you have an answer,' he says to Tawren, and exits.

Tawren drifts back into the dataverse. Her serenity is practised and deliberate. A server can manage far greater degrees of data manipulation whilst in a calm state of mind. In truth, she is fighting a core of anxiety.

With the data-engine active, she can see it all. Or, at least, she can see more of the situation's totality than anyone except the enemy. She can see the truly frightening scale of the losses: the death toll, the crippling injury to the XIII Legion, the burning cities, the slaughtered populations, the devastated geography and the systematic annihilation of the fleet. Under any other circumstances, Calth would be considered a loss, and the battle a defeat.

The Ultramarines' characteristic determination is the only thing keeping them going: their fearless resolve to devise a new practical, to circumvent and outplay even hopeless odds.

These are worse than hopeless odds. Tawren can see

that. She has a simultaneous dataview of the globe, and she can see that even the surviving loyalist forces are hard-pressed and dying, cornered, fighting off attack from all sides, slowly facing elimination. They are too scattered and too isolated. The enemy has superiority in every way.

This is extinction. The grid might have made a difference, but there is no way of accessing or controlling it.

This is extinction. This is the death of Calth. This is the end of the XIII Legion.

[mark: 12.07.21]

'I THOUGHT YOU needed to see this,' says Selaton. He leads Ventanus outside, onto the cratered lawns of the palace.

'A prisoner?' Ventanus asks dubiously.

Most of the enemy fled after the 4th ripped into them. Many stood their ground and fought to the death. But this one has accepted capture.

He is standing on the lawn by the broken fountain, guarded by four Ultramarines.

Ventanus leaves Selaton to his duties and approaches the Word Bearer. The warrior's armour is dented and bloody. His face is smeared with gore. He looks at Ventanus, and almost seems to smile.

'Name,' says Ventanus.

'Morpal Cxir,' replies the Word Bearer.

One of the guarding Ultramarines shows Ventanus the weapons that the Word Bearer was carrying when he was captured. A broken boltgun. A large dagger made of black metal with a wire-wound handle. The dagger is curious. It looks ritualistic and ceremonial: less of a weapon and more a totem of status.

'Were you the ranking officer?' Ventanus asks.

'I was in command,' Cxir admits.

'Any reason I shouldn't just kill you, you bastard?'
Ventanus asks.

'Because you still live by a code. Your Imperial truth.
Your honour. Your ethics.'

'All of which you have forgotten.'

'All of which we have specifically renounced,' Cxir
corrects.

'This is the old enmity?' asks Ventanus.

Cxir laughs.

'How typically arrogant! How characteristic of the
Ultramar mindset. Yes, we slaked our dislike of you
today. But that is not why we attacked Calth.'

'Why then?' asks Ventanus.

'The galaxy is at war,' replies Cxir. 'A war against the
False Emperor. We follow Horus.'

Ventanus doesn't answer. It makes no sense, but the
apparent senselessness must at least be set in the context
of the day's unimaginable events. He takes another look
at the ritual knife. It is ugly. Its shape and design make
him uncomfortable. He believes that the brotherhood
cultists were carrying similar weapons. He slides it into
his belt. He will show it to the server. Perhaps the data-
engine can provide some illuminating information.

'So the galaxy is at war?' he asks.

'Yes.'

'A civil war?'

'*The* civil war,' replies Cxir, as though proud of it.

'Warmaster Horus has turned against the Emperor?'

Cxir nods.

'News takes time to travel,' he says convivially. 'You
will hear of it soon enough. Except *you* won't. None of
you. None of the XIII. Accept the fact that you have just
hours to live.'

'If you allowed yourself to become a captive just so
you could try to threaten us,' says Sullus, walking up to
join them, 'then you are a fool.'

'I am not here to threaten you,' says Cxir. 'I would have

preferred to have died, but I have a duty as commander. A duty to offer you terms.'

Sullus draws his sword.

'Give me permission to silence this traitor,' he says.

'Wait,' replies Ventanus. He looks at the Word Bearer. Cxir's expression is scornful and confident.

'He knows we won't hurt him while he is a captive, Sullus,' Ventanus says. 'He has mocked us for it. He has mocked our civilised code and our principles. He taunts us for having humanitarian ethics. If that's the worst thing he can say, let him.'

Sullus growls.

'Seriously, Teus,' says Ventanus, 'he thinks *that's* an insult? That we have moral standards and he does not?'

Cxir looks Ventanus in the eyes.

'Your ethical stance is admirable, captain,' he says. 'Do not misunderstand me. We of the XVII admire you. We always have. There is much to be admired about the august Ultramarines. Your resolve. Your sense of duty. Your loyalty, especially. These comments are not intended to appear snide, captain. I am being genuine. What you stand for and represent is anathema to us, and we have taken arms against it. We will not rest until it is dead and overthrown. That does not prevent us, all the while, from admiring the strength with which you champion it.'

Cxir looks from Ventanus to Sullus and then back again.

'You were everything we could not be,' he says. 'Then the truth was revealed to us. The Primordial Truth. And we realised that you were everything we *should* not be.'

'His jabbering bores me,' Sullus says to Ventanus.

'You are creatures of honour and reason,' says Cxir. 'You understand terms. That is why I refrained from seizing a death I was happy to embrace, and undertook this humiliation. I have come to offer you terms.'

'You have one minute to express them,' says Ventanus.

'In failing to take the palace and destroy you,' Cxir begins, 'I have disappointed my field commander. Leptius Numinus was identified as a primary target. Do you understand what I'm saying, captain? Just because you've defeated my force, it will not prevent others from coming. At the time of my capture, Commander Foedral Fell was advancing on Leptius with his battlehost. They can't be long away. Fell will crush you. You barely broke my force. His is twenty times the size. And he is not a creature of honour, captain, not as you understand the principle. Surrender now. Surrender to me, and I will vouch on your behalf. You, your forces here, their lives will be spared.'

'Spared for what?' asks Sullus. 'A life spared under those terms is not a life I'd care for.'

Cxir nods.

'I understand. I anticipated as much. There can be no rapprochement between us. We have waded into blood too far.'

'Then what did you expect?' asked Ventanus. 'That we would surrender to you? Side with you, with the XVII, with – if what you say is true – Horus? Against Terra?'

'Of course not,' replies Cxir. 'But I did, perhaps, expect that you might at least listen to our truth. It is not what you think, captain. It is beautiful. Your understanding of the galaxy will change. A paradigm shift. You will wonder why you ever thought the things you think. You will wonder how and why they ever made any sense.'

'Cxir,' says Ventanus. 'I have listened to your terms, and I have heard your offer. I formally reject both.'

'But you will die,' says Cxir.

'Everyone dies,' replies Ventanus, turning away.

'It will not be a good death,' Cxir calls after him. 'There will be no glory in it. It will be a sad and miserable end.'

'Even in glory, death is miserable,' Ventanus replies.

'Fell will punish you! He will punish you in unimaginable ways! He will trample your flesh into the earth!'

'Ignore him,' Ventanus says to Sullus.

'Just like we did to your primarch!' Cxir yells. 'We will cut you and bleed you and kill you, like we cut and bled him! He begged for death in the end. Pleaded for it! Begged us like a coward! He wept! He pleaded for us to finish him. To end his pain! We just laughed and pissed on his heart because we knew he was afraid.'

Ventanus can't stop him. Sullus moves like a blur. Cxir's torso is slashed open from the left hip to the throat in one ripping cut. The end of Sullus's sword embeds itself in the underside of Cxir's jaw.

Blood pours out of the Word Bearer. He sways. Black blood floods from the wound, down his legs, back down the wedged blade and up Sullus's arm. It streams from Cxir's mouth. His mouth is half-open. Ventanus can see the fine steel edge of the sword blade running between two of the lower teeth.

Cxir is laughing.

He murmurs something, choking on blood, gagged by the sword.

Ventanus pushes Sullus away and grasps the sword to wrench it out and deliver the mercy of a quick kill.

'Finally,' Cxir gurgles. 'I w-wondered w-what it w-would take... I knew o-one of you would have the balls...'

He begins to collapse, dropping to his knees before Ventanus can withdraw the sword. The blood pools around him on the dry earth, rolling out like a purple mirror in all directions. The four Ultramarines guards step back in quiet disapproval. Sullus is staring, cursing himself for letting his anger out.

Something else is being let out, too.

Cxir is laughing. The laughter throbs tidal surges of blood out of his mouth. It is thick. There are clots in it. Shreds of tissue. The laughter is a gurgle, like a blocked storm drain.

Cxir divides along the line of the sword wound. He

splits from the hip to the throat. Then his skull parts too in a vertical line, like a pea-pod dividing. Flesh tears and shreds apart like fibrous matter. The sword, unseated, falls onto the bloody earth.

Cxir is on his knees, opened from the waist like a bloody flower. He is still, somehow, laughing.

Then he turns inside out.

Ventanus, Sullus and the guards recoil in dismay. Blood spatters them. Cxir's backbone sprouts like a calcified tree trunk, growing weird branches that look as if they are composed of arm bones. His ribcage opens like skeletal wings. His organs pulse and grow, smearing tissue and sinew across the reshaping skeleton.

Cxir becomes a vessel. Whatever is hidden inside him, whatever is germinating and shooting through him from the warp, is much much bigger than his physical form could have contained.

Sprouting limbs turn black and scaly. They grow bristles and thorns. They stretch out like the legs of a giant arachnid. Scorpion tails twist and thrash like a nightmare wreath as they grow out of the open ribs. Stings glitter like knives.

Cxir's new head buds and unfolds, slowly turning up from a bowed stance. Mouthparts chatter. Huge multifaceted eyes twinkle and glitter, iridescent. Horns sprout from the cranium; the huge, upright horns of some ancient Aegean bull-daemon.

Cxir is still laughing, but it's not Cxir any more.

The air is full of blowflies, like a storm of buzzing ash.

'Samus,' laughs Cxir. 'Samus is here!'

USHKUL//THU

'In the End Phase of any combat, or at any point after the Decisive Strike has been accomplished, loss must be recognised. This is often the hardest lesson for a warrior to learn. It is seldom written about, and it is not valued or defined. You must understand when you have lost. Perceiving this state is as important as accomplishing victory. Once you appreciate that you have, by any theoretical measure, been defeated, you can decide what practical outcome you can best afford. You may, for example, choose to withdraw, thus preserving force strength and materiels that would otherwise be wasted. You may choose to surrender, if anything may be accomplished by the continuation of your life, even in captivity. You may choose to expend your last efforts doing as much punitive damage to the victor as possible, to weaken him for other adversaries. You may choose to die. The manner in which a warrior deals with defeat is a truer mark of his mettle than his comportment in victory.'

– Guilliman, *Notes Towards Martial Codification*, 26.16.*xxxv*

1

'WHO IS... SAMUS?' asks the Master of Vox. Then he flinches, and pulls his headset away from his ears.

'Report!' snaps Gage.

'Sudden and chronic interrupt, sir,' says the Master of Vox, working his console deftly to reconnect. 'Interference patterns. It sounded like huge storm-pattern distortion, as if bad weather had closed in on the Leptius Numinus area.'

'Have you lost vox?' asks Gage.

'Vox-link with Leptius Numinus is suspended,' the Master of Vox reports.

'The datalink is still active, however,' says the magos at the next station. 'Information is still being processed and relayed by the palace's data-engine.'

'Restore that link,' Gage says to the Master of Vox.

Gage crosses to the strategium where Shipmaster Hommed and his officers are examining the rapidly building tactical plot. It is a three-dimensional hololithic representation of Calth and its nearspace regions.

The story it tells is a bitter one.

Virtually all the orbital yards are gone, or so damaged

323

that they will need to be destroyed and replaced rather than rebuilt. XVII fleet formations are bombarding the southern hemisphere of Calth. The rest of the fleet has established a clear orbital superiority position.

The Ultramar fleet is scattered. It has been reduced to about a fifth of its original strength. Those vessels remaining are either fleeing to the far side of the local star to avoid fleet attack or the inexorable fire of the weapons grid or, like the *Macragge's Honour*, they are lying helpless and drifting in the high anchor zone.

There's virtually nothing left to fight with. They are done. It is over. It is simply a matter of the Word Bearers picking off the last few fighting ships of the XIII fleet.

The weapons grid seems to be having no difficulty doing that. It has destroyed the local forge world, a small moon with offensive capabilities, a starfort near the system's Mandeville Point, and several capital ships.

'We have sensors,' says the shipmaster, 'and power is coming to yield. I anticipate capacity for weapons or drive in fifteen minutes. Not both.'

'What about shields?' asks Gage.

'It seemed to me that weapons or drive were greater priorities.'

Gage nods. The theoretical is sound. There are three Word Bearers cruisers effectively docked to the flagship. The weapons grid will not fire at the *Macragge's Honour* while they are so close. The cruisers will not fire, because they would have done so by now. They have come in close to begin boarding actions.

The enemy wants the flagship intact.

Gage sees the pattern. For a moment, he couldn't understand why, of the surviving Ultramarines vessels, many were the largest and most powerful capital ships. Surely an adversary with control of the weapons grid would pick off the most serious threats first?

The ships that have been spared are all helpless and drifting, like the *Macragge's Honour*. The moment they shake off the effects of the scrapcode or the electromagnetic pulse, and move, or raise shields, the grid destroys them.

The Word Bearers intend to take as many of his Legion's capital ships intact as they can. They want to bolster their fleet with warships. They want to build their strike power.

They want to turn Ultramarines ships *against* the Imperium.

What was that nonsense Lorgar was ranting at the end? Horus turning? A civil war? He was demented and, besides, it wasn't Lorgar. It was some xenos manipulation. It was some empyrean breach effect.

Gage knows he's lying to himself. Today has changed the shape of the galaxy in a way that the wildest theoretical could not have anticipated. He hopes he will not live to endure the new order.

However long the rest of his life turns out to be, he will not allow ships of Ultramar to be used against the Imperium.

He turns to Empion.

'Are your squads assembled?'

'They are,' says Empion.

'Mobilise,' orders Gage. 'Repel boarders. Find them and drive them off this ship.'

[mark: 12.20.59]

OLL PERSSON TELLS them to wait.

Smoke covers the river, covers the wharfs, covers the docks. Two container ships are on fire out in the estuary, making dancing yellow fuzzes in the stagnant fog. It's as if the whole world is reducing to a vaporous state.

He tells them to wait: Graft, Zybes, the two troopers and the silent girl. They take cover in a pilot's house overlooking the landing. They're all armed, except Graft

and the girl. She has still to speak a word or look anyone
in the eye.

Oll shoulders his rifle sling and finds a quiet spot in
one of the packing sheds. Back in the day, he'd often
come to Neride Point for the markets. There was always
a fresh catch coming in, even though the wharf spaces
were primarily industrial. Hundreds of boats would
bob along the jetties and landings, in between the bulk
containers.

It's all messed up now. More than one huge sea-surge
has swept boats into the streets and smashed them
against habs and factory structures. The streets are wet,
and covered with an ankle-deep litter of garbage and
debris. The water is worse. It's like brown oil, and there
are bodies floating in it, thousands of bodies, all choking
the landings and under the pier walks and bridges, gathered up by the prevailing currents like jettisoned trash.

The place smells of death. Waterlogged death.

Oll sits down and opens his old kitbag. He turns out
the few items he rescued from his bedroom and sorts
through them on the top of an old packing case.

There's a little tin, a tobacco tin for rough cut lho
leaf. He hasn't smoked in a long time, but several older
versions of him did. He pops the tin open, smells the
captured scent of lho, and tips the cloth bundle into his
palm. He opens it.

They are just as he remembered them. A little silver
compass and a jet pendulum. Well, they look like silver
and jet, and he's never corrected anyone who said that's
what they were. The jet stone is suspended on a very fine
silver chain. It's been years since he last used these objects
– Oll suspects it might be more than a hundred – but the
polished black orb on the end of the chain is warm.

The compass is fashioned in the form of a human
skull, a beautiful piece of metalwork no bigger than his
thumb. The cranium is slightly elongated, slightly longer
than standard human proportions, suggesting that it was

not actually a human skull that formed the model for the design. The skull, a box, opens along the jawline on minutely engineered hinges, so that the roof of the mouth is revealed as the dial of the compass. The markings on the compass rim are so small and intricate you'd need a watchmaker's loup to read them. Oll has one of those too.

The simple gold and black pointer spins fluidly as he moves the tiny instrument.

He sets it down, aligns it north. He watches the pointer twitch.

Oll takes a little clasp notebook out of his kit and opens it to a fresh page. Half the book is filled with old handwriting. He slides out the notebook's stylus, opens it, and writes down the date and the place.

It takes a few minutes. He suspends the pendulum over the compass on its silver chain and lets it swing. He repeats the process several times, noting down, in a neat column, the angles and directions of the spin and the twitches of the compass needle. He calculates and writes down the azimuth. Then he flips the pages of the notebook to the back, opens out a folded, yellow sheet of paper that has been glued into the back cover, and studies the chart. It was written on Terra, twenty-two thousand years earlier, a copy of a chart that had been drawn twenty-two thousand years before that. His handwriting was rather different in those days. The chart shows a wind rose of cardinal points. It is a piece of sublime mystery recorded in ink. Oll thinks of the two forces clashing on Calth and reflects that they are both right about one thing. It's the one thing they agree on. Words are power, some of them at least. Information is victory.

'Thrascias,' he says to himself. As he suspected, they're going to need a boat.

He packs his things away as carefully as he unwrapped them, preps his gun, and goes to find the others.

* * *

BALE RANE LOOKS dubiously at the skiff.

'Hurry up and get in,' says Oll.

The skiff's a fishing craft, good for a dozen people, with a small covered cabin and a long narrow hull.

'Where are we going?' asks Zybes.

'Away from here,' says Oll, lifting some of the boxes aboard. 'Far away. Thrascias.'

'What?' asks Zybes.

'North-north-west,' Oll corrects himself.

'Why?' asks Rane.

'It's where we have to go. Help me with the boxes.'

They've packed some canned food, some foil-wrapped ration packs, some medical supplies and some other essentials, looted from the pilot house. Krank and Graft have gone back down the landing to fill four big plastek drums with drinking water from the dockside tanks.

'Are we rowing?' asks Rane.

'No, it's got an engine. A little fusion plant. But it makes a noise, and there are times when we'll have to be quiet, so we're taking oars too.'

'I'm not rowing,' says Rane.

'I'm not asking you to, boy. That's why we brought Graft. He doesn't get tired.'

The boy, Rane, is getting fidgety. Oll can see it. They're all nervous. All except Katt, who's just sitting on a bollard, gazing at the bodies in the water. There's gunfire in the streets up in the Point, and the sound of tanks. Tanks and dogs.

Except Oll knows they're not dogs.

'Go help your friend with the water,' says Oll. He climbs aboard to check the electrics and tick the engine over.

Rane goes back up the landing towards the tanks. Gusting wind drives black smoke across the wharf, and it makes him cough.

He's not even thinking about Neve. Not at all.

She's just there, suddenly. Right there in front of him,

as though she stepped out of the smoke.

She smiles. She's never looked more beautiful to him.

'I've been looking for you, Bale,' she says. 'I thought I'd never see you again.'

He can't speak. He goes to her, his arms wide, eyes wet.

By the tanks, Krank looks up. He sees Rane, down the boardwalk. He sees what he's doing.

'Bale!' Krank screams. 'Bale, don't! Don't!'

He starts to run to help, but there are suddenly men in his way. Men on the jetty. Men looming out of the smoke. They are hard and dirty, dressed in black. They are scrawny, as if they're underfed. They have guns, rifles. They have knives made of black glass and dirty metal.

Krank's rifle is leaning against the tank. He backs away. There's no hope of him reaching it.

The knife brothers laugh at him.

'Kill him,' Criol Fowst tells the Ushmetar Kaul.

[mark: 12.39.22]

SUITS SEALED, KILL squad six exits the Port 86 airgate. Thiel has command. Empion has personally given him the responsibility, even though there are several captains among the assembled shipboard survivors who would have seen the duty as an honour.

Forty squads move through the hull of the *Macragge's Honour*. Forty kill squads, each of thirty men. They carry bolters and close-combat weapons. Three brothers in each squad lug mag-mines.

Thiel's squad emerges aft of one of the main port-side attitude thrusters. It's a giant, solid mass like the tower of a habitat block, mounting exhaust bells on each aspect that could form the domes of decent-sized temples.

Calth rises above the thruster assembly: bright plan-etrise above a haunted tower. Calth has the look of Old

Terra: green landmasses and blue seas, laced in white cloud.

But Thiel can see its terminal injuries, however. A spiral of soot-brown stormcloud caps part of the sphere, and other areas look like bruises on the skin of a fruit. The atmospheric discolorations are immense. Behind the curved shadow of the daylight terminator, sections of the southern continent are suffused with a luminous orange glitter, like the hot coals at the bottom of a furnace grate.

Mag-locks in his boots keep him on the hullskin. Advancing, he extends his view. He can see across Calth nearspace with extraordinary clarity. He can see the orbitals glowing with wildfire energy as they are consumed by conflagration. He can see the closest of the planet's natural satellites blackened and stippled with fire-spots.

Nearer at hand, there are ships. Thousands of ships. Ships on fire. Ships drifting, spilled and butchered, shredded and ruined; slow swarms of wreckage, silent clouds of glinting metal debris. Beams of energy lick and flicker through the void.

The starfield, the vast unending spread of the galaxy, looks down on it all, unengaged and unimpressed.

The starlight is cold. It is like a sharp, clear evening of tremendous luminosity. There is nothing to interrupt the cool blue-white brilliance of the Veridian sun. All shadows are hard-edged and deep. Around him, it is either painfully bright sunlight or pitch black shadow.

All legionaries are trained for hard-void and zero gravity combat. This is strictly neither. The flagship supplies a limited gravity source, and a skin of thin atmosphere – the atmospheric envelope – clings to the ship's hull, maintained by the gravitic field generators to facilitate the function of open launch hangars and docking bays.

There is, still, little sense of up or down. The landscape of the ship's port-side opens before them like a hive's skyline. It is a dense and complex architecture of pipes and towers, vents and arches, blocks and pylons. The scale is huge. The kill squad advances in giant bounds from one surface to the next, extending down the side of the ship as though they were acrobats moving across an urban sprawl from rooftop to rooftop.

The low gravity amplifies their strength. One firm step becomes a bound of ten metres. The practical takes a second to master, despite the hours of theoretical and drill. It is too easy to overstep, to push too hard, to fly too far. Across the wider gulfs, the ravines of the port-side cooling vents and the immense canyons of the interdeck crenellations, members of the kill squad switch to quick burns of their void-harnesses, clearing the divides of adamantium and steel chasms.

The Word Bearers cruiser *Liber Colchis*, a vast scarlet beast, has clamped itself to the aft port-side of the *Macragge's Honour* like a blood-sucking parasite. The hullspace between the two ships is solid black, all light from the star blocked.

There are, however, lights within the blackness. Advancing with his team, Thiel resolves the spark and glow of cutting tools and clamped floodlights. Evac-ready squads of Word Bearers are surgically opening the flagship's hull in order to attach bulk airgates and allow their storm forces to cross directly.

Kill squads Four and Eight are supposed to be arriving from other evac points to combine against this invasion, but Thiel sees no sign of them. How long should he give them? In Thiel's opinion, the threat of boarding has remained unaddressed for far too long.

He glances at Anteros, his second in command.

He makes the signal.

They go in.

They hard-burn with their void-harnesses, following the wide canyon of a brightly lit heat exchange channel, and passing under the stark shadow of a power coupling the size of a suspension bridge. Their tiny black shadows chase them along the hull.

One half of their target group stands on the flagship's hull itself. The other half stands on the side of a docking tower at ninety degrees to the rest. Melta-tools are being used on the hull plates. Bulk cutting heads are being extended from the open cargo hatches of the clamped cruiser. From Thiel's orientation, the cruiser is above them, and the extended cutters are hanging down from it, biting into the flagship's hull. Plumes of white-hot sparks are sheeting off the cutting heads into the darkness.

Thiel fires his boltgun, and the shells burn away ahead of him on trembling blow-torch tails. There is no sound. They explode the chest plate of a Word Bearer who was standing guard on a heat exchange port but looking the wrong way. His torso erupts in a ball of flame, expanding shrapnel and globules of blood. The impact convulses him, and sends him tumbling backwards, end over end. Thiel streaks past the spinning corpse, firing again. His third shot misses, gouging a silent crater in the hull. His fourth takes the face off a Word Bearer, turning him hard in a spray of flame and sparks. Blood balloons out from his ruined skull, wobbling and squirming in the near-void.

The rest of the kill squad fires. They streak across the target area like a strafing pack of Thunderbolts, and Word Bearers die as the bolter fire drums across them and punches through them. Bodies tumble and bounce. Some disintegrate, releasing clouds of blood beads that ripple like mercury. One Word Bearer is hit with such force his body flies away at great speed, dwindling as it leaves the flagship behind. Another is hit by a blast that causes his own void-harness to malfunction, and he lofts on a fork of fire, colliding brutally with the armoured hull of the cruiser above them.

Four Word Bearers die without breaking the magnetic anchor lock of their boots, and they simply remain standing on the hull, arms limp, like statues, or like bodies sunk to a seabed with their feet weighted.

The environment is full of drifting, swirling blood masses. They splash against Thiel, burst into smaller blood beads, slicking across his armour. For one second, his visor is awash and visibility is lost.

He brakes hard, jets back, makes a landing.

He clears his vision in time to see a Word Bearer bounding at him across the hull. They are both on the side of the docking tower, their 'ground' at ninety degrees to the level of the ship. The Word Bearer's motion, assisted by the light gravity, seems exaggerated, almost comical. He fires his weapon. A bolt burns past Thiel. Thiel fires back. Silent, streaming shots blow the enemy's right leg off and shred both of his shoulder guards. The impacts immediately and violently alter his course, turning his forward leap into a severe backwards tumble and spin. He cannons off a thruster mount and rebounds at a different angle.

Thiel turns. He barely avoids a power axe that slices out of the darkness. He kills the wielder with a single shot that smacks the figure backwards out of shadow into light. But there are two more. Both come at him with cutting tools: a particle torch, fizzing hot, and a power cutter. The Word Bearers bound at him, in big, slow leaps.

Thiel carries his electromagnetic longsword. He draws it from the scabbard, and puts two bolter rounds into the chest of the Word Bearer with the cutter, creating a shoal of dancing blood beads. Then he meets the torch as it flares at him.

It can slice through void hulls. It can certainly slice through him.

Thiel uses the reach and sharpness of the longsword to maximum effect. He cuts through the torch fairing, and the arm holding it. Blood spills out of the severed arm, and energy roasts out of the ruptured torch. Caught in the ball of white fire, the Word Bearer struggles backwards, thrashing, melting, incinerating. Thiel risks one hard kick to the enemy's chest to launch him clear. Immolating, too bright to look at, the Word Bearer rotates as he falls away. The unleashed energy reaches the torch's power cell, and ignites it. Blast-shock and light, both silent, surge up the docking tower, channelled by the hull. The fireball hits the skin of the cruiser, and ripples outwards, exhausting its fury.

Thiel is rocked back. His armour sensors white-out for a second, and he gets a burst of static and crackle.

He tries to lock down on the hull, to re-anchor.

The blast light fades. He makes a swift assessment of the combat. He's lost two men, so far as he can see, but the Word Bearers force has been crippled. There are drifting, broken bodies all around him, surrounded by a sea of quivering, non-symmetrical blood droplets. There is still, however, no sign of the other kill squads.

Thiel jets down to the bulk cutting heads. They are huge instruments, each one bigger than a Rhino, extended on titanic articulated servo arms from the interior of the enemy cruiser. Thiel signals to Bormarus, who is one of the men assigned to carry the mag-mines. They start to clamp them onto the first of the cutting heads. Thiel leaves Bormarus working, and jets up the servo arm to a control platform mounted halfway up. If he can retract the mechanism into the enemy ship...

Like a comet shower, mass-reactive shells blizzard down around him. Some hit the platform and the guard rail, exploding with bright flashes. The deluge of fire is immense. In what is, to him, below, half a dozen of his men die, cut down. Blue-armoured bodies start to drift alongside the red-armoured ones. All the gleaming, trembling blood beads are the same colour.

He looks 'up'.

His kill squad's strike has not gone unnoticed. A main force of Word Bearers are making evac from the open cargo hatches of the cruiser. They emerge firing, their own void-harnesses flaring.

Thiel and his men are outnumbered eight to one.

[mark: 12.40.22]

OLL PERSSON STEPS off the skiff onto the landing. He's got his lasrifle.

One flick of his calloused right thumb flips off the safety and arms the gun. Oll's not even looking at the weapon. He's looking straight ahead, looking up the length of the landing, looking at the figures gathered there. His face is set grim. It makes the care lines harder. His frown gives him a squint as though the sun is out and it's too bright.

He doesn't hesitate. One pace, two, and then he's jogging, then running, running straight up the landing, bringing the armed rifle up to his shoulder, pushing it into his cheek, taking aim as he runs.

Shot one. A knife brother, in the spine between the shoulder blades, just before he stabs the screaming Krank in the neck. Shots two and three. A knife brother, in the face, the man pinning Krank down. Shot four. A knife brother, in the lower jaw as he turns, knocking him backwards into the water. Shots five, six and seven. Two knife brothers turning with their rifles, the trio grouping punching through both of them.

Two more start firing back down the landing stage.

Shot eight. One of the shooters, wings him. Shot nine. Kills him. Shot ten. The other shooter, top of the head.

Shot eleven. Misfire. Clip's out. He's been shooting a lot today. Ejects, still running up the landing, drops the empty cell *thump* onto the decking. Slams home the fresh one.

He reaches them, he's in amongst them. Close combat. Oll swings a block, smacks the gun stock into a face.

Trench war style, like they were taught all those years
ago in the mud outside... Verdun? Oh, for a bayonet!
The bare gunsnout will have to do. It cracks a forehead.

A sideways stamp breaks an ankle, another stock-
smash fractures a cheek. He blocks a knife-thrust with
the rifle like a quarterstaff, turning it aside. He shoots
again. Point blank. Through the sternum. Blood sprays
out the back.

Las shots rip past him in the dark. He doesn't flinch.
Four knife brothers are scrambling over the jetty-end
railings to join the fight, to get at him.

Oll turns, lasrifle at the hip, thumbs to full-auto. One
burst, muzzle-flash ripping like a strobe light.

There's a bone-crack behind him. Oll whips around. A
cultist he hadn't spotted is laid out in a spreading pool
of blood. Graft has punched him with one of his hoist
limbs.

'Thank you,' says Oll.

'He was going to hurt you, Trooper Persson.'

At times like this, Oll wishes he could have taught the
old work servitor to shoot.

At times like this...

How many times has he prayed there would never be
any more times like this? The sad truth of the matter,
there is only war. There's always another war to fight. Oll
knows this. He knows it better than just about anyone.

Maybe this is it. Maybe Grammaticus was right, for
once. Maybe this is the end war. Maybe this *will* be the
last fight.

Krank's trying to get up. He's shaken. Oll looks for
Rane. He sees the boy being dragged into the shadows
by something.

'It got him, it got him!' Krank is gabbling.

'It's all right,' Oll tells him, not looking at him, just
looking at Rane. 'Grab the water. Get to the skiff. We're
going.'

The boy might be dead. Might just be passed out. A

lasgun won't do any good now. The thing that's got him has stepped right out of the warp. Oll doesn't know what Rane or Krank are seeing. Probably something out of an illuminated bestiary. Oll sees it for what it is. Filthy matter, fused into a humanoid shape, clothed in the trappings of a nightmare. It's real enough, real enough to kill, but it's *not* real all the same. It's just a reflection in the energy of this world of something out in the Immaterium. Something hungry, and agitated, and impatient to get in.

Call it a daemon, if you like. Too specific a word, really, though maybe that's all that daemons are.

Oll glances down at the bodies he has killed, the ragged warriors in black. They knew about warpmagick. Not much, but enough to tinker with it. Enough to believe they'd found the unbearable truth. Enough to form a cult, a religion. Enough to lose their minds. Like the idiot Word Bearers. Warp-stuff is pernicious. Once you touch it, it sticks. Hard to ever get it off you again.

The black knives of their brotherhood. Ritual knives. Athames. He picks one up, the nearest, and wedges the pommel of it into his rifle's barrel. An improvised plug bayonet will do in a pinch. He managed well enough at Austerlitz.

Oll jams it in, then steps forward and rams the black blade into the thing pawing at Rane. Black light spurts in all directions. There is a stink of bad eggs and rotten meat, a cloud of smoke.

The daemon-thing screams like a woman, then dies, and the matter of it collapses into black slime. The stuff is all over Rane, and the boy is out cold. But he's still got a pulse.

Oll looks around. The girl, Katt, is standing behind him, staring at Rane.

'Give me a hand carrying him,' Oll says.

She doesn't say anything, but she takes hold of Rane's

feet. Zybes appears, fear in his eyes, and helps her with the boy.

Oll yanks what's left of the knife out of his gun, and tosses it into the soiled water. He touches the symbol at his throat, and murmurs a thanks to his god for deliverance. Adrenaline is spiking in his old limbs. He hates the rush, the burn of it. He thought he was past that nonsense.

He turns back to the skiff. The shooting will have attracted attention, but he reckons they've got time to pull clear and head out into the channel.

He sees the knife brother Graft felled. A commander, an officer, the leader of the pack. A *majir*. Face down. Blood everywhere from that head wound. There's a knife on the decking beside him, another athame.

But the leader's is a good one. A crafted one. A special one to mark his authority and significance. It's a finer thing than the crude ritual spikes the others are wielding, if something so inherently warped and evil can be said to be fine.

It may not be exactly what Oll's looking for, but it's the closest he's seen yet, and he'd be a fool to leave it.

He picks it up, wraps it in a rag, and stuffs it into his thigh pouch.

Three minutes later, the skiff engine rumbles into life, and the boat edges out into the dark water, away from the landing.

CRIOL FOWST SNAPS awake. He sits up, pulling his face off the cool, damp decking. There's blood everywhere, blood all over him. He fingers his scalp, and finds a patch of skull that hurts really badly and shouldn't be quite so mobile.

He is sick several times.

He knows something's been taken from him, something very special and precious, something given to him by Arune Xen. Fowst's future depended on it. He needed it to get all the power and the control he dreamed of possessing.

Someone's going to die for taking it.

No, *worse* than die.

[mark: 12.41.11]

MUFFLED POUNDING. As if his ears are blocked. As if everything's foggy. Like blood thumping in his temples.

A noise. A scratchy, reedy noise. It's a vox. The vox in his helmet. A transmission. What's it saying?

Ventanus tries to answer. His mouth is numb, slack. He's upside down. He can smell blood. It's his.

What is that transmission? What is the message? So tinny, so far away, so muffled.

He struggles to hear. It starts to get louder, louder, sweeping up through the layers that muffle it, like sound coming up through water, until it becomes clear and loud and comprehensible.

'Samus. That's the only name you'll hear. Samus. It means the end and the death. Samus. I am Samus. Samus is all around you. Samus is the man beside you. Samus will gnaw on your bones. Look out! Samus is here.'

'Who's talking? Who is this?' Ventanus stammers. 'Who's on this channel? Identify yourself!'

He is lying on the ground, on his back, on a slope of rubble and chewed-up lawn. He's in the grounds of the palace of Leptius Numinus.

He gets up. Two Ultramarines are dead nearby, one crushed, one torn in half.

Ventanus remembers. He remembers Cxir changing.

He looks around.

The daemon is huge. It's got immensely long arms, thin and bony, and it walks on them the way a bat uses its furled wings to walk. The twin horns on its head are immense.

It is attacking the palace. It is ripping the front walls down. The collapsing sections spew out in great, dust-thick torrents of stonework and plaster.

Battle-brothers and Army are retreating ahead of it, blasting up at it with everything they have: bolters, las, plasma, hard rounds. The shots pepper and puncture the thing's grotesque black bulk, but it doesn't seem to feel the damage inflicted. Ventanus can hear its voice in his ear, gabbling over the vox.

'Samus. It means the end and the death. Samus. I am Samus. Samus will gnaw on your bones. Look out! Samus is here.'

Ventanus sees Sullus. Sullus has picked up his sword, the sword he used on Cxir. Ventanus knows, he simply *knows*, that Sullus is trying to make amends for the evil his mistake has unleashed.

Sullus is rushing the daemon, hacking at it.

Ventanus moves forward. He starts to run.

'Sullus!' he yells.

Sullus isn't listening. He is covered in spatters of ichor, hacking at the thing's rancid flesh.

The daemon finally seems to notice the cobalt-blue figure chopping at the base of its backbone.

It steps on him.

Then it moves on, oblivious to the mass-reactives streaking into its flesh. Another part of the palace front-age crashes down.

Ventanus reaches Sullus. His body is compressed into the lawn in a steaming, scorched depression that oozes slime. He tries to pull him out. Sullus is alive. His armour has protected him, though there are crush injuries. Bones are broken.

Ventanus hears a crash and a trundling sound. One of the Shadowswords ploughs into the palace grounds. It has come over the bridge, and rammed down the gatehouse to get into the compound. It has brought down the gate the Word Bearers lost hundreds trying to destroy.

The super-heavy rumbles across the mangled lawns, knocking down some of Sparzi's emplacements. It lines up its volcano cannon. Ventanus hears the characteristic *sigh-moan* of the capacitors charging for a shot.

The blast is savage. A light flash. A searing beam. It hits the daemon in the body. The blindingly bright light seems to dislocate against the daemon's darkness, obscured. Dark vapour wafts from the creature's body, but it shows no sign of damage.

It turns on the tank.

Ventanus starts to run again, across the shredded lawn, past the bodies of men killed by the daemon, towards the palace wall. He has a theoretical. It isn't much, but it's all he has. The daemon is impervious to harm in its body, but its head might be vulnerable. Brain or skull injuries might slow it down or impair its function. Maybe even drive the damn thing away.

It's got the Shadowsword. The superheavy tries to recharge its cannon, but that famous slow rate of fire...

The daemon seizes the tank by the front of the hull, buckling the armour skirts and tearing the track guards. It shoves the three-hundred-tonne tank backwards, gouging up the turf like a tablecloth. The tank revs, pluming exhaust, trying to drive against the horned thing, tracks slipping and squirming. Mud sprays. Divots fly. The Shadowsword tries to traverse to aim at the daemon point-blank. The daemon slaps at the massive cannon muzzle, ripping the assembly around like a chin turned by a punch. Ventanus hears internal gearing and rotation drivers shred and blow out. The gun mounting falls slack and loose, lolling on the mighty chassis, weapon flopping sideways.

The daemon bends down, snuffling, and takes a bite out of the hull. Then it shoves the tank again, driving it back through an ornamental bed of fruit trees, and smashes it into the terraced wall.

Ventanus runs up a slope of rubble, leaps, arms wide,

and lands on the flat roof of a garden colonnade. He runs along it, leaping over a section brought down by the daemon's attack, and then jumps again, this time onto the marble parapet of the palace roof itself. He runs along it, drawing level with the daemon, almost above it. It is killing the tank, killing it like a hound killing a rabbit.

Ventanus can see the nape of its neck, wrinkled and pale, almost human. He can see the tufts and wisps of foul black hair roped across it. He can see the back of the skull, where mottled skin hangs slack behind the knotted bur of the preposterous horns.

Ventanus accelerates. He reaches for his sword, but the scabbard is empty.

All he has is Cxir's ritual knife.

He rips it out, holds it in both hands, blade tip down, and runs off the roof, arms raised above his head.

[mark: 12.42.16]

THERE'S NOWHERE TO go. Word Bearers stream from the cargo spaces, blitzing the area with gunfire.

Thiel ducks and dodges, bolts slicing past him on silent flame trails.

His kill squad is done. Mission over. The odds are too great.

'Break!' he voxes, and fires his void-harness on full burn.

The violent acceleration lifts him in a wide turn, up and curling back, streaking clear of the killing field. Four, maybe five of his squad lift clear with him. Zaridus, the last to come, is shot by down-raking fire, and his slack body spins away into the stars, jerking and zagging as the harness jets cough and misfire.

Shots chase them. Banking, Thiel sees flashes of noiseless light burst against the flagship hull below him and spark off the buttresses and struts.

He lands, hoping he has decent cover. He has to reload. He tries to calculate the enemy spread and assess the angles they will be coming from. He shouts marshalling orders to his surviving squad members.

The Word Bearers are on him anyway. Two come over the top of a thermal vent, another two around the side of the plating buffer. He gets off two shots. Something wings him in the shoulder.

No, it's a hand. A hand dragging him backwards.

Guilliman pushes Thiel aside and propels himself towards the Word Bearers. His armoured feet bite into the hullskin as he gains traction. He seems vast, like a titan. Not an engine of Mars. A titan of myth.

His head is bare. Impossible. His flesh is bleached with cold. His mouth opens in a silent scream as he smashes into them.

He kills one. He crushes the legionary's head into his chest with the base of his fist. Globules of blood squirt sideways, jiggling and jostling. The body topples back in slow motion.

Guilliman turns, finds another, punches his giant fist through the legionary's torso, and pulls it out, ripping out his backbone. A third comes, eager for the glory of killing a primarch. Thiel guns him apart with his reloaded boltgun, two-handed brace, feet anchored.

The fourth storms in.

Guilliman twists and punches his head off. Clean off. Head and helm as one, tumbling away like a ball, trailing beads of blood.

Cover fire comes across. Another kill squad finally reaches the hull section. A fierce, silent bolter battle licks back and forth across a heat exchanger canyon. Struck bodies, leaking fluid shapes, rotate away into the freezing darkness.

Thiel triangulates his position. He signals to the bridge to open the Port 88 airgate.

He looks at Guilliman. He gestures to the airgate.

The primarch wants to fight. Thiel knows that look. That *need*. Guilliman wants to keep fighting. There's blood around him like red petals, and he wants to add to it.

It's time to stop this fight, however, and fight the one that matters.

2

EREBUS STANDS, SURROUNDED by daemonkind.

He is still high in the north, on the now-accursed Satric Plateau. The sky is blood red, the colour of his Legion's armour. The horizon is a ring of fire. The earth is a cinderheap. The black stones marking out the ritual circle, the stones taken from the graveworld of Isstvan V, throb with an incandescent power. A wind howls. In its plangent notes, like voices chanting, is the truth. The Primordial Truth.

The truth of Lorgar.

The truth of the words they bear.

The surviving Tzenvar Kaul have long since retreated to a safe distance some fifteen kilometres away down the valley. Only the Gal Vorbak warriors remain, led by Zote, their obdurate forms proof against the lethal wind and the unnatural fire.

Erebus is tired, but he is also elated. It is almost time for the second sunrise. The second, greater Ushkul Thu.

He signals to Essember Zote.

Around Erebus, on the charred slopes and blackened

345

rocks, the daemons slither and chatter, disturbed by his movement. They are basking in the luciferous glow, glistening, glinting, chirring; some sluggish, others eager to be loosed.

He calms them with soft words. Their forms stretch out around him as far as he can see, like a colony of pinnipeds basking on a blasted shore. They loop around one another, bodies entwined, embraced, conjoined. They writhe and whine, yelp and murmur, raising their heads to utter their unworldly cries into the dying sky. Fat blowflies buzz, blackening the filthy air. Horns and crests sway in ghastly rhythm. Batwings spread and flutter. Segmented legs stir and rattle.

Erebus sings to them. He knows their names. Algolath. Surgotha. Etelelid. Mubonicus. Baalkarah. Uunn. Jarabael. Faedrobael. N'kari. Epidemius. Seth Ash, who aspects change. Ormanus. Tarik reborn, he-who-is-now-Tormaggedon. Laceratus. Protael. Gowlgoth. Azmodeh. A hundred thousand more.

Samus has just returned, dipping into the circle to clothe himself in new flesh. There is still some fight left in the enemy then, for the likes of Samus to be turned back.

It will not be enough. It will not overcome what is descending.

Reality is caving in. Erebus can hear it creaking and ripping as it buckles. Calth can only stand so much stress.

Then ruin will break, like a storm.

Zote carries over the warp-flask.

Erebus tunes it to link with Zetsun Verid Yard, with Kor Phaeron.

Erebus realises he is bleeding from the mouth. He wipes the blood away.

'Begin,' he says.

* * *

[mark: 12.59.45]

SOROT TCHURE WATCHES Kor Phaeron's face as he receives the message from the surface. There is glee. The time is at hand.

The bulk coordinates are already set. At a simple nod from Kor Phaeron, Tchure instructs the magi at their control consoles. The entire planetary weapons grid is re-trained on a single new target.

Kor Phaeron's eagerness is evident. He has played with the grid, annihilating battleships, orbitals and moons, but quickly wearied of the sport. A pure purpose awaits.

The Word Bearers affect a communion with the stars. The suns of the heavens hold deep meaning for them. The strata of their Legion's organisation are named after solar symbols. Through superhuman effort, Erebus and Kor Phaeron have transformed the entire planet of Calth into a solar temple, an altar on which to make their final tribute.

Erebus has worn the skin of reality thin, and opened the membrane enclosing the Immaterium. The altar is anointed.

Kor Phaeron steps forward and places his left hand upon the master control.

He presses it.

The weapons grid begins to fire. Concentrated and coherent energy. Shoals of missiles. Destructive beams. Warheads of antimatter sheathed in heavy metals. The rays and beams will take almost eight minutes to reach their target. The hard projectiles will take considerably longer. But they will all hit in turn, and continue to strike again and again and again as the merciless bombardment continues.

The target is the blue-white star of the Veridian system.

Kor Phaeron begins to murder the sun.

* * *

[mark: 13.10.05]

'WE FEARED YOU had perished,' says Marius Gage.

Guilliman has just walked onto the auxiliary bridge of the *Macragge's Honour* with his battered kill squad escort.

'What does not kill me,' replies Guilliman, 'is not trying hard enough.'

He makes them smile. He's good at that. But they can all read the change in him. He was never a man you could warm to. He was too hard, too driven, too austere. Now he is wounded. Wounded like an animal might be wounded. Wounded in a way that makes that animal dangerous.

'Voided without a helm,' Guilliman says. 'Primarch biology helped, but the atmospheric envelope was my true saviour.'

'What...' Gage begins.

'What was that thing?' Guilliman finishes. Everyone is staring, everyone listening.

'Should this be a conversation we finish in private?' asks Gage.

Guilliman shakes his head.

'As I understand it from Thiel,' he says, gesturing to the sergeant at his side, 'you have all spent hours fighting your way through this ship against other fiends like it. It has cost you. I can see it has cost you, Marius.'

Gage is suddenly painfully aware of his truncated arm.

'I can't see any point in hiding the truth from anybody here,' says Guilliman. 'You have all served Ultramar today with more than duty might have reason to expect. And the day is not done. It seems unlikely that we will win anything, or even survive, but I would dearly like to wound our treacherous foe before we die.'

The primarch looks around the room. His armour is sheened and sticky with filth. His face is dirty, and there is blood in his hair.

'Let us share what we know, and build some strategy.

I welcome theoreticals from anybody at this stage. Anything will be considered.'

He walks over to the strategium.

'We can use the word daemon, I think. A warp entity manifested and destroyed the bridge. You have fought others. Daemon is as good a word as any. It was Lorgar, or at least...'

He pauses, and looks back at them.

'I don't know where Lorgar is. I don't know if my brother was ever in this system in the flesh, but it was his voice and his presence that visited me, and it was him that transformed. It was no trick. Lorgar and his Legion have consorted with the powers of the warp. They have forged an unholy covenant. It has twisted them. It has started a war.'

Guilliman sighs.

'I don't know how to fight them. I know how to fight most things. I can even work out how to fight warriors of the Legiones Astartes, though the notion seems heretical. Like Thiel here, I can think the unthinkable, and make theoreticals out of the blasphemous. But daemons? It seems to me, with the Council of Nikaea, that we voluntarily rid ourselves of the one weapon we might have had against the warp. We could dearly use the Librarius now.'

His warriors nod in silent agreement.

'We should petition for their reinstatement,' he adds, 'if we ever get the chance. We cannot do it now. There is no time, no means. But if any of us survive this, know that the edict must be overturned.'

He pauses, thoughtful.

'It is almost as though,' he muses, 'someone *knew*. Nikaea disarmed us. It is as though our enemy knew what was coming, and orchestrated events so that we would voluntarily cast aside our only practical weapon the moment before it was needed.'

There is a murmur of quiet dismay.

'We are all being used,' Guilliman says, lifting his eyes and looking at Gage. 'All of us. Even Lorgar. When he tried to kill me, to rip me into space, I could feel the pain in him. I have never been close to him, but there is a fraternal link. I could feel his horror. His agony at the way fate had twisted on us all.'

'He said Horus–' Gage begins.

'I know what he said,' replies Guilliman.

'He said others were already dead. At Isstvan,' Gage presses. 'Manus. Vulkan. Corax.'

'If that is true,' says Empion, 'it is a tragedy beyond belief.'

'Three sons. Three primarchs, the loss is appalling,' agrees Guilliman. 'Four, if you count Lorgar. Five, if what he says of Horus is true. And *others*, he said, had turned...'

Guilliman takes a deep breath.

'Corax and Vulkan I will mourn dearly. Manus I will miss most of all.'

Gage knows what his primarch means. In all tactical simulations, Guilliman shows particular favour for certain of his brothers. He refers to them as *the dauntless few*, the ones he can most truly depend upon to do what they were made to do. Dorn and his Legion are one. Ill-tempered, argumentative Russ is another. Sanguinius is a third. Guilliman admires the Khan greatly, but the White Scars are neither predictable nor trustworthy. Ferrus Manus and the Iron Hands were always the fourth of the dauntless few. With any one of those key four – Dorn, Russ, Manus or Sanguinius – Guilliman always claimed he could win any war. *Outright*. Against any foe. Even in extremis, the Ultramarines could compact with any one of those four allies and take down any foe. It was *primary theoretical*. In any doomsday scenario that faced the Imperium, Guilliman could play it out to a practical win provided he could rely on one of those four. And of them, Manus was the key. Implacable. Unshakeable. If he was at your side, he would never break.

Now, it seems, he is gone. Gone. Dead. Brother. Friend. Warrior. Leader. Ultramar's most stalwart ally.

Guilliman breaks the bleak silence.

'Show me tactical. The nearspace combat. Someone said there was a vox from the surface finally?'

'From Leptius Numinus, lord,' says the Master of Vox.

'Who was it?'

'Captain Ventanus,' says Gage. 'We had a good signal for a while, and were getting a vital datafeed, but the vox cut off suddenly about an hour ago. A violent interrupt.'

'I don't need to ask if you're trying to re-establish the link?' says Guilliman.

'You do not, lord,' replies the Master of Vox.

Guilliman turns to Empion.

'Assemble all the strengths we have aboard this ship. Kill squads. Every heavy weapon we can find. Forget Chapter and company lines, just divide and group the men we have into viable fighting parties. Have the squad leaders mark their helms in red.'

'Red, sir?' asks Empion.

'We do not have reliable vox, Klord, so I want firm and simple visual cues for the chain of command.'

Guilliman looks across at Thiel.

'Besides,' he says, 'I think after Thiel's efforts today, it's high time that stopped being a mark of censure.'

'Yes, sir,' says Empion.

'My lord!' Shipmaster Hommed calls out.

'What is it?'

'The weapons grid, my lord. It's firing.'

'At whom?'

'At... the sun.'

3

THUNDER ROLLS THROUGH the glowering skies above the shattered palace of Leptius Numinus. It starts to rain torrentially. The weather patterns of the abused planet are convulsing again.

Ventanus stands for a moment and lets the streaming rain wash the foul black ichor off his armour. He feels the water hitting his face. He opens his eyes and watches Sparzi's flamer squads burning the slime, the blubbery black flesh and the noxious inky entrails the daemon left behind when it exploded. The flame jets sizzle and hiss ferociously in the rain.

He walks up to what's left of the palace atrium. Selaton is waiting for him.

'You killed it,' Selaton notes.

'I don't agree with your definition.'

'You sent it away, then. How did you do that?'

'Luck. Luck of the very worst kind.'

Ventanus glances back at the ruined gardens, the ragged walls, the rubble of the gate.

'We can't stay here,' he says. 'Cxir said other forces were coming. This place was hard to defend before. It will be impossible again. This was never a fortress.'

'Agreed, but what about the data-engine?' asks Selaton.

'Good question.'

Ventanus notices that his sergeant is holding a sack. He takes it from him and looks inside.

It is full of black daggers. Ritual knives. Some are black metal, some glass, some knapped flint; some handles are wire, some leather, some snakeskin. Selaton has collected them from the brotherhood dead.

'You used Cxir's weapon against the daemon,' says Selaton simply. 'Theoretical: these blades work. Their own weapons work.'

'You may be right,' says Ventanus. He looks into the sack. The blades shine and glint in the shadows of the bag. 'But I'm afraid these things are as toxic and dangerous as the monsters we want to use them against. Throw them away, Selaton. Drop them into a well. Put a grenade in the sack and hurl it into the ditch. We can't start using these.'

'But–'

Ventanus looks at him.

'Theoretical: that's how it began with the XVII,' he says. 'Expedient use of an exotic weapon to turn back an unexpectedly resistant new foe. Strange daggers found in some xenos tomb or temple? What harm can they do? They cut daemon flesh. It's worth the risk.'

A look of utter distaste crosses Selaton's face.

'I'll dispose of them, sir,' he says.

Ventanus walks to the stack room. He passes the chambers where Sydance is watching the magi trying to reconnect the vox.

'Well fought,' Sydance says, clasping his hand.

'I was the thirteenth eldar this time,' replies Ventanus, 'but we won't get that grace again. Is the vox up?'

'They're working on it. The datalink is still active. The server wants to see you.'

'Good. I want to see her.'

Ventanus enters the stack room. Tawren has disconnected herself from the chattering data-engine. One of her magi, Uldort, has taken her place in the MIU link to maintain processing.

'Captain,' Tawren says.

'Server.'

'This data-engine is not powerful enough to seize control of the grid,' she says flatly. 'Moreover, it is not powerful enough to run the grid.'

'So that's it?' asks Ventanus. 'Our contribution now is... to collate and supply data to the fleet until such time as we are exterminated?'

'That will be the fate of Leptius Numinus,' she agrees. 'However, please place that contribution in context. This is the only loyalist data-engine at work on Calth. It is not just a vital source of data. It is the *only* source of data.'

She shows him data-slate displays.

'We have built a picture of resistance across the planet. It is broken and scattered, but it is fierce. Spread across hundreds of locations, as many as thirty thousand of your battle-brothers and two hundred thousand Army and Mechanicum warriors are still active. Coordinated, they can achieve more than if they remain uncoordinated.'

'This palace can only provide coordination for a short time,' says Ventanus. 'The enemy is on its way.'

'The picture is not totally dark, captain. About fifteen minutes ago, I made one profound discovery.'

The memory of that revelation makes Tawren smile. It is bittersweet, almost painful to think of, and yet uplifting. She found Hesst's gift. She found what he was working on when he died, what he hid so scrupulously so it would be safe until she uncovered it.

'My predecessor,' she says, 'managed to configure a killcode to combat the enemy scrapcode sequence. He achieved this feat shortly before he died. It was an act of desperation and genius. It is a sublime and intuitive piece of coding, and only Hesst could have done it.'

'We can use it to purge?' asks Ventanus.

'Hesst hid the killcode in a secure data-engine which he then closed off and sealed. The data-engine is the manifest cogitator of the cargo handling guild at the starport. It is in a secure bunker in the industrial zone between Numinus Starport and Lanshear landing grounds. It runs cargo operations for both ports, and thus is more than powerful enough to manage the dataload of the planetary weapons grid. As a civilian engine, it was not a primary military target. Hesst cleaned it with his killcode and then shut it away.'

It was why he kept going until the very last moment, Tawren now realises. It was why he wouldn't leave his post, even when the scrapcode had maimed his mind. He had to finish. He was determined to finish. He was hanging on as long as he could to get it done.

'Can you control this engine remotely?' asks Ventanus.

'No, captain. I need direct MIU access to launch the killcode. Once I have purged a pathway into the system, I can create a new manifold and assume command of the grid.'

'Getting to the port zone won't be easy.'

'Of course it won't,' she agrees. 'There is an additional issue.'

'Go on,' says Ventanus.

'The enemy is controlling the grid using a captured data-engine on one of the surviving orbital platforms. I can purge the system, but I cannot override that control. We need fleet assistance to target the platform.'

He nods.

'What about the engine here?' he asks.

'It must remain functional for the greatest period possible,' Tawren replies. 'Magos Uldort has volunteered to stay with the engine and keep it running as long as she can.'

'It is a death sentence,' says Ventanus, looking at the young magos at the MIU link. 'The Word Bearers are coming.'

'Calth is a death sentence, captain,' the server replies. 'All that matters is how we face it.'

He is silent for a moment.

'Prepare your staff for travel, server,' he says. 'See what you can do via the datalink to coordinate force response to support our assault on the port zone.'

He walks back to the vox chamber. In the doorway, he tells Sydance, Selaton and Greavus to mobilise the forces.

'We're evacuating this site,' he says. 'We're going back to the port. Gather as much punch as you can. Fighting vehicles especially. We're going to have to cut our way into it.'

'This doesn't sound good,' says Sydance.

'It sounds like it sounds,' says Ventanus. 'It's the only worthwhile practical we have left. I need that link. I need the vox. We'll be wasting our time without fleet coordination. Tell the magi I need vox.'

They move off, urgent. He waits. He thinks.

Arook appears.

'I'm staying,' says the skitarii.

'I could use you.'

'My duty is to the Mechanicum, Ventanus. This data-engine needs to stay alive for as long as possible. You understand duty.'

Ventanus nods. He holds out his hand.

Arook looks at it for a moment, baffled by the unfamiliar business of social interaction.

He grips Ventanus's hand.

'We march for Macragge,' says Ventanus.

'We stand for Mars,' replies Arook. 'It means the same thing.'

They turn as Sullus approaches. The captain's armour is badly scratched and dented. He is limping. It will take a long while for his bones to knit.

'I will remain here too, Ventanus,' he says. 'The skitarii could use a few Legion guns. Right now, I'm not fit to

DAN ABNETT

march far. But I can stand and shoot.'

Ventanus looks Sullus in the eyes.

'Teus, this wasn't your fault,' he says. 'It–'

'This isn't atonement, Remus,' Sullus replies. 'I don't feel sorry for myself. This wasn't anybody's fault, but we're all going to end up paying whatever we can. Take the port, win the grid, kill their fleet. Remember my name while you're doing it.'

'We have vox!' Sydance yells.

VENTANUS TAKES THE speaker horn the magos offers him.

'This is Ventanus, commanding Leptius Numinus. Ventanus, Ventanus. Requesting priority encrypt link with the XIII Fleet. Respond.'

'This is XIII Fleet flagship,' the vox crackles. 'Your authority codes are recognised. Stand by.'

A new voice comes onto the link.

'Remus.'

'My primarch,' says Ventanus.

'You sound surprised.'

'I thought you had officers to run vox-nets for you, sir.'

'I do. But just this once. I was worried that your surprise might stem from rumours of my death.'

'That too, my primarch. It will boost spirits here to know that you are healthy.'

The vox fizzles and whines.

'I said, you've done a good day's work, captain,' says the vox. 'The data you are sending is invaluable. Gage is coordinating our forces.'

'It's a bad day, sir.'

'I can't remember a worse one, Remus.'

'This facility may not remain functional for very much longer, sir. Expect to lose the data feed in the next few hours. But we're going to get the grid, sir. We're going to retake the grid.'

'Good news, Remus. It's killing us. It's killing the sun, too. I think the XVII want to kill everything that ever lived.'

'It looks that way down here too, sir. Sir, this is important. We–'

The vox washes and crackles again.

'–say again, Leptius. Say again. Ventanus, do you copy?'

'Ventanus, sir. I read you. The interrupts are getting worse. Sir, we can't complete our control of the grid unless the fleet can take out the orbital the enemy is running it from. We can purge their code once we're in, but we can't break it. The fleet needs to target and destroy their grid command location as a priority.'

'Understood, Remus. A priority. Can you identify the target?'

Ventanus looks at Sydance. Sydance hands him a data-slate.

'I can, sir,' says Ventanus.

[mark: 14.01.01]

'REMUS? SAY AGAIN!' demands Guilliman. 'Ventanus, respond! Respond! What is the target? What is the target?'

He looks at the Master of Vox.

'Vox lost, sir,' says the Master of Vox. Electromagnetic screeches issue from the speakers.

'Datalink from Leptius also just went down,' says Gage.

'Did we lose them?' asks Guilliman. 'Damn it, did we just lose Ventanus and his force?'

'No, sir,' says the Master of Vox. 'It's an interrupt. A severe interrupt.'

'It's the sun,' says Empion.

They all look at the main viewer.

Bombarded by concentrated energy and laced with toxic, reactive heavy metals, the Veridian star is suffering a gross imbalance in its solar metabolism. Its natural, internal chain reactions and energetic processes have been disrupted and agitated. Its radiation levels are rising. Its output is visibly increasing as it starts to burn through its fuel resources at an unnaturally accelerated rate.

Its blue-white wrath is growing more fierce, like a malignant light. A daemonic light. Black sunspot crusts seethe across its tortured surface. Staggering, lethal flares rip away from it in tongues of flame and lashing arcs of energy millions of kilometres across.

It is going nova.

[mark: 14.01.59]

THUNDER ROLLS.

Out in the dismal fog of the channel, Oll steers the skiff through the black water, passing burning water craft that are half sunk, passing pale, ballooned corpses floating in the brown scum.

He thinks there's a boat behind them, a way behind. Another skiff or a launch. But it might just be the echo of their own engine in the fog.

Krank is sleeping. Zybes sits staring off the bow. Katt and Graft are wherever their minds go to.

Rane twitches, in the clutch of a nightmare. They have bundled him in blankets. He probably won't recover from his ordeal.

Oll takes out his compass, and checks the bearing as best he can.

Thrascias. It still seems to be *Thrascias.* That used to be the word for the wind from the north-north-west, before the cardinal points of the compass rose were co-opted for other purposes and given more esoteric meanings. *Thrascias.* That's what the Grekans called it. That's what they called it when he sailed back across the sun-kissed waters to Thessaly in Iason's crew, with a witch and a sheep-skin to show for their efforts. The Romanii, they called it *Circius*. Down in the oardecks of the galleys, he hadn't much cared about the names of the winds they were rowing against. The Franks called it *Nordvuestroni*.

Oll looks up. A star has suddenly appeared, visible even through the black fog and atmospheric filth. It is harsh, bright, blue-white. It is malevolent. A star of ill omen.

It means the end is coming, and coming fast.

But at least he now has a star to steer by.

RUIN//STORM

'Everything is an enemy.'

– Guilliman, *Notes Towards Martial
Codification, 645.93.vi*

1

ABOVE GROUND, IT is raining. It has been raining for about seven hours without a break. The evaporated southern oceans, thrust into the upper atmosphere as steam, have returned, first as poison fog, and then as an apocalyptic deluge.

The burning population centres steam and sizzle, their fires inextinguishable. The molten cores of city-graves glow in sinkholes hundreds of kilometres across. Craters and impact scars fill with water, from the most massive hive sinkhole to the smallest bullet pock-mark. Plains turn to mud, an ooze as dark as blood. River basins flood. The forested sweeps of Calth's highlands and valley systems crackle and roar as they combust, fire-fronts a thousand kilometres broad.

The rain forms a curtain as thick as the fog that preceded it.

There is a plague of rainbows. The downpour combines with the swelling blue-white radiance of the terminal star to decorate every prospect, every ruined street, every burning hab-block, every fire-blackened forest, with a scintillating rainbow.

4th Company moves underground.

The fighting group built around the elements of 4th Company retraces Ventanus's steps through the sub-branch of the arcology, along the safe route built in colonial times by the early governors.

Despite subsidence from shock-damaged earth, which has split or slumped the tunnels in places, the passageways are intact and commodious. They offer an arterial that can take even the largest fighting vehicles.

Long stretches of the tunnel system are partially flooded, with still more water sluicing down through broken pipes and drains, and running through clefts and cracks in the roof. The rain is getting in wherever it can. Men wade, up to their waists. Tanks and carriers glide, pressing through the silty black water like reptiles, their slow-moving hulls stirring up little, flowing wakes.

Ventanus moves along at the front, with Vattian and the scouts. He leads the way, standard in hand.

Two hours after they leave the palace, the data and vox links are finally restored, thanks to Magos Uldort's unstinting efforts. From the datalink, Ventanus learns that several strikeforces are closing to conjunct with him at the port zone, including a major taskforce punching down from Sharud Province, the assembled remains of the 111th and 112th under the command of a sergeant called Anchise. On another day, in another history, Anchise's efforts to rally, compose, turn, and redirect his forces would become the stuff of instruction text and legend.

Today, on Calth, it is just another story of a man's last hours alive.

Ventanus hopes that Anchise's force arrives in time to render support. He doubts it will. The 4th is moving fast, and it cannot afford to wait or hesitate. Even if Anchise, or any of the other projected support units, make it through, there are still no guarantees. The port zone is in enemy hands. Numinus Port is a burning ruin, and Lanshear and the foundries have been overrun by the predatory hosts of Hol Beloth.

Beloth circles from the south. Foedral Fell approaches from the north-west. Ventanus wonders how much longer Uldort's valuable datalink can remain active.

They have passed below the Shield Wall, and are drawing close to the service linkage where they will be obliged to surface, and move in the open.

Ventanus stops briefly to talk to his unit leaders: Cyramica, commanding the skitarii strength; Colonel Sparzi of the Army; Sydance and the company sergeants, Vattian of the scout force.

He has the battered golden standard in his hands as he talks to them. There are no orders, and no feeble efforts at oratory. He tells them how it is, and what has to be done. He tells them the practical, and he tells them what he expects from them.

They say nothing. They nod.

That's all he needs.

[mark: 19.29.37]

THEY HAVE WHAT they need. They have their target. They have their practical.

They are ready.

It took the primarch about ten minutes to determine the target. Ten minutes. Thiel watched him work it out. Guilliman did it by eye, by observation, by consulting the reams of notes and scraps and stylus jottings he had scattered over the strategium.

He had the resolution long before the datalink from Leptius was re-established.

'It has to be a functioning facility,' he reasoned. 'It has to have a data-engine rating of at least, what, 46nCog? It needs to have an active datalink, which we can probably detect using back-trace. The Word Bearers have done such a good job of destroying platform facilities, it makes it easier to spot the ones they've deliberately left alone.'

He pointed to the display.

Zetsun Verid Yard.

Then the practical had to be decided. Shipmaster Hommed recommended a ranged bombardment: primary spinals, lances. The *Macragge's Honour* certainly has firepower enough. Gage seconded the suggestion. But if they didn't make a direct kill with the first salvo, there was a real danger that the enemy could retaliate with the grid and finish the flagship.

Empion was all for close attack: flagship power to yield, shields up, throw off the enemy cruisers suckling around them and go for the yard. Blow it out of nearspace. Ram it, if necessary.

Except, the moment they moved, the moment they even rated a power condition, the *Macragge's Honour* would become a target. The flagship could move rapidly, and with devastating effect, but faster than the weapons grid could be retrained and discharged? That was even supposing nothing got in their way, like a drive issue, or an enemy ship.

So Empion's plan had also been dismissed, and Gage's alternative considered: put all power into the teleport system. Transfer a kill squad, maybe two if the power lasted, direct to the Zetsun Verid. Do it the old way.

'I will lead it, of course,' said Guilliman.

'I hardly think so,' retorted Gage. Almost everybody present physically recoiled from the look the primarch shot his Chapter Master.

'Very well,' said Gage.

'Damn it, Marius,' growled Guilliman. 'If not now, when?'

THE FIRST KILL squad of fifty Ultramarines, led by Guilliman, Heutonicus and Thiel, assembles in the flagship's teleportation terminal. If enough power remains, a second squad led by Empion will follow them.

The helms of Heutonicus and the section leaders are painted red to match Thiel's.

Guilliman's cleaned and polished wargear makes him look more like a vengeful martial god than ever. There are golden wings spread across his helm's faceplate. His left fist is a massive power claw, and his right holds a superb bolter weapon, decorated to match his armour.

There is a stink of ozone in the chamber, a metallic tang rising from the heavy, matt-grey platform of the teleport system. Coolant vapour rolls like mist in the yellow light. Guilliman takes a cue from his squad leaders, then signals to the Magi of Portation behind their lead-lined screens.

Power builds. It builds to a painful pitch.

Like a storm, about to break and unload its fury.

[mark: 19.39.12]

SULLUS CAN HEAR the rain beating on the roof. He watches the magos, Uldort, working in communion with the data-engine. It is as though she is in a trance. Data chatters and whirrs. Her hands make haptic motions across invisible touchpads.

Sullus hurts. He never told Ventanus or any of the others quite how much he had been damaged. He can feel bones grinding, refusing to mend despite the fever heat of biological repair throbbing through his body.

Pain, death, he doesn't fear any of that. Only failure.

His helmet link bleeps. He gets up, picks up his sword and his boltgun, and limps up the passageway to the west entrance.

In the rain, the ruined grounds and collapsed frontage of the palace seem even more dismal. Water streams and patters down from the shattered roof, dripping on grand

370   DAN ABNETT

tiles and mosaics, cascading down inlaid staircases, turning fallen drapes and tapestries into lank shrouds.

He limps out onto the rubble. Rain drums on his armour. The sun, a toxic blue, burns malignantly through the cloud cover.

Arook Serotid is waiting for him.

'They are here,' says the master of skitarii.

Sullus looks out into the rain. Beyond the crumpled walls, beyond the earthwork ditch, beyond the ragged bridge, the enemy has assembled. They have come silently out of the downpour. They are not chanting. The black ranks of the brotherhoods line the ditch in rows a hundred deep, but behind them are the shapes of war machines, and the ominous gleam of red armour.

Behind that mass, there are larger shapes still. Giant things, obscured by rain, horned and hunched.

There are even more than Sullus imagined. Foedral Fell's assault force numbers in the tens of thousands.

'Now it ends,' says Arook.

Sullus draws his sword.

'Oh please, skitarii,' he says, head up. 'It's only just beginning.'

2

4TH COMPANY STRIKES.

The first that the Word Bearers know of it is a savage, serial bombardment of light cannon and field pieces, supported by the immense firepower of a Shadowsword and a handful of other significant machines.

The Word Bearers had forces positioned along Ketar Transit, a main access way that linked the container stores to the northern facilities of Lanshear port. The forces were supposed to ward Hol Beloth's main army from any counter-attack that came around the eastern sweep of the Shield Wall into Numinus territory.

The forces do not realise that, by occupying the zone around Ketar Transit, they are also effectively guarding the data-engine of the cargo handling guild in the bunker system below the majestic prospect of the guildhall.

It *was* a majestic prospect. Stippled with shell holes, the guildhall remains an inspiring building, crowned by statues of toiling guild porters and the proud Ultima symbol.

The area has not been razed wholesale. It is not military, it is commercial. Server Hesst chose it very well.

The barrage pummels the roadway, levels three blocks of habs, and scatters the enemy formation. Hundreds of knife brother warriors are killed by the shellfire, dozens of Word Bearers too. Armoured vehicles are destroyed and left burning in the rain. A traitor Warhound engine, suddenly alert and striding forward like an angry moa, hunts for a hot target. A torrent of cannonfire catches it, hammers it, and beats its void shields down with sheer relentless insolence. Then the Shadowsword speaks, and a spear of white light kills the Warhound like the lance of some vengeful god.

Debris showers for hundreds of metres, felling some of the retreating cultists. Others, urged by their raging crimson lords, dig in behind walls and barriers of wreckage, and begin to return fire.

Warp-flask messages chime and shrill across the zone; desperate calls for support.

The Land Raiders spur forward, hulls streaming with rainwater, kicking out spray from the rain-sheeted roadway. They drive down walls, rolling over the rubble, crunching over the knife brothers trapped and killed by the cover they had chosen to use. Sponson-mount lascannons rasp into the blue-white twilight, causing the rain to steam and swirl. Heavy bolters shred the air with their noise and drench the enemy positions with destruction.

Ventanus leads the foot advance behind the Land Raiders, double-time across the broken streets. To his left, the units led by Sydance, Lorchas and Selaton. To his right, the units led by Greavus, Archo and Barkha. Cyramica's skitarii form a wide right flank, blocking and punishing an attempt by the Jeharwanate to regroup and counter-charge. Sparzi's infantry mob in behind and to the left of the legionary assault, evicting knife brothers from their strongpoints and foxholes along the north-western end of the massive carriageway.

Word Bearers, a scarlet line in the rain, rise up to block

the main charge. Missiles cripple the first of Ventanus's Land Raiders, leaving it trackless and burning. There is fire from autocannons, the streaks of mass-reactive rounds, both of which drop cobalt-blue figures from the charge.

But the Word Bearers have developed a taste for cutting, an appetite for bladework. Perhaps it has come from their knife brother slave-hosts. Perhaps it is simply to do with the sacrificial symbolism of the sharpened edge.

Concentrated and well-directed firepower might have broken or turned Ventanus's charge, but it is not used. The Word Bearers simply wait for the clash, relishing the prospect. They draw their blades. They want to test their mettle against the vaunted XIII in a skirmish, the outcome of which cannot possibly influence the final resolution of the Calth War.

The traitors want to prove themselves against the paradigms to which they have been compared so many times.

There is a crashing, hyperkinetic impact. The charging cobalt-blue bodies reach the solid red line. They tear into it. They rip through it, they mangle it, red and blue together, a blur. Blows are traded. Huge power, huge force, huge transhuman strength. Blood squirts in the driving rain. Bodies crash to the ground, spraying up water. Blade grips grow slick with rainwater, oil and blood. Shields chip and break. Armour fractures. There is a spark of ozone and power mechanics, the crackle of electrical discharge.

Ventanus is in the thick of it. Boltgun. Power sword. Standard across his back. He shoots away a head in a cloud of bloodsmoke. He impales. He chops off an arm, and smites a helm in two, diagonally.

He has never felt this strong. This driven.

This *justified*.

He has never known such an entirely fearless state.

There is nothing the Word Bearers can do to him any more. They have done their worst. They have burned his world, his fleet, his brothers; they have shed his blood and unleashed their daemons.

They can shoot him. They can stab him. They can grab him and tear him down. They can kill him.

It doesn't matter.

It's his turn. This is his turn.

This is what happens when you leave an Ultramarine alive. This is what happens when you make the foulest treachery your instrument. This is how it comes back to reward you. This is how Ultramar pays you back.

Carnage. *Carnage*. Absolute and total slaughter. The visitation of death in the form of a gold and cobalt-blue storm. A Word Bearer, reeling, arms spread, his carapace sliced open to the core, releasing a profusion of blood. Another, hands lost, stumps smouldering, sinking slowly to his knees with a bolter shell blast hole clean through his torso. Another, red helm caved across the left half, the bite of a power sword. Another, jerking and convulsing as mass-reactive shells blow out his body and overwhelm his transhuman redundancies. Another, cleft by a power axe. Another, disarticulated by a Land Raider's cannons. Another, with the toothmarks of a chainsword.

Another.

Another.

Another. Grunt and spit and curse and gasp and bleed and strike and turn and move and kill and die.

Ventanus reaches the guildhall, leaps the barricades, and lands amongst knife brothers who shriek and flee before him. Red armour comes at him, a sergeant of the XVII, bringing down a thunder hammer. Ventanus dodges the swing, lets it pulverise rockcrete. He lunges and drives his sword, tip-first, through visor, face, skull, brain and the back plate of a helmet.

He snatches the blade out. The sergeant falls, flops

over, blood welling up out of his holed visor like oil from a freshly drilled reserve.

The gutter is running with blood. Ventanus smashes down two of the Tzenvar Kaul foolish enough to attack him, and then shoots a Word Bearer who is coming down the shot-chewed front steps at him. The blast blows out the brute's hip, drops him sideways. Ventanus kills him with his power sword before he can rise again.

Sydance passes Ventanus, ascending the steps. He's firing his boltgun ahead of him, targeting Word Bearers at the top by the main doors of the guildhall. Shots streak back at him. The Ultramarine beside him, Brother Taeks, ends his service there, brains spilled. Sydance's bolter shells put Taeks's killer backwards through the panelled doors.

The first of the XIII are in the building. Ventanus is with them. Blood and rain drips from them onto the marble floor.

'Back up,' warns Greavus.

They make space.

A Land Raider drives in through the doors, collapsing them, splintering the wooden bulk of them.

Ventanus and his men cover the side hatch as it opens and skitarii lead Tawren out.

'Haste,' the server says to Ventanus.

'Not a point that needs to be emphasised, server,' he replies.

It will not take Hol Beloth's assault leaders long to realise that this is not a counter-punch into Lanshear. The guildhall was a specific target.

Small-arms fire *pinks* at them from upper galleries in the huge atrium. Sergeant Archo waves up a kill team and heads away to scour the knife brothers out.

Artillery and heavy weapons continue to pound outside. The suspended lamps in the atrium swing and sway. Pieces of glass and roof tile fall in from the damaged clerestory far above.

Selaton locates the armoured elevator to the guildhall's sublevels. They can rig power from the Land Raider to light and run the system, but it needs an override code.

Tawren enters it.

'My birthdate,' she says, noticing Ventanus watching her.

'There were two codes,' he says.

'I have two birthdays. My organic incept, and my date of full-plug modification. Hesst knew both.'

'You were close,' notes Ventanus.

'Yes,' she replies. 'He was, I suppose, my husband. My life partner. The Mechanicum does not think in such old-fashioned terms, and our social connections are more subtle. But yes, captain, we were close. A binary form. I miss him. I do this for him.'

The lift shutters open. For a second, Ventanus envies her loss. However approximate to standard human her relationship with Hesst might have been, it was still something. An analogue.

He is transhuman. He knows no fear, and there are many other simple emotions he will similarly never experience.

OUTSIDE, SOAKED IN rain, Colonel Sparzi turns as gunfire kisses the walls behind him.

'Oh damn and fug,' he groans.

His men see it too.

Hol Beloth is coming.

He is descending on the guildhall with a vengeance. He is coming with punishment. He is coming with Titans and cataphractii and the Gal Vorbak.

3

THE TELEPORT BURST scorches and jolts every molecule of their bodies.

It is an intensely risky operation. A considerable nearspace distance. A vast energy expenditure. Mass transfer – an entire armoured kill squad. A comparatively small target zone.

Thiel loathes teleports. It feels like you're being pushed through the mesh of an electrified sieve. There is always a bang like a fusion bomb in your brain. There is always an aftertaste like bile and burned paper left in your mouth.

They materialise.

He stumbles, his balance screwed for a second. He's on a deck. He hears a scream.

Given the risk factor and the atrocious error margins, the teleport can be considered a success. Forty-six of the squad have appeared with Guilliman on the transverse assembly deck of Zetsun Verid Yard. They have lost four.

Two of them are fused into the bulkhead wall behind them, parts of their visors and gauntlets and knees protruding seamlessly from the grey adamantium. Another

377

has been reduced to a glistening red sludge by re-formation failure. He is spread over a wide area.

A fourth, Brother Verkus, has materialised bonded into the deck plates from the waist down. He is the one screaming. It's not as though he can be pulled out. He *is* the deck now, and the deck is him.

It is troubling to hear a legionary scream with such a lack of restraint, but they say teleportation overlap is the most unimaginable pain.

Guilliman cradles his head and kills him quickly to end his suffering.

'Move,' he instructs the squad.

There's no time for reflection, no time to take a breath. There's no time to get over the stinging discomfort of the transfer. The squad confirms its arrival site against schematics of the yard and fans out. There is caution, but there is no loss of pace. They are transhumans moving with all the speed and efficiency they possess.

The transverse assembly deck was chosen because it was the largest interior space, and thus allowed for the greatest transfer imprecision. Their assault target is the yard's master control room, two decks up.

The Word Bearers will have read the teleport flare. You can't mask an energy signature like that.

Heutonicus confirms their transfer by vox to the *Macragge's Honour*. Gage replies that there is insufficient power for a second transfer. Empion's kill squad will not be following them, not for a while at least.

They move up through the deck gantries, past the massive airgate and mooring assemblies where ships are docked. The interior superstructure is brightly lit and filled with a vast network of chrome pipes, rods and cablework.

Word Bearers open fire on them from above. Shots rip past them, exploding against the bare metal and ceramite fabric of the yard. The blasts and impacts make huge booming sounds inside the artificial structure.

Two Ultramarines, Pelius and Dyractus, die in the first hail of shells. They are cut apart by sustained fire. Then Brother Lycidor topples over a rail, headshot. His cobalt-blue figure drops into the assembly area below, arms outstretched.

The Ultramarines fire back, covering the structures above them in a cloud of bolter blasts. Word Bearers topple, but there are more to fill their places. Many more.

Guilliman roars a challenge to them. He condemns them to death. He condemns their master to a worse fate.

He hurls himself at them.

The primarch is, of course, their greatest asset, Thiel realises. Not because of his physical superiority, though that is hard to overestimate.

It is because he is a primarch. Because he is Roboute Guilliman. Because he is simply one of the greatest warriors in the Imperium. How many beings could measure favourably against him? Honestly? All seventeen of his brothers? Not all seventeen. Nothing *like* all seventeen. Four or five at best. At *best*.

The Word Bearers on the upper structures see him coming. They are kill squad strength at least, the best part of a full company. At least a proportion of them are the vaunted Gal Vorbak elite.

But they see him coming, and they know what that means. It doesn't matter what cosmic dementia has corrupted their minds and souls. It doesn't matter what eternal promises the Dark Gods are whispering in their ears. It doesn't matter what inflated courage the warp has poured into their veins along with madness.

Guilliman of Ultramar is coming right at them. To kill them. To kill them all.

Even though they stand a chance of hurting him, they waste it. They baulk. For a second, their twisted hearts know fear. *Real* fear.

And then he has them.

And then he is killing them.

'With him! With him!' Thiel yells. They surge forward. Mangled Word Bearers fly overhead, or crash into the decks around them. When Thiel reaches his primarch's side, Guilliman has slain a dozen at least. His boltgun is roaring. His power fist crackles with cooking blood.

It is brutal close quarters. Thiel has the exotic longsword that has served him so well on this darkest of days. Two-handed, he wields it, cutting crimson ceramite like silk. Word Bearers blood looks black, as if it is sour and polluted. Thiel flanks his primarch, advancing steadily with the press of the assault towards the primary hatch.

They lose eight men. Eight Ultramarines. But they break through into the master control room leaving a carpet of enemy dead in their wake.

The real fight awaits them there.

A stunning barrage of bolter-fire greets them, killing Stetius, killing Ascretis, killing Heutonicus.

Kor Phaeron, master of the dark faith, master of the unspeakable word, orders his men forward.

Then he flies at Guilliman, trailing dark vapour, coruscating with black energies torn from the pits of the warp.

'Bastard!' Guilliman howls.

He does not flinch.

Not for a second.

[mark: 20.06.23]

THE GUILDHALL SHAKES. Titans are firing at it.

'I need an update,' Ventanus yells into the vox as blizzards of glass and masonry swirl around him.

He's stayed on the surface to command the repulse. Selaton has ridden down into the armoured bunker with Tawren. All data and vox-links from Leptius Numinus shut down about five minutes ago. The palace has fallen.

The only feed Ventanus has is close-range comms with his company.

'The server has activated the engine,' Selàton voxes back. 'She is connecting. Connecting to the MIU.'

'Is it working?' Ventanus demands.

'I don't know what it looks like if it *is* working,' Selaton replies.

'I can guarantee it looks better than this!' Ventanus responds.

Armour loyal to the Word Bearers is pushing relentlessly along the transit, covering their positions with a hail of shells and bulk las. Smoke and rain have cut visibility to almost nothing. Fabricatory buildings on the far side of the road have collapsed in welters of flame and stone. Two Reaver Titans, weapons mounts glowing from relentless discharge, are approaching through the smoke at full stride.

Cyramica is dead. Lorchas is dead. Sparzi is probably dead too. Ventanus can't find Greavus or Sydance. The company line is broken. The 4th has done all it can.

It cannot match the overwhelming strength of Hol Beloth's offensive.

'The server has launched the killcode,' Selaton reports. 'She is launching it into the grid system. She is preparing for a purge.'

Ventanus ducks as Titan fire hurls a Land Raider into the air a few dozen metres ahead of him. It lands, burning, buckled, hitting the torn ground so loudly it sounds as though the sky is caving in.

The sky *is* caving in, of course. Blue-white fire crackles above the rain. Solar flares are searing Calth's upper atmosphere, irradiating the stricken world, triggering massive, unnatural aurora displays as energetic charged particles strike the thermosphere. Light and colour jump and twist around Ventanus: light from the explosions, light from the agonised sky.

'That's good, isn't it?' Ventanus voxes back. 'That's good?'

'Yes, captain,' Selaton responds, 'but it's useless without control. She can't take control of the grid until enemy control is taken away. And that hasn't happened. She is telling me that hasn't happened.'

A Gal Vorbak beast looms at Ventanus through the murk, swinging a power axe. He wears no helmet. His face is... not human.

Ventanus meets the charge and plants his blade across the haft of the axe, blocking the swing. They struggle. Ventanus is forced back by the killer's bruising power. The locked weapons break apart, and Ventanus ducks hard to avoid the scything chop that follows.

Ventanus recovers quickly, ramming his blade upwards. His sword-tip glances off the Gal Vorbak's axe, deflects into the enemy's mouth, and skewers his head.

The Gal Vorbak doesn't die. Not fast enough. He laughs around the blade impaling his mouth. Black blood pumps out over the sword hilt and Ventanus's hand and arm. The Gal Vorbak puts his axe deep into Ventanus's side.

Then he obliges, and dies.

Ventanus sinks to one knee.

'A-anything?' he voxes.

'Captain? Are you all right?' Selaton replies.

'Is there anything yet?'

'Your voice sounds strange.'

'Selaton, has she got it yet?' Ventanus growls.

'No, sir. Enemy control is still in place.'

The Titans are close now. The last Shadowsword remaining with the 4th fires and damages one of the striding giants, but they reply together and turn the super-heavy tank into a vast conflagration that levels the city blocks behind it.

Nothing else is coming. None of the support that they hoped might arrive to stand with them. None of the reinforcements.

Their hope was a good hope, but it was not strong enough.

The XVII Legion has won the Battle of Calth.

[mark: 20.09.41]

THE SATRIC PLATEAU is bathed in aurora light. The local star spews energy across the entire Veridian System.

Erebus watches.

Rain is falling. The rain is blood. The daemons scream. The storm breaks.

[mark: 20.10.04]

KOR PHAERON GREETS Guilliman with a beam of smoke-light, a column of wretched darkness that bursts from the palm of his right hand and smashes the XIII primarch into the chamber wall.

Guilliman gets back up, but he is shaken. The wall is crumpled where he struck it.

Kor Phaeron cries out, a bark of straining effort, and manufactures another ray of smoke-light. Guilliman is charging, but the beam slams him back into the bulkhead with a kinetic slap so powerful that it rings out with a deafening sonic boom.

Guilliman staggers up, falls, and then half rises, clenching his power fist. The ceramite of his breastplate is cracked. Guilliman coughs, and blood drips from his mouth. He tries to stand.

Kor Phaeron blasts him again, this time with a weird, negative electricity that crackles around Guilliman and causes him to seize in violent spasms.

Guilliman is left on his hands and knees, his cobalt-blue plating scorched, his head bowed, his whole form smouldering as the superheated armour burns his skin.

The Word Bearer draws his athame and steps forward.

Kor Phaeron can see a choice, and it delights him. He can end the life of the great Guilliman. A personal kill is so much more valuable than a distant or mass killing.

With his own hand, he can murder Roboute Guilliman.

Or, with his own hand, he can *turn* him.

Just as the Warmaster was turned.

Erebus did it. So Kor Phaeron can do it.

Guilliman is hurt, weak, vulnerable. The bite of the athame will free Guilliman's sanity while he is in such a state, slice away his inhibitions. The painful burn of the athame wound will fester in him, and ultimately, through the lens of delirium, reveal the Primordial Truth in all its hellish glory.

They came to Calth to kill Guilliman and his perfect warriors. How much more will it mean to return to the court of Lorgar and Horus Lupercal with Guilliman as a willing and pliant ally?

Guilliman, crowned with horns. Guilliman, invested in the iridescent cloak of daemonhood.

Kor Phaeron stoops beside the crumpled primarch. Guilliman's breathing is fast and ragged. His armour smokes, discoloured, and his blood pools beneath him.

'There is so much you don't understand,' says Kor Phaeron. 'The truth will shock you, Roboute. I'm sorry, it will. But you will learn to accommodate it. I'm happy to share my knowledge with you. To help you understand. To grow in appreciation.'

'Get away from me,' Guilliman gasps.

'Too late. Embrace this.'

Thiel is too far away to stop it. Locked in the unyielding fight raging on the opposite side of the control chamber, Thiel glimpses what he knows is likely to be the final few seconds of Roboute Guilliman's life.

He tries to break through, screaming out his rage and frustration. The Word Bearers have driven Guilliman's kill squad back, slaying most of them. Thiel and the others fight to reach their primarch's side, but they cannot. There are too many of the enemy. And these are the enemy elite.

Three warriors obstruct Aeonid Thiel. One is Sorot Tchure. Tchure blocks every strike and thrust Thiel makes, as surely as a practice cage set on maximum extremity level.

Kor Phaeron puts the blade of the athame to Guilliman's throat.

4

THE UPPER STOREYS of the guildhall collapse. Ventanus finds Sydance, Greavus and the remnants of their squads, and backs across the outer concourse. The severity of his wound is making him shuffle, his gait uneven.

The enemy is all around them. Two more Titans have just loomed out of vapour to the east. Two more. It is laughable. It is academic. The enemy strength has long since passed the tipping point. Hol Beloth has employed maximum overkill.

At least, Ventanus considers, they have taken a lot of them down. A *lot* of them. The Word Bearers have had to pay dearly to reach the end of this world.

Sadly, they do not seem to care.

The guildhall will fall next, and no matter how well-armoured the bunker in the sub-levels is, the XVII will dig it out, kill Tawren, and smash the data-engine.

One of the Titans opens fire.

Another of the Titans explodes from the waist up. A giant fireball bellies out from its upper section, consuming it, swirling yellow and white flames into the sky.

* * *

THREE HUNDRED METRES below the guildhall, the bunker trembles. The noise of the terminal war overhead is a dull grumble, a vibration masked by the whirr and rattle of the powerful data-engine.

Tawren, connected in machine communion by the MIU, frowns.

Selaton sees her expression change. The Ultramarine has never experienced such exasperation. He is absent from the fight, useless, destined to do nothing except monitor and report on the silent haptic operations of an inscrutable Mechanicum magos.

'What?' he asks. 'What is it?'

'Two Titans have vectored into the fight,' she says quietly, scanning streams of moving data invisible to him. 'The Titans that have just appeared are *not* traitor machines.'

'What?'

'They are loyalist instruments,' she says. 'The *Burning Cloud* and *Kaskardus Killstroke*. One has just made an engine-kill against the Word Bearers-aligned Titan *Mortis Maxor*.'

'We are supported?' Selaton asks.

'It seems–'

'Server, are you telling me that reinforcement forces are arriving to supplement the 4th?'

'Yes, sergeant, I am. The data supports this supposition. According to the data, that is the case.'

Tawren remains entirely calm. She seems to show no relief. She studies the rapidly updating datastream, winnowing out its information.

'Captain Ventanus's force was facing an annihilation projection of three minutes and sixteen seconds. That limit is being revised up to six minutes and twelve seconds. To eight min... to ten minutes and fifty-one seconds.'

Tawren watches the datafeed. It streams from a thousand different picture and data sources: the visor capture of the Ultramarines legionaries, the optic feeds of the skitarii, the auspexes of loyalist vehicles, the guildhall zone sensors, the parts of the city cogitation network still operating. She watches events unfold.

The reinforcement strength explodes into the Lanshear Belt from the east, fast and mobile. It comes along Tarxis Traverse, Malonik Transit, Bedrus Oblique and the Lanshear Arterials. It pushes through the conurb structures behind the cargo depots and the ring of habitats to the east of Port Dock 18. A column of Land Raiders and armour support three Titans: two Reavers and a Warlord. An infantry force follows, moving rapidly. She identifies them by insignia, heraldry, trace codes and unit marker transponders. The force is mostly XIII and Mechanicum elements from Barrtor and the Sharud muster, but there are twenty thousand Army troopers too, bringing lighter armour and support weapons.

She switches rapidly between pict-supporting feed views to track the advance. The relief force forms two prongs of assault. One is a Legion force led by a sergeant of the 112th called Anchise, and a captain of the 19th called Aethon. The other is predominantly Army, and is commanded by a colonel of the Neride 41st called Bartol, but it is physically being led by Eikos Lamiad and a lumbering Ultramarines Dreadnought.

Before she was lost, Tawren's loyal junior Uldort fulfilled her duties with extraordinary diligence, and coordinated all the force and firepower she could contact.

Lamiad. Eikos Lamiad, Tetrarch of Ultramar, Primarch's Champion. He leads a ragged host of soldiery collected from the desert and the burning hills around the Holophusikon. He raises his sword in his one good arm and sweeps his warriors into the street fight.

Telemechrus, the Contemptor, strides beside him, expending ammunition as he drives a wedge into the enemy formations. His munitions tally records two kills among Hol Beloth's senior commanders. Assault cannon. Most efficient.

Tawren switches views again. She follows other code tags.

Justarius, the venerable, walks with Aethon's squads. A second Dreadnought brought to the fight. And in the shadow of the Titans, a second tetrarch too: Tauro Nicodemus, who has spent the day fighting up from the south and the slaughterfields at Komesh.

Switch view. Switch view. Tawren watches the data, almost startled by the speed of update, the rapid turn of the battle's balance.

She finally becomes aware of Selaton's desperation, and starts to tell him what she can see.

Hol Beloth's forces flinch at the unbridled force of the attack. It is not just the firepower, it is the coordinated strength of it. The shattered survivors of the XIII should not have been able to organise with such precision and effect. In the midst of chaos, confusion, a world ablaze, they should not have been able to rally and focus around such a strategically specific point.

Tawren checks her annihilation projection.

It now stands at forty-seven minutes and thirty-one seconds.

In that time, the assembled survivors of the Calth Atrocity will express their fury and their vengeance, and they will do massive damage to the enemy. They may even temporarily drive the Word Bearers back out of the Lanshear Belt.

But it is only a last, gratifying chance to rage into the face of death.

For Hol Beloth, it will simply add an hour or two to the fight. In many ways, it serves to concentrate his victims in one convenient killing ground. He can draw in supporting divisions from all directions.

The XIII cannot.

If they hoped to fall in glory, they are about to get their wish.

Tawren has no grid control with which to shift the combat dynamic. She has the killcode, but no damned control.

[mark: 20.13.29]

THE ATHAME BITES. Guilliman's blood wells up around the sliced flesh. He grunts through clenched teeth.

'Let it go,' whispers Kor Phaeron. 'This is the beginning of wisdom.'

Guilliman mutters something in reply.

'What?' asks Kor Phaeron, cupping a hand to his ear, mocking him. 'What did you say, Roboute?'

Every single word is an effort.

'You made an error,' Guilliman gasps.

'An error?'

'You chose the wrong practical. You had a choice. Toy with me. Kill me. You chose the wrong one.'

'Really?' smiles Kor Phaeron.

'You should not have let me live.'

'I let you live so I could share the truth, Roboute.'

'Yes,' says Guilliman, sucking in each ragged breath. 'But all the while I'm alive, I can do this.'

There is a sharp sound. A sudden, wet crack. An explosive spray of blood, as though a skin of red wine has burst between them. Kor Phaeron makes a tiny noise; a thin, ceramic sound like a wet finger sliding down glass.

Guilliman rises. Though its power has long since shorted out and failed, he has buried his armour claw in Kor Phaeron's chest. He has crunched through plate, through muscle, through augmented ribs. Kor Phaeron twitches, impaled on Guilliman's fist. His feet are off the deck, his elbows digging into his sides. He shudders, head flopping on his neck.

The athame falls from his fingers and rebounds off the deck.

Sorot Tchure hears the noise his master makes. He is focused on his combat with the Ultramarines raiders, but he cannot help but turn his eyes for a second. Less than a second. A microsecond.

Thiel sees his opening. His practical. It is infinitesimal, a tiny chink in the Word Bearer's guard. It lasts a microsecond, and it will not be repeated.

He puts his sword through it.

The longsword shears the right side of Tchure's helm away. Cheek, ear and part of the skull separate with it. Tchure stumbles, bewildered by the pain, the shock, the disorientation.

For a moment, Tchure thinks it is Luciel. He thinks it is Luciel who has risen up to punish him for a trust so miserably betrayed.

Thiel shoulder-slams him aside into one of the other Word Bearers, spattering blood over them all. He ducks the sword slash of the third, and decapitates him.

He is the first to break clear and rush to Guilliman's side.

Guilliman looks Kor Phaeron in the eyes. Kor Phaeron's lips quiver. He blinks hard and bubbles of saliva form around the corners of his trembling mouth.

Guilliman wrenches the claw out. It is clutching Kor Phaeron's heart.

Kor Phaeron crashes to the deck, bitter black blood coursing from under him in all directions. He retches, and covers the floor with a vile lactic spatter.

Guilliman throws the mangled heart aside.

Thiel steadies him to stop him falling.

'Never mind me, sergeant,' Guilliman rasps. 'Kill the damned systems. Do what we came to do.'

Thiel races to the system consoles. The brass cogitation banks of the data-engine chatter and clack in front of him. He doesn't know where to start.

'In the name of Terra,' Guilliman snarls. 'Thiel, shoot the bloody thing!'

Thiel is out of ammo. But he has his sword. It has one more job to do today.

[mark: 20.20.19]

THE CONTROL CODES release. Tawren sees it happen. She sees the digital sequence suddenly shift across the noospherics. *Control suspended (engine failure). Control suspended (engine failure). Control suspended (engine failure). Control suspended (engine failure)...*

It is like a moment of data-revelation. A profound data sequence change. All values alter. All authorities reset.

She doesn't hesitate. Hesst would not have. She runs the killcode directly into the suddenly *open* system, and watches as it burns through the corrupted numerics of the Octed scrapcode.

The killcode is her vanguard. Her praetorians. Her Ultramarines kill squad. Her Ventanus. She follows it in with her authority codes.

She takes control. She selects the discretionary mode. Thousands of automatically generated firing solutions instantly present themselves. She sorts them using subtle haptics, code-forms and binaric cant.

'Server?' Selaton is addressing her. 'Server?'

Tawren ignores him. She opens a vox-link.

'Server Tawren, addressing the XIII Legion Ultramarines, and all forces allied to their standard. Brace for impact. Repeat, brace for impact.'

[mark: 20.21.22]

THE FIRST BEAM-WEAPON strikes hit Lanshear. They come straight out of the sky, columns of dazzling vertical light. They stream from orbital weapon platforms, platforms that the Word Bearers left intact for their own use.

The beams, generated by lance batteries, particle tunnels and meson weapons, strike with surgical accuracy. They cauterise the city-zone around the guildhall in the northern depot area. They obliterate Titans, dissolve armoured vehicles, and reduce brotherhood and Word Bearers formations to ash.

Sheltering, in some cases, less than half a kilometre from the impact sites, Ultramarines and Army forces are untouched. Their eardrums burst. Their skin burns. They are half-blinded by the light, and hammered by the concussion, e-mag pulse and violent after-pressure, but they endure.

The negative pressure causes the rain to swirl cyclonically around the zone, a whirlpool of smoke and ravaged climate.

Ventanus looks up, dazed by the blast. Hot ash has plastered their wet armour, covering them all; ash that was Word Bearers only seconds before.

The Ultramarines around him look pumice grey, gun metal grey, the colour of the XVII's old livery.

[mark: 20.21.25]

TAWREN HAS NOT finished. She deploys the grid elements available to her, she hits other surface targets. Simultaneously, she retasks orbital platforms, and retrains lance stations. She begins to systematically exact punishment on the Word Bearers fleet.

For the first time since the cataclysmic orbital strike, it's the crimson-hulled warships that explode and die in nearspace. Cruisers and barges detonate in multi-megaton conflagrations, or are crippled by devastating impacts.

This is a dynamic combat shift. This is the game *changed*. Hesst would approve. *Guilliman* would approve.

* * *

[mark: 20.21.30]

ON THE AUXILIARY bridge of the *Macragge*, Marius Gage sees the first of his enemy's ships sputter and torch out. He watches as phosphorescent green and white beams stripe out from the orbital grid, spearing Word Bearers vessels.

He looks at Hommed.

'Statement of yield, please?'

'We are currently at fifty-seven per cent yield, Chapter Master,' says Hommed. 'Enough to transport Empion's kill squad.'

'I intend to take rather more direct action than that. Engage the drive and move towards the yards. Raise the shields.'

'Sir, there are three enemy cruisers clamped to our hull.'

'Then I imagine they will suffer, shipmaster. Raise void shields. While you're at it, shoot them off our back.'

The titanic flagship lights its shields. One of the cruisers buckles as it is caught and torn in the void field, blowing out along its centre line and voiding significant compartments to space. Its wrecked bulk remains clamped to the *Macragge's Honour* as the flagship surges forward, drives glowing white hot.

A second cruiser falls free, clamps blown and cut. The flagship's batteries begin to pick it apart before it can stabilise its motion.

The third is pounded repeatedly at close range by the flagship's starboard guns. Gage refuses to order cease firing until the side of the cruiser facing him is a molten hell, burning up, with inner decks exposed.

The executed cruiser drops away, glowing like an ember, and falls out of the plane of the ecliptic.

* * *

[mark: 20.24.10]

THE MASTER CONTROL room is on fire. Flames and smoke are rapidly filling the habitats of the Zetsun Verid Yard. Thiel and the remainder of the kill squad retreat rapidly towards the transverse assembly deck. They pack tight around the wounded, limping primarch.

'The flagship is inbound,' says Thiel.

Guilliman nods. He seems to be recovering some strength.

'The sun,' murmurs one of the squad.

They look up through the vast crystalflex observation ports and see the Veridian star. It is stricken, its light ugly and sick. A bubonic rash of sunspots freckles its surface.

'I think we have won something just in time to lose everything,' says Guilliman.

Thiel asks him what they should do, but the primarch is not listening. He has turned his attention down, to something he can see on the through-deck beneath the assembly layer.

'Bastards!' he hisses. 'Can't they just burn?'

Thiel looks.

He can see half a dozen of the surviving Word Bearers. They carry the bloody carcass of Kor Phaeron. Somehow, the wretched Master of the Faith seems to be alive, despite the fact that Guilliman tore out his primary heart. He is twitching, writhing.

Leading the party, Thiel sees the Word Bearer whose helm and skull he cut away.

Tchure turns to look at them, sensing them. The side of his face is gore, teeth and bone exposed.

Thiel draws his boltgun, reloaded with ammunition from a fallen brother. The other Ultramarines start to fire too.

The Word Bearers shimmer. Spontaneous frost crackles out in a circle around their feet, and corposant winds around them. They vanish in a blink of teleport energy.

'Gage! Gage!' Guilliman yells.

'My primarch!' Gage responds over the vox-link.

'Kor Phaeron is running. He's gone from here, teleported out! He'll have run to his ship.'

'Yes, sir.'

'Just stop him, Marius. Stop him dead, and send him to hell.'

'My primarch–'

'Marius Gage, that's an order.'

'What about you, sir? We are moving into the yard to recover you.'

'There are ships docked here,' Guilliman replies. 'The *Samothrace*, a couple of escorts. We'll board one and be secure enough. Just get after him, Marius. Get after the damned *Infidus Imperator*.'

[mark: 20.27.17]

THE WORD BEARERS battle-barge *Infidus Imperator* turns in the debris-rich belt of Calth nearspace, ships dying in flames behind it. It engages its drive and begins a long, hard burn towards the outsystem reaches.

As it accelerates away, raising yield to maximum, the *Macragge's Honour* turns in pursuit, its main drives lighting with an equally furious vigour.

It is the beginning of one of the most infamous naval duels in Imperial history.

[mark: 20.59.10]

FATE HAS TWISTED, dislocated. Erebus can see that plainly. He does not care, and he is not surprised. Ways change. He knows this. It is one of the first truths the darkness taught him.

Calth is dead. The XIII is crippled and finished. His

ritual is complete, and it is entirely successful. The Ruinstorm rises, a warp-storm beyond anything space-faring humanity has witnessed since the Age of Strife. It will split the void asunder. It will divide the galaxy in two. It will render vast tracts of the Imperium impassable for centuries.

It will isolate and trap forces loyal to the Emperor. It will divide them, and block their attempts to combine and support one another. It will shatter communication and chains of contact. It will even prevent them from *warning* each other of the heretical war breaking across their realm. The Ruinstorm will cripple the loyalists, and leave Terra raw and alone, infinitely vulnerable to the approaching shadow of Horus.

But... somehow the enemy salvaged *something*. They were defeated from the very start, and they remained defeated throughout, and in the aftermath, the Word Bearers can salt the XIII's scattered bones. Yet they won something back. Some measure of retribution. Some degree of pride. They did not yield, and they forced a surprising price for their lives.

Erebus is sorry to leave any of them alive. They say you should always kill them. Ultramarines. If you make one your enemy, do not allow him to live. Do not spare him. Leave an Ultramarine alive, and you leave room for retribution. Only when he is dead are you safe from harm. That is what they say.

They are fine words. The proud boast of an unfailingly arrogant Legion. They mean little. The Ultramarines are done. Calth has gutted them. They will never more be a force to be reckoned with.

Horus no longer has to worry about the threat of the XIII.

The poison light of the sun falls across the Satric Plateau. Erebus basks in it. He raises his hands. The daemons sing in adulation.

The Dark Apostle feels the rising winds of the

Ruinstorm snatching at his cloak. He is finished here. He has carried out the duty that was entrusted to him by Lorgar. It is time for his departure.

Reality has worn thin at the edge of the black stone circle, thin like bleached and ancient cloth. Erebus takes out his own ornate athame dagger, and cuts a slit in the material fabric of the universe.

He steps through.

5

GUILLIMAN WATCHES THE rising storm from the bridge of the *Samothrace*, a replacement command crew at the control stations. Every reliable authority says it will be the worst in living memory.

'We must translate from the system, my primarch,' says the shipmaster. 'The fleet must exit before we are swept away.'

Guilliman nods. He understands the imperative. If nothing else, firm and clear warnings of the daemonic threat must be conveyed to the Imperial core sectors, and to the Five Hundred Worlds of Ultramar.

'There are still hundreds of thousands down there,' he says to Thiel, looking at scans of the ravaged planet.

'We extracted as many as we could, with whatever ships we had, sir,' Thiel replies. 'Further evacuation is now impossible.'

'What about the rest?' Guilliman asks.

'They are fleeing to the arcologies,' Thiel says. 'There is a good chance that the subterranean hab systems and catacombs will protect them from the effect of the solar radiation. They may be able to ride out the storm until

401

such time as we can return with a Legion fleet to evacuate them.'

'That could be years.'

'It could,' agrees Thiel.

'If ever.'

'At worst, years,' says Thiel. 'We *will* return. They *will*
be saved.'

Guilliman nods.

'You'll excuse my mood, Thiel. I have lost a world of
Ultramar. I have lost... too much. You are not seeing the
best of me.'

'Theoretical,' replies Thiel. 'The reverse of that statement is true.'

Guilliman snorts. His face is grey with lingering pain.

'Anything from Gage?'

'Nothing, sir.'

'And of the forces we extracted, was Ventanus among
them?'

'No, sir,' replies Thiel. 'He was not.'

[mark: 23.49.20]

VENTANUS TAKES THE vox-horn.

'This is Ventanus, Captain, 4th,' he begins. 'I am
making an emergency broadcast on the global vox-cast
setting. The surface of Calth is no longer a safe environment. The local star is suffering a flare trauma, and will
shortly irradiate Calth to human-lethal levels. It is no
longer possible to evacuate the planet. Therefore, if you
are a citizen, a member of the Imperial Army, a legionary
of the XIII, or any other loyal servant of the Imperium,
move with all haste to the arcology or arcology system
closest to you. The arcology systems may offer sufficient
protection to allow us to survive this solar event. We
will shelter there until further notice. Do not hesitate.
Move directly to the nearest arcology. Arcology location

and access information will be appended to this repeat broadcast as a code file. In the name of the Imperium, make haste. Message ends.'

He lowers the device and looks at Tawren.

'I have set it to repeat transmit,' she says.

'Then we must go. There is very little time, server. Disengage from the data-engine.'

'I do not know about these caves,' she says. 'I think it will be unpleasant down there.'

'Not as unpleasant as it will be on the surface,' says Selaton.

'This is not a discussion,' says Ventanus. 'It is not an elective matter. We are retreating to the arcologies. We will endure there. End of debate.'

'I understand,' she says. 'You realise that enemy strengths left on the planet will flee underground too?'

'I do,' says Ventanus.

'So what do we do?' asks Tawren.

'We keep fighting,' Ventanus tells her. 'That's what we always do.'

6

THE WORLD HAS never seemed so dark. It is impossible to tell where the rolling blackness of the sea ends and the twisted darkness of the sky begins.

Only the star remains, poisonous and fierce, like a baleful eye, gleaming through the smoke and fog.

They ground the skiff off a shingle beach and come ashore. Oll checks his compass. They start trudging up the beach, heading inland.

'Where are we?' asks Bale Rane.

'North,' says Oll. 'The Satric Coast. The great plateau is that way.'

He gestures at the darkness.

'Fine country,' Oll says. 'Even been up that way and seen it?'

Rane shakes his head.

'What are we doing here?' asks Zybes.

Strange, daemonic voices hoot and gibber in the distance, echoing down the inlet.

Zybes repeats his question with more urgency.

'I don't understand any of this,' he says. 'We've come all this way in that damned boat! Why? It's no safer here. It sounds like it's worse, if that's possible!'

Oll glances at him, tired and impatient.

'We've come here,' he says, 'because this is the only place we can get out through. The only place. It's our one chance to live and do something.'

'Do what?' asks Krank.

'Something that matters,' Oll replies, not really listening. He's seen something. Something on the beach by the boat.

'Who is that, Trooper Persson?' Graft asks.

There is a man on the beach behind them. He's following them. He passes their grounded skiff, walking briskly. Another small launch, presumably the one that brought him in, is turning slowly in the black water off the beach, abandoned.

'Shit,' murmurs Oll. 'Get behind me, all of you. Keep moving.'

He turns, sliding his rifle off his shoulder.

Criol Fowst is black on black, a shadow of a figure. Only his face is pale, the drawn skin white and streaked with dried blood from his head wound. He approaches, his feet crunching over the shingle. A laspistol hangs in his right hand. Oll faces him, weapon ready.

'No closer,' Oll calls out.

'Give it back,' Fowst shouts. 'Give it back to me!'

'I don't want to fire a weapon or spill blood here,' Oll warns, 'but I will if you make me. Go back and leave us alone.'

'Give me my blade. *My* blade.'

'Go back.'

Fowst takes a step forward.

'They can smell it, you know,' he hisses. 'They can smell it.'

'Let them smell it,' replies Oll.

'They'll come. You don't want them to come.'

'Let them come.'

'You don't want them to come, old man. Give it back to me. I need it.'

'I need it more,' says Oll. 'I need it for something. It's why I came here. I need it for something more important than you can possibly imagine.'

'Nothing is more important than what I can imagine,' replies Fowst.

'Last chance,' says Oll.

Fowst screams. He screams at the top of his voice.

'He's here! Here! Right here! Come and get him! Come and feast on him! Here! Here!'

The rifle cracks. Silenced, Fowst falls back on the stones of the beach.

But things are stirring. Things disturbed and drawn by the sound of Fowst's cry and the noise of the shot. Oll can hear them. He can hear batwings flap in the darkness, hooves scrape on stone, scales slither. Voices mutter and growl abhuman sounds.

'Hey!' Oll shouts to his travelling companions, who are cowering in the dark. 'Come back to me! Come back. Gather round.'

They hurry to him. Krank and Rane. Zybes. The girl. Graft is the slowest.

'What is that?' Krank asks, hearing the sounds that the things are making as they close in around them through the darkness. 'What's making that noise?'

'Don't think about it,' Oll says, working hard, trying to remember a simple sequence of gestures. 'Just stay close beside me. It might be all right here. It might be thin enough.'

'What might be thin enough?' asks Rane.

'What's making that noise?' Krank repeats, agitated.

'Something's coming,' says Zybes.

'It's all right,' says Oll. 'We're just leaving anyway.'

He has the dagger in his hand. The athame, unwrapped. He murmurs to his god for protection and forgiveness. Then he makes a cut.

'How are you doing that?' asks Katt.

They all look at her.

Oll smiles.

'Trust me,' he says. He pushes the knife harder, deepens the cut. He makes the slit vertical, the height of a man. He makes a slit in the air, so that reality parts.

The daemon sounds come closer.

Oll draws back the edge of the cut like a curtain. They gasp as they see what's on the other side. It isn't here. It isn't Calth. It isn't a broken, pitch-black beach.

Oll looks at them.

'I won't pretend this is going to be easy,' he says, 'because it isn't. But it's better than staying here.'

They stare at him.

'Follow me,' he says.

UN//DOING

'We keep fighting.'

–Ventanus, on Calth, prior to the
start of the Underworld War

EPILOGUE

[mark: 219,479.25.03]

COLCHIS, AT THE bitter, broken end; the mark of Calth still running after all these damned years. It is essentially a futile measurement, merely symbolic, but sometimes symbolism is all you have left. A ritual. The scum of Colchis should understand that much, at least.

The world burns, devastated. A world for a world. There is little retribution left to be extracted, little punitive satisfaction to be savoured. But the deed must be finished, so the count can be finished, and this is one great step towards completing the process.

Ventanus, veteran captain, battered by fortune and service, stands on the outcrop of rock, looking out over the benighted landscape. The firestorms reflect off his polished plate and his grim visor, bright orange patterns dancing on the cobalt-blue and gold. So much has passed since this began. The galaxy has changed, and changed again. The revolutions that stunned his mind on Calth seem insignificant beside what he has witnessed since. The end. The fall. The start. The loss.

He has not known fear, but he has known pain. The breaking of the order of things. He has seen his species discover that the greatest enemy of all is itself.

The years spent waging the Underworld War seem so distant. They are fading, almost unremembered, like the empire that followed them, and the Heresy that ended it all.

His officers are waiting, sergeants in red helms, junior captains with their crests and swords. Ventanus can still remember a time when a red helm meant–

Times change. Things change. Ways change. They are waiting for him, impatient to get on, wondering what the old bastard is thinking about, wondering what's taking him so long.

In low orbit above, the barge *Octavius* waits, cyclonic torpedoes primed.

Ventanus turns. He thinks of brothers lost, and looks at the brothers with him. He holds out his mailed hand.

The colour sergeant passes him the standard. It is old and battered, dented, with a slight twist or two in the haft. Surely, the sergeant thinks, the damned thing could have been cleaned and mended.

Ventanus takes it, honouring every mark upon it.

He plants it upright in the burning rock of Colchis. The flickering firelight catches at the golden crest of the standard.

'We march for Macragge!' the sergeant declares.

'No, not today,' Ventanus replies. 'Today, we march for Calth.'

[mark: unspecified]

WHILE WORD BEARERS still live, in the madness of the Maelstrom or in the depths of the warp, the mark of Calth will continue to run.

It is running now.

Thanks to
Aaron Dembski-Bowden, Richard Dugher,
Bruce Euans, Laurie Goulding, the High Lords
of Lenton, Nick Kyme, Graham McNeill,
Lindsey Priestley and Nik Vincent.

ABOUT THE AUTHOR

Dan Abnett is a multiple *New York Times* bestselling author and an award-winning comic book writer. He has written over forty novels, including the acclaimed Gaunt's Ghosts series, and the Eisenhorn and Ravenor trilogies. His previous Horus Heresy novel, *Prospero Burns*, topped the SF charts in the UK and the US. In addition to writing for Black Library, Dan scripts audio dramas, movies, games, and comics for major publishers in Britain and America. He is also the author of other bestselling novels, including *Torchwood: Border Princes*, *Doctor Who: The Silent Stars Go By*, *Triumff: Her Majesty's Hero*, and *Embedded*. He lives and works in Maidstone, Kent.

Dan's blog and website can be found at
www.danabnett.com

and you can follow him on Twitter
@VincentAbnett